Peter Lancaster was born and educated in Lancashire. He continues to pursue a professional career in Sussex where he lives with his partner and two dogs. A life-long interest in aviation, which led to a private pilot's licence, and in the Second World War, in particular the parts played by the RAF and various clandestine organisations such as SOE, prompted this novel, intended to be the first in a series.

Dedicated to the memory of all those who did in reality the sort of things portrayed in this work of historical fiction.

Peter Lancaster

KNIGHT'S BATTLES

AUSTIN MACAULEY PUBLISHERS™

LONDON • CAMBRIDGE • NEW YORK • SHARJAH

A CIP catalogue record for this title is available from the British Library.

ISBN 9781528935173 (Paperback)
ISBN 9781528968157 (ePub e-book)

www.austinmacauley.com

First Published (2020)
Austin Macauley Publishers Ltd
25 Canada Square
Canary Wharf
London
E14 5LQ

With thanks to all family and friends who helped in whatever way in bringing this labour to fruition.

Prologue

With the sun at its back the fighter falls through the sky like a stooping hawk, aiming remorselessly for its prey.

The mode of attack is not unexpected; in fact it has been anticipated. Pilot Officer George Knight, the objective, shades his eyes with one hand as he squints into the glare. He knows where to look because he has learned his profession well. The Great War maxim 'beware the Hun in the sun' still holds good. He continues to watch for a few seconds more as it hurtles towards him, gauging its approach. Just as it seems he has left it too late, he opens the throttle and pulls the stick sharply to the right, giving a shout of exhilaration as his Hurricane rolls smoothly into a turn; taking it safely inside the trajectory of his assailant – and slap, bang into trouble.

The shout dies on his lips as he sees two more fighters; not diving down but curving in towards him on the same level; he has turned straight into them. The fighter leader is a clever tactician and George knows he has fallen into his trap. His mind races – try to climb? He will present an easy target – dive? And concede the advantage of height; only one answer – keep the turn going – hard. He pushes the throttle 'through the gate' and pulls the stick right back into his stomach. The roar of the engine increases and the Hurricane surges forward as the emergency boost takes effect. His vision blurs as the manoeuvre forces the blood from his head. Resisting the weight pressing down on him he holds the turn through a half-circle before rolling level. Relieved of g-force his vision returns, permitting a quick glance over his left shoulder. His two opponents are chasing, but not yet in shooting range. Looking over his other shoulder, he can't see the third. It will be there somewhere, probably using the speed from its dive to climb back above him and do the same again. He has evaded the ambush but, outnumbered, to run is his only option. 'Right', he says to himself, pushing the stick forward, 'let's go flying.' The hands of the altimeter spin round the dial as he dives earthwards. He is soon less than a hundred feet above the ground, jinking and weaving. Cattle and sheep scatter in terror as his Hurricane roars over their fields. A village flashes underneath giving fleeting glimpses of rooftops and, in the streets, white, upturned faces. He swerves to avoid a steeple. His heart pounds, his whole body aches; he has to keep going.

He clears a stand of trees. Behind, the two fighters are still there. He scans the sky above him anxiously – where the hell is the third? Beyond the trees the ground slopes away into a valley. At the far end a bridge spans the gap between the hillsides. He roars down the valley, the bridge growing in front of him. Over or under? In a split second he elects to go under, between the supports. At the last moment, he rolls his wings almost vertically. The Hurricane shoots through the gap with feet to spare. Glancing back, he sees that he has shaken-off two pursuers.

Playing safe, they have pulled up to clear the bridge and lost way. He looks again for the third and, at last, he can see it, high in the sky over his right shoulder and slanting down towards him. George is ready to stand and fight now the odds are level; just he and the leader. Throttling back to normal boost, he starts climbing, reduced speed allowing the other aircraft to gain on him, gauging its approach as before. As it closes, he begins a shallow dive, picking up speed. It follows, overhauling him rapidly. It is almost in a firing position when he kicks in full left rudder and hauls back on the stick. The Hurricane goes into a flick roll, rolling and yawing to the left at the same time. His head feels ready to fly off his shoulders but he maintains concentration, watching earth, horizon and sky chasing each other round in a crazy ballet until he puts in full opposite rudder and pushes the stick forward, cancelling the forces that are tumbling his aircraft through the sky. Coming out of the roll he is now behind his opponent who has overshot him, surprised by the sudden manoeuvre. Hunted has become hunter. A quick burst of power and he is in firing position. The aircraft fills his gun- sight. His thumb hovers over the firing button, ready to blast it from the sky.

Instead, he flicks his R/T switch, "Bang, bang you're dead – sir!"

The laconic tones of F/L Brian Underhill, Red One and leader of 'A' Flight, 686 Squadron, crackle in his earphones. "Well done George – top hole! You're operational as of now. One thing though, save the split-arse flying for the enemy. I've neither the time nor the inclination to scrape you off some bloody bridge!"

Elation fills George. A year after joining the RAF he has made the grade; he is a fighter pilot. "Wizard! Can I stand you a beer, sir?"

George steps out of the flight hut and looks at the Hurricane he has just flown. The sun has sunk low in the sky and silhouettes the aircraft. He studies the outline. He has seen the Spitfire, whose sleek, almost artistic, lines have already caused it to be called the thoroughbred of fighter aircraft. If the Spitfire is the thoroughbred then the Hurricane is a steeplechaser; robust, uncomplaining, big-hearted. He relives his flight again. The surge of power as he opened the throttle wide, unleashing all of the thousand and thirty horsepower of the Rolls-Royce Merlin engine; the positive controls, the ready response and the feeling of freedom and invincibility as he swooped and soared through the heavens.

The ground crew finish refuelling and the fuel bowser drives away. As silence descends he approaches the Hurricane. Despite having a metal structure, the control surfaces and rear fuselage are covered with fabric; the last link with the bi-planes of the Great War. George breathes in the smell of the cellulose dope which shrinks the fabric onto the airframe. He walks around the wing to the nose, absent-mindedly but affectionately trailing his hand along the leading edge. The short stubby exhausts, protruding pugnaciously from the engine cowling, tick periodically as they cool. The odour of warm engine oil reaches him and he can feel himself sitting once again in the cockpit. A surge of pride and affection sweeps over him as he steps back and admires the aircraft; standing twice as tall as he, on a wide sturdy undercarriage, solid, aggressive, menacing; a fighter pilot's aeroplane – his aeroplane – all that he has been working for.

Unknown to George, Underhill has been watching. He understands the bond between man and machine. He joins him and asks the question even though he knows what the answer will be. "Think you'll enjoy flying Hurricanes on ops?"

"You bet, sir. She's my best friend already."

"Splendid – I think you mentioned a beer?"

Part I
The Battle of France

'Fair stood the wind for France
When we our sails advance,
Nor now to prove our chance
Longer will tarry;'

from 'Agincourt' by Michael Drayton (1563-1631)

1: September, 1939

"Cripes – this sounds serious!" said 'Edge' Alderley.

"The papers said, 'No war this year'!" protested Giles Frobisher.

"That was last year, so they were right. I doubt that Hitler reads the *Daily Express* anyway," retorted 'Shorty' Lewis.

"Perhaps they'll withdraw, now that we've stood up to them," ventured Reg Pearson.

"Unfortunately, I doubt it," said F/L Parsons, the Adjutant, gravely, "we've let them get away with too much already. They don't believe we will go through with it."

He was referring to the news they had just heard on the Mess wireless. German forces had that morning crossed the frontier into Poland and heavy fighting was taking place. The Governments of Great Britain and France had delivered an ultimatum – withdraw from Poland by 3rd September or they would be at war.

"So we'll have to show them the error of their ways," said George. It was five weeks since he had achieved operational status. Like many a nineteen-year-old fighter pilot his confidence was sky high and he was eager to test himself against real opposition. Parsons smiled at the youthful bravado. The row of medal ribbons on his tunic bore silent witness to his own experiences; 1917 when German ascendancy meant that the life expectancy of RFC pilots could be measured in days and 1918 when the fledgling RAF had seized control of the skies, never again in that war to relinquish it. He had heard the brave words before, uttered them himself even, twenty-odd years ago, and knew what was in store for the new generation, but he was here to support and encourage, not demoralise; they would find out soon enough, would have their steel tempered in the heat of battle. The ribbons served another purpose. They signalled to this group of confident, self-reliant youngsters that this older man, greying at the temples and no longer as vigorous as they, was to be respected; he had fought the kind of battles they would have to fight and he had not only survived but triumphed. Therefore, instead of dismissing the man they knew as Richard or 'Adj', they listened to him; sought advice from him; made him their father – confessor.

His thoughts were interrupted by the arrival of S/L Sullivan, the C/O; his manner brisk and authoritative. "Sit down please, gentlemen. I'm afraid the days of the RAF being the best flying club in the world have just ended. With immediate effect, we are on a war footing so, firstly, gasmasks are to be carried at all times. Secondly, there is a great deal of work to be done in a very short space of time. All aircraft have to be dispersed; there are shelter trenches to be dug, sandbags to be filled and, if you want somewhere to sleep tonight, tents to be erected." Groans met this last remark. "You cannot use the airfield buildings in case of bombing. By the way, were any of you in the Boy Scouts?" Three hands were raised. His face broke into a grin. "Good, you're in charge of pitching tents. Take any more help you need. The rest of you can go and ask F/Sgts Mackay and Robertson what assistance you can offer."

"Christ, I ache all over. Two days of torture under a blazing sun. Bring on the war, it can't be any worse," groaned Giles.

"I thought officers weren't supposed to do manual labour anyway," added 'Edge'.

"Technically, you're right but the C/O thought it would be better for morale if we are seen to be pulling our weight alongside the other ranks," said Underhill.

"Wouldn't be so bad if everyone had pulled their weight," rejoined Giles, looking accusingly in the direction of P/O 'Foggy' Hayes, "instead of turning up when the job's finished and claiming their recall telegram was delayed."

"But it was delayed," protested 'Foggy', "it was lunchtime yesterday when it arrived and it's a long drive from Cornwall – I left immediately; well almost – I had to drop Felicity at the railway station." He grimaced, "Doubt if I'll be seeing her again!" George had been looking out at the Hurricanes, now dotted around the perimeter of the airfield. Faintly, he could see his own reflection in one window. His sisters had told him that, if he added a moustache, with his looks he could be a matinee idol. They had even said he bore a passing resemblance to David Niven but he had always discounted that as an excess of sibling loyalty. He re-considered their advice for a second and dismissed it. His tall, athletic figure contrasted with Giles' bulky frame. "You're not fit, Giles. Must be all the beer you've been drinking. Better put some time in with the PTI or you won't get into the cockpit."

"George's right," added 'Edge', "if you're not careful in your Sidcot suit, you could be mistaken for a barrage balloon."

"Bloody nerve!" retorted Giles "To think I've been chauffeuring you ingrates to the local hostelries. Have I been holding vipers to my bosom?"

Richard Parsons listened to the banter with quiet amusement. He had heard exchanges like these many times before and knew the unspoken tensions which prompted them. He checked his watch again. It was time. "Silence, gentlemen, please," he called, turning on the radio, "for the Prime Minister."

Each of them was left with his own thoughts as they listened to the sombre tones of Neville Chamberlain, "…This morning the British Ambassador in Berlin handed the German Government a final note stating that, unless we heard from them by eleven o'clock that they were prepared at once to withdraw their troops from Poland, a state of war would exist between us. I have to tell you now that no such undertaking has been received, and consequently this country is at war with Germany…"

As soon as the broadcast finished, S/L Sullivan stood up and motioned for silence. "Gentlemen, all of your training, and in particular that of the last few weeks, is now going to be put to the test. You are some of the best pilots in the best air force in the world. I know that you will not fail that test. 'A' Flight will go to standby, and 'B' Flight, thirty minutes readiness – good luck to you all."

A hubbub breaks out. "Thank God we've got a decision, it's the uncertainty I can't stand," said 'Roy' Rogers.

"Me too," said 'Foggy', "now we can get on and teach these bloody Germans a lesson!" All around the room, the mood was similarly upbeat. The only reservation was held, silently, by Richard Parsons. He had heard 'Edge' say that 'it will all be over by Christmas'; he had heard that once before.

'B' Flight pilots, with the benefit of thirty minutes notice, remain in the Mess, able to contemplate the day's events from the comfort of armchairs, while 'A' Flight, consisting of Red and Yellow Sections, head for dispersal. Within five minutes, George, Red Three, is strapped into his aircraft, his ground crew standing by, awaiting the signal to scramble. He shares the general relief that the waiting is over. As he sits, ready to go to war, a jumble of thoughts crowd his mind.

Five summers ago, he had had his first flight in an aeroplane, a ten-shilling flip in a rickety bi-plane from Weston-super-Mare sands. From that point on, he knew that the only thing he wanted to do was fly, although it would mean turning his back on the family business – their last four generations had been stockbrokers. After leaving school, he had spent an agreed year with the firm before joining the RAF in the summer of 1938. Nothing was ever said or done to give it substance, but he could not escape the feeling that his family felt he had let them down in some way and it had planted in him a fierce determination to succeed in his chosen career, to demonstrate that he had done the right thing. In this respect, he had been fortunate to find that he was one of that happy breed, a born pilot. From his first solo to his last training exercise, the whole thing had come easily – but he had not flirted with his gift – he had applied himself as diligently as the least talented of his colleagues and as a result had received his coveted wings with the rating 'exceptional' – as good as it was possible to be and remain mortal. So why was he sitting here now on the first day of the war, about to do or die? Why the RAF? Why hadn't he joined Imperial Airways and flown to exotic locations instead? Simple – he was seduced by the chance to fly high performance fighter aircraft, and by the image; Hendon Air Displays, the aerobatic display teams; the boys in blue, collars and cuffs undone and silk scarves insouciantly worn like cravats; as the C/O had said a couple of days ago, the best flying club in the world – a few hours a day flying then a game of squash, beers in the Mess or, for those stationed within fifty miles or so of London, a trip up to town and dinner at Quaglino's or the Savoy Grill or a score of other fashionable restaurants with a cool blonde on his arm. He laughs ironically to himself at that thought. He who had had one girlfriend in his life. He had known Dorothy for as long as he could remember. Sweet, homely, doe-eyed Dorothy whom he loves dearly. Whilst Great Britain had been sleepwalking its way towards war, he and Dorothy had been sleepwalking towards a life together – after all, hadn't he proposed to her when he was seven and been accepted? But just as voices of warning had been raised in the country, so voices of doubt would sometimes whisper in his head. As on the national stage, they had made little difference. The war will delay things, but everyone knows that one day he will marry Dorothy and raise a houseful of children. That's for the future, what of now? He had been able to enjoy the best flying club in the world for only a few weeks and now it had been snatched away from him. From here on, the possibility of finishing every day in a smoking hole in the ground or at the bottom of the English Channel instead of in the arms of the cool blonde. No surprise really – he had joined the RAF around the time of Munich. Since then, war had been 'when' rather than 'if'. At least now, the RAF has forty-odd squadrons of modem fighters instead of the handful it had then. A fly strays into the open cockpit and buzzes around the inside of the windscreen. He swats at it unsuccessfully a couple of times before it disappears the way it came. He looks to his left. Giles, Yellow Two, in the next aircraft makes a rude gesture and laughs; he reciprocates. Giles Frobisher, portly, easy-going, the butt of many a joke, who can fly formation with the precision of a surgeon. To George's right is Brian Underhill, a born leader who exercises authority with a feather-light touch, but woe betide anyone who steps over the line; and beyond him 'Roy' Rogers, Red Two, a ragamuffin in uniform but another Hurricane virtuoso. To Giles' left Edgar 'Woody' Woodrow, Yellow Section leader, due to leave any day for promotion and a new squadron and beyond him, Ivor 'Taff' Evans, Yellow Three, farmer's son and bass baritone from Pembrokeshire, another born pilot; all of them professionals of the highest calibre. George feels privileged to have been admitted into their company and proud of what that means. Would he rather have been with Imperial Airways? No, and in one sense the question is irrelevant. Everything he has and is, he owes to his family and his country – so if they are threatened, there is no question but that he will fight to defend them. He has read the arguments of the intellectuals and the pacifists – he knows that turning the other cheek is not for him, that he will do his utmost to defend those things and people that matter; so whichever path he had taken would have led to this point anyway. He finds himself chewing at a fingernail as they continue to wait. It is the generally held belief that when hostilities commence, enemy bombers will deliver a series of devastating blows to knock Britain out of the war; several years earlier had Prime Minister Baldwin not announced that 'the bomber would always get through'? George and his comrades-in-arms don't accept this – they are going to shoot the enemy out of the sky before they can strike home. Under the late summer sun, it is warm in the cockpit, even with the hood open. He uses one end of his scarf to wipe sweat away from his eyes. He has already come to know that for fighter pilots, the silk scarves are not an affectation but a necessity. The collar and tie has yet to be invented; that doesn't chafe as a result of the repeated head turning needed to keep a lookout in the air; God it's hot!… and still they continue to wait.

Suddenly, a green flare shoots skywards before arcing lazily over the airfield – the signal to scramble. The almost rural tranquillity is shattered. "Contact!" shouts George, priming the engine then pressing the starter-motor and booster coil buttons. The aeroplane shudders as, with a belch of black smoke from the exhausts, the engine bursts into life. He checks oil pressure immediately; satisfactory. A ground crewman disappears from view under the nose to remove the chocks. He reappears seconds later with thumbs up. All along the line of aircraft the same routines are being followed. George checks engine temperature and hydraulic pressure. Both OK. He takes a deep breath to still the last of the butterflies in his stomach, pulls the stick back, releases the brakes and begins taxiing in concert with the rest of 'A' Flight.

Keeping the stick back to prevent the tail from lifting too early, he opens the throttle. The aircraft accelerates across the airfield, bumping over the uneven grass, gathering speed until he moves the stick gently forward allowing the tail to lift and then, pulling back again, he is airborne. Seven, not six, Hurricanes start climbing away from the airfield. They are led, on this, the squadron's first wartime operation, by their C/O. His voice sounds over the R/T, "Bad Hat Control. Shuttlecock aircraft airborne."

"Shuttlecock leader, Bad Hat Control. Head for the Big House and make Angels twenty."

George and his friends are heading for London again. Today, however, it will not be Quaglino's or the Savoy Grill. Today, they are going to meet the Luftwaffe.

They have been flying in silence for ten minutes, each man thinking about what lies ahead of him – for each his first action – a strange hollow feeling in his stomach. How will I cope? Will I be good enough? Will my nerve hold? Please God, don't let me let the other chaps down.

The R/T breaks into the tension. "Shuttlecock Leader, Bad Hat Control. Return to base, repeat, return to base."

"Bad Hat Control, Shuttlecock Leader. What the blue blazes is going on? We're on our way to intercept a horde of Huns."

"Not any more. The plot has disappeared."

"For Christ's sake! You mean you've had us chasing bloody shadows?"

"Sorry, Shuttlecock Leader. It appears there never were any bandits."

After a pregnant pause, Sullivan speaks again, this time in a measured tone. "Shuttlecock aircraft, you all heard that. Let's go home."

As he joins his colleagues en route to the Mess, George feels a mixture of emotions; disappointment that he was unable to mix it with the enemy, satisfaction that he has kept his end up, annoyance at the wild goose-chase and relief that he will not die today; but mainly disappointment. "What a bloody balls up!"

"Seems like some serious finger trouble to me," says 'Taff' Evans.

"To be honest, I'm not surprised," adds 'Roy' Rogers, pulling off his flying helmet and unleashing a barely-regulation mop of black hair, "consider how tense everyone has been here in the last couple of days and apply that across the board. Someone at Ops has seen or heard something unexpected and, hey presto, there's a flap on. I bet it'll happen some more before everyone settles down."

Giles nods in agreement. "I think you're right. Pity you didn't pass that sweet reason on to the C/O, though. I think he's phoning Ops to 'discuss' the matter, and he didn't look happy as he passed me."

"Ouch!" adds Underhill, grimacing, "still, there were some positives – our first op went off without a hitch, even if it was a false alarm; and nobody pranged their kite. I think that warrants a party tonight."

Because he had been flying, he did not see the newcomer's arrival. The last of the introductions was being made when he got to the Mess. The new man had his back to George and turned at Richard's prompting. George recognised him before he had turned fully, and the split second enabled him to master his surprise.

"Marcus, this is P/O George Knight. George, this is F/O Marcus Stanhope-Smith, replacement for F/O Woodrow, and therefore Yellow Section's new leader." George's gaze was firmly fixed on Stanhope-Smith's eyes. He saw them register shock, almost panic, followed for a fleeting second by a look of pure malevolence before their owner composed himself and gave a disarming smile. "Knight, good to see you. It must be what, six years?" The proffered handshake was perfunctory and his hand felt clammy. He turned to address Richard in a stage whisper before George could reply, "We were at school together. Knight was three years below me so we weren't bosom pals or anything, but it's always good to meet a former school-chum. Against my wishes, my father decided I needed a more rounded education, so he sent me to Switzerland for my final year but I still have fond memories of the old place."

Whilst Stanhope-Smith was talking, George's mind travelled back six years to their last encounter. It was three o'clock in the morning when Stanhope-Smith's 'lieutenants' had entered the dormitory, dragging a sleepy George from his bed and up to an attic room to face their leader. The light from a bare bulb had added an air of bleakness to the proceedings. He had spoken menacingly. "So Knight, are you going to pay or do you have to be disciplined?"

"You can whistle!" spat George defiantly, wide awake now and trying to contain his fear. Stanhope-Smith was just sixteen, the other two fifteen, whilst George was only thirteen. He was, however, worth his place in the under-fifteens rugby team and as he struggled, his captors were working hard to contain him.

"Right! You've asked for it," said Stanhope-Smith, driving his fist into George's stomach. George doubled up, winded, and sagged so that he had to be supported. He hit George twice more; this time the blows were to his ribs. George continued to hang limply. "One last chance, pay up!"

"No, go to hell!" groaned George.

Stanhope-Smith addressed the other two. "Your turn – but don't mark his face." As one of them released his grip, George seized his opportunity. He leaped upwards from his sagged position, twisting free of the other's grip. He lunged forward towards Stanhope-Smith and in one fluid movement landed his fist squarely on his nose, which exploded with a crack and a spray of blood. Stanhope-Smith gave a howl of pain and toppled back into a pile of packing cases, causing them to collapse with a loud crash. George hurdled these and turned to face the other two, who, after a moment of uncertainty started to advance on him. He looked around desperately and spotted some old ornamental shields stacked in a corner. He ran to these, picked one up and threw it towards his assailants. They dodged easily but it landed with a resounding clang, followed soon after by another and then another. "For Gob's sake, stob him!" cried Stanhope-Smith desperately through a bloody handkerchief, "he'll wake der whole sgool ub." Spurred on by their leader, they dodged another shield and charged George. The three of them fell to the floor in a yelling, flailing heap just as the attic door opened to reveal Mr Hipkiss, the Housemaster, flanked by two prefects. Within minutes, the four combatants were before the Headmaster. Initially, things had looked black for George. Stanhope-Smith and his cohorts tried to bluff their way out by claiming that their presence in the attic had just been a prank and that George had launched an unprovoked assault but by now the whole school was awake and, emboldened by the rapidly spreading tale of George's fight, some of Stanhope-Smith's victims started to come forward. Within a few hours, the whole shameful extortion business had become known, resulting in expulsion for Stanhope-Smith and his two associates. Word reached George that before leaving, Stanhope-Smith had threatened revenge, but he had heard no more after that and had put the whole episode to the back of his mind. Until now.

As Stanhope-Smith turned back from speaking to Richard, George was surprised to feel a dislike for him, which he thought had died away in the intervening years. He appraised him. His hair was fair as it had been six years ago. Although he was still smiling, his cold grey eyes were not. George remembered the nose as being aquiline but noticed with quiet satisfaction that it was now rather misshapen. Beneath it, a pencil-thin moustache sat over a lip that, just as George recalled, seemed to have a permanent curl, as if everything that its owner saw displeased him.

George spoke. "So what did you do after Switzerland?"

"I had two years at University in Germany. I was recommended to go there by one of my Swiss tutors. It was a good time but I saw the workings of the Nazi party at first hand. I came to realise that sooner or later Germany would come into conflict with Britain so I came home in '36 and volunteered for the RAF, to be in a position to do my bit for the old country."

"Good show!" said 'Foggy'

"Hear, hear!" added Giles, 'Edge' and several others.

Stanhope-Smith smiled again. This time George saw a flash of triumph in his eyes. His mind was racing. Something was wrong but he couldn't put his finger on it. Yes, he could understand Stanhope-Smith's look of panic and covering up his expulsion from school. Had that been made known he wouldn't even have got into the RAF. He must have used some nimble footwork to get through the interviews. Yes, the flash of hatred he had displayed was understandable as well. Patriotism – that was it – the last refuge of the scoundrel, Dr Johnson had said – and Stanhope-Smith had certainly been a scoundrel. Try as he might, he could not reconcile the Stanhope-Smith that he knew with the man who had come back to do his bit for the 'old country'. Or was he being harsh? Was he a changed man? Had he mended his ways? He doubted it but he did not know for sure. One thing he did know – and Stanhope-Smith's look of triumph confirmed it – he had sold himself to the rest of them, at least for the time being, so there was no point trying to denounce him now. All he could do was to watch him carefully and, if he was up to something, hope to find out what.

Stanhope-Smith spoke again, this time to the pilots at large. "So how have you chaps been getting on?"

"Speaking for myself, I'm pretty browned-off," Reg replied, "the war's nearly four weeks old and so far we haven't had as much as a sniff of Jerry."

"Just so," added 'Shorty' Lewis, "we spent the first week or so either sweltering in our cockpits or going off on wild goose-chases. Since then it's been convoy patrols, stooging about over a fleet of rusty old merchant ships –"

"Or freezing our chuffs off on a windswept airfield," interjected 'Edge', "I think we got the convoy detail as penance. The C/O kept ringing up and bollocking Ops over the false alarms."

"You're probably right," added Reg, "and convoy patrols are not only boring but downright dangerous on occasions. Last week, the cloud base came down below two hundred feet. The only reason we got back in one piece is because the Suffolk coast is as flat as a witch's tit. Then to top it all, we had to stay the night there, Wattisham that is – definitely one of the Good Lord's lesser works. We're using it each day as a forward base, patrolling at section strength."

"Life has its compensations though," 'Foggy' added, "it meant we spent the evening in the local pub in the company of the most delightful of barmaids. I'm hoping to get weathered-in some more this autumn."

Dinner was a pleasant aftertaste and George was on his way from his room to join one of Giles' motorised pub-crawls. As he passed a part-open doorway, Stanhope-Smith's voice hailed him. "I say, George – I hope you don't mind me calling you George. Please come in, and do call me Marcus. After all, schooldays are behind us now." George stepped into the room. It contained the same utilitarian furnishings as his own. There were no personal touches as yet. It was obvious he was in the middle of unpacking his possessions. He was holding a camera he had just taken from his case. George could read the name, Rollei, around the lens of the camera. "An interest of mine – photography – I picked this up while I was in Germany. Whatever else the Germans may be they do produce good cameras." He pressed a button and the back of the camera swung open. He presented it for George's inspection. To his untutored eye it meant little but he nodded approvingly. Stanhope-Smith snapped the case shut. "Do you dabble?"

"Not really," said George, "I know which way up to hold a camera for holiday snaps but that's about it."

"I'm thinking of making a photographic record of the war. Then even if I don't survive there will be something for people to remember me by – those that want to anyway," he added ruefully. There was an awkward pause before he continued, "I just wanted to say thanks for not bringing up our past history today. I really do appreciate it. I know I behaved abominably at school and there's absolutely no excuse for it. I also want to apologise and assure you that I am a changed man. I've grown up. I've had to. I can tell you it was a major shock when my father sent me to school in Switzerland but I can see now that he did the right thing. It gave me time to think, to reflect on my wrongdoing. I suppose I ought to thank you again, because if you hadn't stood up to me when you did, who knows where things might have finished up? Anyway, if you will accept my humble apology, I would like to think we can put all that behind us. After all, we face a common foe now. Shoulder to shoulder and all that, eh?" He offered his hand. George was in turmoil, completely surprised by what Stanhope-Smith had said. He was even more surprised to find himself wanting to believe it, but the flash of malevolence he had seen earlier was still fresh in mind and he knew the leopard hadn't changed its spots; it was only hiding them. He just didn't know why – yet.

He took Stanhope-Smith's hand and hoped he sounded convincing, "As far as I am concerned, the past is over and done with." Stanhope-Smith's handshake was firmer than it had been earlier, but still lacked sincerity. Any temptation that George had to cast aside his doubts was dispelled by Stanhope-Smith's eyes. They showed again the same triumphant look they had shown when he had received the approbation of the Squadron. A half-forgotten adage flashed into his mind – something about'…keeping your enemies closer'.

"I'm just joining Giles and a few other chums for a pub-crawl. Fancy tagging along? I'm sure if we all crush up there'll be room in his car for one more."

"Another time and I would love to but I have some letters to write. Thanks for asking though, I do appreciate it."

No matter where they had been earlier, Giles' pub-crawls always ended at *The Kings Head,* which meant that whoever drove the final leg only had to weave three-quarters of a mile back to the aerodrome, hoping that the village bobby was otherwise engaged. The advent of petrol rationing should have halted these excursions but they had somehow carried on unabated. It was whispered that 100-octane aviation fuel had given a new lease on life to the tired old Sunbeam.

There were six of them sitting around the table with the final pint of the night; Giles, Reg, 'Foggy', 'Shorty', 'Edge' and George.

"I'm fed up with this bloody war," said 'Foggy', staring into his glass, "it's played havoc with my love life."

"You can hardly call it a war. Apart from convoy patrols and sleeping in tents for a couple of weeks, nothing has happened," said 'Edge', "the real thing is still to come."

"You're a fine one to talk. Not long ago you said it would all be over by Christmas," said George accusingly.

"Well maybe it will. Everyone will get so brassed off they will just push off home and that will be it," he replied lamely.

"Oh come on!" jeered Giles, "I've heard some tosh in my time but that takes the biscuit."

"So what do we make of the new type?" asked 'Shorty' deciding it was time to change the subject.

"Sheems a damn fine fellow to me," slurred Reg, "coming back to fight for King and country!"

"I'll second that," said 'Edge', looking to regain some credibility, "a grand chap. Must have been an inspirational sort at school, eh George?"

"He was three years older than me and you know that at school even a year is a gap as wide as the ocean. I scarcely knew him but I don't remember him as anything special." George hated deceiving his friends but at this point he could see no alternative. He found himself almost admiring the man. Within a few hours, he had captured the hearts and minds of the squadron and had George lying on his behalf. "Nonshense, the man is a scholar and a gentleman." Reg struggled to an upright position and raised his glass. "A toasht! To F/O Shtanhope-Smith."

"And all who sail in him!" added Giles irreverently.

Reluctantly, George raised his glass. "Stanhope-Smith," he murmured, reflecting that last time their paths had crossed the outcome had been explosive. What lay in store this time?

2: October, 1939

The familiar exhilaration was still with George as he climbed from the cockpit. He had come to enjoy air tests the more since the outbreak of war because he could do what he liked best, fly as freely as a bird. No formation to keep to, no specific orders to follow, no particular place to go; just swoop and soar and loop and roll, the Hurricane his plaything and the limitless sky his playground. The contrast was the more marked since they had been assigned to convoy patrols. The whole squadron disliked the mind-numbing tedium of flying to and fro, to and fro over the ships, gradually edging their patrol line forward in concert with their charges. So far, there had been no sign of the enemy and little else to relieve the monotony. He was also glad to take his mind off Stanhope-Smith, who had been with the squadron for nearly a month and hadn't put a foot wrong. His popularity remained high despite being only a moderate socialiser; boosted in part by his sideline in taking portrait photographs of the other pilots. Despite himself, George was increasingly finding himself prepared to believe that Stanhope-Smith was a new man and then the feeling that the whole thing was a charade would overtake him once more. He was becoming frustrated by the whole business.

He turned his attention to Cpl Owen, his fitter. "Message from the C/O, sir – all pilots to assemble in the Officers' Mess at sixteen hundred hours."

"Thanks, Owen, any idea why?" George had learned that Owen usually knew anything worthwhile long before it was announced officially.

"Grapevine says we're going overseas, sir; Eastern France."

At four o'clock, S/L Sullivan strode into the Officers Mess, flanked by the Adjutant and Intelligence Officer. Sullivan was a robust looking man of above average height with short brown hair. A career officer and product of RAF College Cranwell, his sun-tanned face radiated drive and energy. He had been in command for only a few months but he was fiercely proud of 686, *his* squadron, and fiercely protective of *his* pilots, by whom he was liked and respected. His steely gaze swept around the room. "At ease, gentlemen. I am pleased to tell you that convoy patrols are no more." He smiled indulgently and paused to let the cheers subside. "We're being sent to France. We're going there to provide cover for our Fairey Battle Squadrons."

"Whereabouts in France, sir?" asked 'Edge', enthusiastically.

"The airfield lies on the outskirts of St Jean-sur-Moselle, a small village on the river Moselle, between Epinal and Chatel-sur-Moselle in Lorraine. That's about two hundred miles southeast of Paris, in the Maginot Line." A murmur ran round the room. He turned to the Intelligence Officer, "Can you show us on the map?"

The I/O looked embarrassed, "I'm afraid maps of France are in short supply at the moment, sir. GHQ has promised us a consignment before we move to St Jean but for now, this is the best I could manage." He put a dog-eared 1937 AA

Continental Touring Guide on the table, open at a map of Eastern France. A red circle just north of Epinal signified their destination.

After everyone had had a look at the map, Sullivan continued "We leave in three days, and en route we will make a courtesy visit to our French comrades-in-arms at Anglure. It's all been fixed up by the propaganda merchants so there'll be cameras there; lots of photos of us and the French with arms around each other, smiling and shaking hands; that sort of thing. Bit of a bind but orders are orders. As of now, the squadron is non-operational. That means you chaps will be hanging about getting under everyone's feet, so to avoid that you are going on forty-eight hours embarkation leave. No doubt you'll celebrate the news in your own inimitable fashion."

They stood to attention as he left. 'Roy' Rogers' broke the silence, "One thing I don't understand. How do we shake hands if we've got our arms around each other?" He was answered by a volley of cushions.

"*La belle* France – champagne!" exclaimed Reg.

"Not to mention all those French popsies," added 'Foggy', grinning broadly. "*Oui, oui, l'amour, l'amour!*" returned Reg, warming to the theme.

"Sounds wizard, but first things first," said George, "I'm going to enjoy some leave."

"Thanks for picking me up."

"My very great pleasure, don't get to use the car much now. Petrol rationing for non-essential users. Eighteen hundred miles per year rather clips one's wings so it's nice to have an outing, despite the blackout," said his father as they emerged from the station. With a pencil-beam torch they began feeling their way towards the car.

"How are you coping?"

"Much as the rest of the country, groping about, banging into things and hoping for the best. I think the blackout is a lot more dangerous than the Germans at present."

"That sounds like a London cabbie I was with earlier except he put it a bit more pithily – 'this 'ere bleedin' blackaht's killing more folk than the bleedin' Luftwaffy' were his exact words. Mind you, he had just had a bump at the time so he was probably a little emotional."

His father laughed. "So long as there are London cabbies, there'll always be an England. They seem to know every inch of London, day or night. Luckily it's simpler here." They reached the car and gratefully climbed in.

"How's Mother?" George asked as the engine came to life.

"Fine; and bursting to see you. She's been like a cat on hot bricks since you phoned."

"Sorry, it was such short notice but I only knew I was on leave at five o'clock."

"Don't apologise – I understand the vagaries of service life. Is there a story?"

"Yes, we're off to France. I'll tell you both later. Its strange hearing you talk of service life. You were always reticent about your war service when I was younger. All I ever found out was that you were in the Yeomanry and served in the desert."

"It's not easy to talk about to someone who hasn't been through it themselves or shared one's experiences. You'll find the same thing."

"One day I shall be able to swap yams with you."

"I'll look forward to that. So, any other news?"

"Yes, there is one thing. A name from the past – Stanhope-Smith."

"I remember that name – the extortionist?"

George smiled, "That's him – F/O Stanhope-Smith is a Section Leader in 686 now."

"Good Lord! How did he get a commission with his record?"

"That's been bothering me. That and what he's doing in the RAF at all; claiming to be a reformed character and oozing patriotic zeal, but I can't bring myself to accept it. I have to go along with it for now but underneath the facade I don't think he's changed – just a smoother operator."

"I take it you've not told anyone about him."

"He's so popular at the moment I don't think they would take me seriously. Also I want to be absolutely sure. It's fine to unmask him if he is up to no good but if I'm wrong and he has joined up for the right reasons then I should leave the school business in the past where it would belong."

"Has he actually done anything to arouse your suspicions?"

"Nothing tangible. It's just his manner and…a feeling – based on past experience."

"What's he been doing since he was expelled?"

His father thought for a moment after George had told him. "If you are correct then you need to be careful. Given your history I doubt he'd have any qualms about harming you now were he to see you as a threat but, having said that, I have to say his story sounds perfectly plausible. He could well have come to his senses while he's been away. Don't be hard on yourself though. It's understandable that past events have influenced your thinking."

George felt deflated and a little annoyed; he had automatically assumed that his father would view things his way. He respected his judgement though; so if he didn't see anything sinister then perhaps he needed to re-examine the matter.

"We're nearly there. There's one thing that I want to mention before we arrive." George, peering into the gloom and unable to identify anything, wondered idly if there was a London cabbie in his father's ancestry.

"What's that?"

"Your mother is no wilting violet but she worries about you, it's only natural after all. Try not to say anything that gives her too clear an idea of the dangers you're facing. I know she was a nurse in the last lot and saw the horrors of war at first hand but she could distance herself from what happened to strangers. At the moment, she only has a vague idea of what you are doing and therefore only a vague fear. We all build a sort of bubble in our minds which keeps out the worst. Don't burst your mother's bubble; I wouldn't mention Stanhope-Smith either – no point bothering her with conjecture." The crunch of gravel under the tyres announced that they had turned into the driveway. His father stopped the car and the front door opened revealing a darkened interior. As they walked up the steps into the house, the door shut behind them and suddenly the lights came on. "George!"

"Mother, it's good to see you," he said throwing his arms around her and kissing her on the cheek. At forty, she looked younger than her years; ash-blonde, blue eyed, elegant and poised, a reflection of the life she had enjoyed, he thought.

The subtle hint of perfume that she wore overlaid the old familiar, comforting smells of the house, his home.

"Sorry about the melodramatic entrance but the blackout regulations are strictly enforced. There are more fascists in the local ARP than Oswald Moseley ever managed to muster."

"They have a job to do, dear," said his father, soothingly.

"And don't they enjoy doing it! Little men and great power. It's a dangerous combination. Anyway, enough of minor irritations. How are you?"

"I'll tell you what, Mother, I'm hungry. Hardly eaten a bite all day."

"Dinner will be half an hour or so. Let's have an aperitif," she said motioning him into the drawing room, "and there's someone else who's dying to see you."

Dinner had been cleared and his father and mother had discreetly melted away. George and Dorothy were walking in the garden, arm in arm in the moonlight. They stopped under an oak tree and kissed. Dorothy was an apt name, George reflected; she was very reminiscent of a photo he had seen of her namesake in the *Wizard of Oz*. "Will it be dangerous in France?" she asked at length.

"No more than it would have been here if the Jerries had shown up."

"That doesn't really answer the question," she chided gently.

"Yes, I suppose it will – be dangerous."

She put her head against his chest, "Please be careful, Georgie. I don't want anything bad to happen to you."

"I'll be all right. After all, I'm with a good crowd. We'll give the Jerries a bloody nose, and when it's all over, we'll come home and pick up where we left off."

"I'll be waiting, like all the other times you've been away. I'll always wait for you." He hugged her.

"That's a date then." Some phantom made her shiver. "Are you cold?"

"Yes," she lied.

He slipped his uniform jacket over her shoulders. "Perhaps we should go in."

When he returned from seeing Dorothy home, George made his way to bed. Except for the blackout curtain covering the window, his room was just as it had always been. Bookshelves, pictures, the trunk containing his cricket and rugger kit; fishing rods and basket in one corner; shotgun and air rifle in a rack in another; wardrobe, chest of drawers and his bed – old friends almost; and between the window and the fireplace was the desk at which he had done the homework that every school holiday had entailed. On the corner, where it had been for a dozen years, was a photograph, taken at the wedding of Dorothy's uncle. It showed George and Dorothy, Page and Bridesmaid, arm in arm, walking out of the church.

The following morning, he awoke at six o'clock, remembered where he was, turned over and went back to sleep. It was nearly ten when he crept guiltily downstairs. "Morning dear," his mother said cheerily, "have a good lie-in?"

"Yes, thanks."

"Fancy some breakfast?"

"Just some toast, please. I think I've slept through feeling hungry."

"Well, you can always catch up at lunchtime. Your father asked me to tell you he's had to go into the office this morning but he will be back this afternoon if you fancy some shooting."

"I'd like that. I'm meeting Dorothy for lunch but she's got an appointment in London this afternoon. Something to do with war work. Will you feel deserted?"

"Not at all. I've a busy day today – WVS meeting and Comforts for the Troops Committee."

"Does Father know you're comforting the troops?"

She laughed. "Don't be coarse, George. Is this what service life has done to you?"

"Seriously though, is a woman of your talents happy with a couple of committees?"

"You're too kind, dear. The short answer is no. I intend to go back to nursing but only if there is a real need. At the moment, we have what our American cousins have dubbed the 'phoney war' – which basically means there isn't a lot of nursing to do; and I'm too long in the tooth for a lot of menial tasks like rolling bandages and stacking bedpans to fill the time. When the need arises, I will volunteer. Until then, I shall be happy with my committees – and comforting the troops." She continued after a short pause, "So you're lunching with Dorothy. Anything you want to tell me?"

"Such as?"

"Engagements, weddings?"

"No."

"Good Heavens, George! For a man who flies high-speed aircraft, you're awfully slow in some departments. I know you proposed when you were seven but that really doesn't count."

"I know, though it has sufficed until now. I don't feel ready to commit at the moment. I want to have some excitement before I settle down."

"Well I imagine Herr Hitler and his friends will provide that for you. But what about Dorothy? She's a lovely girl. Don't you worry someone else will steal her from you?"

"Dorothy will still be here when this lot's over."

"How can you be so sure?"

"She told me so."

He had taken leave of his mother and Dorothy at the house. They had stood by the front steps as the car went down the drive, each waving with one hand and dabbing a handkerchief to her eyes with the other. George turned to face forwards. His father spoke first. "Well George, it's been wonderful having you home again and I know your mother feels the same, even if you have spoiled her plans slightly."

"What do you mean?"

"She was hoping to apply her considerable administrative talents to organising a wartime wedding, but I gather that's not in prospect at the moment. Is everything alright between you and Dorothy?"

"Yes." He was silent for a few moments. His father watched the road ahead and waited. The words came in a rush. "I sometimes wonder if I am doing the right thing. I love her but I also love my sisters and brother and I'm not going to marry them. I've had no serious girlfriends besides her so I've nothing to compare."

"Having observed your relationship with Dorothy over the years I know it's not *Elizabeth and Essex* but we're all different and perhaps that's what suits you. I won't give you a litany of advice but I will say two things. The first is that neither your mother nor I had a long list of suitors or suitresses before we met but when we did it felt right and we knew it. We didn't need to compare. It felt right then and I'm happy to say it still feels right now. The second is that when, God willing, you come back from the war you won't be the same man you are now. It will change you as war changes everyone that it touches. I didn't meet your mother until our war was all but over so we didn't have to re-adjust to each other. If you're uncertain now about Dorothy then I think you're doing the right thing in waiting."

George was silent again for a while. Eventually he spoke, "Thank you, Father."

"All part of the service," he said lightly, "as you'll find out one day when you're a father too."

They drew up outside the station and while his father retrieved his case from the boot George took a last look around him. A man in a dark suit and a trilby, a raincoat over his arm, alighted from a car, heading for the ticket office; otherwise just the rural tranquillity he was going to war to defend. His father cleared his throat. To George, the brown eyes looked a little shiny and the firm jaw he had known all his life showed a hint of a tremor. Although there were only flecks of grey in his dark hair, for a moment he looked old and vulnerable. "I'm not going to make a speech. Suffice to say that you're a fine son and I'm damned proud of you. Just make sure you come home in one piece – and for God's sake, be careful!" They shook hands and embraced. George picked up his case. "Bye Father. Love to Mother and everyone." He glanced back once as he headed for the platform. Still standing by the car, his father waved.

When the train arrived, he found an empty compartment and settled himself down for the hour or so that it would take to reach Victoria. His solitude didn't last long. The man who had passed him outside the station entered and sat across from him. He felt irritated; 'there must be lots of empty compartments, why come and disturb my peace?' He was considering going to look for another himself when there was a jolt and the train started to move. Smoke from the engine billowed past the window as it laboured to overcome the inertia of the coaches. With increasing speed, station, sidings, and a knot of houses slipped behind and then they were into open country. Without any warning the man spoke. "Good afternoon, P/O Knight."

"How do you know my name? Who are you?"

"Wing Commander Ellitson – Intelligence. I know your name and a lot more besides, because it's my job to do so. I know we haven't got long so listen carefully but feel free to ask questions. I know you once went to the same school as a Marcus Stanhope-Smith, who is now a Section Commander in the same fighter

29

squadron as you, and I know that you were instrumental in his being unmasked as an extortionist, resulting in his expulsion from that school."

"That's history."

"But history has a habit of repeating itself and you may be able to help thwart him again. We suspect that during his time in Germany, he has been seduced by Nazi propaganda and recruited to spy for Germany. He is classic spy material, a man who feels slighted by his own people, seeking revenge in betrayal; and a major coup for German Intelligence, placing an agent right in our armed forces."

"Good Lord! I should have seen it before. It fits him to a tee." He suddenly felt vindicated – he hadn't imagined any of it – but still a little bit irritated that his father had chosen to see things differently. "What do I have to do?"

"You are to do nothing whatsoever which could let Stanhope-Smith know that you suspect him. Just observe and tell nobody what you are doing. Don't put anything in letters home. For the time being, no one below the level of AHQ will be aware of this situation, which means your C/O will have to be kept in the dark. With you going overseas, we can't give you any support, so it will be down to your judgement; if you think something is brewing, go to your C/O or I/O and tell him to contact the Intelligence Section at AHQ, who will fill him in on things and decide in concert with London what to do next."

"Why don't you just grab him and give him the third degree?"

"At the moment there's no evidence that he is a spy and, if he is, we don't know yet how many others are involved. He may also make contacts in France. We want to catch as many of them as possible."

"What do you think he is after?"

"He hasn't gone to the trouble of training as a fighter pilot to find out how soft the pillows are. The chances are he'll be after top secret stuff like the new reflector sight or how our air defence system operates."

"Doesn't he know that already, we practice intercepts quite often?"

"All he knows from that, like you, your fellow pilots and very probably the Germans, is that you are given a course to intercept the enemy. None of you know how that is achieved and for the foreseeable future that's how we want to keep it."

"He's been operational for two years already."

"I've seen his service record. Until three months ago, he was flying biplanes – not much there worth reporting back on. We feel fairly confident he's been lying low until the war began, consolidating his position and waiting for worthwhile opportunities. So – it's down to you now – eyes and ears open and the best of luck!" The train was slowing for a station. When it came to a stop, Ellitson opened the door and was gone in an instant, leaving George to reflect on what had been said.

Fifteen Hurricanes took off on a late-October morning better suited to summer. They flew in five vics of three aircraft, in line astern. George was in his now accustomed position of Red Three, tucked in to the left of and behind Brian Underhill, their wingtips overlapping and just feet apart, as the squadron made the customary beat-up of the airfield before setting course for France. As 686 climbed away, the order was given to relax formation and the vics widened and dropped back from each other. They flew across the verdant fields of Kent and then, passing over the White Cliffs of Dover, the enormity struck George that he was leaving England to go to war. He felt a lump in his throat as it came to him that he might never see home again. He was glad for those moments to be alone in the cockpit.

From 5,000 feet the channel looked calm and blue under the bright sun. Far to the north, he could see a coastal convoy heading towards the Thames Estuary; he was pleased not to be escorting it. Otherwise the whole expanse of sea was virtually empty. Two months ago, before war had been declared, it had been full of cross channel steamers bustling to and fro, merchant traffic and all manner of pleasure craft. Shortly after crossing the French coast, they arrived at Norrent-Fontes where they refreshed themselves with NAAFI tea while the aircraft were being refuelled. Then it was a south-easterly course for Anglure, and lunch with the French.

After an uneventful arrival, the sections were guided to dispersal points by ground crews. As Red Section climbed from their aircraft they were greeted individually by French pilots. George's escort, a tall, dark, individual with a slight stoop and a lugubrious expression gave a well-practised salute. *"Bonjour!* I am *Sous-lieutenant* Thierry Gautier and on behalf of *Groupe de Chasse III/5 of L'Armee de l'Air,* I welcome you to Anglure."

George returned the salute, *"Enchante, je suis Pilot Officer George Knight."*

The Frenchman looked surprised, "You speak French? Those of us who are able have been ordered to speak English today."

George smiled. "I speak some French but I rarely get the chance to use it. People keep talking to me in English."

Gautier laughed and the ice was broken between them. "Orders are orders. Can I ask you to accompany me?" He gestured in the general direction of the Officers' Mess. As they walked, George could see the *Escadrille's* mounts, Morane Saulnier 406 fighters, dispersed at intervals around the airfield. Nearing the Mess, his attention was caught by a solitary plane, parked in the shadow of a hangar, without squadron markings or camouflage, but, far from being an abandoned relic as may have been assumed, it looked modem and new.

"Is that a Dewoitine 520?"

Gautier registered surprise again. "It is supposed to be top secret."

"We were shown silhouettes before we came here. Better than attacking them out of ignorance." Gautier nodded his agreement. "Is that one a prototype?" He was obviously reluctant to reply. "We are on the same side, you know," prompted George.

Gautier shrugged. "We will be receiving many more in January. This is for us to acclimatise ourselves. It is the French Spitfire, you know." He looked a little conspiratorial, "It would be better if no one knows I have told you these things."

"Bien sur," said George. Like the Spitfire the D520 had a long nose but to him it was a less elegant aeroplane. He decided not to share his opinion.

They joined with a throng of French and British airmen that was forming near the Mess. On the balcony, a man with a cine camera was filming the gathering. "Looks like we're on Pathe News," George said to Reg, who had appeared beside him. "And 'Picture Post' or 'Paris Match'," he replied, indicating a man in a rumpled Macintosh with a large camera, obviously from the 'Press', "not to mention our own roving cameraman."

George turned to see Stanhope-Smith, camera in hand, arranging a group photograph.

"Excusez-moi un moment," he said to Gautier and moved nearer to observe the proceedings. Stanhope-Smith, his back to George, was on the farther side of the gathering from the Mess and as George approached, he could hear him giving directions. "I need you a little further left because of the light. Just a step more… that's perfect. Now hold it… OK! Anyone else?" A group of British and French pilots stepped forward. "Can you move that way a bit please? Otherwise the light will be wrong. A bit more, a bit more. Spot on. Hold it there and… say cheese! Got it! Who's next?" George was puzzled because all Stanhope-Smith's subjects seemed to be off to one side. Realisation hit him like a slap in the face. Stanhope-Smith was using them as a decoy and manoeuvring them out of the photo. There was no more room for doubt in George's mind now. "You cunning bastard!" he muttered under his breath, "You're photographing the D520. You really are working for the Germans." Presumably, there would follow a regretful announcement that the photos had failed to develop; by which time they would be on their way to Germany. George swung away and headed back to Gautier and Reg, not wanting Stanhope-Smith to catch sight of him at that moment lest his face betrayed his thoughts.

His mind whirls, trying to decide what to do – it would be futile and probably self-defeating to denounce Stanhope-Smith here, as well as contrary to the orders he has been given; from what he has seen of the camera it is solidly built and unlikely to be damaged by all but the most severe of 'accidents'; the only answer he can find is to get possession for long enough to open it and allow daylight to spoil the film inside; but he has to do this without Stanhope-Smith knowing or suspecting his involvement, and obviously before the film is removed, which most probably means he has to act in the next couple of hours, before 686 leave Anglure.

His thoughts are interrupted by the announcement that lunch is served. He knows that he must be seated close, but not too close, to Stanhope-Smith. He spots him making his way towards the Mess entrance and pushes his way through the throng in order to claim a suitable seat, completely abandoning Gautier, who endeavours to follow with a mixture of surprise and irritation. When he catches up, George is three places away from Stanhope-Smith. His chagrin is eased when George indicates the seat he has saved for him. "I 'ad not realised you were so 'ungry," he says tetchily.

"Forgive me – bad habit from schooldays – it used to be first-come, first-served." He knows the excuse sounds feeble even as he says it, but it is all he can think of. He has achieved one small objective. The camera is in his view, placed on the table at Stanhope-Smith's right hand – just three places away; Gautier, Hewartson of Green Section and another Frenchman intervene. But what could he do even if he were sitting next to it? He can't just grab it and open it in full view of everyone. He is vaguely aware that he is eating a fine lunch and that Gautier is trying to make polite conversation. His mind is hardly on either; it is filled with a succession of schemes, ranging from hopeful to fantastic. When his opportunity comes, it is in a manner he has not expected – an announcement that before coffee is served there will be a ten-minute break. George is on the alert – this has to be the moment. Most of the company rise and leave the room immediately. He wants to go too but knows he must not. Gautier, baffled by George's reluctance to move, excuses himself. Hewartson and his companion have already gone. George watches with bated breath as Stanhope-Smith rises to leave. He pauses and reaches for the camera. George's heart sinks. The opportunity is gone. No! He's had second thoughts and is heading for the door without it chatting amiably to his Frenchman. George glances round. The room is virtually empty. A couple of people have remained but they are deep in conversation. It's now or never. His heart in his mouth, George stands up and moves towards the camera, trying to look nonchalant; inwardly more nervous than he can ever remember. He is standing over it. A furtive glance. No one seems to be looking. Slowly and casually he reaches out. His hand touches the camera and he gently feels his way to the back. He finds the catch that he once saw Stanhope-Smith operate. He explores it with his fingertips for a couple of seconds and then, holding his breath, with one finger, he presses. He feels, more than hears, a gentle click. The back is unlatched.

"I say, George!" His hand recoils from the camera as though he has been stung. Guiltily, he turns to face... Giles, who does not appear to notice his discomfiture. "Have you seen my Frog? I seem to have misplaced him."

"I don't think so. Wouldn't know him anyway." George replies, relieved.

"Dapper chap, looks like a young Claude Rains."

"Sorry, Giles. Definitely not seen him. Must still be outside," he replies calmly, hiding his mounting agitation – *for God's sake go away!*

"You're probably right. Better go and look for him there. Wizard lunch don't you think, especially that pate? I'll remember that for some time to come."

Oh please bugger off! - "Yes, wizard!" Giles lingers for a few moments more before turning to head back whence he has come. "See you later, then." George does not respond. He has missed his chance. In numbers people are drifting back into the dining room. He feels crushed. He knows he should re-latch the camera and move away. Utter numbing disappointment leaves him rooted to the spot. He is aware of someone approaching. Must be Stanhope-Smith, come to catch him red handed. He doesn't care. Instead, it is Gautier, with concern on his face.

"Are you alright? You look unwell." Before George can answer, Gautier picks up the camera. "What a fine... *Zut alors!*" It is Gautier's turn to be crestfallen. The back of the camera has swung open. His face registers dismay. George is ecstatic. He cannot believe his luck. He could almost hug Gautier. The pall of gloom is lifted and his mind is sharp again. He takes the camera from Gautier's tentative grasp, making sure that the door is kept open for a few seconds longer, then snaps it shut and replaces it on the table. A glance round convinces him that no one has seen what occurred; the camera having been between them. He seizes Gautier by the elbow and propels him towards the door.

"I think I could do with a breath of air after all."

"But I must apologise to your colleague. I 'ave ruined his film."

"I don't think that would be a good idea. The chap concerned would probably make a scene and neither your *Commandant* nor my Squadron Leader would be very happy about that – today of all days. This way he'll be well away from here when he discovers the film is spoiled and he won't have any idea it was you."

"But the pictures 'e took..."

"Were only a few souvenir photos – nothing special. I'm sure the official photographs will make up for what has been lost. It was an accident, so don't blame yourself. In England we have a saying – 'least said, soonest mended'."

Five minutes later, they return to the dining room. George glances in Stanhope-Smith's direction, taking care not to catch his eye. He is talking, looking relaxed and unconcerned; possibly, George thinks to himself, a little smug. The camera is where he had replaced it. All is well. Inwardly, he is very happy. He has foiled Stanhope-Smith. To do so, he has exceeded his orders just to observe but he is certain he has done the right thing in the circumstances. Moreover, it will be plainly obvious that a faulty film has spoiled his photos so why will Stanhope-Smith have reason to think that George or anyone else is involved?

After coffee and an exchange of compliments between the Commandant and S/L Sullivan it was time for 686 to leave. British and French once more made their way onto the aerodrome; the British to head for their aircraft, the French to watch; for it was the unwritten rule that the visiting Squadron would put on a 'show' for their hosts. George turned to Gautier. He felt he had made a friend and regretted that he had to some extent used him. "Thank you for your excellent company. It has been a pleasure and an honour to meet you."

Gautier looked shrewdly at George. "I 'ave 'eard it said that the English are mad and at times today, I thought I was seeing it for myself. But you are not mad, and I don't think you are bad," he smirked at the unintended rhyme, "and I doubt that you are ready to let me into your secret, so I would like you to assure me that whatever you have involved me in is nothing for which I should feel regret."

George made no attempt to protest innocence but looked him straight in the eye. "I give you my word as an officer and a gentleman that you have done nothing for which you should feel ashamed. In fact, very much the opposite. I hope we shall meet again at a time when I can tell you more. In the meantime," he gave a conspiratorial wink, "It would be better if no one knows I 'ave told you these things." He climbed into his cockpit accompanied by a roar of laughter from Gautier.

The squadron took off together in an enlarged vee comprising five sections. Once in the air, they went into sections line astern and, as they climbed, circled round to fly over the airfield again. S/L Sullivan's section had climbed higher than the others and dived steeply down at the airfield before pulling up into a loop and half-rolling off the top in the direction they had come from. The remaining sections flew low over the airfield respectively exhibiting upward rolls, hesitation rolls, barrel rolls and slow rolls before orbiting round for a final pass. This time, each section dived almost to ground level before breaking away into Prince of Wales' feathers; the performance orchestrated by the crisp commands of S/L Sullivan and his section leaders over the R/T. Climbing away, George could see the French pilots waving enthusiastically. It had been a hard ten minute's flying and he was pleased with his own contribution but, above all, he felt a fierce pride in the group of which he was so obviously now a part.

S/L Sullivan addressed them briefly when they reached their new airfield. "Congratulations to you all on a fine display of flying for our allies at Anglure. Today you have upheld the finest traditions of the service. Now there is nothing more for you to do other than go and find your accommodation, to which end I will hand you over to the Adjutant who, whilst you have been living off the fat of the land, has been bribing and corrupting on an unimaginable scale to ensure your continuing comfort." Richard cleared his throat and the cheers and laughter subsided. "Your personal possessions are awaiting you in the 'Billet Bus' over there," he said indicating a lorry standing nearby, "and I will now distribute directions to your respective billets. For the foreseeable future you will be fed by your hosts. Tonight is yours. You are due back here at 0700 tomorrow. Your transport will be outside the *Mairie* at 0645. The Officers' Mess is to be in the *Mairie* but it will not be ready for you until tomorrow. Thank you, gentlemen."

George and the other pilots climbed from the 'Billet Bus' and surveyed the village square. On one side, where he stood, was the *Mairie,* the largest and grandest of the buildings. It was flanked by lesser structures, one of which was a library; of the rest he was unsure. Opposite stood *le Cafe Georges* which he took to be a good omen. It was a brightly painted building with a large gaily-striped awning which shaded a number of tables and chairs. Either side of it and continuing around the other two sides of the square were shops whose signboards displayed words he had not seen since school French lessons — *Boucher, Boulangier, Epicier, Legumier et Fruitier* and *Tabac.* In the middle of the square, encircled by a cobbled road was a paved area with more tables and chairs and a number of trees which now retained only a handful of brown leaves from the dense green canopies which they had sported in summer. Even as he looked a few more fluttered down to lie forlornly on the tables or the paving. At each corner of the square, a road led off to other parts of the village and beyond.

"I say," suggested Giles, "how about a snifter before we head off to our billets?"

"Good plan," said 'Foggy', "let's try *le Cafe Georges* — you never said you owned a cafe, George!"

"One doesn't like to brag," countered George, "and one likes to keep the riff-raff out." He ducked an attempted cuff from 'Foggy' and tried, unsuccessfully, to return the compliment. By this time, they had reached the cafe and as they filed noisily inside they were met by the unmistakeable smell of French cigarettes. Several patrons, seeing the RAF uniforms, nodded their appreciation and there was the odd murmur of 'bravo'.

Behind the wooden bar with its forest of pumps and bottles stood a short, stocky man of about fifty with receding dark hair, clad in black waistcoat and trousers, white shirt and apron. A *Gauloise* drooped from his mouth. He looked bored. His greeting sounded rehearsed and uninspiring. The *Gauloise* danced as he spoke, one eye closed against the rising smoke. *"Bonjour messieurs, le Cafe Georges* welcomes our brave RAF allies. What can I offer you?"

Giles had been first to enter and now he was at the front of the press of bodies at the bar. He managed to turn enough to count his compatriots. *"Douze bieres, s'il vous plait,"* and then to the throng, "If you think I'm paying for this lot you're jolly well mistaken, someone pass a hat round." The first round disappeared quickly. "Who's for another?" called Giles.

"Not for me thanks," said Stanhope-Smith, placing his glass on the bar, "I'm off to find my billet. See you chaps in the morning."

Reg was returning to the bar from a call of nature. "Was that Stanhope-Smith I saw leaving? The one-pint wonder."

"Yes, I don't think he's ready for a Frobisher tour yet," said Giles, "what say you, George?"

"No, you're right, not really a drinking man," he replied abstractedly. His attention was on a sullen looking Frenchman, seemingly a farm labourer, sitting at the end of the bar, who had been staring moodily into his drink ever since the pilots had arrived, as if he did not share the general goodwill towards the RAF. When Stanhope-Smith's name had been mentioned, he had exchanged a quick glance with the cafe owner, before resuming his study. Some twenty seconds later, he emptied his glass, dropped a few coins on the bar and left without a word. It seemed to George that Stanhope-Smith was expected.

At the suggestion of a third, George and several others demurred, "I don't think it'll make a good impression if we arrive at our new billets blotto." He put some money into the hat and made for the door. Outside, he picked up his belongings and looked at the piece of paper he had been given. It read – 'Madame Delacroix – School House'. He looked around the square. To his left *'Rue d'Ecole'* seemed to provide the answer. The road was cobbled and ran up a slight incline. He had passed a couple of houses before he recognised what was different from home – each had shutters to its windows. The sun was now low in the sky and the evening becoming chilly; the smell of wood smoke hung in the air. He quickened his pace and within a couple of minutes, he had arrived at the school, next to which, and built of the same stone, was the School House. It was larger than the houses he had passed and obviously intended to look more important. In the garden, a woman in a large overcoat was clearing up leaves. Blonde hair tumbled from under her beret. As he opened the gate, she put down the rake and turned to face him. *"Bonjour Madame Delacroix, Je suis* Pilot Officer Knight."

She came towards him, her pretty face radiating a pleasant, unaffected smile which was reinforced by her grey-green eyes, and spoke English, made alluring by a hint of French accent, "Pleased to meet you Pilot Officer. I am *Mademoiselle Delacroix,* but I would prefer you to call me Justine."

He smiled "Only if you will call me George." As he took her proffered hand, their eyes met. He was completely unprepared for the feelings that came over him at that moment. They stood for several seconds, as though locked together in eternity; and then the spell was broken. George looked at his feet and tried to still his racing heart. Justine, hoping to hide her confusion, turned towards the house and, with a catch in her voice, called, *"Mamam, c'est le Pilote Anglais qui tu attends!"*

Madame Delacroix bustled excitedly down the path, oblivious to what had occurred.

"Monsieur, oh monsieur, bienvenu a notre maison – pardonnez moi – welcome to our 'ouse, Justine has been teaching me the English but in my excitation I forget." Her greying hair was in a bun and her face had lines, but she was clearly Justine's mother.

George had recovered some semblance of composure. *"Enchante Madame. Je voudrais que vous m'appelez Georges aussi."* He leaned forward and kissed her hand. "Zen you must call me, *Mamam."* Her joy seemed to be complete and she stood for a few seconds not knowing what to say next.

"Perhaps we should show George his room, Mamam," said Justine, taking the initiative, her voice still a little unsteady. As she turned, their eyes met again: briefly, but enough for both to know they hadn't imagined what had passed between them.

He followed them into the house and upstairs. The furnishings were simple, the decoration tasteful. Beeswax vied for his attention with kitchen aromas. His room was sparsely furnished but opposite the fireplace, in which the remains of logs glowed, and below a small wooden crucifix, was a wrought iron bedstead and what looked like a feather mattress; a big improvement, he thought, on the service beds he had known for the last fifteen months.

Justine and her mother left him to unpack his belongings. Instead, he sat on the bed and tried to make sense of the last few minutes.

In Sussex, the day better suited to summer ended like many a summer's day. Dirty grey clouds rolled in, bringing squalls of rain and ferocious gusts of wind. George's mother was giving the house a final airing before November damp would make the process impractical. As the wind rose, she and the maid scurried to close the windows. Having secured George's room, she noticed that the photograph had been blown off his desk and was lying, face down, on the fire surround. She picked it up and gasped; there was a jagged crack lengthways in the glass, separating George from Dorothy.

A clock chimed the quarter hour. A shadowy figure moved swiftly across the darkened square and made for the equally darkened *Cafe Georges*. A double tap and the door opened soundlessly. The figure ducked in under the blackout curtain and the door closed. "Good evening *mi'lor*, I 'ave been expecting you."

The interior was gloomy but, after the dark outside, Stanhope-Smith could see well enough to confirm that there were only the two of them; there was no sign of the man who had earlier followed him and thrust a crumpled note into his hand. It had read 'Cafe Georges – 11.15 – knock twice.' "Have you anything to say to me?" he demanded.

"The lights are bright on the Wilhelmstrasse despite the war,"

"But Piccadilly is in darkness. I take it you're Georges?" He relaxed visibly. "Jacques, actually – Jacques Dubois. The name came with the cafe and I didn't..."

"I don't have long. My landlady thinks I'm out for a breath of fresh air. God knows I need one. The bloody house stinks like a pigsty. Is there anyone else?"

"Just Marcel, *mi'lor*. You met 'im this afternoon."

"The peasant?" Away from the squadron he saw no reason to be the 'new' Stanhope- Smith. His manner was already starting to grate. Jacques knew he could grow to dislike this man even more than he had grown to dislike himself.

"Marcel fought in Spain. 'E knows about guerrilla fighting and silent killing. I was in the engineers in the last war. We are ready when you give the word."

"Which won't be anytime soon!" snapped Stanhope-Smith, "the last thing we need at the moment is to draw attention to ourselves with pointless stunts. For the time being we watch and listen, until something worthwhile comes along." He waited for a moment. "I take it you have a contact?"

"Yes, *mi'lor*. I meet 'im when I go to Nancy for provisions. 'E receives my reports and issues instructions."

"From now on he will receive reports and relay messages. I will be issuing your instructions."

"Yes, *mi'lor*." He tried to keep the growing resentment out of his voice.

"Why do you keep calling me *mi'lor*?"

"You are an Englishman with two names so you must be a lord."

Stanhope-Smith decided not to correct him. "I have to get back. I will contact you again in a few days." He drew a small package from his pocket. "In the meantime this must get to Berlin as quickly as possible."

"Do I say what it is?"

"Just say the contents will be self-explanatory. One more thing, no more notes unless there is a serious problem. Our future meetings will be arranged by a signal and will be here at 11.00 pm. If I need to see you I will come into the cafe, drink a coffee and leave a cigarette in the saucer, two if I need Marcel as well. Do you have a bicycle?" He nodded. "Then leave a sign outside – *bicyclette a louer* – if you want to see me."

Jacques locked the door behind Stanhope-Smith and as he made his way across the café, he caught his reflection in the large mirror behind the bar. *'Stupide idiot!'* Five years ago he and his wife were running one of the best cafes in Paris. But the lure of cards and horses had proved to be his undoing. Two years later, he was sitting, alone and drunk, in the ruins of his business waiting for the bailiffs, when he was approached by a man he had seen increasingly in the cafe in its declining months. The man made an astonishing offer. If Jacques promised to give up gambling he would set him up in another cafe – not in Paris but in a small village near the Maginot Line. The loan, for that is what he had said it was, could be paid off over a period of time in exchange for information – information picked up by listening to the soldiers, from the nearby army camp, who frequented the cafe. Three years on, the loan had not been paid off. The soldiers had gone and the airmen had come in their place. Now he was in league with an ex-guerrilla and a turncoat English lord, selling the country he had once fought for with each 'installment' of the loan. There was no getting off; he was trapped on a runaway train and he knew that one day it would hit the buffers.

Despite the comfort of the feather bed, George was finding it difficult to sleep. It had been an extraordinary day and his mind was working overtime. He was in France – only a few miles to the east lay Nazi Germany. Now there was a real chance of seeing action. If nothing else it was a change from the Stanhope-Smith business. He had no doubt now that he was a spy; but, as one question had resolved itself another had arisen – how could he watch three of them, assuming, of course, that they were only three? Was it time now to involve others? He knew he must decide, and soon, but there was a subject he would much rather be thinking about – Justine. Dinner had been a sublime experience. Mamam's food was first class but he would have settled for bread and water to be at that table with Justine. He could recollect every detail; the tilt of her head when she listened; the magic of her smile; the lips which he couldn't wait to kiss: the way she flicked her hair; the music of her laughter and, above all, the sparkle of her eyes. Did she share his feelings? The indications were good – their eyes had met several times; he had seen shyness but not rejection. And what feelings! He had never known anything like this before – this had to be love, real love, an overwhelming desire for her, not like the sedate affection he had felt for – Oh God – Dorothy – he had quite forgotten her! One thing he knew with certainty; whatever happened between him and Justine he would not be marrying Dorothy now, it would neither be right for him nor fair to her – he would only ever be going through the motions and he had more respect for her than that. He must write to her immediately; try to break it gently, but what should he say?

Dear Dorothy,... He was still trying to compose his letter when sleep finally overtook him.

Stanhope-Smith was finding sleep elusive too. He lay in the dark, watching the glow as he drew on his cigarette; and thinking. He had done well today; the photographs would be well received in Berlin. It felt good to be contributing after two frustrating years flying Gloster Gauntlets; biplanes so outdated that all he could report was that the RAF was ready for a rerun of the last war. He had been counselled to contain his impatience by his contact, Max; ostensibly an Austrian refugee who eked out a living teaching violin from a dusty little flat off the Edgeware Road. And Max had been right. To his surprise, not long after his squadron had converted to Hurricanes he had been promoted Flying Officer and transferred to 686. He had visited Max on the first day of his embarkation leave, the first time since his transfer. "Your patience is paying off. In France I think you will find more scope for your mission. Ring me in three days and I will tell you of your contact in St Jean. Have you anything for me?"

"Only that George Knight, the person responsible for my expulsion from school is in the squadron. Initially I was frightened he would reveal my past but I spun him a tale about being a reformed character and he swallowed it hook, line and sinker. He's like the rest of them; overgrown schoolboys who want to drink beer and talk about girls. My countrymen have no great vision or purpose like the Fuehrer has given Germany: that is why they will lose this war."

"Never underestimate the British," he had tapped his lower leg, producing a metallic sound, "that is the mistake we made last time. I am not so sure about this Knight." Stanhope-Smith had been surprised at the steel which the seemingly gentle older man had revealed, "if you get the chance I think you should kill him. Do not let him jeopardise your mission. I expect great things of you."

He was not squeamish but if it came to killing George he knew who would be ideal for the job – Marcel. He had recognised him as a killer in their brief encounter after leaving the cafe. He could see Marcel being an asset. He was less certain of Jacques. He was neither a psychopath nor an idealist – he was in this for money and men who can be bought once can be bought by a higher bidder. He would have to keep his eye on Jacques.

He stubbed out his cigarette and turned over. He needed to sleep, for tomorrow he would begin the next stage of his efforts to help the Third Reich towards world domination. And if George Knight had to be killed – so be it; it was well overdue as far as he was concerned.

Justine awoke with a start. She had gone to sleep contentedly, suffused with the warm glow that comes from contentment. She too had been surprised by what she had felt when she met George; but not unpleasantly. She knew she had met a special man; charming, handsome, intelligent and, as a fighter pilot, obviously dashing and brave; yet in his eyes she saw a gentleness and she sensed a certain endearing shyness. This was a man to whom she could give herself willingly. Above all this, however, was the sensation when they first met; the feeling that he was meant for her and she for him. But sleep had brought dreams and she had seen another man, broken by war, slowly coughing his life away.

She took a sip from the glass of water at her bedside and lay down again to sleep. But doubts had begun to seep into her mind.

3: November, 1939

George left the house before Justine was awake, his spirits undampened by the drizzle which accompanied him on his walk to the *Mairie.* The first hint of dawn revealed a solid layer of low, grey cloud stretching across the sky.

Before the war, the airfield had belonged to a private flying club and boasted a small hangar and a couple of brick-built buildings. Of these one had become offices for Squadron Leader, Adjutant and Intelligence Officer and the other the dispersal hut for pilots on duty. Here the pilots learned that the C/O had gone to Area HQ with the Adjutant and that they were to maintain thirty-minute readiness until he returned.

The morning passed slowly. A strong feeling of anti-climax produced a subdued atmosphere. Some talked, others smoked or read. George was mainly occupied with thoughts of Justine. At midday, the rain stopped and he was having a breath of fresh air when the squadron Humber returned. S/L Sullivan emerged grim faced and headed straight for his office. Richard was about to do the same when he saw George approaching. "Hello Adj, good trip?"

"Not really, it seems there's been a monumental cock-up and we shouldn't be here."

George's heart sank. "What do you mean?"

"As you know, we were sent here to protect some of our Battles after a formation got shot up rather badly. But they've gone back to the Reims area and someone else moved a couple of Hurricane squadrons already in France to give them cover. By the time the right hand found out what the left hand was doing we were here; surplus to requirements."

"So are we going back then?" He waited with his heart in his mouth. He didn't want to leave – not now.

"No, the Brass think it wouldn't look good to our allies if we were to scuttle back to England. German propaganda is already saying that the British will only fight to the last Frenchman. So it seems we are here for the duration. As you would expect, the C/O isn't very pleased."

"I can imagine." He almost sagged with relief.

"Anyway, you'll hear it from him. He wants all pilots in the dispersal hut at fourteen hundred hours."

After reprising what George had learned from the Adjutant, Sullivan continued, "Whatever the circumstances of our coming here, the fact is that we are here to stay and with your help I intend to make sure that the only ones who have cause to regret it will be the Germans; which leads me to operational matters. AHQ believe that the next few months will be fairly quiet. The armies on both sides are unlikely to make a major offensive through the winter months and aerial activity is going to be correspondingly quiet – reconnaissance flights and possibly some fighter incursions to test our response. It will be spring before the balloon goes up, which gives us five months or so to prepare. Unfortunately, we don't have the kind of fighter control we had in England. Keep this under your hats because it's absolutely hush-hush but I've just heard we're going to get a portable version. Until it arrives, unlike the controlled intercepts we practised at home, we will have to rely on the French Observer Corps. Not ideal, bearing in mind the speed of modern aircraft; the bandit will have travelled some distance by the time we get an alert, so we will have to chase after him. However, Jerry has been sending over an early morning recce flight on a regular basis which, weather permitting, we can expect to continue, so, from tomorrow, we will put up a morning patrol at Section strength with the intention of knocking him down. Standing patrols are wasteful so otherwise we will only scramble in response to observer plots. Until the military or aerial situations show signs of changing, I intend to have only one Flight on readiness each day, on an alternating basis. Within each Flight, Sections will alternate the morning patrol. I hope you will thus all have gained actual combat experience by next spring. Initially, I want the Flight not at readiness each day to put in some time getting to know the lie of the land; I don't want you getting lost. Finally, I will draw your attention to standing orders which for the present forbid crossing the frontier. You may be tempted to do so, either in pursuit of a fleeing Jerry or to provoke a response from their fighters but for the time being the order is – don't. Your chance will come soon enough. Any questions?"

"When do you think we will get this... portable control stuff, sir?" asked 'Roy'.

"I can't say with any certainty but I would hope we'll have it by Christmas."

"Is it the same system we had at home, sir?"

"Less range I understand, but enough for our needs – and smaller – apparently it all fits into a couple of trucks." Stanhope-Smith had put the last question, deadpan, concealing his mounting excitement. George, sitting behind him, had been daydreaming about Justine through the C/O's talk but suddenly he was alert; he knew the time had come to share his burden.

Stanhope-Smith ducked under the blackout curtain. Locking the door behind him, Jacques wondered what had caused the excitement which showed in his face. He held out a plain white envelope. "Make sure this gets to Berlin immediately; make a special trip to Nancy if necessary."

"I take it I am not to know what it contains?" Jacques said tartly.

"Correct," he said bluntly, "just let me know the minute that you get a response. In the meantime, that bicycle of yours – I need it."

"Now?"

"No – on my days off. I have decided to photograph the countryside."

It was three days before George got his opportunity. Stanhope-Smith was airborne with Yellow Section and 'B' Flight had gone on a familiarisation trip. 'Roy' and Brian were at dispersal, in discussion with F/Sgt Robertson. George had

42

wanted as few as possible seeing him go to the C/O; it was bound to lead to questions. He was happy therefore to find that S/L Sullivan was again at AHQ; no one would take notice of him talking with 'Einstein'.

Albert Howlett, a mathematics teacher in peacetime, had applied to join the RAF as a pilot even though he knew his eyesight left something to be desired. His attempt to pass the eye test by memory had failed because he found himself myopically reciting a different chart from that which was before him. The RAF, possibly impressed by his feats of memory, decided that he had something to offer and after a few weeks learning the essentials of service life he found himself, in the uniform of a Flying Officer, posted to 686 Squadron. Albert the mathematician had soon become known to one and all as 'Einstein'.

George entered his sanctum and closed the door. "Morning sir, can you spare me a few minutes?"

'Einstein' looked up from the sea of forms on his desk. "You're very formal today, George. Ought I to call you P/O Knight? I'd be glad to give you a few minutes, anything's better than this." He smiled, "Sorry, didn't mean it like that."

His smile turned to incredulous laughter when George began by saying that Stanhope-Smith was a Gennan agent but twenty minutes later, a serious looking 'Einstein' made the telephone call. It was several minutes before he replaced the receiver. He looked grim. "When I made this call half of me was hoping it was some elaborate practical joke, but it isn't. When did you know for certain?"

"Anglure, when he was taking the photographs."

"The Air Commodore told me to give you a pat on the back for your initiative over the camera. To use his words 'Richard Hannay wouldn't have done it better'." George felt a glow of pride but kept a straight face. "So what happens next?"

"The responsibility is off your shoulders now. Things will be controlled via AHQ but here, apart from you and I, only the C/O will know – they're telling him as we speak, glad that job didn't fall to me – so we're to continue to observe and report."

"Aren't they going to nab him?"

"Apparently not. I think they want to give him a bit more rope."

"But what about the fighter control system – I'm sure that's his objective?"

"It's not here yet, so no point worrying. They probably know what they're doing."

A week after their last meeting, Stanhope-Smith had received the 'bicycle for hire' signal from Jacques. "I hope this is important."

"But of course mi'lor. I have two messages. First, the packet you sent containing a film. Unfortunately no pictures could be saved. It has been suggested that you take more care in handling films."

Stanhope-Smith was seized with a wild anger. He had taken a big risk photographing the D520 and it had all been for nothing. He shouted at Jacques. "I was bloody well careful! I removed that film from the camera in absolute darkness. It must have been faulty – or they handled it wrongly in Berlin."

Jacques shrugged, "Per'aps you are right mi'lor, I am only the messenger, after all."

43

Stanhope-Smith sensed that Jacques was enjoying his discomfiture and it angered him further. "What is the second thing?" he demanded.

"Your plan is approved in outline. You are to keep Berlin informed of developments and you will be given all possible assistance." He produced an envelope, "The information you requested is in here. In addition, I've been given a small portable transmitter. It is to be used sparingly, when the usual channels will not suffice." Stanhope-Smith's anger dissolved, replaced by exultation. This would more than make up for the camera fiasco. He glanced at the envelope to see if it had been opened.

"Am I to know what this plan is, *mi'lor*?" There was a hint of frustration in his voice.

"I'll tell you when I'm ready." He felt no inclination to trust Jacques until he had to.

"Have you ever been to England?"

"I was there for eighteen months, studying English. I had to abandon it in January and come home when Papa died."

"I'm sorry." He regretted the question. He would not have asked it if he had known where it would lead. Her sadness was almost tangible.

"Thank you, but it was probably a mercy – for him and Mamam. He was gassed in 1917 and never completely recovered. Winters were the worst because of the damage to his lungs and in the last couple of years his health declined quite rapidly. Mamam nursed him but beyond that there was nothing she could do."

She fell silent and he could sense the conversation was drying up. He tried to revive it; he did not want the evening to end like this. "Will you finish your studies?"

"I have found my vocation so there is no need. I was going to go back to England but Mamam was brought low by Papa's death, spiritually and financially, and I knew I couldn't leave her. By a happy chance the village school needed a teacher. I was given some glowing references and everything just fell into place."

They were talking in the kitchen. These were the moments George looked forward to. As usual, Mamam had been with them earlier but she had gone to bed. He felt guilty at being pleased when she retired but it left just him and Justine, together. It should have been perfect – but it wasn't. After that first night some unseen barrier had been progressively raised. She still smiled, she still laughed, she still talked and he felt she was still attracted to him but she was not giving herself wholeheartedly as he was to her; she was holding back and he had no idea why. He only knew how much he wanted her and that he would do whatever it took to break the barrier down. He decided to try a new gambit. "I hear there's a cinema in Epinal. Fancy going with me one evening?"

It seemed an eternity before she answered and when she did the words were like daggers to his heart. "I don't think so, but thank you for asking."

As he looked out of the dispersal hut window across the rain-soaked airfield, George thought back to that conversation. She had been still more distant since then. But he was convinced that she was suppressing her true feelings – or was it just wishful thinking on his part?

If things were going badly regarding Justine they were no better on the flying front. Fog, rain and gales in the first three weeks of November meant there had been few opportunities; He had yet to do a morning patrol and had had just one local flight so far. The squadron's only contact with the enemy had been by Yellow Section on the day he had been to see 'Einstein' – they had stalked a Dornier but lost it in cloud.

The morning's patrol had been cancelled yet again but the seemingly limitless expanse of low grey cloud was gradually breaking up as the day wore on. Ironically, 'B' Flight had taken to the air an hour ago on a 'local' leaving 'A' Flight hoping for an intruder.

They were still waiting when they heard the approaching sound of Merlin engines and seconds later, the dispersal hut shuddered as 'B' Flight roared low overhead. They ran outside to watch the 'beat-up'.

"Maybe they've got a Jerry," suggested Giles.

"Nonsense," retorted Underhill, "they're celebrating because they've found the airfield; 'B' Flight never could navigate."

Thirty seconds later, the Hurricanes came roaring back. One of their number had detached itself and was flying lower. Over the airfield perimeter it began a slow roll. "Who's that?" called Evans.

"I think its Alderley," Stanhope-Smith responded, squinting to make out the identification letters.

"He's bloody low!" added Giles.

"If you didn't know before, that's why we call him 'Edge'," 'Roy' shouted to George above the din, "nothing to do with his surname – it's because he likes to live on the edge of... Oh Christ!"

The crack was like a rifle shot. They stood in dreadful fascination and watched. The Hurricane was three-quarters of the way through the slow roll, its wings vertical. The rudder, which at that stage was pointing skywards to provide lift, sagged and the aircraft staggered in the air. The pilot tried to regain control but he was flying too low and too fast. A wing tip dug into the turf and the aircraft cartwheeled before slamming into the ground. Pandemonium broke out. Instinctively, the watchers began running, some towards the crash, and others towards the fire tender. Their shouts were drowned by the roar as ruptured fuel tanks exploded in a sheet of flame. They stopped, knowing that even if he had survived the impact, 'Edge' would not have survived the explosion and fire. George found himself hoping that he had died before the flames took hold. In silence, they watched his funeral pyre burn.

The word was that some of 'B' Flight had stumbled across a Dornier and attacked it. It was last seen heading eastwards with both engines trailing smoke after putting up a spirited defence, making good use of available cloud cover and scoring hits on the attacking Hurricanes, including 'Edge's'. They had been waiting for nearly an hour, talking in subdued tones, after being ordered to assemble in the Mess. S/L Sullivan entered, his face pale. His voice was hard and angry. "Today, one of your colleagues died – needlessly and pointlessly; he wasn't

45

killed in action, he was killed doing low- level aerobatics after combat. His aircraft failed because it had sustained damage, although he didn't realise it. Tonight, I have to write a letter to his next of kin – do I tell them he died bravely, fighting for King and country, or uselessly, fooling about?" He paused to let his words sink in; no one made a sound. "Never again, as long as I am in charge of this squadron, will this folly be repeated. If anyone chooses to ignore me, they will be court-martialled and finish their service career cleaning latrines – with a bloody toothbrush." He strode from the room. Initially no one spoke. Gradually the buzz of conversation returned.

George noticed Richard and 'Einstein' at the back of the room. He joined them, "I think he got his point across!"

"If you inspect the paintwork you will find it blistered," said 'Einstein'.

"But he's quite right," added Richard, "there's a time and a place for aerobatics and a hundred feet after a scrap isn't it. Anyway, he's said what had to be said, no need for me to harp on. Anyone want a beer?" George looked surprised. Richard read the look. "Let me give you some advice. Flying's a dangerous game, with or without a war. I've seen a lot of good chaps go west. If you let it affect you every time someone dies it'll prey on your mind and you'll reach the point where you won't be able to carry on. Whatever you do you can't bring them back. The trick is to just accept it – old so–and–so's bought it – and move on. There's no disrespect – it's just a way of coping."

It was nearly eight o'clock when George opened the door of the School House. Mamam ran to him and threw her arms around him. "Oh, thank God you are safe. We 'eard about the crash and when you were late…"

"I'm sorry, I didn't think…"

"No, you didn't," Justine appeared; she had obviously been crying, "you are just a thoughtless pig and I wish you had never come here. Why don't you go back where you came from and leave us alone?" She pushed past him and ran upstairs.

There was an awkward silence before Mamam spoke. "I'm sorry, but with all this, I 'aven't made anything. You can 'ave some bread and 'am, if you wish."

"No thank you, I'm not hungry. I'm late because the C/O kept us for an ear bashing."

She gave him a sympathetic smile. He suddenly felt very, very tired. "I'm going to my room." He paused, "I'll speak to the Adjutant tomorrow and sort out another billet, it's probably for the best." Mamam said nothing as he closed the door.

He realised he had left his cap downstairs. As he opened his bedroom door, he heard voices along the corridor; Mamam and Justine, talking in French. Curiosity overcame manners and he stayed where he was and listened; it was a severe test of his French, made more difficult by the partly closed door to Justine's room.

"Why are you being… with George?"

"Like what?"

"Trying to… him away. I don't understand. I know you love him; I saw it in your face… he first arrived and again tonight when you thought… bad had

happened to him; and in between I... watched you trying to live a lie, making it... *as if you don 't care but I know it is not from the heart.*" The concern in her voice would have been obvious in any language.

There was a silence before Justine sighed. She began to speak, slowly, deliberately; choosing her words. "*You are right, I do love him but I'm frightened Mamam, frightened of loving him and losing him like you lost Papa or like the young man who died today. So I want him... away before it is too late.*"

"*Can you not see it is already too late? Whether you are parted now or in the future you are locked... And your separation will mean pain whenever it... You are hurting him and yourself for... that might not happen. And if it does, at least know the joy of being together. I was desolate... Papa died but I have twenty-two years which no one can... from me. As it is, if George were to die next week or next......you will have had nothing and you will be left with nothing. If I had my time again, and knew what I do now I wouldn't do anything differently. This is your... for happiness, my child, however short or long it may be – don't throw it away.*"

There was a long silence. "*I shall... you have said.*"

"*Don't think about... too long. He is talking about... to another house.*" Her response was lost to him. He quietly closed the door; the cap could wait. He felt elation – she loved him – but tempered by the fact that she didn't want to admit it. What could he do? One thing was certain now. He would not move out. He would stay here and fight for her.

As George made his way back to the School House, the thoughts he had gone to sleep with the previous night returned to him, having been kept at bay by other matters for most of the day. After a poor start, the weather had improved steadily and an impromptu 'local' sortie was arranged for 'A' Flight. Stanhope-Smith arrived at dispersal in the nick of time on his borrowed bicycle.

"Where the hell have you been?" demanded Underhill.

"Out with my camera, sir," responded Stanhope-Smith brightly, "I'm making a study of the countryside."

"All fine and well if it doesn't clash with duty but, until we have finished the business of getting to know the local area, check with me before you go gadding off!"

It was George's first intimation of this new activity. He passed the flight and an hour beyond impatient to talk to 'Einstein'.

"Yes, I witnessed the wanderer's return," said 'Einstein', "any idea what he was up to?"

"He told F/L Underhill he's making a photographic study of the countryside."

"He probably is, but not for its own sake, I imagine."

"I agree and I've had an idea. We think he's interested in the portable air defence stuff and we are told it fits into a couple of lorries. Suppose he and his friends could steal them; what would they do then? They couldn't just drive over the border into Germany but they could load the stuff into a plane and fly it out. I think he's looking for suitable landing grounds."

"I have to say it sounds a bit far-fetched, but I haven't come up with anything better. I'll talk to the Old Man and AHQ."

George's mind returned to the present as he entered the kitchen. Mamam turned to greet him. She looked apprehensive as she pre-empted his question. "I am sorry that Justine will not be wiz us tonight. She 'as... *mal a la tete* – a 'eadache."

"That's a pity. Can I do anything? Perhaps take her meal up?" asked George. He was determined to see her if it was possible. "I have some news."

Mamam had tried diplomacy and failed. "I am sorry; she told me to say that she does not want to see you this evening." It would not have hurt more if she had hit him with one of her iron pans. She busied herself, not wanting to face him. "Is the news about your new billet?" she asked guardedly.

"No. The forecast is good so I'm finally doing a morning patrol tomorrow. Might meet up with a Hun at last."

A mixture of excitement and thinking about Justine meant that he had slept little; however determined he was to win Justine's hand, it was not looking good. He rose before dawn, dressed hurriedly, shivering in the cold, and shaved by the light of a candle. He was vaguely aware of the smell of freshly baked bread when Mamam tapped on his door and he descended to his breakfast. He normally relished her food but today he hardly noticed what he was eating. The hollow feeling in his stomach remained with him despite the meal.

When it was time to leave, she accompanied him to the door and stretched to plant a kiss on his cheek, *"Bonne chance, mon brave,* kill some Boche for me and may God go wiz you."

He returned the kiss, *"Merci, Mamam; merci beaucoup,"* and then hesitated, trying to hide his disappointment. "Say *au revoir* to Justine for me."

A mischievous smile played round her mouth, "I sink it would be better if you did so yourself – she is outside."

He held his breath as he stepped into the garden. As soon as he saw her, his heart leapt. She rose from a bench and came to him. The woollen cardigan and print dress she was wearing gave only subtle hints of the shapely figure within and her hair was covered by a headscarf but to him she was a goddess. Being taller than her mother, she tilted her head only slightly as she looked up into his eyes. Her face was unnaturally pale in the dawn twilight and her eyes were moist. She was trembling and he realised that it wasn't only because of the early morning chill. "Please come back safely – for me." With this she darted a chaste peck to his lips and made to move away. He caught her in his arms and drew her to him. Their mouths melded in a kiss that told each that there would be no more barriers. At length, reluctantly, they drew apart.

"Je doit partir. Au revoir, ma cherie," he said.

"Au revoir, my love," she replied, dragging herself away from him.

She was joined by her mother as he closed the gate. Standing on the doorstep, they returned his wave and watched until he was out of sight.

He felt as if he were walking on air, and at the same time ready to burst with joy. At that moment nothing was beyond him. Today he hoped to destroy a

German aircraft. Only one? Today he could shoot down the whole bloody Luftwaffe!

Again he makes the sweep; from behind his left shoulder, overhead and beyond his right, then looking past his two companions, across to his left and finally up and back to the beginning, trying to cover every inch of sky. He has seen nothing except wisps of cirrus cloud, probably ten or fifteen thousand feet above him. No sign of the enemy. But he is certain there will be today. After the time lost to bad weather the Germans will be eager to resume their reconnaissance. He starts another sweep. Suddenly he checks – a flash – must be something metallic. He blinks hard, looks again and realises he can see the outline of an aeroplane. He flicks the R/T, "Red Leader, bandit ten o'clock high. Dornier I think, heading westwards."

"Roger, Red Three, I see him. Looks like he's alone. Well spotted," Underhill responds. "Climb in line astern to approach from below, try to keep in the sun until we get close enough to clobber the bastard."

It is not long after sunrise. The morning is virtually cloudless, the sun a brilliant orb but still low in the sky, yet to make an impression on the blankets of mist draped over the fields. If they climb with it at their backs they will be virtually invisible to the enemy crew. As he opens the throttle the vibration in the aircraft increases and the roar of the engine grows louder. In the climb he adjusts his oxygen flow for 20,000 feet, and checks oil temperature, oil pressure and engine temperature – all within limits. Performing the routines helps him to contain his mounting excitement; he knows that the successful hunters are those who can stalk and kill in a detached manner, like the aces of the last war, containing their emotions until the job is done. As tail-end Charlie, he continues sweeping the sky for other aircraft whilst the quarry grows in his windscreen. Still it flies on, the crew seemingly oblivious to the danger stalking them, every mile reducing their prospects of returning home. Eventually, the R/T comes to life, "We will attack individually, on my command. Tally-ho!" George watches as Underhill's Hurricane surges ahead. Eight lines of tracer spring from it, like long sinewy fingers, reaching out towards their target. Immediately, an answering line of tracer streaks from the Dornier's ventral machine gun, missing by a cat's whisker as the Hurricane jinks wildly in response before breaking away to port and out of range. A thin plume of white smoke streams from the port engine but the bomber shows no perceptible loss of speed. "Your turn Red Two, and watch out for that bloody gunner, he's no mug."

"Roger, leader." 'Roy' swings his Hurricane left so he can curve back in for a beam attack. The Dornier begins a turn to starboard, trying, he decides, to keep him astern where the gunners can reach him; perhaps also because heading for home is its only hope. He opens the throttle wide and overhauls it. Like tiny explosions, his tracers strike the bomber's midriff. A maelstrom of death and destruction blasts through the fuselage. The ventral and dorsal guns, firing wildly as they strain to draw a bead on him, fall silent; the gunners annihilated. To avoid a collision 'Roy' pushes the stick hard forward and his Hurricane darts underneath as the damaged aircraft flies on.

"Good work, Red Two. OK Red Three, it's all down to you now. Let's see what you can do." George's mouth is dry. He licks his lips and struggles to swallow, heart beating fast. Automatically he checks temperatures and pressures again; the reflector sight is 'on'; gun-ring turned to 'fire'. He wonders whether the gunners are dead or still capable of shooting him down. No point asking for trouble. He swings right to place himself beyond their arc off fire and begins closing. The Hurricane shudders under the recoil of eight Browning machine guns as he delivers a brief burst from extreme range. Pieces fly off as his tracers smash into the starboard wing, outboard of the engine. A new smell in the cockpit; cordite. He is calm now, almost clinical. The quarry is wounded, but not mortally. It has fallen to him to administer the *coup de grace.* Time seems to pass slowly. He closes in; a little left rudder to correct his aim; throttle back to avoid overshooting. He fires a three second burst. Five hundred bullets hammer into the engine. The propeller stops as black smoke billows and flames begin to lick back over the wing. The port engine, already damaged, is unequal to the extra burden placed upon it and the stricken Dornier curves gracefully down to the right. "Break off Red Three, break off and rejoin section." Fascinated, almost mesmerised, George has been following it down. Underhill's sharp command regains his attention and he pulls away into a climbing turn to rejoin his comrades, now some thousand feet above him. The Dornier speeds earthwards; trailing fire like a comet until it buries itself in a field; a ball of flame and an expanding cloud of black smoke mark its grave. Two parachutes float earthwards.

"They're for the bag," 'Roy's' voice breaks the silence, "pity about the rest."

"Good show everyone; and remember – no victory rolls."

The rest of the patrol proves uneventful and, one after another, the three Hurricanes swoop low over the boundary hedge before throttling back and settling gently onto the sodden airfield. They taxy to the dispersal area. Ground crews appear as if by magic and head for the mud splattered aircraft, to re-arm and refuel ready for the next sortie. Three propellers slow to a stop and the growl of engines dies away to be replaced by the clink of ammunition belts and the clang of nozzles against fuel tanks. The cockpit odours of glycol, rubber and warm oil give way to the sickly smell of high-octane fuel. Harnesses spring open and the pilots emerge. Expectant faces look up, eagerly. "How'd it go, sir?" a voice calls out.

"Chalk one up to 686!" Underhill responds; a heartfelt cheer from those around. "Pilot Officer Knight, a moment please."

George, who has been recounting the combat to his eager fitter and rigger, sees Underhill indicating that he should walk a short distance away, out of earshot of everyone else. Underhill's fury is controlled and the words spit out like the bullets he had been firing earlier. "Right, you stupid bugger! If you ever follow an enemy plane down like that again in my sight I'll shoot you myself to deny the bloody Jerries the satisfaction. All the hours we've spent teaching you to be a fighter pilot and first time out you go on a bloody sightseeing trip. Today we were shooting a rat in a barrel – three fighters against one unescorted bomber; no contest – but just think what could have happened if there had been Jerry fighters about while you were fannying around gawping at that Dornier."

"Sorry sir, you're right. It was my first scrap and I got carried away. I realise I committed a cardinal sin. It won't happen again."

George's obvious contrition takes the heat out of Underhill. "Good, then enough said." He is the same height as George, with dark pomaded hair. His brown eyes, angry to begin with, adopt his easy smile. "That was first class shooting today. I'll bet there aren't too many who can match it. Another reason not to get shot to blazes by an opportunist Jerry; sooner or later we're going to need all the good pilots we can get."

"Thank you, sir." George starts to feel better after his chastisement.

"Bollocking's over now, so you can call me Brian again. Apart from that howler you put up a good show so I'll stand you a beer later. Meanwhile, we'd better cut along and tell 'Einstein' what we've been up to."

He was sitting, pen in mouth, clad in woollen scarf and greatcoat in an attempt to keep warm, hair rumpled and horn-rimmed glasses perched halfway down his nose, contemplating yet another Air Ministry form when Red Section entered his office. "Morning 'Einstein'!" they choroused.

"Morning gentlemen, have you reduced the Luftwaffe to submission yet?"

"Not quite, but we bagged a Dornier," Underhill responded as he draped a leg over one corner of 'Einstein's' desk.

"Only eight hundred to go then," said 'Einstein'.

"You can be shot for talking like that," 'Roy' responded, settling himself on another corner.

"Unlikely, if you chaps are pointing the rifles," countered 'Einstein'.

"Not so fast," said Underhill, "we have in our midst a crack shot," indicating George, who, feeling pleased with himself by now, was leaning with affected nonchalance against the wall opposite 'Einstein'; between a window, crisscrossed with tape to prevent blast damage, and an aircraft identification chart.

"Tell me more," he said, producing a pile of buff report forms.

"So, that amounts to one-third of a kill each," said 'Einstein', proffering the completed reports for signature. "Sorry to rob you of a victory George, but on the evidence, you all contributed significantly to bringing down the Dornier."

George shrugged, pushing his report back across the desk. "Can't argue with that. At the very least Brian and 'Roy' softened it up."

"Not to worry George, plenty more Dorniers in the sky," said 'Roy', clapping him on the back.

"My point earlier," responded 'Einstein'. "Anyway, congratulations are in order as you three have achieved 686's first kill."

"What about the Dornier that did for 'Edge'?" asked 'Roy'.

"No one saw it crash so it can only be recorded as a probable. We know yours did. Just before you returned the C/O had a call from the local gendarmerie asking if he wanted the survivors brought to the Mess this evening."

"What did he say?"

"That 'the Geneva Convention required prisoners to be treated humanely but that didn't mean wining and dining the bastards'. One last thing. It'll be in the

Order of the Day, but I might as well tell you. Apparently not everyone in France is on our side. There have been reports of unusual activity around some of our airfields and AHQ has issued orders for all personnel to be vigilant. Also, you are to carry your service revolvers with you if you are out on your own at night, or in isolated locations."

"What, spies and saboteurs?" said 'Roy'.

"That sort of thing," said Einstein, looking at George.

"Don't be long George; unless you prefer cold tea!" Neither Underhill nor 'Roy' had showed any curiosity when 'Einstein' asked him to remain behind.

"I put your theory to the C/O and AHQ," said 'Einstein'. "The consensus was that you should lie down in a dark room." George looked disappointed. "Unfortunately they outrank me, because I have been considering it further and think your idea has merit." He unfolded a large-scale map of the area as he continued. "In ideal conditions, the Junkers 52 transport aircraft requires approximately 450 yards to take-off or land. Doubling that to allow for adverse conditions means a field of half a mile in length with no obstructions to takeoff and landing." There were pencilled crosses on the map. "As you can see, there are several candidates within a ten mile radius and between them they cover all wind directions. What the map doesn't show is general condition."

"So what are you suggesting?"

"I, too, will rediscover the joys of cycling and conduct my own survey."

"Is there any point? Surely they won't let Stanhope-Smith get hold of the equipment."

"I do hope not but, to use a metaphor, they might end up giving the fish too much line. If the line breaks then this," he tapped the map, "might be the landing net."

As he jumped from the 'Billet Bus', George faced a problem of divided loyalties. There was to be a party in the *Mairie* to celebrate the day's success; on the other hand he wanted to be with Justine. He was still grappling with the problem when he was greeted by a beaming Mamam. *"Georges,* 'ow are you, 'ow many Boche did you shoot up?"

He suppressed a chuckle. "I got a third of a Dornier."

"A third, 'ow is this, what 'appened to the rest of it?"

"Three of us shot it 'down'," he emphasised the word, and she laughed, "so we are all given a score of one-third."

"Je comprends. What 'appened to the German flyers?"

"Two baled out and were captured. The others died."

"In Germany, mothers will be weeping for their sons. I should feel sympathy for them but I cannot. I don't think I will ever forgive the Boche for killing Alain."

"Who was Alain?"

"My brother – a boy of sixteen, shot as a saboteur even though he was innocent." She faltered. Twenty-one years later the memory was still poignant.

"I don't think I would find it easy to forgive if they killed one of my family." It was time to change the subject. "Is Justine home?"

She smiled indulgently, *"Non,* she 'as gone to give extra teaching to one of 'er *enfants* so she will be late."

"When are you expecting her?"

"It is usually about *huit*... eight-thirty, so not before then."

"Wizard!" said George as his difficulties dissolved. "I have to be at the *Mairie* at seven, to celebrate today's victory, but I'm going to make sure I'm away by eight-thirty."

"I will save some food for you and Justine."

"You're very kind."

"Il n'importe pas. She will come 'ome past the *Mairie,* so you can look out for her per'aps. I know she is eager to see you."

"Smile please, gentlemen." A battered machine gun, retrieved from the wreck, had been installed on the Mess wall as the squadron's first trophy. Underhill, 'Roy' and George, the proud victors, were photographed, tankards in hand, admiring it. The party was in full swing, plenty of drink, gramophone music and madcap games. George's mind was elsewhere though.

"Something wrong old man?" asked Giles, "You've hardly touched your beer."

"You are rather subdued," added 'Roy', "not feeling sorry for the Huns are you?"

"No, I'm just..."

"I may be wrong but, as an expert in these matters, I would say he's got a lady on his mind." interjected 'Foggy'.

"How can you tell?" asked Giles.

"Preoccupied air, reduced alcohol consumption," responded 'Foggy'.

"Dopey look," added Reg.

"I am here, you know!" protested George.

"I do believe you're right," said Giles, peering at him intently, "guilty as charged."

"Well, well, well – George has been bounced by Cupid; so who is the lovely lady?" asked Underhill.

"Only those of you who reside in the seclusion of the C/O's chateau would ask that," said 'Foggy' disdainfully. "It's obviously that rather scrumptious school teacher he's billeted with. What's her name? Christine?"

"Justine," said George.

"Well you sly old dog," said 'Foggy'. "So what are you doing here with us old soaks when the fair Justine awaits?"

"She's giving extra tuition to one of her pupils."

"I see," said Giles with mock indignation, "nothing better to do so pass the empty hours with your squadron chums."

"It's not like that." countered George, defensively.

"So when are you expecting her?" asked Underhill.

"About eight-thirty."

"Well, its twenty-past now so if I were you, I'd buzz off and save yourself further mauling from this crowd."

"I'll do that," said George, eagerly. He drained his tankard and left.

"Spoilsport," said Giles to Underhill.

"There's always tomorrow," said 'Foggy' mischievously.

"Tonight's not over yet," said Reg, "follow me, and keep it quiet."

George stood under the trees in the middle of the square. The sky was clear and the cold night air made a pleasant change from the smoke-laden atmosphere in the *Mairie.* He felt an anticipatory tingle at the sound of footsteps coming from the direction of *Rue Foch.* He peered into the gloom and called softly, "Justine?"

"George, where are you?"

"Over here, under the trees."

With an excited squeal, she ran across the cobbles and threw her arms around him. The reserve of earlier days had been banished that morning; she kissed him passionately. They stood locked in their embrace for a couple of minutes before she spoke. "It's wonderful to see you. I have been worried about you. How did you get on?"

"We got a Jerry – no need to worry – it was a piece of cake."

"How can you say don't worry when you go off to fight?" she asked reproachfully.

"You're right," he conceded, "but it really was no contest; three of us queuing up to shoot it down. It should be like that for the next few months so I don't want you fretting every time I fly."

"Easy for you to say; but it's dangerous even without the Germans. What about the crash two days ago?"

He took her hands, squeezed them and looked into her eyes. "That happened, I hate to say, because he did a stupid thing. If he'd followed the rules he'd still be here."

She looked into his for reassurance, "How do I know you'll follow the rules?"

"Because I've got you to come back to."

They kissed again.

"Have you eaten?" she asked.

"No, but Mamam has left supper for us."

"Well, let's go home," she said, pulling George by the hand.

As they emerged from under the trees torchlight flashed across the square, the illumination catching them hand in hand. A storm of whoops and catcalls erupted.

"What is that?" she asked, startled.

He grinned "I'm afraid my colleagues have found out about us."

She laughed, "You English, you are like schoolboys in matters of the heart."

The following afternoon, although 'A' Flight was not on duty George made his way to dispersal; his success had left him eager for a chance of tackling the enemy again. After a fruitless patrol, 'B' Flight had spent the morning sitting around the pot-bellied stove, trying to keep warm and waiting for some enemy activity. News of George's romance had spread rapidly. They were relieving their boredom with the predictable ribbing when F/Sgt Robertson entered. He addressed F/L Stewart. "Sir, I have a Hurricane requiring an air-test."

Alistair Stewart's speech was deliberate and precise like that of the Edinburgh lawyer he would have become had the RAF not claimed him. "Well F/Sgt, 'B'

Flight is on Readiness so I can't spare any of them but there is someone who may be willing to assist." Stewart looked at George and, with mock gravitas, enquired. "P/O Knight, would you be so kind as to run the rule over the F/Sgt's handiwork?"

"Delighted, sir." He headed for his locker.

"So what was wrong, Flight?" he asked as they made their way to the Hurricane.

"Flying left wing low, sir," replied Robertson, "but we've fixed that."

"Anything else I should know?"

"P/O Evans was unhappy with the gun button. It's been checked and tested on the firing butts. We've also re-harmonised the guns to two hundred and fifty yards at the C/O's suggestion."

"Interesting. Is it armed?"

"A full load minus what we fired. Fuel is under half-full but plenty for an air test, sir."

Thirty minutes later, George is fifteen thousand feet above the airfield putting the Hurricane through its paces. Ten minutes of aerobatics is enough to satisfy him that it has no remaining trim problems. An experimental push on the gun-button produces the satisfying roar of eight Brownings. He is once more enjoying unfettered flight and in no hurry to return to the ground. Above him, an infinity of blue, and below, the fields of France, here and there hidden behind cotton-wool clumps of cumulus cloud. Routinely sweeping the sky he spots movement below, to the east. He can make out three aeroplanes, all twin-engined, with a south-westerly heading but not moving in unison. Recognising that two are attacking the third, he rolls the Hurricane into a dive, heading for the melee; initially uncertain which is friend or foe. As the planes grow larger he identifies two Messerschmitt 110 fighters attacking a Potez 63.11, a French reconnaissance machine. The French pilot is putting up a determined fight, twisting and turning to avoid his attackers and trying to give his gunner the opportunity to fight back, but without assistance there can be only one end to the contest. The Potez's port engine is trailing smoke and one undercarriage leg is dangling. Like an arrow, George points his Hurricane at one of the Me110s. Airspeed is in excess of 360 mph and engine screaming as if in protest. The Me110 looms large in his sights. He is in perfect position for a beam attack, able to rake it from port engine across to starboard. He presses the firing button. Nothing happens. He curses, jabbing at it. This time the guns fire. The split-second delay means he only achieves strikes on the starboard engine. Immediately it streams smoke. The German pilot, suddenly alive to the danger, pulls sharp left to pass under his line of flight. George's guns continue blazing at an empty sky. He jabs the button several times more before they stop. Pulling hard back on the stick he uses the speed gained in the dive to zoom climb. At the top he stall turns and dives again, this time for a quarter attack on the other Me110. Although aware of his presence, it has persisted in attacking the Potez, attempting to finish it off. Now it starts to dive away but it has delayed too long. The speed of his dive means he continues to close. The rear gunner rushes his shot and a stream of tracer passes wide of the Hurricane. George presses the gun button hard. The gunner pays for his haste, annihilated in a torrent of bullets. The return fire stops but so do his guns. Cursing again, he thumbs the button but all he gets is the clank of empty breechblocks and the hiss of compressed air – he is out of ammunition. Seething with frustration he pulls away, leaving the Messerschmitt to limp homewards; there is no sign of the first one.

Deprived of further opponents, his battle fury ebbs away. His ears ache after the dive and he works his jaw to relieve them. He isn't sure of his whereabouts. He has been uncharacteristically careless; only intending a local flight, he hasn't brought a map. Beneath is a bewildering patchwork of fields. To make matters worse his gauges only show about twenty minutes worth of fuel. The rage of a few moments before is replaced by uncertainty. He remembers the Potez. If it is still airborne it will be heading for some friendly airfield. It was on a south-westerly course so he turns that way and begins searching the sky ahead. He sees the trail of smoke first then the aircraft; it has lost height since he last saw it. Opening the throttle in pursuit, he quickly overhauls it. Understandably, the crew will be jumpy so he stays out of shooting range and half rolls one way to display his Hurricane's black and white underside and then the other to show the large blue and red roundels on top of the wings. The rear gunner waves to him. He closes in. Alongside now, he can see just how much punishment the Potez has suffered. The pilot waves. George shrugs his shoulders and spreads both hands in front of him. The pilot responds by pointing downwards then gesturing 'ten'. Hoping he means ten minutes to an airfield, George takes up station above and behind to escort the Potez home.

It continues to lose height. They are now flying at about five hundred feet so that when he sees a town ahead it is from an oblique angle and difficult to identify. The Potez waggles its wings and starts a deliberate descent. Finally he recognises some landmarks. It is Epinal. They are approaching the airfield which lies to the northeast. His fuel gauges show he still has a few minutes flying time left. His first concern now is for the Potez. He circles overhead watching its approach. He reckons the pilot has only one chance at a landing, doubting that the battered aeroplane could summon the power to climb out and go round again. The pilot does not lower the undamaged undercarriage leg, obviously intending a belly landing. His approach over the perimeter fence is slightly high. George holds his breath. He assumes the remaining engine has been cut, but the Potez still floats some way across the airfield. The pilot flares early to create a nose-high attitude, hoping to prevent the dangling leg locking in a down position. Luck is with him; as it touches the ground the leg folds back under the wing allowing the plane to settle in a level attitude. It strikes the ground a glancing blow, bounces and strikes again before slithering to a halt in a cloud of mud and debris. A fire tender and ground crew rush to it but there is no fire, just some smoke from the engines, which receive a precautionary dousing. Pilot and rear gunner climb from the top of the cockpit. The pilot gesticulates to the waiting ambulance and the crew dismount and run across to the plane with their stretcher, joined by ground crew equipped with axes and other cutting tools, and begin the process of removing the third crewmember from the wreck. The gunner shades his eyes and searches the sky. He spots George's Hurricane curving in onto its final approach.

As the Hurricane slows, George swings the rudder and opens the throttle to taxi towards dispersal. He glances at the fuel gauges. Empty, to all intents and purposes. He makes a silent prayer of thanks. By the time he has reached dispersal, switched off and undone his harness a small gathering has formed and more are joining. As he jumps to the ground, he is greeted with loud cheers and 'bravos'. A dark, swarthy individual of a similar age to himself pushes through the throng, hugs him, slaps him repeatedly on the back, then steps back and shakes him vigorously by the hand. "Lieutenant Desfors at your service. It was my aircraft you saved."

"My pleasure. You helped me too, though. I was lost after the fight."

"The two things don't equate. You saved our lives."

"Are all of your crew safe?" asks George, feeling bashful and trying to change the subject "I only saw two of you from the air. Potez's carry three don't they?"

"Unfortunately, Maurice, my observer stopped a piece of cannon shell in his stomach. The doctor says he will live but I doubt he will fly with us again. He's alive, though, as are Francois, my gunner, and I, thanks to you."

George is bracing himself for more backslapping from the Lieutenant when salvation arrives in the form of the *Escadrille's* immaculately attired commander who stands to attention and gives an equally smart salute. "Commandant Henri Laval. I have the honour to command *Group Aerien d'Observation 549* – I think in the RAF we would be called a Reconnaissance Squadron."

"Pilot Officer George Knight, 686 Squadron, sir." George, being hatless, does not salute but stands to attention.

"You are well named Pilot Officer; I think today you have been," he indicates the mud-spattered Hurricane and smiles, "a knight in not-so-shining armour."

George is starting to feel embarrassed again. "It was nothing, sir – all part of the job."

"Your modesty does you credit – however we are in your debt; is there anything we can do?"

"I would appreciate some fuel, sir; and I've no map – I was only on a test flight."

"Consider it done, but I hope you are not leaving us so soon. By the time your plane is refuelled, it will be nearly dusk. You must stay with us this evening and we will celebrate Lieutenant Desfors' deliverance."

"I don't know what my C/O will say, sir."

"It is no problem – I will speak with him and tell him that you are helping to seal the *entente* between our two great nations. You are with the squadron based at St Jean-sur-Moselle I imagine?"

"Yes, sir. Could you also ask him to pass a message to Madam Delacroix with whom I am billeted?"

"Bien sur, although it is uncommonly civil to notify your... landlady. She is pretty *n'est pas?"*

"Yes sir. It would be ungallant of me to say otherwise; but she is only my landlady."

"Then her daughter is pretty?"

"Yes, sir, very," he admits, defeated "were you an *Avocat* before the war?"

Laval claps him amiably on the shoulder as they start to walk towards the airfield buildings, *"Non,* but I am French; we understand these things. Now, let us repair to the Mess; I am intrigued to know more of this English 'knight' who has captured the heart of a French maiden; and now the formalities are over I think we can dispense with 'sir' – Henri will be fine."

George's head was pounding the following morning and he had an unpleasant taste in his mouth as he set course for St Jean. Low stratus cloud stretched from horizon to horizon but would present no problem as there was no intervening high ground. He had learned the best way that Armee de l'Air Mess evenings were little different from RAF ones. After an uneventful return flight, he was met at dispersal by F/Sgt Robertson. "I believe congratulations are in order, sir. How was the aircraft?" he enquired.

"Trim's OK, but the bloody gun button isn't fixed. Cost me the chance to blow a couple of Me110s to glory."

"I'm sorry to hear that, sir."

Despite flying back on oxygen, George's head was still hurting and he wasn't in the best of moods, "So you bloody should be, there's not much point getting us into the air if all we can throw at Jerry is insults."

"Yes sir, there's no excuse, it should have been fixed. I'll have it attended to at once. I've been told to give you a message – you're to report to the Intelligence Officer, immediately on landing."

"Hail the conquering hero, and how are you this dull morning."

"Morning 'Einstein', head hurts but otherwise OK. I was told to report to you immediately; has Stanhope-Smith been up to something?"

"No. I'm to take your combat report and then you're on ninety-six hours leave, effective immediately. Once you've finished here away you go."

"Have I put up some sort of a black?"

"Far from it but you have created a problem for the Old Man. We've had the French C/O on the phone singing your praises and word of your exploits has gone straight to the French High Command and thence to our upper echelons. Things like this are an absolute Godsend for the propaganda merchants – the *entente* in action, our boys fighting alongside their boys etc. – so it follows that we can expect a 'phone call any minute asking us to play host to a crowd of Pressmen. In case you've ever wondered why we've never had a visit, it's because the C/O's made it known to AHQ that he doesn't want 'a horde of gin soaked hacks' crawling over his squadron; not least because he thinks your heads are inflated enough without getting your photos in 'Picture Post', and after 'Edge', he doesn't want you living up to the fighter ace image that they will create for you all. He can't disobey a direct order to produce you for the Press but obviously if you're not here that rather scotches things. He and the Adj have made themselves scarce this morning and my orders are to get you out of here before they return so they can deny all knowledge of seeing you. You're about due for leave anyway so he can claim that there was a mix-up and you went on pre-arranged leave in his absence."

"So what happens when I return – won't they still be looking for me?"

"Chances are something else will happen in the meantime to take their attention plus neither they nor AHQ will want to wait so between them they'll cook up a story without you. Now, to business. Tell me about yesterday's events."

"First of all – are you sure they were Me110s you tackled? It's just that we have had no reports of any units being deployed on the western front so far."

"Well I'm positive they weren't Dorniers and they definitely weren't Ju88s so they must have been. Perhaps they were a detachment or something."

"Fair enough. The Old Man won't be happy about that gun button, it should have been fixed first time round," said 'Einstein', working through the report.

"I tore F/Sgt Robertson off a strip this morning; he's said he'll sort it out. I have to say it's unusual; the erks are usually first class."

"No doubt, but he will have some more to say, I'm sure. This is sloppy in the extreme and could have cost you your life. Bad enough it cost you a victory."

"So I didn't down it then? I lost sight of it in the fight."

"French observers spotted two twins heading for home yesterday afternoon. Too far away for a positive identification, unfortunately. One quite low and flying on one engine. We don't know whether it made it home or crashed somewhere in Germany, so we can only credit you with a 'damaged' and the other makes two 'damaged'."

"Damn! If the guns had worked properly, I'd have blown both to Kingdom Come – I couldn't miss from that range."

"So you're happy with the guns being harmonised to two hundred and fifty yards?"

"Definitely! Less chance of missing and more punch when you hit."

What did you make of the Me110; we don't have much gen at the moment?"

"Can't help much. Didn't really dogfight. The first one I bounced did turn under me a bit sharpish when I hit his engine, but the second didn't have any chance to perform because I was on him so quickly."

"The C/O will talk to you when you get back, among others. He's keen on the gun experiment as you'll find out. By the way, he asked me to tell you that you're starting to live up to your 'exceptional' rating. So, enjoy your leave. You're due back here at," he looked at his watch, "10.00 hours on the 1st. Any idea what you're going to do?"

"Except when Justine's off school, none whatsoever, it's all a bit sudden. I will have to amuse myself for the rest of the time. I could try to get to Epinal for a few hours – there's something I want to do there. Otherwise it's a chance for some lie-ins and to write some letters. No doubt you'll keep an eye on our mutual friend."

Marcel and Jacques were waiting when Stanhope-Smith arrived. He wasted no time on small-talk. "Where can I hide two lorries?" He fired the question at Marcel, who responded with an uncomprehending shrug.

"He speaks little or no English, *mi'lor*," said Jacques, "so unless your French is good, I suggest I translate." He received an impatient gesture to carry on and repeated the question in French. "... He knows such a place."

"Where? Describe it."

"... *Le Trou* – 'The Pit' – On the farther side of the forest, well hidden. He says lorries can get to it despite the trees."

"Does anyone else know of it?"

"… He doubts it. No one else from the village ventures far in. Apart from the difficult going, there's the legend of *le Bete Sauvage* – the Wild Beast – that stalks the forest." Marcel crossed himself as Jacques translated.

Stanhope-Smith made no attempt to hide his scorn. "People don't believe that medieval tosh in the twentieth century do they?"

Jacques answered without referring to Marcel. "Until recent times maybe not, but fourteen years ago a boy from the village died a bad death in the forest. Country folk are superstitious. It is rumoured that he was killed by the Beast."

"I need to see this place for myself."

"… Whenever you like."

"Tomorrow morning then, nine o'clock, unless you hear aircraft operating. How shall I find you?"

"… Marcel says enter the forest. *He* will find you."

4: December, 1939

It was the kind of mist which wets everything it comes into contact with. By the time he was passing the School House, it had soaked through Stanhope-Smith's greatcoat. After passing another three houses, he left the village behind. The forest edge, which had stopped, as if respectfully, some twenty yards short of the buildings, now came right to the side of the road. A short distance further on, he saw an opening among the trees. As he swung his bicycle into the forest, he pulled a small compass from his pocket and made a mental note of his direction. The track he was on had obviously been hewn and trampled out of the surrounding forest by generations of foragers; on either side were areas of stumps and at their edges, partly chopped trunks and branches from recent felling. After a few hundred yards, the track petered out and the ground suddenly became rough; too rough for the bicycle. Fearing punctures he dismounted and propped it against a tree. He took another compass bearing and commenced walking. Despite his recent campaign of cycling, he found the going hard and stopped for a rest. The musty smell of decay was all around and the dull day left little light to spare. He listened – only silence. He barked out Marcel's name several times and was answered once by the shrill cry of a bird somewhere in the canopy above. Standing in the eerie silence the forest seemed to close in on him. He cursed Marcel – where was the bloody man? He was out of the mist now but his clothes had been saturated and the bitter cold was starting to seep into him and gnaw at his resolve. It wasn't difficult here to understand how tales of mythical beasts gained credence. He told himself to get a grip and started walking again. He stepped on a fallen branch. The rotten wood gave way. His foot sank into a pulpy mess; woodlice and beetles erupted from it and ran crazily in all directions, some onto his shoe and even up his leg. He had always loathed insects. Involuntarily, he sprang back dashing at them with his gloved hands. Something grasped his shoulder. A spasm of terror coursed through him and he spun round, eyes and mouth wide, face pale.

"Bonjour mi'lor."

The hint of amusement on Marcel's face was too much for Stanhope-Smith. "You stupid fucking idiot! If you ever do that again I'll blow your whoreson brains out!" Marcel spoke no worthwhile English but after his years in the International Brigade, he could swear in most European languages. The knife was at Stanhope-Smith's throat in a second. There was no amusement now, just controlled anger. *"Insultez-moi peut-etre, mais pas ma mere!"* he hissed menacingly. Stanhope-Smith froze. Vaguely aware of Marcel's foul breath, he stood there helpless, between life and death. Marcel held the knife there for a few seconds to emphasise his message and then the anger subsided. He sheathed the knife and stepped away. *"Suivez-moi!"* It was more a command than an invitation. He set off walking in the direction Stanhope-Smith had been heading. Stanhope-Smith took a few moments to gather himself and then stumbled after him. As the prospect of imminent death receded and his mind began to embrace life again his anger returned. He was not going to be humiliated by some stinking peasant. When Marcel was no longer useful, he would pay for threatening Marcus Stanhope-Smith. He struggled to match his pace. Only when Marcel finally stopped did he catch him up. His breathing was laboured but Marcel appeared not to notice. Instead he pointed ahead of them. *"Voila, le Trou!"*

He looked around. The trees were less dense and the better light had encouraged bushes to grow but he could not see anywhere to hide two lorries. "Where… *Ou est-il?"*

"La bas!" Marcel said tetchily, pointing again in the direction of the shrubbery.

Stanhope-Smith approached. Encircled by the bushes was a large, crater-like pit. It was not man-made and he had no idea what force had fashioned it. Two sides were almost sheer drops of twelve to fifteen feet and the others were slopes which he knew a lorry could cope with. Most importantly, it was wide enough to accommodate three or four lorries, side by side. He looked up. Patches of sky were visible because the canopy of trees was less dense but from his flying experience he knew not much would be seen from above, particularly if camouflage netting were used. The muffled sound of a vehicle reached him from, he guessed, the main road. *"La route?"* he asked, pointing.

"Oui, environ d'un kilometre."

He indicated the trees, wider spread than those they had come through but still a potential problem. "A lorry can… *Un camion peut venir ici?"* He sought assurance. *"Sans doubt,"* Marcel confirmed.

For the first time that morning, his spirits soared. He even felt a fleeting moment of gratitude towards Marcel. Piece by piece, his plan was coming together. A shiver reminded him how cold he was. There was no more to be done here for the present; he would return to his billet and thaw out in a hot bath. Then he would await the coming of the lorries.

The little dog danced around them, barking excitedly. George took a step towards it and it retreated, still barking. He stepped back and it advanced again, tail wagging. A child's voice called, *"Gaspard, fermez! Asseyez-vous!"* Quieted, the dog sat. A small boy burst from the trees and stopped when he saw them. *"Bonjour, mademoiselle!"*

"Bonjour, Pascal. C'est votre chien? Il est bon."

"Oui, mademoiselle. Un cadeau de Pere Noel," he replied proudly.

"Puis-je presenter George, mon ami?"

"Bonjour m'sieu." Pascal had not noticed until now that they were holding hands. His eyes opened wide. *"Votre ami!"* He clapped a hand to his mouth and ran off giggling, followed by Gaspard. George laughed and squeezed her hand.

Justine smiled. "The whole village will know about us by tonight. His mother is the biggest gossip in Lorraine."

It was Thursday so she was not at school. A glance at the leaden sky was sufficient to know why George was not on duty. They had been in the forest collecting wood for over an hour and the old pram that served as a cart was nearly full. As Pascal's laughter faded to nothing, George hefted the axe and approached a fallen branch. He caught her eye and smiled. "This one then call it a day?" he asked. She returned his smile, nodding her agreement, and leaned against a tree to watch, admiring him, drinking him in as he chopped the wood. It had been three weeks since she had abandoned her doubts but she had no regrets; just the reverse, despite knowing what she had known before – that he could be snatched from her at any moment by a cruel fate – but instead of being an obstacle that truth now served as a spur, made what she had more exquisite – each moment needed to be lived and loved to its fullest extent. One more bridge remained to be crossed and she yearned for that final fulfilment when, in all ways, she would have become one with him, but she knew that it offered risk as well as reward. She ached for him yet any hint of immorality or breath of scandal would mean the end of her brief teaching career. She knew that he desired her too; he had made it obvious, but he had respected her when she had forced herself to check his advances. No doubt the gossips were already placing her on the other side of the bridge but she knew she could look the world in the eye and deny it – for now.

Having reached the northern limit of their patrol, they turned and flew a reciprocal course which took them south of their starting point before turning northwards once more. Underhill's voice broke into their concentration. "Right chaps; Jerry's either weathered in or funked it today so we might as well head home for a cuppa." Within twenty minutes, they were back at the dispersal hut where they were surprised to find not only Yellow Section but the rest of the squadron as well.

"It looks like they've finally realised we're here, see..." Evans was telling George in his Welsh lilt when S/L Sullivan entered the room.

"At ease, gentlemen. Unless the grapevine has failed for once to get here ahead of me you will know that AHQ has asked us to carry out a practice escort mission with two Battle squadrons. Protecting the Battles was our reason for coming here so I am determined that we will acquit ourselves well today. Our task is to rendezvous with them here," on the wall map he indicated Chalons-sur-Mame, south-east of Reims, and then moved his pointer eastwards to an area south of Thionville, "Escort them to here and then back again. The whole Squadron will take part, that is, fourteen aircraft whilst F/O Stanhope-Smith remains indisposed, as I want everyone on this show for the experience. The Battles will be flying at 5,000 feet so all sections will fly at that level, except Red Section who will be top cover at 15,000 feet. We will be flying close to the German border and, you might say, trailing our coats, so there could well be trouble. Don't forget the Battles have previously suffered at the hands of the Jerries so everyone keep their eyes peeled. Take-off will be 11.30 hours; refuel at Bar-le-Duc and rendezvous 14.00. Any questions?"

It occurred to George as they flew towards the rendezvous that for Stanhope-Smith it was a blessing in disguise to be rendered non-operational today. If 686 were to meet up with the Germans, he would not have wanted to be fighting his friends. It followed then that whatever he was planning would have to come to fruition before long; he would want to get away before the war started in earnest.

His watch shows 14.04 and there is no sign of the Battles. He scans the terrain below; it matches the area marked as the rendezvous point on his map. He knows the rest of the squadron will be searching too and no doubt S/L Sullivan is particularly anxious. Giles, Yellow Leader for the day, breaks the tension. "Battles at ten o'clock."

George can see them now, closing from the north-west but still five miles or so away. After the two formations have combined, he resumes his general scan and, whilst doing so, he contemplates the Battles as Red Section weaves above them in a manner reminiscent of convoy patrols, forced to do so to maintain formation with their slower charges. Powered by the same Merlin engine as his Hurricane but larger, and carrying three crew instead of one plus a bomb load, the Fairey Battle is about 100mph slower than the Hurricane and comparable fighters, and far less manoeuvrable. It had effectively become obsolescent when monoplane fighters entered service and, as had already been demonstrated, without an escort it was virtually helpless. He feels a pang of sympathy for those who have to operate these flying coffins and remembers his friend from training days, Peter Templeton, expressing his disappointment at being posted to Battles; wondering at the same time if he is among those beneath him.

They are nearing Thionville and the border when he sees specks in the north-eastern sky at about his own level, heading towards the Battles. The direction they are coming from means only one thing – Germans. He thumbs his R/T. "Shuttlecock Leader, Red Three, bandits two o'clock, probably 109s."

"Roger, Red Three. Red and Yellow Sections, engage enemy. Remaining sections cover the Battles and prepare to intercept anything that breaks through." The aircraft of Red Section adjust their course slightly to aim for a point between the Battles and the advancing enemy aircraft. Below him, George can see the three aircraft of Yellow Section climbing hard to join them; throttles doubtless wide open as they surge upwards. When they reach Red Section, the six aircraft are facing what now are obviously eight Bf 109s; barring the way to their quarry. The 109s respond by splitting into two groups of four, threatening to fly either side of them. Underhill's voice is calm. "They're trying to sneak in for a quick squirt. Yellow Section, take the gaggle on the right. Red Section, follow me." The sections turn towards their allotted targets. The two groups of 109s split again. One pair from each dive towards the Battles while the others change course towards Red and Yellow Sections. "The bastards are taking us on!" The opposing aircraft close rapidly in their headlong charge; both sides committed. For either to turn away now would provide the other with a sitting target. The next few seconds are a blur; winking lights on the front of the 109s; thumbing the gun-button to fire back; senses pummelled by the roar of the engine, clatter of machine guns and stench of cordite. Distantly George hears Sullivan ordering Green and Blue Sections to intercept the diving Messerschmitts. There are jolts; the bottom corner of his bulletproof windscreen goes opaque; pieces fall off a 109. They close at over six hundred miles per hour. A new threat looms; collision. Every fibre of his being is screaming to pull away. Discipline prevails over instinct; he holds firm, silently imploring Underhill to order him to break. The enemy blinks first. The 109s lift their noses. He glimpses yellow markings as the outline of an aircraft flashes over him, the tailwheel feet from his cockpit, the snarl of its engine plainly audible. Instinctively he ducks. The sky is suddenly clear.

Miraculously, neither side has inflicted serious damage. Red Section roar round in the tightest of turns but the aircraft they faced, re-joined by those that challenged Yellow Section, are already far ahead. Below, they can see the other four aircraft streaking for home, one trailing white smoke. Underhill judges he can catch them in a dive. "Bandits eleven o'clock low. Tallyho, Red and Yellow Sections!"

Sullivan breaks in. "Break off pursuit, Red and Yellow Sections. Maintain Angels fifteen and cover main formation. All Shuttlecock aircraft, keep a sharp lookout. Good work Red Leader. Well done everybody."

George slowly starts to unwind. He feels lightheaded, heart thumping and hands trembling. For the first time in his flying career, he has known real fear. Death had been seconds away. He seeks comfort in the humdrum of routine, checking gauges and testing controls to ensure the aircraft is not badly damaged. Gradually his composure returns and with it comes a bonus – the realisation that he has been tested to the limit and not found wanting.

The formation reaches its destination. The Battles perform their mock attack while the Hurricane pilots, mindful of their proximity to the German border and the amount of fuel and ammunition they have used, scan the skies anxiously. "Bogeys, one o'clock!" All eyes turn to a group of aircraft, probably fifteen miles inside Germany. Anxious minutes pass. Sullivan is laconic, "They don't want to play, let's go home."

At Chalons, the Battles take their leave, waggling their wings in farewell. It is dusk by the time 686 land at their airfield. To a man, the pilots dump their kit in the dispersal hut and head for the 'Billet' bus. Parsons' head appears over the tailgate as they are about to set off. "Message from the C/O – 'Well done chaps, Officers' Mess, half an hour, first round's on me'."

The mood in the Mess was exuberant. A hubbub of excited conversation filled the room. "I had a split second as he came across me so, quick guess at deflection, press the tit and hey presto, white smoke!" said 'Shorty'. "With any luck his engine seized on the way home."

"Our Jerries ran when we turned towards them," said 'Foggy'.

"It would have been much better if they'd stayed to mix it," rejoined 'Shorty', "Fourteen to eight – we'd have downed the lot."

"Which is probably why they didn't." added 'Einstein', joining the group.

"What brings you here? Don't tell me the old man's bought you a beer too," said Reg.

"I'm here to get your reports on this afternoon's events before alcohol once more reduces your brains to mush," 'Einstein' replied with some asperity, "And as a matter of fact, he *has* bought me a beer, perhaps because he's like a dog with two tails at the moment. He's had messages of thanks from the Battle Squadrons and congratulations from AHQ for a job well done. I think it's fair to say that 686 Squadron is now well and truly on the map. It seems as though you have been gainfully employed for once; my congratulations, gentlemen. As if to underline your newfound status, you will be pleased to learn that the portable control equipment turned up this afternoon; just as the C/O foretold, two lorries; each towing a generator."

"I didn't see anything. Where are they?" asked George.

"On the hill to the west of the aerodrome. It's the highest point for miles around so I suppose that's where you'd put what is effectively a lookout post."

"Are they working yet?" asked 'Roy'.

"A couple of weeks. I gather they have to calibrate things and test everything. However, none of this is getting any reports done. Can I start with Red Section?"

"Thank you for your submissions, gentlemen; I can see that you in particular have earned your corn today," said 'Einstein', "but before you go I'd like to do some intelligence gathering. This was the Squadron's first brush with 109s; is there anything you can add besides what you've written. For instance, what formation did the Jerries employ initially?"

"They looked like an uneven line, made from two parts," Underhill responded. "That's right; before they split you could see that they were essentially two groups of four; in each group one was in front of and slightly above the others," added 'Roy'. "Like this?" asked 'Einstein'. He held his hand out with the thumb curled underneath and his four fingers spread widely. "Picture my finger nails as the 109s."

"Spot on!" said Underhill. George and 'Roy' nodded agreement.

"This is the tactical formation they developed in the Spanish Civil War," explained 'Einstein', "the four together are known as a *Schwarm,* composed of two pairs or *Rotten.* In a dogfight, they split up into pairs – the leader of each pair attacks a target, protected by his wingman – or on occasions, like today, they combine into larger units. They swept all before them in Spain and Poland but we don't know yet whether that's because of superior aircraft or superior tactics – or perhaps both. However, for the time being the brass hats want you to continue with vic formations."

"I'm not sure that's the right thing," said Underhill, "I think we won today because we outnumbered them. I had the feeling that tactically they were capable of flying rings round us; and that's no criticism of the way the Old Man handled us."

"I think you're right," added George, "after all they've had three years of actual combat to sort this out while we've been doing air displays and stooging around with Battles and so forth."

The dying embers flickered and sparkled as they gazed into the fire; her head on his shoulder. George had been subdued this evening. She had sensed that it had been hard; she knew that it couldn't always be a 'piece of cake' despite what he had said previously. He had only mentioned briefly the day's events and she was aware that he had left a lot unspoken. She had seen fourteen Hurricanes fly out – it would have been difficult to have missed them – and later she had counted them back in again; her man was safe and that was what mattered. He would tell her the rest when he was ready; and whenever that was, she would be there to listen.

Perhaps a bit of suffering had knocked some humanity into him, thought Jacques. Stanhope-Smith had never been so affable. They waited as he struggled to clear his throat; the aftermath of a bad cold, the legacy of the day he had met Marcel. He began to speak, pausing periodically so that Jacques could translate. "As you may know, two lorries arrived today, carrying secret equipment. My intention is to seize that equipment and put it onto a plane bound for Germany. Once we have them, the lorries will be hidden in the forest until the moon is right for the aircraft to land and take off again; the operation will be timed to keep that period to a minimum. Two things still remain to be done before planning can be completed. First, Marcel; for the next seven nights, I require you to observe the guard on the lorries; how many men, what times they change and where they patrol. Second, we need three powerful torches. Jacques, purchase them when you are next in Nancy. Any questions?"

"The legend may keep the villagers out of the woods but a thorough military search would find the lorries," Jacques suggested, apparently undaunted by the proposition.

"I agree," Stanhope-Smith nodded. "Both lorries have trailers. Once they are in the forest, you will use your van to take a trailer and abandon it twenty or thirty miles up the road, to throw everyone off the scent. Any more questions? Right! We'll meet here a week tonight for Marcel's report."

The 109s were flying straight at him, one after another. He was firing at them and cursing because he couldn't shoot any down. In turn they broke away but each was leaving it later before doing so. Suddenly, he knew that the next one was going to fly right into him. It was closing rapidly. He tried to turn away. The controls wouldn't respond. He tried to open the hood to bale out. He tugged at it but it wouldn't budge. His Hurricane flew on. With a cry of despair he waited for the impact…

"George, George, wake up, you're having a bad dream!" Two arms enveloped his head and he was drawn into a warm cushion. As the nightmare receded and his mind began to clear, he realised that the arms were Justine's; that she was holding his head to her chest, her head on top of his. He put his arms around her waist and held her tightly. His fear was ebbing away, being replaced by a new emotion, prompted by the softness of her skin and the scent of her. She sensed the change and felt a stirring within herself. His hands moved to the swell of her buttocks and pressed her to him. The flicker of desire within her became a raging fire. She knew she should pull away but her last vestiges of resolve were dwindling rapidly…

"Is anything wrong?" It was Mamam's voice, from beyond the room, etched with concern. "I thought I heard shouts."

"Everything is fine, Mamam. George was having a nightmare but he's alright now." Still trembling with the intensity of the moment, she drew away from him. He caught her arm. She looked longingly at him, her eyes filled with yearning. He kissed her hand and then she was gone. For a while longer at least, the bridge would remain to be crossed.

The walk from the Billet Bus had been cold. George was warming himself in front of the kitchen fire as Mamam prepared the evening meal. "It is Christmas Eve tomorrow. Will you come to Midnight Mass wiz us? We are not very religious but Christmas is special."

"I'd love to. If it's not a silly question, what time?"

"After eleven o'clock. You will still 'ave time to be wiz your friends in the squadron, there is no meal here tomorrow evening."

"Why is that?"

"Because after Mass you can join us for a traditional French Christmas. We will enjoy *Le Reveillon* – the feast after Mass. We will 'ave a… a… *une oie.*"

"A goose?" ventured George. She nodded. "Sounds wizard!"

"What is wizzard?"

"It's an expression – like *formidable.*"

"Ah, je comprends. There is one other thing," she coloured slightly, "zer will be four of us. I 'ave asked a friend. I 'ope you do not mind."

Marcel and Jacques looked on expectantly as Stanhope-Smith began to speak. "Here is the plan. There is to be an invitation dance in the Officers' Mess on December 31st commencing at seven-thirty. It will occupy the squadron and most of the village so it is the obvious time to act. You will be in position on the hilltop for eight thirty; that is half-an-hour after one guard change and three and a half hours before the next. Marcel has found that except on changeovers there are only two guards. They patrol individually, meeting up every six minutes; so the two of you will be capable of dealing with them and then taking the lorries to the forest. After that, Jacques will take a trailer and dump it on the road to Nancy before returning to the cafe by midnight. Marcel will stay with the lorries."

"What will you be doing, *mi'lor*?" asked Jacques.

"I shall attend the dance. No one knows of my involvement and if I am there when the lorries are taken no one has cause to suspect me. Equally, no one knows you are involved. If you open your cafe as usual the next day there should be no reason to suspect you either. You will run the cafe as normal until the night of the pickup when you will next be needed. As Marcel spends much of his time in the forest, his absence is not likely to attract attention in the village. The squadron has already been warned about fifth columnists so it will look as if some unknown group is responsible.

We will keep the radio with the lorries so that, on the day, we can notify which landing field is to be used without going to the cafe. Whichever field we use will be over five kilometres from the village so the aircraft shouldn't be heard. The moon will be sufficient for landings for several nights starting on the 2nd and 3rd January. We will take the first opportunity that the weather allows. The aircraft will arrive at eleven o'clock. If it is unable to land within an hour of that time, it will abandon the attempt and try again another night. We will guide it in to the field using the torches Jacques has obtained. There will be extra men on the plane to help us with the loading. The whole thing should be done within an hour." Stanhope-Smith looked triumphantly at the others.

"How long will you stay here after the equipment has gone?"

"A few days. I have some business with one of my 'comrades', then I shall steal a Hurricane and return to Germany in triumph!" There was a strange look in his eyes; a look which disturbed Jacques.

"And what of Marcel and I?"

"I am authorised to say that your 'loan' will be deemed repaid after this and you can revert to running your cafe; although you might still be called upon to do the odd 'favour'. I have something particular in mind for Marcel. I want to make sure he gets what he deserves."

Jacques felt a sudden surge of optimism; there was a way off the runaway train after all. He poured three large brandies and raised his glass. "To success!"

Half an hour before midnight, through a fall of snow, they approached the church to the sound of bells ringing out carols. A figure in RAF uniform stepped from the shadows. "Good evening Juliette, Justine and George." He kissed Mamam and Justine on the cheek and nodded to George before offering Mamam his arm.

"Evening Adj," said George. He squeezed Justine's hand and they exchanged amused looks as they followed on into the Church.

Three hours later, they sat talking over the remains of *Le Reveillon.*

"That was *formidable,* Mamam," said George.

"I'll second that," said Richard, removing the pipe from his mouth. "Christmas 1939; I could never have imagined a year ago what I'd be doing now or who I'd be doing it with; nor even that I would be enjoying myself again. 1938 was my first Christmas as a widower. It all seemed very bleak then, like the ghost of Christmas future, but since then, I've got back into the RAF and never looked back. I give you a toast – friends."

"Friends," they responded.

"On the subject of friends, how did you two meet?" asked Justine, still surprised.

"As a certain lady emerged from *l'epicier* her shopping bag broke…" Richard began.

"…and a certain gentleman was on 'and to assist," Mamam looked at Justine and laughed, "I suppose you could say 'e is *my* knight."

"I'd never seen so many onions," Richard added. Mamam giggled. "Since then we've been meeting for coffee at *Le Cafe Georges.* It's been six weeks."

"Why didn't you say anything?" Justine asked, looking at Mamam.

She hesitated, "At the beginning you 'ad other things on your mind. I was also worried what you'd think."

"Oh Mamam, it is two years since Papa died. I will always miss him and I know how you loved him but that doesn't mean you can't have someone else who is special."

Mamam's lip quivered for a moment. Then she reached out and squeezed Justine's hand. *"Merci, ma petite."*

George spoke, "I want to toast love; a flower that grows in the most unexpected places and at the most unexpected times." Justine looked deep into his eyes as she raised her glass.

"To love."

"And I want to thank the RAF for providing George and Richard," Justine added.

"The RAF," they chorused, and then sat for a few moments in contemplation.

Richard broke the silence. "If you will excuse us for a moment I need a private word with George." Puzzled, George followed him from the room. "I imagine you've got a present for Justine, but have you given it to her yet?"

"I bought her something in Epinal but I was waiting for Christmas Day."

"Which it now is. Hold on a minute, I've got something for Juliette."

They returned with their parcels. Richard spoke. "If you'll excuse an English custom being tagged on *to Le Reveillon* we have something for you." Mamam opened hers first; unwrapping it to reveal a wireless set. "I know you are here a lot on your own, I thought it would be company for you."

Her eyes brimmed with tears. She kissed Richard on the cheek. "Sank you so much, it is a wonderful present. You are so very kind."

Justine removed the wrapping paper from hers and just stared at the box within.

"Mamam," she whispered hoarsely, *"c'est Paquin."*

"Formidable!" Mamam cried.

"Why don't you try it on?" said George.

"While she's gone, let's see if there's any dance music on the radio," said Richard, "I know it's late but perhaps Hilversum or Luxemburg are still broadcasting."

She returned a few minutes later, seeming to float into the room like some celestial being. "I say!" said Richard, busy twiddling the dial.

Mamam was in tears for the second time in minutes. *"Mon dieu,* you look like an 'ollywood star. It is so beautiful."

George spoke, "No Mamam, it is just a dress. It is Justine that is beautiful." Dance music suddenly filled the room. "I thought I'd find something. Ladies and gentlemen, take your partners please."

A few minutes after seven-thirty on New Year's Eve, Jacques' van emerged from the back yard of *Le Cafe Georges.* He had closed the cafe early, ostensibly in deference to the dance at the *Mairie.* He turned into *Rue de L'Ecole* and drove out of the village to the spot where Stanhope-Smith had entered the forest a few weeks before. He pulled over, opened the window and gave a short whistle. Marcel emerged from the trees and climbed in. The van set off for the far side of the forest.

George, Justine and Mamam walked up the steps into the *Mairie.* The first person they met was Richard, who offered his arm to Mamam and led her into the hall. When George and Justine followed, they were surrounded by his colleagues. He introduced her, "Gentlemen, I give you Mademoiselle Justine Delacroix."

"I wouldn't if I were you," said 'Foggy' archly, "because we won't give her back."

"They've all asked me for a dance, George. Do you mind?"

He smiled. "Not so long as I get the waltzes."

"Are you going to introduce me to this ravishing young lady, George?" asked S/L Sullivan, joining the group.

"Sir, may I present Mademoiselle Justine Delacroix. Justine, this is S/L John Sullivan to whom we sometimes refer as 'the Old Man'."

He laughed. "Less of the 'Old Man' you young whippersnapper. For that bit of insubordination I'm going to pull rank and claim the first dance. This will make a nice change from the wives of Air Marshals." He turned to Justine. "May I have the pleasure?"

She inclined her head and took his outstretched hand, *"Enchante."* She winked as she passed George. A seven-piece band had been hired for the occasion and they launched into a foxtrot. Sullivan was clearly a practised dancer but Justine matched him as they glided smoothly round the floor.

They bounced and rattled their way through the trees until Jacques stopped at the edge of the pit. He did not try to hide his van as he would need it again and doubted anyone would be there in the meantime. From the back, he produced his bicycle. Marcel, the younger man, mounted the saddle and Jacques climbed onto the step. They set off gingerly back the way they had come, en route to the hill.

The dance floor was already nearly full. Apart from the squadron, a large number of villagers were present. George noticed Stanhope-Smith across the room, a cigarette in his hand, watching the dancing and looking, he thought, tense. The dance ended and Sullivan led Justine back. He made a small bow. "Thank you, Mademoiselle. May I presume to ask for another dance later?"

"It would be my pleasure, Squadron Leader." George took her hand. "He is a good dancer, and a perfect gentleman."

"There aren't many of us left." The band started to play a waltz. "I think this is my dance," he said, leading her onto the floor.

It was nothing exceptional; it could have been taller and still been classed as a hill. Its gentle slopes had provided no difficulties to the two lorries, which stood on the broad, flat summit; ideal for the purpose which had brought them there. They were arranged in an 'L' shape, almost back to back and attended by their two trailers; the whole covered by an array of camouflage netting. Two figures were standing in the lee of the assembly, hunched against the cold. There was a brief spark of light as one lit a cigarette. LAC Harry Beale took a long drag before he spoke. "New Year's bleeding Eve. Freezing to death on a bleeding French hilltop while a bunch of la-di-dah bleeding officers get their hands down some French tarts' knickers." Beale was a Londoner, from the East End. Having grown up in the Depression and seen its effect on his family he had joined the Communist Party of Great Britain, from where, before Stalin's non-aggression pact with Hitler had confused the issue, it was a natural progression to enlist in the fight against fascism; and to him the RAF had promised to be the most egalitarian of His Majesty's forces.

71

AC1 Sydenham Napper, his companion, rubbed his gloved hands together and stamped his feet as he spoke. "It's a goodwill exercise. Foster relations with the locals. Mind you, I wouldn't mind being there myself, maybe I will when I'm aircrew."

"I wouldn't bank on it, the system is designed to keep the likes of you and me down; and call it what you like, it's no way to fight a bleeding war!"

Although the words were inaudible the murmur of voices reached the ears of Jacques and Marcel, watching from behind a small patch of shrubs. After a week of reconnaissance, Marcel knew the area like the back of his hand and despite the dark, they had reached their location without difficulty. Jacques peered at his watch and could just make out 8:25. They were on schedule. The next thing was to observe the guards and satisfy themselves that the routines Marcel had observed remained unchanged. Only then would they make their move.

He had to be there until midnight so he had decided to enjoy himself. Stanhope-Smith had asked and the girl had eagerly accepted his invitation to dance, flattered by his approach. Unfortunately the only impression he made was on her toes. After two dances, he was on his own again. His watch said 8.55.

AC1 Napper was nearly halfway round his patrol line. He was marching briskly, trying to keep warm. Away from the meagre shelter of the lorries, it was even colder. The frozen snow crunched under his boots. It had snowed at Christmas and on several days since. Only a matter of time before it starts again – shouldn't be doing this for much longer though, he thought to himself; as soon as my application for aircrew training is approved I'll be on my way back to Blighty and… "Halt, who goes there?" He had seen a shadowy form ahead, darker than the surrounding gloom. "Friend!" came the reply. The accent didn't sound English.

"Advance friend and be recognised!" He had unslung his rifle and he stood with it at the ready pointing at the advancing figure. There was a click as he worked the bolt to cock it. He did not hear Marcel stealthily approaching from behind. The first he knew was when the loop came around his neck. As it had countless times in Spain, the cheese wire did its deadly work, slicing through flesh and cartilage. ACl Napper and his dreams of aircrew died with a choking sound.

"*Vite!*" hissed Marcel as Jacques bent to remove the bayonet from the fallen rifle.

"*D'accord!*" He knew they must be at the lorries when the other guard returned.

The band struck up again, this time for another foxtrot. "There are a couple of chairs over there, just crying out to be sat on," said Justine.

"Good idea. Would you like a drink?"

"Later, thank you. Let's just be together for a few moments."

As the dance ended and another started she raised her head from his shoulder. "Happy?" he asked.

"Very, and you?"

"Never more so."

"I think I'd like that drink now. Should we get one for Mamam and Richard too?"

George felt guilty. "I never gave them a thought. Any idea where they are?"

"I saw them earlier." She looked around the floor and caught sight of Mamam. She giggled, "Look, they're still going strong – she will sleep like a log tonight." There was a pause before she added, meaningfully, "I doubt that any amount of noise will wake her."

Something in the way she had said it sent a frisson through him. He looked into her eyes and knew he had not misunderstood.

LAC Beale was concerned. Napper normally got back ahead of him, if anything, and certainly not this long afterwards. "Syd, where the 'ell are you?" he called into the darkness. Like Napper he didn't hear Marcel, but, whether it was overconfidence or the darkness, Marcel had miscalculated. Beale was left-handed and, away from the prying eyes of officers and sergeants, he liked to sling his rifle on the opposite shoulder to everyone else. The cheesewire, instead of dropping over Beale's head, was impeded by the bayonet attached to the muzzle and Marcel stumbled into him. The East End was a hard school and Beale had graduated as a street fighter; Cable Street his battle honour. Driving his elbow backwards he caught Marcel full in the face, sending him sprawling. A street fighter too, although his eyes were blurred by pain, Marcel knew he had to get up immediately. He did; a knife instantly appearing in his hand, just as Beale, no time to cock his rifle, attempted to bayonet him. With speed and nimbleness acquired in Spain, Marcel dodged the thrust and stabbed. This time he was thwarted by one of the packs on Beale's webbing belt. Beale dropped the rifle and grasped his wrist, starting to force the knife back towards him. Marcel had learned to carry two knives, and the second dropped from his sleeve into his other hand. He tried to stab under Beale's greatcoat for his stomach. Beale checked his arm with his free hand and head-butted him. At that moment Marcel nearly died. He lost concentration as waves of agony coursed through his already broken nose. His first knife was pushed dangerously near his neck before he renewed the struggle. He knew he was losing the fight. He was desperately searching for a means of salvation when, suddenly, Beale stiffened, gave a sigh and slumped forward. Although he recognised the man was dying, Marcel did not slacken his resistance until the life had gone from him. He stepped back and let the body crumple to the ground. *"Merci!"* he gasped. Jacques was standing behind Beale, wiping something. It had been twenty-one years since he had last done it, in a German trench, and in that time he had forgotten many things, but he had not forgotten how to kill a man with a bayonet.

Richard left Mamam seated with Justine and George while he did a round of the room. As Adjutant, he explained, he felt it was his duty to make sure that everyone was enjoying themselves. Stanhope-Smith checked his watch again – quarter to ten. "Evening Marcus, not bored I hope?"

"No Adj… well, only a little."

"Dances not your thing?"

"Not altogether, two left feet I'm afraid."

"Well you've given it a good shot. I don't suppose anyone would mind if you sloped off now."

"I think I'll stay, thank you sir. I'd like to see the New Year in."

"Good man!" A thought struck him. "You're keen on photography aren't you? Upstairs in the office is a portfolio of photographs taken at Anglure. Only arrived today; haven't had a chance to even glance at them. Why don't you go and sort them out for me? By the time you've done that, it will be getting on towards twelve and your problems will be solved."

It hadn't taken too long to dismantle the camouflage netting and stow it in one of the lorries along with Jacques' bicycle, retrieved from the shrubbery, and the dead men's rifles and ammunition. The trailers were hitched to the lorries and everything was ready. Marcel lit a cigarette. In the glow from the match Jacques caught sight of his battered face. *"Mon pauvre!"* he said, sympathetically.

Marcel shrugged, *"C'est rien – allons!"* and climbed into the leading lorry.

Stanhope-Smith settled in the Adjutant's chair, put his feet on the desk, lit a cigarette, and started to flick through the photographs. Memories of the day and his efforts to photograph the D520 came back to him. Suddenly he froze. In front of him was a picture of the officers' dining room at Anglure. The room was half-empty but there were groups of pilots here and there. To the right of centre were two figures, a French pilot and George Knight, and between them, in George's outstretched hand was Stanhope-Smith's camera, with the back open. His instantaneous anger quickly gave way to panic as the implications became clear. He tried to marshal his tumbling thoughts. Damn Knight to hell! He knew, and he had sabotaged his camera; he was too much an English gentleman to have said nothing if it had been an accident. Max had been right – he should have killed him. It was inconceivable that Knight had kept this to himself, so who else knew? Not the squadron at large; their attitude to him showed no animus whatsoever. Obviously the C/O; come to think of it he had seemed a bit terse on the odd occasion he had had contact with him. Probably 'Einstein'. Unlikely the Adjutant, given that he had suggested he sort the pictures. Unless… no, unlikely. But why had they done nothing? There was a wider picture here. They were letting him run and seeing where he went. He must therefore assume that they knew about Jacques and Marcel. Perhaps they had also followed Jacques to Nancy. Bugger and damn, what a mess! But hold on! They obviously hadn't tumbled to the lorries; there would be more than two guards unless it was some very clever trap. He checked his watch – 10.20 – getting on for two hours since the plan started. It must have succeeded! If not, someone would have come to arrest him by now. In which case come midnight and the changing of the guard all hell was going to break loose. No future now in stopping around as he had planned. He must warn Jacques not to go back to the Cafe and then they had to hide in the woods, for two days, maybe more. If the trailer decoy worked it could be done – time to go!

At the end of the corridor, was a second staircase. He descended quietly, let himself into the back lane and cautiously made his way round. Music and light spilled from the front door of the *Mairie* into the otherwise darkened square. There were a few couples outside but they were too preoccupied to notice him. Keeping to the shadows he skirted the square and made his way to the back of *Le Cafe Georges.* Jacques' van wasn't there so he was still out, presumably dealing with the trailer. He started to walk along *Rue de L'Ecole,* out of the village. The sounds of revelry faded behind him as he headed for the fork where the incoming road split to go into the village or past the other side of the forest.

Richard came to reclaim Mamam. George had seen him talking with Stanhope-Smith and was curious. "Everything alright?" he asked innocently.

"Yes, everything's going swimmingly."

"I thought Marcus looked a bit browned off."

"Oh, he's OK, he's gone to…"

"Come on you two," interrupted Justine, "you can talk shop tomorrow. It's the Hokey-Cokey next and Mamam wants to learn."

Thirty kilometres along the road to Nancy, Jacques pulled over. He walked back to the trailer and briefly shone a torch on the wheel. The tyre was ruined, chewed and shredded by the wheel rim. He had bayoneted it, ten kilometres back, and then driven fast to this point. He unhooked the trailer and, with a struggle, pushed it into the ditch at the side of the road. It looked just as he had hoped – abandoned in haste. He climbed into the cab and turned around to head back to St Jean. The world felt good – fate had given him a second chance – a few days more and he would be rid of the vile English Lord, the cafe would be his and this time he wouldn't gamble it away. It had all gone like clockwork, or, as he had heard the English pilots say, 'a piece of cake'. The lorries were safely in the forest, being watched over by Marcel; the decoy was in place; he was on his way to bed and he didn't give two hoots where *mi'lor* was.

Marcel sat on the edge of the pit and rolled a cigarette. His face was hurting like hell and he would need to see a doctor tomorrow but despite that, he felt good. The plan had worked and he had struck a major blow against the village and the nation that had spumed him and his family. His life had been happy until his father had gone off to war; ending up in 1917 being shot as one of the French army mutineers. His mother was left with a son to raise and no pension. She was pretty then and there were those in the village who offered insults by day and money by night. As he grew, Marcel started ignoring school and spending his time in the forest hunting and snaring to supplement his mother's earnings. His mind went back fourteen years as he looked down onto the lorries. The boy had called him the son of a whore. At the time, he only understood that it was an insult. It was said later that the boy's neck was broken. He had dragged the battered body from the forest, claiming to have found it. For two days gendarme, priest and several others had probed his story but in the end, having neither evidence nor confession they had let him go, and the legend of the beast was reborn. He saw it now as his first act of retribution. In 1936, he went to Spain for adventure and joined the Republican cause, returning three years later. Crocodile tears from the Cure who had so often reviled her, and the news that in his absence his mother, worn down by life, had gone to her rest rekindled his desire for revenge. Providentially, he met Jacques, the first for a long time to show him any humanity, then the obnoxious Englishman; together they had provided opportunity.

Jacques was approaching the fork in the road when, in the faint beams which his masked headlights produced he saw a figure in front of him, flagging him down. Stanhope-Smith's face appeared as he opened the window. "You can't go back to the Cafe, they're on to us!"

A feeling of dread came over him. "How? It went perfectly."

"Head for the forest, I'll explain on the way."

"Wait! If you're suggesting that we hide with the lorries, we're going to need water and food – there's none in the forest. I've plenty at the cafe."

Stanhope-Smith squinted at his watch – 11.40. "We've got to be quick – the guard changes at midnight and five minutes could be enough for news to reach the *Mairie*. We mustn't be seen in the area at all now, it will compromise the decoy."

"It's five minutes to the Cafe and another ten minutes to collect what we need. It will be tight but we've no choice." He gunned the engine.

F/Sgt Angus MacKay was not a happy man; he was rostered for the midnight guard-change. It was Hogmanay and not one Sassenach bastard in the Sergeants' Mess would swap with him, to allow him the time-honoured celebration. As a consequence, he hadn't had a dram all night. The replacements were waiting by the truck. He gave them a searching inspection, hoping to find fault and vent his spleen, but they were immaculately turned out. He climbed in beside the driver and waved him on his way.

They had coasted the last few yards, lights off, and swung into the lane behind the Cafe. Inside, Stanhope-Smith peered round the blackout curtains whilst Jacques had scurried about collecting their requirements. "Ready!" Jacques finally called.

"We can't go yet," he replied, disbelief in his voice, "they're doing a bloody conga round the square." He waited, fretfully, checking his watch every few seconds, while Jacques fidgeted near the back door. After what seemed an eternity, the revellers disappeared into the *Mairie*. "Come on, let's go!"

While they were loading the van faint strains of 'Auld Lang Syne' reached them.

"Happy New Year," said Jacques, without conviction.

5: January, 1940

As the truck crested the hill F/Sgt MacKay knew he wouldn't be drinking a dram for a while yet. The lorries had gone. The headlights picked out a bundle. He realised as he dismounted what the bundle was. He put a finger to Beale's neck. "Dead, and nae very recently," he announced. "Dinnae just stand there, search for ACl Napper!" It was several minutes before a shout drew him across the hilltop. When he got there A/Cl Dorking was off to one side retching and LAC Mitchell had tears in his eyes. A quick flash of his torch told the gory tale.

"Sorry F/Sgt, N-never seen a body before, n-not like that, anyway," faltered Mitchell. "Aye laddie," he said gently, "but ah shouldnae wonder ye'll see worse than that before this war's over. Ah'd like to get mah hands on the bastards that did this."

The *Marseillaise* and God Save the King had been played. "Gosh, I'll sleep tonight," said Mamam, stifling a yawn. Justine discreetly squeezed George's hand.

"You'll soon have your chance," said George, "I think things are just about winding down here."

"That looks like F/Sgt MacKay," said Richard, "I'd better see what he wants."

They were joined by S/L Sullivan. George could see from their faces that something was wrong. MacKay and Sullivan left the room and Richard mounted the stage and motioned for silence. "*M'sieu* LeMaire, Ladies and Gentlemen. I'm afraid that ends the proceedings for tonight. I'd like to thank you all for coming and on behalf of 686 Squadron to wish you all a very happy New Year." He repeated it in French and then added a final message. "All Officers are to re-assemble here with sidearms at 00.45 hours." A buzz ran round the room as he re-joined his party. "I'm sorry George; the Old Man wants to see you right away. I'll take Justine home with Juliette."

George took Justine to one side; disappointment was etched on both their faces. "I'll be back as soon as I can. I'm so –"

She put a finger to his lips. "Come back safe. Better late than never."

"Come in, George. Take a seat." Sullivan was looking at the photographs. "Haven't had the chance to commend you for what you did at Anglure." He handed George the picture of the camera incident. There was a cigarette burn where George's midriff had been but the picture otherwise told its story. "I think you'll get the gist. Sorry to curtail your evening but unfortunately our bird has flown the coop tonight. Even worse, he's taken the lorries containing the equipment and two A/Cs are lying dead up on the hill."

77

"Oh Christ – sir!"

"Precisely. I've spoken to the Duty Officer at AHQ and there's nothing they can do until morning. I'm determined to have this bugger's hide. It should never have got to this. You know him better than anyone – what do you think his plan is?"

"My feeling is that he will try to fly the stuff out, as I said a few weeks ago." He left the rest unsaid.

"Perhaps we should have listened to you then," Sullivan acknowledged, "so how do you think he will do it?"

"I think he and his chums are hiding somewhere in the area, waiting for the full moon that's a couple of days away I believe – and then he has a number of suitable fields to choose from – depending on wind. They're marked on a map and 'Einstein' has been checking them." Sullivan raised an eyebrow.

"Fetch him and the map, then. If they are hiding around here we can start searching tonight; the forest and the fields."

When George returned with 'Einstein' the other officers had assembled and been briefed on the situation. George had wondered what their response would be to the news about Stanhope-Smith. As he walked into the Mess, they cheered him. Sullivan studied 'Einstein's' map for a few moments. "Right, gather round. Red Section, you take the forest. Yellow, Blue and Green Sections take these fields and their surroundings," he pointed at the map, "Take six A/Cs each and flush the bastard out. Recall will be a red flare. Any questions?"

"We may not see a flare under trees, sir," said Underhill.

"Fair point – each section can take an extra man to act as a runner."

Jacques was thinking, sitting next to the pit in his old army greatcoat. He had tried to sleep, down below in his van, but couldn't. At least keeping watch was a useful way of passing time, although it was bloody cold. He had heard Stanhope-Smith's story, and, adding insult to injury, with mounting anger had to translate it for Marcel. 'You stupid, cocksure, arrogant, puffed-up fucking idiot' he had wanted to shout at him.

But he had been a soldier, and a good soldier too, he allowed himself; so he knew that you didn't get out of a mess like this by fighting among yourselves. There would be time for recriminations later, when they had got away; and if the decoy worked, it should buy them the time they needed. But what was there for him if he did get away? He couldn't go back to the Cafe now. He didn't want to go to Germany either. He would be a wanted man elsewhere so he would have to change his identity. He could try his luck in Belgium or Switzerland; better perhaps in Spain or North Africa. He had the means; whilst Stanhope-Smith had been keeping watch at the café, he had taken the opportunity to lift a certain floorboard and extract his nest egg – he'd done rather well since he had come to St Jean. He glanced across to where he sensed Marcel was. Poor sod! His face was a real mess. He needed a doctor for that or he could end up… He stiffened. Instincts honed in the trenches had not deserted him. He could hear faint noises coming to him through the forest. Marcel was at his side in an instant. *"Restez!"* he said and vanished silently into the night. A few minutes later, he was back, *"Les Anglais – neuf hommes."* He went off to fetch Stanhope-Smith. By the time they joined

Jacques, the noise of the searchers was quite discernible and torchlight was flashing through the forest, making bizarre patterns of the trees. Marcel brought the captured rifles, cocked them and gave one to Jacques. Stanhope-Smith was lacking his usual hauteur. He sounded uncertain, panicky.

"We must go – immediately – before they find us. How could they know we were here?"

Jacques recognised the signs. The last few hours had dealt serious blows to Stanhope-Smith's self-assurance. In four years of war, he had seen several officers facing crises of confidence; their trusty *Sergeant Dubois* had steadied them all. "We must stay where we are, *mi'lor*. If we run, now they will see us. As it is, they are only searching. If they knew we were here, they would send more than nine men. And see, their line of advance; unless it changes they will bypass us."

They squirmed under the bushes and waited tensely as the searchers followed their oblique track. Jacques watched the shadowy figures over the sights of his rifle. A stray beam of light illuminated the face of one man. He recognised him as the pilot who was courting the schoolteacher. Kill the officers first, they were always told. He took aim and started to track him; 'just one wrong move, *m'sieu*.' The group halted. His target seemed to be looking straight at him, staring at him through the darkness, although he was a hundred and fifty metres away. Jacques' finger tightened on the trigger, taking up the slack in the action. Any further movement of his finger now and the man would die. Seconds passed. He could hear the thumping of his heart in his chest. There was a shout from somewhere deep in the wood and he thought he heard the word 'recall'. A muffled command and the searchers turned and headed whence they had come, the dome of light from their torches receding with them. He waited until he could no longer hear them, then, with a long exhalation, he un-cocked the rifle.

"You were right," said Stanhope-Smith, before making his way back to the lorries. 'And that,' thought Jacques, 'is as close to 'thank you' as I'm ever going to get.'

Sullivan was waiting when they returned to the *Mairie.* "Sorry George, but your intuition was wide of the mark. One of the missing trailers has been found abandoned near Nancy – they've obviously made a run for it. There's no more to be done tonight, so get some rest here. At first light Red, Blue and Green Sections will carry out sweeps in the Nancy area."

"I'm glad I'm out of that forest," said 'Roy', "I half-expected to bump into Dracula!"

"It's a toss-up who'd have been more frightened if you had," Underhill suggested.

"It's strange," said George, thinking aloud, "I could have sworn they were in there. I almost felt I could reach out and touch them."

"Hello, George," said Justine lightly, "been busy?"

"I'll say! I've done more flying today than all the time I've been in France. Haven't found them yet though. I take it you know who I'm talking about?"

"Not really," she replied, "although I gather that it involves the Cafe. Quite a day for St Jean. A group of gendarmes broke in, searched it thoroughly, and then boarded it up – amid protests from the regulars of course! Then there's all the flying you've been doing and villagers being questioned. I thought I'd have to sedate Mamam!"

He related the story. "I'm not surprised at Marcel being involved," said Mamam, "'E's a bad lot. I think 'e murdered little Leon all those years ago. It makes more sense than that *Bete Sauvage* nonsense."

"But he was only a boy himself then. I don't see how he could have caused the terrible injuries everyone talked about," Justine responded.

"'e probably threw him into *le Trou."* Mamam replied, "'e was only ten or eleven but 'e lived almost wild and 'e was a lot tougher than other boys of 'is age. 'E gave your brother a bad beating one day for calling him names."

George couldn't contain his surprise. "You have a brother?" In over two months, he had heard no mention, seen no photographs.

"Yes, Alain," said Justine wistfully, "my big brother. I should have told you but we don't talk of him because it upsets Mamam. As you might guess, he is named after Mamam's brother. Papa wanted Alain to follow him into local government but he was…is, not the right person for office work. Papa was not a well man but he had a strong will and they quarrelled bitterly. When Alain was fifteen, he ran away. He left a note to say he was going to Marseilles to join the navy, and we haven't heard from him since."

Mamam had slipped from the room. When she returned, George could see that she had been crying. Questions about *Le Trou* were left for another day.

In the forest, spirits were high, despite the cold. At dawn, they had sat with bated breath as the first patrol of the day took off. The aircraft had flown over them but continued until out of earshot in a northerly direction; and so it had been all day, and no more search parties on the ground – no one knew they were there. Stanhope-Smith had recovered his poise. The ruse with the trailer, *his* idea, was working. Now, the evening had come and the patrols had ceased. They would be safe for the night.

Mamam returned from the shops to find Justine sitting at the kitchen table, an envelope in her hands and tears in her eyes. Without a word, she passed it to her. It had come that day though the postmark was a month earlier. Blue crayon lines and a clumsy attempt at resealing it testified that the letter had been through the censor. She read the address:

To my fiance. P/O G. Knight, c/o The School House, St Jean-sur-Moselle, Lorraine, France; and she sniffed the scent of the envelope. "When I was in England, it was called Californian Poppy," Justine said dully, and then with anguish "I have come to terms with the possibility of him being killed, but not this." All Mamam's instincts told her it could not be this simple. She had talked with George, looked into his eyes, lived under the same roof. Please God, he couldn't be so cold-blooded. "Wait until he comes 'ome, *ma cherie,* I am sure there is an explanation."

She looked up at her mother, wanting to believe it was true. "I hope you're right, but I'm going to go mad sitting here. I need a walk."

Gaspard flushes a rabbit and starts to chase it. Whenever it finds cover, he is there again to keep it running, deeper into the woods. Trailing behind, shouting desperately at his unheeding dog, is Pascal. The rabbit breaks cover yet again and is racing across the ground when there is a sudden swirl and it is hanging by its back legs. *Gaspard,* in hot pursuit, blunders into another snare but, too heavy to be lifted like the rabbit, ends up with one leg held in the air. Pascal, guided by *Gaspard's* frantic barking, finds his pet and begins sawing at the snare with the small penknife his father allows him to carry. He has almost severed the noose when he is suddenly looking into the bruised and blood-caked face of Marcel. He screams and drops his knife. He is cowering from the ghastly apparition when Jacques puts a hand on his shoulder. *"Qu'est ce que vous faites ici?"*

He spins round. *"Mon chien a chasse le lapin,"* he sobs.

Alerted by the noise, Stanhope-Smith appears. "What the hell is going on?"

"The boy's dog chased this rabbit into Marcel's snares and got caught itself. He was trying to free it when Marcel surprised him."

"Well shut the bloody dog up!" he turns to Marcel and, indicating *Gaspard,* who has started barking again, draws his finger across his throat.

"Non!" screams Pascal, realising what he means. As Marcel draws his knife, *Gaspard* senses the danger and, making a supreme effort, seizes the snare in his mouth. The last strand parts and, before anyone can react, he disappears into the forest.

"Marvellous!" says Stanhope-Smith disgustedly. "Sooner or later, probably sooner if someone finds that bloody dog, somebody's going to come looking for the brat. Perhaps we should kill him and leave him somewhere for them to find…"

"Over my dead body!" Jacques squares up to Stanhope-Smith, making no attempt to hide his anger. "I've sunk pretty low recently – but not to this."

Stanhope-Smith thinks quickly. Even if Marcel would go along with the idea, he still needs both of them and he knows Jacques isn't bluffing. "Just thinking aloud," he says emolliently, "the fact is that we're going to have to bring things forward because 'beast' or no beast they will start combing the forest once they realise he's missing. I reckon that will be around dusk when he fails to return home. We need to stay here until it's properly dark – two hours or so from now – then head for the landing field. I'm going to signal Germany and bring the landing forward to seven o'clock; that's the earliest we can manage because there'll be no moon before then. While I'm doing that, tie the brat up and put him in a lorry." He turns then pauses. "If it doesn't offend your delicate sensibilities, tell him that if he makes a sound, Marcel will eat him."

Justine shivers despite her winter coat and looks at her watch; dusk in an hour or so. George will probably be back soon after that and then she will know the truth. She has been walking for over two hours, her head bursting with conflicting thoughts. She cannot believe that he has been deceiving her, yet there it was in writing, 'to my fiance'; what other explanation was there? He had never mentioned other women; was that good or bad? True, she hadn't talked to him of past boyfriends – but they were over and done with and she hadn't been engaged to any of them. Last evening, and all the others she has spent with him, had been so wonderful; now they seem lost forever. She is filled with misery.

Heading back towards the village, she reaches the point where the houses begin but follows the line of the forest behind them instead of *Rue d'Ecole.* Suddenly *Gaspard* is there, jumping around her and barking excitedly, darting into the forest and then running back to her, barking each time. She looks around and calls for Pascal. Receiving no response she studies the dog. The remains of the snare on his leg alarm her. Has Pascal blundered into a trap too or is he lying injured somewhere?

She follows *Gaspard* into the forest; stumbling after him for ten hard minutes until there is a lighter area ahead. She knows she is approaching the pit; she has been there once with her brother; mainly because they had been told not to. She stops to catch her breath and the dog runs back to her, barking again. There is no response when she calls Pascal's name. To one side, near a sapling, there is a small object on the ground.

She picks it up. It is Pascal's pocketknife. Turning towards the pit, she calls his name more urgently, her voice betraying her fear for him. She stops, heart in mouth; down below she can see two lorries and Jacques' van. All is clear now. She has to get help. She turns away from the pit and gasps. Marcel has appeared as if from nowhere, blocking her escape. She controls her revulsion at his battered appearance and glares at him defiantly. Someone speaks from behind her, mockingly. "Good afternoon, *Mademoiselle*, is there something we can do for you?"

She swivels to see Stanhope-Smith, wearing an amused expression, and behind him, deadpan, is Jacques. Stifling her fear she replies. "I'm looking for a missing boy, Pascal, I'm worried that he is hurt."

"He is here, safe and well," Jacques answers.

She tries to bluff. "Thank you. I'll take him home then – his mother will be worried." Stanhope-Smith speaks again, a harsh edge to his voice. "You won't be taking him anywhere. He will be released tonight, when he can no longer pose a threat to us; but you are Knight's girl and because of that, I shall take you to Germany. I intended to kill him before I left but he is out of my reach now. However, fate has compensated me by delivering you instead."

She is defiant again. "I will never be yours!"

"Perhaps not. Denying you to Knight will be satisfaction enough; any more would be a bonus." His tone becomes menacing, "But if you do decide to spurn my protection the Third Reich will have a use for you."

She maintains her composure despite the icy fingers of fear clutching at her heart.

"People are searching as we speak. You've no chance."

He comes close to her and his face twists into a snarl. "Don't insult my intelligence Mademoiselle. We know how long the boy has been out. It is most unlikely he will be missed before dusk; even then it will take time to organise a search. In an hour or so we leave for a place where no one will think to look for him or you. Another two hours and we shall be on our way to Germany. Your boyfriend won't save you, either. He's chasing shadows thirty miles away. Say your adieus to George Knight."

He motions to Marcel who advances with a piece of cord in his hands. She can smell his rasping breath and feel it on her neck as he seizes her roughly, tying her wrists together behind her back. As he does so, *Gaspard* appears and hurls himself at his ankle. With his free leg he kicks the dog savagely. It yelps pitifully and limps away into the forest. He leads her down the slope and bundles her into the back of a lorry, tying her ankles with more cord before locking the tailgate in place. She lies there for a minute, breathing hard, accustoming her eyes to the gloom, and then struggles into a sitting position. A small, frightened, face is watching her. *"Pascal, vous etes bien?"* He nods hesitantly. *"Pouvez vous parler?"* His eyes fill with tears and he shakes his head. Shuffling across the floor until she is beside him, she puts her mouth to his ear. *"Pourquoi non?"*

He whispers in response. *He can't speak because Marcel will eat him* – she doesn't know whether to laugh or cry, but sitting almost back to back has given her an idea. She whispers again and he nods enthusiastically.

The novelty of flying to and around Nancy had worn thin. The unspoken feeling in the squadron was that it was a wild goose-chase; that Stanhope-Smith and friends had got clean away. George was feeling browned-off as he returned through the gloaming to the School House. He was met by Mamam, minus her usual smile.

"Is Justine not in?"

"She went for a walk – to think." There was steel in her voice.

"About what?"

"Zis!" she thrust out the letter. He didn't know the scent but he recognised the hand. He opened it and read. Mamam watched him, arms folded. He handed it to her.

"I can imagine what you're thinking so I'd like you to read this."

Pangley Vale
2nd Dec '39

Dearest Georgie,

I have had your letter for <u>three weeks</u> now. I couldn't believe it when you said that you had met and <u>fallen in love</u> with <u>someone else</u> and that you knew you <u>couldn't</u> ever <u>marry</u> me!! After <u>twelve</u> years <u>engaged</u> as well!! But now I realise that it's just a passing fancy!! Apparently lots of soldiers in the last war got infatuations for French girls and then <u>forgot</u> about them when they came back to England!! I can't say I'm mad about the idea of you <u>consorting</u> with some French floozy but Maudie says that these are the kind of things men do under the <u>stress</u> of war and it's not as if you will be <u>marrying</u> her or anything like that!! So as long as you <u>forget</u> her and come <u>back</u> to me, I suppose I can <u>forgive</u> and forget about Mademoiselle from Armentieres – I have no wish to write <u>her</u> name.

I've got a job now, helping the war effort. Maudie works with me. Can't say any more – all dreadfully <u>hush-hush</u> as they say!

Must dash, simply <u>loads</u> to do!!
Yours <u>always</u> and forever.

"I asked her to marry me when I was seven," said George as Mamam handed the letter back, "since then we've drifted along and things have been taken for granted. I met Justine and I knew then what love really was. That's why I wrote to say I could never marry her. This is no infatuation or dalliance, Mamam, I truly love Justine."

Mamam's face lit up. "She loves you too. She was heartbroken when the letter carne. What are you going to do?"

"About Dorothy? This letter isn't from the Dorothy I thought I knew – she clearly can't accept what I am saying. I must write again. About Justine – I shall ask her to marry me – with your permission, of course – I should have done it before now."

She threw her arms around him, elated. *"Bravo, mon brave!* I won't stand in her way. I can't wait to see her face! She'll be 'ome soon – she should have been 'ere by now."

It has taken an hour but, sitting back to back, Justine has succeeded in untying the cord that binds Pascal's hands. He is now trying to free her but, sobbing with frustration, his fingers aren't strong enough to make an impression on Marcel's knots. She is trying to encourage him when she hears footsteps approaching. *"Vite, asseyez vous!"* she hisses. He scrambles back to his original sitting position, remembering to put his hands behind his back.

Stanhope-Smith makes a cursory sweep with his torch. "It begins, Mademoiselle."

The quiet is shattered as three engines burst into life. The next five minutes for Justine and Pascal are like a bad fairground ride as the lorry climbs from the pit then sways and bounces its way through the forest. Pascal struggles again in vain to undo her bonds. As they turn onto the road, she realises they are running out of time; something else is needed. Against the noise she gives him instructions. As she had expected the lorry slows when it reaches the fork. *"Maintenant, allez!"* He hesitates, fearful. *"Allez, allez, vite!"* she urges, desperation in her voice. Reluctantly, he scrambles over the tailgate. His delay means that the lorry is gathering pace again. She hears a cry as he drops to the ground but the lorry is drawing away. All she can do now is trust in him.

The lorry was at the back of the convoy so no one else saw him drop to the ground or heard his shout of pain as he landed. He has lain in the road scarcely daring to breathe as the taillights faded into the distance. Now he tries to stand. Red-hot pokers stab his ankle. He slumps to the ground and the tears come. The darkness closes in on him. He wants his mother. Sitting there he remembers what Justine had told him. 'Get word to George – they are taking me to Germany. You're my only hope!' Apart from Gaspard and his parents there is no one in the whole world whom he loves more than Mademoiselle. He has to save her. He struggles to his feet. Again the pain assails him. Tears of self-pity turn to tears of determination. He grits his teeth and takes a step. His leg buckles and he collapses. He struggles to his feet and tries again. He finds that turning his foot on its side dulls the pain. He takes a step, then another, and another. He laughs through his tears as he hobbles with growing speed towards the village.

Richard had gone to the kitchen fire to warm himself. "Bit of a flap in the village. I gather they're organising a search party. Little boy went into the woods with his dog. The dog came back on three legs but no sign of the boy."

"Justine's missing as well!" Mamam responds, anxiously. "She went out hours ago; do you think there's a connection?"

George has an ominous feeling. "I think we should join the search."

"Lead on!" says Richard.

"I'll stay 'ere in case…"As Mamam opens the door, Pascal stumbles in and collapses into her arms. Between sobs he blurts out his story as Mamam tends his injured ankle. *Gaspard* and the rabbit… the pit… Marcel, Jacques, and a pilot like George… the lorries… they are taking Mademoiselle away. Mamam translates with mounting agitation.

"Good Lord! They've been here all the time!"

"But they won't be here much longer! It's five past six. The moon rises about seven so any time after that they can be away."

"Where from though?" asks Richard.

"There are three possible fields, but only two are likely today. 'Einstein's' got a map."

"Let's go and find him then. We've got to organise an assault party."

George draws Richard out of Mamam's earshot. "I'm sure that if we attack them Stanhope-Smith will kill her, to get even with me. I've got to try to free her first."

"How will you find her?"

"Between them, the three fields cover all wind directions but the wind today has been negligible so, bearing in mind the amount of equipment they're stealing and the icy conditions, if I were them I'd ignore the wind and go for the longest runway. When you see 'Einstein's' map there's one field that is noticeably longer than the others. It has a slight slope too. That's got to be the one."

"What if you're wrong?"

"I daren't think about it."

Richard is silent for a moment. George's whole plan is based on supposition but from what he has heard and seen George's intuition in the whole affair has been spot-on so far. He doesn't like the idea of him launching a one-man rescue mission but he can see his point. He can also see from his determined manner that any alternative would have to be achieved at gunpoint. He hesitates only a moment longer. "Right, I'll organise the cavalry. Good luck!" He kisses Mamam. "I'll pass word about the boy." George gathers Justine's bicycle and a torch. He runs upstairs and returns, buckling on his service pistol, having filled the empty chambers from a box and tipped the other bullets into his greatcoat pocket.

"What is 'appening?" asks Mamam anxiously.

He speaks quietly, with determination rather than bravado. "I'm going to rescue her."

Silence descends; the convoy is at the landing field. In the back of the lorry Justine shivers. It is cold but that isn't all. She has followed the twists and turns of the road in her mind and calculated that she is seven or eight kilometres north-west of the village. Will anyone else though? Has Pascal delivered her message? If not, she is lost anyway. Despair is a heartbeat away but she resists it. The sound of Stanhope-Smith's voice reaches her. "Its forty minutes until the moon rises. Walk the field and ensure that no obstructions have arisen since I last inspected it. If the field is clear, Jacques, take up position at the far end; Marcel, in the middle. When you hear the aircraft, shine your torches to the south-west. After it's landed, get back here to help load it." As they set off she hears him climb into the other lorry and switch something on, followed a couple of minutes later by tapping. Unable to read Morse she doesn't know he has transmitted a single word – *Freya*. The tapping stops. He approaches.

"About now, Mademoiselle, an aircraft is taking off from an airfield just inside Germany." As he speaks, he flashes his torch into the lorry. "It will be here about the time the moon rises and then... where is the boy?"

She spars with him, "About now, *m'sieu*, he will be safely home with his mother." He drops the tailgate and scrambles in. A quick search shows that there are no places among the equipment where Pascal can have hidden. He raises his arm to strike her, his face contorted with rage; and then he checks himself. "A woman of spirit. I like that. Definitely worth more than a place in the Fuehrer's baby farms. The boy can't do any harm now; he has no idea where we are."

George has studied Einstein's map enough to know the route to each field, but in the dark it is not so simple; easy to miss a turning. The lanes are rutted and frozen so he struggles to maintain a decent pace. All at once he comes upon a fork. He remembers it from the map. The two roads lead to the two possible fields he has discussed, but they are miles apart. Doubts crowd in on him. What if his analysis is wrong and Stanhope-Smith has chosen the other field? He runs it through his mind again. Today length, not wind, has to be the deciding factor. He sets off pedalling. Suddenly the handlebars twist and he is catapulted over them. He is fortunate; he lands in a bush which breaks his fall. He is also lucky that his torch isn't broken. He flicks it on to look for his bicycle and finds the reason for his crash. He has cycled into a deep rut, filled with water. The ice covering it has been broken by something heavy; so recently that it hasn't had time to re-freeze.

Richard is seething with frustration. It is over half an hour since he raised the alarm and he is still waiting at the *Mairie*. Sullivan had been decisive. "Two lorries – fifteen armed airmen in each. Richard, take 'Roy' and F/Sgt McKay. I'll take 'Shorty' and F/Sgt Robertson in the other. Initially, one lorry for each of the two fields – we can't risk George being wrong – as well as the girl there's the equipment to retrieve. Whichever party finds them, fires a green flare. If the aircraft manages to get airborne, fire a red. There's a section on stand-by to shoot it down." The squeal of brakes outside heralds the lorries – at last.

George creeps through the gate and pauses, crouching. It isn't moonrise yet but it is imminent. In front of him the field stretches away, made faintly white by frozen snow. Off to his left he can see three vehicles in a row, dark against the background. He works his way along the hedgerow towards them and settles in a depression about ten yards away. There appears to be no sign of life, then he becomes aware of a figure doing something at the front of the lorries. The rim of the moon edges above the horizon, bringing a pale luminescence to the field. Faintly at first, and then more distinctly, comes the growl of an aircraft. The figure – he recognises it as Stanhope-Smith comes to the back of the lorry and flashes a torch inside, saying a few words. His heart leaps as he catches a flash of blonde hair – Justine! The aircraft is overhead now. Stanhope-Smith walks beyond the lorry and calls out. "Lights!"

Further down the field George sees two more beams complimenting Stanhope-Smith's torch. He knows now where everyone is. This is his chance. He runs to the lorry and vaults inside. "Ssssh!" he hisses as Justine gasps. He tugs at the knots. "Damn, they're tight! I've no knife."

"Pascal's penknife. I had forgotten! It's in my pocket."

He finds the knife and starts to saw at the cord… He can hear the aircraft on final approach… Her hands are free… A muffled thump… The engine note changes…. It is taxiing up the field… He works frantically on the cord binding her ankles… Damn! The blade has gone blunt…'The roar of engines rises to a crescendo as the Junkers swings round ready for take-off… then silence. He hears a door open, men jumping to the ground. *'Raus, raus, schnell!'* Torchlight flashes into the lorry. "Your carriage awaits, Mad…"The word dies on Stanhope-Smith's lips… He gapes… George drops the knife and reaches for his pistol… Not there… He must have lost it when he crashed the bicycle… He hurls himself at Stanhope-Smith and they hit the ground together… George is on his feet first and grabs him by the collar… *"Hilfe!"* he cries… George's fist crashes into his jaw, knocking him out.

"Was is los? Wer da?" The shouts come from the vicinity of the aircraft.

Justine has freed her ankles and jumped from the lorry. "Run!" George seizes her hand and they bolt for the gate.

"Halte, oder ich schiesse!" Jackboots pound up the field and a German soldier rounds the lorry, sub-machine gun ready. Nothing. He stares suspiciously into the shadows then grunts. His sergeant joins him as he is unceremoniously hauling Stanhope-Smith to his feet, slapping his face to rouse him.

"Name, schweinhund?" the sergeant snarls into his face.

"Stanhope-Smith." They snap to attention. The sergeant tries to splutter an apology.

"Enough. Who are you and how many have you brought?"

"Feldwebel Braun, sir. I have five armed men. May I ask what has occurred?"

"It is unimportant." He waves towards the lorries. "The main thing is to get this lot on the plane, quickly. Put two of your men on guard and get the rest to work. I've two men as well." He goes to a lorry and reaches into the cab. The headlights, which he had unmasked minutes ago, illuminate the Junkers. The sergeant moves the other lorry up to the aircraft and the waiting soldiers set to work.

Marcel joins them. *"Ou est Jacques?"* Stanhope-Smith asks. Marcel shrugs.

For Jacques it was time to leave; the first opportunity since New Year's Eve. He wasn't telling *mi'lor*; he didn't trust him not to put a bullet in him now the job was nearly done. As the Junkers swept in over him he had switched off his torch and melted into the shadows.

When they had run from the field they had dived into a ditch under the hedge to dodge the expected hail of bullets. Instead all they heard was Stanhope-Smith's conversation with the German soldiers. "I've got to do something to stop them," George whispers, "With the men available they'll have that aircraft loaded before anyone else gets here. Work your way along the hedge until you find your bicycle. If the Junkers takes off or you hear shooting and I'm not back, don't try to find me, go, straight away. In case I don't return – the letter that came this morning, it isn't what it seems; and if I get back, I want you to marry me. I love you." Before she can respond he kisses her and is gone.

Back in the field again, he is watching the loading. The first lorry has been emptied and is reversed back into line to provide illumination as the second rolls forward. He is wondering desperately how to sabotage the process. He looks around; the lorries, the aircraft, *Georges'* van: an idea forms and gingerly he begins to move forward.

Stanhope-Smith is thinking about George as he supervises the loading. What was he doing here alone? The brat must have got word back and George come on ahead to rescue his girl; he would have guessed that she would be killed if there were an attack. How did he find the field so quickly? Others must be following, but how soon? Damn him again for his bloody meddling – I should have killed him before now! What's he doing now? Forget the girl, she's free; the issue now is the secret equipment. He's out there somewhere, planning something in case his friends don't arrive in time. At the current rate the loading will be completed within ten minutes or so. He'll be able to see that now if he hadn't overheard when I spoke English to the soldiers. That was a mistake. What will he do? He's unarmed; that was obvious when he was in the lorry.

What would I do in his place, one man against eight or nine? Damage the plane, stop it taking off. How? Crash a vehicle into it; with a bit of luck he could do it *and* get away. That has to be it! Now he knows he can set a trap. He calls the *Feldwebel.*

The two lorries bounce along the lane. When they reach the fork where George had his moment of doubt, Sullivan's lorry stops. Richard's lorry draws level. Sullivan calls across. "We're both five minutes from our field; that means one of us will be ten minutes away; whoever finds the aircraft has got to do the job alone. Good luck!"

From his vantage point *Feldwebel* Braun sees a figure emerge from the shadows and run to the van. As it starts up he fires. The windscreen dissolves in a hail of machine gun bullets. Two stick grenades follow, detonating the fuel tank. The van explodes in a ball of flame. Stanhope-Smith is exultant.

Icy fear grips Justine, not for herself but for George. She is crouching by a hedge at the corner of the field, her bicycle nearby. The flames from the van are dying away. She knows she should leave but can't bring herself to do so. Suddenly a lorry coasts up behind her, lights off. It stops and men begin clambering down and forming up. Orders are quietly given and they start to deploy. Some pass her and head for the gate whilst others go along the side of the field. Another man appears from the shadows, flare pistol in hand. Peering at his watch, he almost falls over her. "Richard!"

"Justine, thank God you're safe! Where's George?"

"He went back into the field. He said he had to stop them. There was shooting and an explosion and he hasn't returned."

"We saw the explosion." Richard raises the pistol. There is a muffled crack and a green flare sails into the sky followed by a fusillade of rifle shots and the answering rattle of Schmeissers. "Stay here and keep your head down. We'll find him."

The loading is complete. They pause as the flare lights up the sky. Suddenly bullets are pinging around them and punching into the Junkers. A soldier grunts and clasps his arm, blood oozing between his fingers. The two men on guard are retreating towards them, keeping up a return fire. The others hurriedly retrieve their weapons. *"Feldwebel,* did they tell you the importance of what we are doing here?"

"Jawohl, Herr Oberleutnant!"

"Then you know what you must do. *Heil Hitler!"* Stanhope-Smith salutes, grabs a gun and climbs into the aircraft. He calls to the pilot. *"Zeit zum zu gehen!"* The engines burst into life and the Junkers begins to roll along the field, slowly gathering pace. Feldwebel Braun shouts orders to his men; they begin advancing across the field, shooting as they go. One of them topples backwards, his Schmeisser firing a last futile burst into the sky. Stanhope-Smith hears a shout and sees Marcel running diagonally across the field, towards the aircraft. "Bastard!" He fires his Schmeisser, swinging it through an arc. A line of bullet holes appear across Marcel's chest and, a look of surprise on his face, he is dead before he hits the ground. The heavily laden Junkers is gradually drawing away from the fight but Stanhope-Smith ducks involuntarily as a bullet ricochets off the doorframe. At length it staggers into the air and starts climbing. As it banks onto a homeward course a red flare climbs up the sky. He contemplates its meaning as he tries vainly to close the door, which is jammed open by some of the cargo.

The Hurricanes are bouncing across the frozen airfield before the flare has reached its zenith. They lift into the air; their pilots aiming to climb quickly for a chance of spotting their quarry silhouetted against the white background.

The last time they had flown at night was in England in August '39. Then the south coast had been lit up like a Christmas tree. Now they are flying by moonlight over a patch-work of woods and fields; relying on six softly lit instruments on their blind- flying panels to do what in the semi-dark their eyes and ears cannot – enable them to maintain controlled flight and prevent them from tumbling to earth. Alone in the night sky, they are held together by one invisible thread; R/T. "The Hun should be passing to the north of us so keep a sharp lookout." Easier said than done, reflects Giles, on the sortie as one of 686's three most experienced night-flyers and aware that the Hurricane is not ideal as a night-fighter; the exhausts, ahead of the cockpit, create a glare and spoil his forward view.

Anxious minutes pass before the silence is broken by F/L Stewart. "I believe I see it, leader. Two o'clock low, heading eastwards, about five hundred feet."

"Well done Alistair!" Unusually, Underhill's voice betrays tension, "we'll only get one chance so make every bullet count. Tallyho!"

"Two Jerries dead and four prisoners, Sah! Three of them wounded." They had surrendered their hopeless fight as soon as the Junkers was safely airborne.

"Thank you F/Sgt; and our own men?"

"Two wounded and all accounted for, Sah!"

"Except P/O Knight," corrects Richard, "where the devil can he…?"

"Sir, over here!" Torchlight illuminates a still, crumpled form.

Justine is the first there. "George!" Her strangled sob as she drops to her knees conveys all the misery a human soul can feel.

The rush of cold air through the open door is bracing and Stanhope-Smith feels triumphant as he watches the fields and woods passing underneath. They must have crossed the German border by now; only a few minutes to the airfield. He and the equipment are on their way to a hero's welcome and at last George Knight is dead, as well as the impertinent peasant. Only the girl got away and she doesn't matter – there will be plenty of women around when he steps out wearing his Iron Cross, presented by the Fuehrer himself. A loud metallic hammering and a deluge of debris is the first he knows of the pursuing fighters as metal cabinets only a few feet from him are blasted to scrap. For three hellish seconds he is immobilised by fear as the storm of bullets crashes through the fuselage. The bedlam stops as suddenly as it began and he is starting to collect his wits, mechanically brushing slivers of glass and metal off himself, when the aircraft shudders as another burst rips into it. He hears an engine cough and stop. The Junkers begins a shallow descent. Moments later, a third torrent of metal strikes and he hears a cry from the front – the pilot must be hit. The nose drops further. The descent steepens. The engine note starts to rise. The way forward is blocked. He can't get to the cockpit. He goes to the door again and sees the dark shape of a wood coming up towards him. Just as a crash seems inevitable the injured pilot jerks the nose up and the aircraft levels off, but it strikes the tops of several trees and staggers, causing

Stanhope-Smith to lose his balance and topple into the void. Instinctively he curls into a ball. He feels himself smashing through branches; pain and then nothing. He is unaware of the crash and explosion a hundred yards beyond.

His foot jerked in response to the MO's rubber hammer. "And the other leg, please… Fine! I thought you'd at least have concussion but you seem to have got away without any serious injury whatsoever. A couple of days in bed and you should be as good as new."

"My head hurts."

"Not surprising considering that wicked gash to your scalp. Still, once your hair has grown back no one will ever know. I must say you were lucky. An inch lower and whatever it was would probably have taken the top off your head; like a boiled egg. I'm going to give you a pill that will make you sleep. Take it as soon as the C/O has spoken to you. And as for you young lady, if I were you I'd get some sleep too, you look all in. He won't need you for the next few hours."

Justine was at his side, where she had been since he had been found, her face weary and streaked with blood and dirt but her eyes shining. Her tears of grief had splashed onto his face causing him to sneeze, the first sign that he was alive. They had gently prised him from her arms and taken him to the *Mairie* where the MO had assessed the extent of his injuries, and thence, stitched and bandaged, to the School House.

Sullivan, accompanied by Richard, replaced the MO. They motioned her to stay but Justine left the room also. "Glad to hear you'll be alright. Any idea what happened?"

"Vaguely, sir. I didn't know if anyone was going to arrive in time so I'd made up my mind to take the Cafe-owner's van and ram the aircraft – to stop it taking off. I was just crawling towards it when, I assume, *Georges* himself suddenly appeared from the bushes and jumped in – he must have been trying to bunk off – and then all hell broke loose. The last thing I remember was a flash and a bang."

"As the MO said, you've been very lucky; and damn brave too, I might add. You'll be happy to hear that we got the Junkers. It crashed and burned so the Jerries didn't get hold of the equipment after all and, better still, that lousy traitor was aboard! So it just remains to follow the doc's advice and you'll be fighting fit again in a few days."

"Thank you, sir. Before you go may I have your permission to get married?"

"My dear fellow, congratulations," said Richard enthusiastically, "but are you sure you want to do this now?"

"It's not the knock on the head if that's what you think. I intend to propose before anything else happens to me but I need to be in a position to deliver," replied George.

Sullivan tried to look suitably magisterial. "Richard, you are the most experienced among us. What do you think?"

"In my day there were two schools of thought, and I don't imagine things have changed: one took the line that while there was a war on everything should be put on hold – no attachments, no commitments, nobody left to grieve if they bought it. The other said 'we pass this way but once, let's enjoy whatever time we've got left'. I began in the first school but converted to the latter."

"So you'd say yes. Isn't he a bit young? Regulations say he should be twenty-eight."

"Old enough to fly the most modern fighters the RAF can offer and old enough to fight and possibly die."

"Well said." He turned to George, "My remaining concern is for the morale and fighting efficiency of this squadron and any effect that your getting married would have. Based on your performance since we arrived here, I do not see any cause for worry. However, I need to remind you that you are a serving officer in His Majesty's forces in time of war and that your first consideration must be to your duty. Secondly, by marrying you, Justine does not become a part of the squadron and the squadron does not assume any responsibility for her. If we are required to remove to another airfield, we will not take her with us and, in the unfortunate event of your death, the squadron will not be able to look after her. Do you accept all I have said?"

"Yes, sir."

He smiled. "It all sounds rather harsh I know, and unofficially we would always do what we could for the wife of a brother officer, but that's the official position. On that basis, I am delighted to give you permission to marry. Good luck to you both!"

"Wizard... I mean, thank you, sir!"

"No doubt you'll want leave. I can't make any promises because if the balloon goes up leave may be cancelled, but subject to that it is approved – seven days. Richard will sort the details out when you have a date."

"You'd better have this," said Justine, proffering his pill and a glass of water. "Before I do there's one thing. Up to the point when I got kyboshed I can remember everything that happened – including what I said before I left you."

She assumed an innocent expression. "What was that?"

"I love you – and will you marry me?"

She walked round the room as if in thought, although there was nothing left to think about; Mamam had shown her Dorothy's letter that morning. She could sense the tension rising in George and, mindful of recent events, decided not to prolong her charade. She hopped lightly onto the bed and touched his nose with hers. "I love you too; just try and stop me, George Knight!"

His arms encircled her, holding her there "It's my head that's injured, not my mouth!"

"When are you to marry?" asked Mamam.

"We're hoping for the Thursday before Easter – Justine will be off school – providing I can get leave and that's ultimately down to the Germans; so fingers crossed. I have the C/O's permission; the next thing is to get a ring."

"I can 'elp you there," she said brightly.

It was George's second day in bed. The headache had gone and apart from a slight tingling in his scalp he felt no after-effects. He was bored and wanted to get up, but Mamam, his nurse now Justine had returned to school, was insistent that he followed doctor's orders. He heard her go to her room and open a drawer. She returned and placed a ring on the table by his bed. It consisted of a large diamond surrounded by several smaller ones. There were a couple of candles burning and the ring caught their light and sparkled. It showed quality without ostentation. "It was my mother's. It would give me great pleasure if you would accept zis to place on Justine's finger."

George was silent for a few moments. "I accept your gift with humility, Mamam. It is very generous and I do not know how to thank you adequately."

"Love 'er and make 'er 'appy, as I know you will; zat is all the thanks I ask. Against zat ze gift is nozzing. *Aussi,* we can enjoy it on 'er finger instead of 'idden away."

Justine and Mamam were in a state of ill-concealed agitation as George returned from the airfield. "What was all the shooting? We thought the Germans had come."

"Oh that." George replied. "Since the Stanhope-Smith affair, it's been decided that we should be proficient with our service pistols so we've been getting some training."

"I thought you knew how to shoot?"

"Rifle and shotgun, yes, but never a pistol before today."

"How did you get on?"

"Better than most, but not brilliantly. Aiming a pistol is more difficult than longer barrelled weapons. They're close-quarter weapons."

"Can you teach me to use one?"

"If you like but Stanhope-Smith and co are dead. They aren't a threat anymore."

"These are dangerous times. Who knows what is in store?"

"True. I'd be happy to show you but they won't allow me the ammunition and, even if they did, I can't let you keep my pistol."

"We have our own pistol," said Mamam. She went upstairs and returned carrying a leather-bound case; slightly scuffed but otherwise intact. "My 'usband acquired zis in a Boche trench in 1916."

George opened it to reveal a Mauser 9mm pistol and several boxes of ammunition. Despite a musty smell the contents were pristine. "It's hardly been used."

"Pierre lost interest in it, but 'e kept it. Perhaps 'e knew it would have a use one day."

"Will this do?" asked Justine, hopefully.

"Admirably, though being unused for so long it will need servicing before we fire it."

"Can you do that?"

"Certainly. It only needs stripping down and oiling."

"I will help you and learn how it is done."

Thursday morning found George and Justine in the woods. They had daubed the outline of a man on a tree. "If you want to defend yourself then aim at the body of an attacker. If you don't kill him outright you are more than likely to disable

93

him. The head is a small target and easy to miss with a handgun so don't aim for it. I learned all this on Tuesday," said George, by way of explanation. "Do you mind if I have a go first?" She nodded assent. He held the gun at arm's length and squeezed the trigger. There was a sharp crack and the bullet ploughed satisfyingly into the target.

"Bravo!" she exclaimed.

He smiled modestly. "Here, you try. There isn't much of a kick. Hold the gun at arm's length, take a breath, relax and fire as you breathe out." She did as he suggested and squeezed the trigger. There was another crack but no obvious damage to the tree. *"Zut!"* she said, "It is heavier than I imagined." She fired again, unsuccessfully.

"Bend your elbow and steady your wrist with your other hand." Another shot went wide of the mark. "Try picturing Stanhope-Smith on the tree." The next three bullets formed a neat group in the middle of the target. "I think you've got the hang of it!"

Winter had taken a firm grip in the second half of January and flying had almost come to a complete stop. The summons to join S/L Sullivan at the *Mairie* promised to be a welcome diversion from another boring day at dispersal. Sullivan was with Richard, 'Einstein' and two other officers. "P/O Knight, may I present Air Commodore Bryce from AHQ and Wing Commander Ellitson who I believe you have met before."

George saluted. "You keep turning up unexpectedly, sir."

Ellitson laughed. "I'm here today to tie up a few loose ends on the Stanhope-Smith matter. Before we start, I must stress that nothing discussed here today is to be spoken of beyond these four walls and nothing in the squadron diary please, Adjutant. Firstly; Squadron Leader Sullivan, can you confirm the Junkers was completely destroyed?"

"I believe so, sir; my chaps hung around and watched it for several minutes. They thought it exploded rather more violently and burned for longer than they would have expected of a normal crash. It must have been carrying extra fuel or munitions."

"Actually, it was because the equipment contained certain modifications to make it tamper proof – booby traps you might say – explosives and accelerants to make sure it was destroyed if it was opened by the wrong hands."

"So the Germans wouldn't have learned anything even if they had got hold of it?"

"Yes and no, possibly what's happening this week on *'ITMA'* and very probably that we were taking them for a ride, but not how our air defence system works." He looked around the puzzled faces. "Let me explain. The Germans have been planning this war for at least the last six years. We had suspected for a long time that their agents were being infiltrated into Britain, and France, come to that, but try as we might we struggled to find their networks. Then word reaches us that P/O Knight's old school adversary and general bad-egg Stanhope-Smith, having come back from two years in Germany to fight for the country that had more or less booted him out, was on his way to France with 686 Squadron. Even before my meeting with P/O Knight, we were monitoring telephone calls in and out of 686

Squadron and a few days after said meeting we hit the jackpot; Stanhope-Smith rang his controller – a music teacher chappie – who gave him details of his contact over here, thus confirming his guilt and giving us our entrees in both England and France. As a direct result, we have either neutralised, or turned – that is to say, in exchange for their lives they now pass on information and messages provided by us – a gaggle of enemy agents in Britain."

"So why didn't you act against Stanhope-Smith?" asked George.

"In co-operation with the French, we were continuing to give him his head, to see who else he involved. As soon as we knew that he was a spy one of my colleagues had come up with a bright idea; instead of letting him find something to spy on we gave it to him on a plate. We thought, correctly in the event, that as soon as he knew that air defence equipment was coming to St Jean, he wouldn't be able to resist it. As a consequence, he and his colleagues put all their energies into our decoy instead of doing something that might have been damaging to us."

"Do you mean the equipment wasn't what it seemed, sir?" asked 'Einstein'.

"Indeed! Hence my remark about *'ITMA'*. We didn't want to risk the real thing so the boffins strung together a load of radios, CRTs, oscilloscopes and suchlike to hoodwink the uninitiated. I gather it had very good reception but couldn't spot aircraft. Of course, if their scientists had got hold they would have got past the booby traps and seen through it very quickly, and when they realised that we were on to Stanhope-Smith, both he and all he had contact with would have been tainted in German eyes. We nearly came unstuck there. We had underestimated Stanhope-Smith. The most we expected was that he'd try taking it apart and get his head blown off. We didn't foresee the airlift, but your chaps pulled our fat out of the fire."

Sullivan had been quietly growing angry. "What about the aircraftsmen who died? Where do they fit into your bloody chess games? What do I tell their families?"

"Steady on, Squadron Leader!" Interjected the Air Commodore.

"It's alright, thank you, sir," said Ellitson. He looked directly at Sullivan. "Squadron Leader, I understand your anger and very much regret the loss of your men. On a different level, I regret having to tap your phones and keep you in the dark about matters concerning your squadron but intelligence is a dirty game. We don't fight with chivalry because our fight is about survival, and a preparedness to do anything and everything to survive. The last war cost this country dear in men and resources and it is debatable whether we have recovered from that when we find ourselves again having to face a formidable enemy. Subterfuge used to good effect can be worth many divisions or save many lives. It is a ghastly decision to make, and the rightness of it is an individual judgement, but sometimes the sacrifice of a few can mean salvation for many." Sullivan made a resigned shrug. Ellitson turned to George and 'Einstein'. "Is either of you aware of Stanhope-Smith having any contacts locally other than the cafe owner and the poacher fellow?" They both responded in the negative. "Good! So with them dead that appears to be it. There are contacts in Nancy and beyond but the French are dealing with them." He paused, "Oh yes! Stanhope-Smith's uncle, who was an RAF officer, shot himself – whether guilt or shame we'll never know now. Thank you, gentlemen. That covers everything I needed. Over to you, Air Commodore."

"Thank you, Wing Commander. I would like to begin by commending the courage of P/O Knight and the outstanding initiative displayed by both him and

F/O Howlett. In ordinary circumstances, I believe both of you would receive a medal but this whole affair is somewhat extraordinary and medals might create unwanted attention. Instead therefore, as soon as your C/O considers it appropriate to put your names forward for promotion, his recommendations will be approved. As for you Squadron Leader, the initiative displayed by these men and the commendable efficiency with which your squadron performed during this affair, neither of which will be specifically mentioned in the citation, and the way you handled the Battle exercise last month, which will, are all indicative of the high standard of leadership which you have brought to bear since you formed this squadron eight months ago. You will therefore be recommended for a decoration forthwith."

The visitors had gone and they were talking over a drink. "Congratulations to all three of you," said Richard, raising his glass, "well deserved in each case."

"I have to say I'm glad it's over, I'm not cut out for this cloak-and-dagger stuff. Maybe now, weather permitting, we can get on with the war in the air," said George.

"I couldn't agree with you more," added Sullivan.

"I found the whole thing quite stimulating," observed 'Einstein'.

Sullivan's face began to darken. Richard intervened. "I didn't get the chance to tell you earlier, sir, because of our visitors, but I received a telephone call from Commandant Laval, the C/O of the French squadron that George visited, inviting a party from 686 to dine with them and…" he hesitated.

Sullivan knew Richard well enough. "Come on man, out with it."

"To take part in a shooting contest."

"Bloody hell!" said Sullivan.

"My fault I think, sir," said George, "among other things we discussed shooting and I think I might have given the impression that we are cracks."

"I gather Laval's chaps want to test our prowess," added Richard.

"Tell him we'd love to but we don't have any shotguns," said Sullivan.

"He's obviously keen; he's offering to provide some."

"So long as it's not pistols, we might stand a chance. That training session was a bloody shambles. How large will our party be?"

"He invited the whole squadron but I explained we always have one Flight on readiness and an orderly officer; so we settled on eight. The new chap's due today so we're back up to strength."

"How many of our chaps can shoot?"

"So far there are F/L Stewart, George, Evans, Frobisher and yourself."

"I thought you could shoot?"

"I haven't done so for a long time."

"Well you make six and 'Einstein' seven."

'Einstein's' face registered surprise and concern, "I've never shot at all, sir."

"Time you learned. You should find it 'stimulating'," he said archly, "Richard, draw lots or something for number eight. When does he want us?"

"February the twelfth, sir."

"Right, let him know we are honoured to accept."

The discussion was terminated by the arrival of the replacement pilot. George guessed that he was about his own age; tall, slender, his hair tending to ginger, and displaying a self-consciously awkward gait as he approached the group. He came to attention and saluted. "P-pilot Officer Pemberton-Harcourt reporting, sir." In addition to the slight stammer, his face flushed as he spoke.

"I'm Sullivan. I'd like to introduce Richard Parsons, Squadron Adjutant, *roué*, war hero and all round good egg; our esteemed and occasionally perverse Intelligence Officer, known to one and all as 'Einstein', and George Knight, one of the villains comprising 'A' Flight, within whose ranks it will be your misfortune to muster." He continued after greetings had been exchanged. "How many hours on Hurricanes?" Pemberton-Harcourt reddened. "Thirty-two, sir, mainly convoy patrols and controlled i-intercepts."

"Neither of which will help you much around here I'm afraid. You'll notice a distinct lack of shipping in the area and the only intercepts so far are what we have managed ourselves. Thirty-two hours suggest you can handle a Hurricane though so I'm sure you'll soon fit in. We've developed an aversion recently to double-barrelled names, and Pemberton-Harcourt is a bit of a mouthful anyway, so we'll have to shorten that."

"My last Squadron called me 'Litmus', sir."

"Derived from pH or a tendency to go red?" enquired 'Einstein'.

"P-probably both, sir."

"That's settled then," said Sullivan, "'Litmus', welcome to 686. Care for a drink?"

"Shandy please, sir. I'm not much of a drinker."

"Not to worry. More for everyone else. Final question – do you shoot?"

"If you mean game, then yes, sir."

"Splendid! Just the man we've been looking for."

6: February, 1940

The Gestapo officer's voice was silky but menacing. *"So, Oberleutnant, not a particularly encouraging set of results. First the film of the new French fighter fails to develop; then you promise secret equipment but turn up here empty handed, having cost us an aeroplane, a pilot and six soldiers..."*

Stanhope-Smith had been lucky so far and he knew it. After falling from the Junkers, he had crashed through several trees and been knocked unconscious yet the only serious injury he had suffered was a badly broken leg. Found before he had the chance to die of exposure, he had been placed in the hands of a surgeon, who had promised him a full recovery; another week and the plaster would be removed for good. Now two men, one Gestapo, the other Abwehr, had come to conduct the inevitable enquiry. His needed his luck to hold a little longer.

"...I have to ask myself whether you are committed to the Third Reich at all or whether, perhaps, another loyalty has always held the ascendancy." As he spoke, his manicured fingers toyed with the wires that supported Stanhope-Smith's leg. The threat was unsubtle.

Stanhope-Smith knew enough of the Gestapo to understand that they did not respect weakness so despite his vulnerable position, he made no attempt to check the surge of anger he felt.

"Perhaps instead, Herr Glauber, you should ask yourself whether anyone in his right mind would have arranged to be shot out of the sky by a section of fighters, because that is the logical extension of what you are suggesting!" Glauber stiffened but added nothing.

Hartmann, the Abwehr man, looked as if he had enjoyed the exchange. Stanhope- Smith was aware that no love was lost between Gestapo and Abwehr and had sensed the tension between the two men; and that he could use it to his advantage. He also knew that Hartmann had been watching, appraising him. Hartmann was the one he had to convince, an old hand in the intelligence game, well-versed in its nuances; not a B-movie gangster like his companion. The Abwehr, which had recruited, trained and launched Stanhope-Smith on his mission, still seemed to be the senior partner in this enterprise. The Gestapo would only take over if he were found to have been disloyal. He suppressed a shudder. Hartmann spoke. *"So, accepting that you are on our side what went wrong?"*

Five weeks in hospital had given him plenty of time to think and work out a story. He knew in truth that, ultimately, the mission had failed because of him, and the only consolation, which he couldn't mention, was the death of Knight; but had their past connection been reported by Max? If so, his version of events would be less than worthless and he would end up in front of a firing squad, or worse. Did they know and were they playing with him? He was about to find out. He swallowed. *"The Cafe owner, Jacques, betrayed us. It all points to him. Everything* was fine from capturing the equipment until the aircraft arrived. Then he disappeared and immediately we were attacked; there was no other way the landing field could have been found so easily. He was my courier too, so he must have sabotaged the film."

"Who else did you have dealings with?"

"Marcel, but I doubt if it was him; I saw him die in the landing field, defending the aircraft."

"What about Bertrand?"

Stanhope-Smith looked blank. "I didn't know anyone named Bertrand. Who was he?"

"Jacques' contact in Nancy. 'Was' is appropriate – we've lost touch with him." Stanhope-Smith could guess why and didn't want to dwell on the subject. "I expect Jacques has betrayed him too."

"It's very convenient that everyone is dead or missing," said Glauber icily.

"Not everyone," said Hartmann, watching Stanhope-Smith intently, "immediately after the crash we sent a message to Max, in England, saying the mission had failed and asking what he knew."

Stanhope-Smith held his breath, hoping to hide the turmoil within, waiting for the blow to fall.

"And?" demanded Glauber.

"He replied that he regarded him as a highly competent agent and that the failure was unlikely to be his fault," replied Hartmann; Glauber frowned; Stanhope-Smith allowed himself to look smug, "so I think that wraps things up."

"What happens next?" asked Stanhope-Smith as they started to leave.

"Your espionage career is at an end. As soon as you're fit, you will be joining the Luftwaffe," he laughed, "to make use of all that expensive training the British put you through! Heil Hitler!" Mindful of his Gestapo companion, Hartmann saluted with more effort than usual. The other two snapped off immaculate responses.

As they were leaving the hospital, Glauber spoke, "Not the most searching examination I have ever witnessed!" He flexed his knuckles. "Perhaps I should question him further?"

Hartmann sounded irritable. "Does the Gestapo try to solve every problem by beating the shit out of it? There's no point. He could tell you anything to stop you hitting him and there's no way of corroborating it. It's simple anyway – either he or the cafe owner was responsible; but I've no doubt he tried to get the equipment back to us. Don't forget that if the fighters had been five minutes later, the Junkers would have made it to the airfield. Then, instead of an interrogation we'd be watching the Fuehrer pinning a medal on him."

"So, it was the cafe owner – recruited by... remind me... ah yes! The Abwehr."

"Duplicity is an occupational hazard in intelligence."

Which, Glauber thought, is why the Gestapo will continue to observe the Abwehr and its activities.

Alone, Stanhope-Smith sagged with relief. Off the hook! Now he could put the whole fiasco behind him and make a new start as a fighter pilot. By the time he was fit again, things should be hotting up in the west. He would get the chance to take his revenge on the RAF for depriving him of his Iron Cross. In fact he could earn one shooting down a bagful of the overgrown schoolboys he so despised. Roll on Spring!

George was in the kitchen, recounting the visit to Laval's squadron. "They greeted us with large coffees – laced with Brandy to keep out the cold."

"*Naturellement!*" Mamam chuckled. "I 'ave 'eard of zese events from my 'usband."

"Then we went to shoot. Ten shots each, at clays."

"I'm glad you weren't shooting birds," said Justine.

"It was so cold they were probably frozen to the trees anyway, so they wouldn't have been much of a challenge. Things started badly – 'Einstein' hadn't shot before – he only hit three – the Old Man had 'volunteered' him in a fit of annoyance, and must have wished he hadn't. Richard was just rusty – he got five so leaving us six behind."

Mamam smiled. "It's a wonder they hit anything after those coffees!"

Justine nudged her. George continued unconcernedly, "F/L Stewart and Giles each pulled one back and the Old Man tied with Laval. 'Taff' Evans pulled back another two."

"So the deficit was only two?" asked Justine, her eyes starting to sparkle.

"That's right; then 'Litmus's' opponent shot and it became nine."

"He's the new boy you've mentioned, the shy one?"

"He wasn't shy with a shotgun – he scored nine and brought us level."

"He probably doesn't drink much." Mamam observed.

"Mother, behave!"

"Actually, she's right."

"See, I told you!" laughed Mamam triumphantly.

"I'm starting to wonder if you've had some brandy too." said Justine.

"Zer is a little devil in me because I 'ave some news which makes me 'appy. But let George tell 'is story first. What 'appened next?"

"My chap got nine as well leaving me to get all ten to win."

"And…?"

"I got the lot – we won!"

"Well done!" Justine hugged him.

"Bravo!" added Mamam.

"After that we had dinner – and then Laval and his men taught us a new game – it's called *Tour Eiffel.*"

"Pierre once told me of zis," said Mamam, nodding sagely.

"What happens?" asked Justine.

"The idea is to build a tower of furniture. One man is on top from the start, building it up from items passed to him and staying on top as each stage is added, until he can touch the ceiling; or he falls off and is caught by his colleagues, using a curtain or something."

"Pierre said they often missed," added Mamam matter-of-factly.

"Anyway, our hosts went first. Apparently their chap had once been in a circus, so he was red hot. Try and picture it – it was sheer bedlam – he's assembling this pile of furniture under him while all around his comrades are egging him on – 'Allez, allez, allez!' – and we, drunk as lords, are trying to put him off, shouting, 'Tombez, tombez!' and other things that I won't repeat here; and throwing rolled up napkins and cushions at him. He got to within a couple of feet of the ceiling but try as he might he couldn't manage the last stage because his tower was too wobbly. In the end it started to collapse. He dived off and – allez-oop – somersaulted neatly into the waiting curtain."

"So how did you get on?" asked Justine.

"On reflection, I think it was a mistake letting Giles volunteer to be our top man; nature hadn't intended him to be a gymnast. He started alright but by the time he was three tables high he was wobbling all over the place – he looked like Eros in an earthquake." She giggled as he continued, "Then a Frenchman hit him on the chin with a piece of bread and it was all over. The tables collapsed and down he came, like a ton of bricks. We managed to catch him in the curtain but he was so heavy we all fell in on top of him. When order had been restored we spent the rest of the night trying to out-sing and out-drink our hosts."

When their laughter had subsided Justine turned to her mother. "So Mamam, what is your news?"

"I have 'ad a letter from my sister. I wrote to her of your engagement and now she wishes me to visit wiz 'er for a week. I leave tomorrow morning."

"Tante Lys lives in Normandy," Justine explained, "she's a widow now but she still runs the farm she shared with her husband."

"Not easy for a woman on her own," observed George.

"She has good and loyal farmhands," said Mamam, "and she is a strong woman."

"Obviously in the genes!"

"Apologise to Richard for me please, I know it is sudden. I 'ope you will manage without me," said Mamam.

Justine and George's hands met under the table, "Don't worry, we'll be fine."

"That was super, I didn't know you could cook at all, let alone coq au vin," said Justine languorously, turning her gaze from the hearth.

"Watching Mamam must have rubbed off on me. All I've ever managed before was bacon and eggs over a campfire."

"Well it was a lovely surprise. I wasn't looking forward to making a meal after an evening's tutelage."

"I wanted to do something for Valentine's Day," he reached for the bottle, "more wine?"

She put her hand over her glass. "You know more than one goes straight to my head. Anyone might think you're trying to seduce a poor defenceless school-mistress."

"They'd be right," he said jauntily.

Her eyes met his. "Well, you don't need to get me drunk."

They lay entwined, peaceful in the after glow, watching the stars through the open curtains; the soft murmur of dance music in the background. "This is heavenly. If only it could last forever. If only the war would stop so we can live like normal people!"

"We have six days to do just that before your mother returns – so let's make the most of them." She gave a shiver of pleasure as he ran his fingers down her back. Their lips met; gentle, darting kisses at first and then with growing intensity.

"I take it the old man's not back yet?" asked Underhill, ambling into dispersal. "He took advantage of the break in the weather and flew to AHQ."

"He'd better get a move on, there's heavy cloud coming in from the east," said Stewart, undoing his parachute, "I curtailed the patrol because I doubt we will be seeing any Jerries today."

"If you don't mind I'll hang around here. See the C/O safely back," Underhill replied.

Stewart smiled. "I think he would be tickled pink to hear you say that. It probably wouldn't do to let him know, though."

They passed an hour talking, by which time Sullivan had still not returned. Cloud now filled the sky and snow was blowing across the aerodrome when, faintly and then more strongly, the sound of a Merlin engine reached their ears. It passed overhead and began to diminish then turned back the way it had come. "He obviously can't see us!" Underhill shouted, "Get the Very pistol, quickly!" 'Shorty' Lewis dashed from the dispersal hut carrying the pistol and some cartridges. "Put a couple of shots ahead of him. Not too close, shooting him down won't look good on your record!" Lewis smirked briefly, listened for a few seconds and then fired into the clouds ahead of the engine noise. He reloaded and fired again. The engine note changed as the pilot throttled back. It became apparent that he was following a circular path and making a shallow descent as they heard him complete one orbit and then a second. A third and a fourth followed. With each orbit the tension grew.

"Good grief, I think he's up there for the day!" said Reg. "Maybe we should have lunch and come back later."

"It's flat round here – no problem if he stays close to the airfield but..." Stewart realised he was thinking aloud and checked himself.

It was becoming unbearable as another one and a half orbits ensued. At last, to relieved cheers, the Hurricane finally broke clear of the cloud base, now down to three hundred feet in places, and completed a trouble-free landing. Sullivan emerged and made his way to the waiting group. "Thanks for the Very lights. I was about to head west to find another airfield when I saw them; it was getting a bit hairy up there above ten-tenths cloud. Bit of a surprise when the first one shot out of the murk but jolly welcome all the same. I'd like to see you all at 1400 hours – I think we can discount flying for today – there are some interesting developments I want to talk about."

"Within a short time, our aircraft will be fitted with steel plate armour on the back of the pilot's seat. You may think it would upset the handling of the aircraft but after thorough testing the conclusion is that there is no adverse effect. It will reduce top speed slightly but I imagine you will agree that this is a small price to pay for the added protection it affords." A murmur of assent ran around the room. "This should anyway be more than compensated for by the fitting of variable pitch propellers." The murmur this time was one of excitement followed by laughter as he added, "I am told that all aircraft will have been refitted by mid-March, so I suggest we read end of April for that," he continued, "During my visit to AHQ today, I had the good fortune to meet the C/O of No. 1 Squadron, who originated the back armour idea. As a result of talking with him, I intend that we make a couple of other changes. First, repainting the underneath of our aircraft. The current black and white colour scheme was developed to make the aircraft conspicuous to our Observer Corps but it also makes them conspicuous to the enemy. Flying line abreast we must resemble a pedestrian crossing." He paused to let the laughter subside. "Henceforth we will take a leaf from the Jerries' book by painting the underneath of our aircraft duck-egg blue so they are more difficult to spot from below." There were nods of agreement. "The second change is re-harmonising the guns of all our aircraft from four hundred down to two hundred and fifty yards. As you know several aircraft had their guns experimentally re-harmonised three months ago. I would like to thank 'Einstein' for analysing our combat reports since we arrived here, few though they are, from which the inescapable conclusion is that attacks made at shorter range are more successful. The 'Dowding' spread, as it is known, was developed for use against bombers, which are fairly large targets. Nonetheless, experience shows that at four hundred yards range a successful attack is by no means guaranteed. If we are to shoot down fighters, a much smaller target, then it is certain that we will have to do so from nearer in. The reduced range will increase the danger of return fire from bombers and other aircraft armed with rear-firing guns but I believe that the rewards will outweigh the risks." Another murmur rippled through his audience. "Finally, battle tactics. I've asked the Adjutant to say a few words on the subject. Richard?"

"Thank you, sir. They say that things will be different in this war but personally I doubt it. My own feeling is that the same type of fighter combats as last time will take place but, because of greater speeds, over a wider area. In which case the old maxims will be important again, derived from the lessons we learned; the man who has height controls the battle, beware of the Hun in the sun, don't fly straight and level in the presence of the enemy for more than ten seconds and get in close, shoot and get out. Unfortunately, between the wars the focus of tactical and strategic thinking has been on bombers – 'the bomber will always get through' and so on – and insufficient attention has been paid to fighter tactics. I have my doubts, and I know S/L Sullivan shares them, about the prescribed tactics. 'Fighting Area Attacks' – the aerial drill book – is fine for displays, practice drills and perhaps bombers but I can't see them working in fighter battles; in close formations, while everyone is concentrating on not bumping into each other, they are not keeping an adequate lookout for the enemy. Given half a chance, the Jerries will 'bounce' you; a quick attack, probably from out of the sun, shoot down a few and be away before you can respond, without any loss to them. Again, manoeuvring in close formation is difficult. Keeping a good lookout and the ability to respond quickly and positively to a threat are the important things and your formations must permit these aims. Believe me when I say that fighter battles will be inevitable; large groups, not just individual skirmishes. Maintaining a rigid formation is impossible under those conditions. In my day, when we met the German fighter 'circuses' it invariably ended up as a collection of individual combats, hence 'dogfight' and I see no reason for that to change. My generation found these things out the hard way. I hope passing on the benefits of those experiences will save you from paying a similar price rediscovering them. In conclusion, I will repeat the two key points – flexibility and lookout. All yours, sir."

"Thank you, Richard. I don't want pilots from this squadron to be lost because we are applying tactics which are either obsolete or wholly unsuitable. At the moment, I don't have a definitive answer for you. Indeed, although the Adj. has given us a start, as he has suggested it is something we will have to work out between us. Initially, we will continue with the Vic formation with which you are familiar. The obvious alternatives are the French variant – more widely spread and augmented by a couple of weavers to provide a lookout for attacks from behind, or the two and four aircraft formations developed by the Germans. Although it is difficult to believe looking outside, spring is round the corner and soon we can expect to start meeting the Germans in some strength. Initially, I will leave it to the Flight Commanders to determine what formations they employ but based on experience gained we will evolve a standard formation. Finally; to relieve the boredom of being snowbound I have something to occupy your minds." He looked around the expectant faces. "I have asked 'Einstein' to prepare a test in aircraft recognition for the end of the month." Groans greeted this announcement. "It's no good having the right formations if you shoot at the wrong targets. Anyone scoring less than seventy-five percent will find themselves doing extra Orderly Officer duty. You have been warned. Good luck gentlemen."

"Here's to armour plate," said 'Roy' Rogers, raising his glass, "and no more bullets up the Khyber."

"I agree," said 'Shorty', "but as someone who has yet to use one I'm keen to try out the variable pitch propeller." In response to a few quizzical looks he added, "Unlike you spoiled youngsters who trained on Harvards with their constant speed props, I came to the Hurricane via a long line of fixed pitch props all the way back to the dear old Avro Tutor; so I've some learning to do."

"Me too," added 'Roy', "Has anyone here flown a Hurricane with a VP prop?"

"I have," volunteered 'Litmus', reddening.

"Well go on," prompted 'Shorty' seeing that he wasn't going to expand.

"W-well there's not a lot to it but it is slightly different from constant speed props. The main thing is to remember to select fine pitch for take-offs, climbs and landings; coarse for level flight. I've seen a few come to grief trying to take off in coarse pitch."

"What happened?" asked 'Shorty'.

"T-they ran into the boundary hedge because they couldn't lift off. Not enough power. It's like trying to drive a car up a steep hill in top gear. In fact the whole thing is a bit like gears in a car." He lapsed into a self-conscious silence as Underhill joined them. "We're talking shop," said Reg "What do you make of re-harmonising the guns?"

104

"I'm all for it," replied Underhill, "I think it will improve our chances considerably. There'll be an increased threat from rear gunners but I think the answer is to dodge and jink a bit in the attack. Don't fly too predictably. I agree with the C/O about formations too, although whilst he's keeping an open mind about what we replace them with I favour the German method." He turned to 'Litmus'. "How did they approach this in your last Squadron?"

'Litmus' flushed, thought for a moment, took a deep breath and then gave his considered response. "I – in the light of today's discussions – have to say not very well. I suppose you could say the C/O was a by-the-book man. When w-we practiced RDF interceptions, we flew in tight vics. For FAAs, we were in tight formation; in f-fact everything we did was in close formation. The more experienced pilots used to say we were flying too close together and that we would r-regret it when we came up against Jerry, but it went no further: we certainly had no forums like this. I v-volunteered to be p-posted here to get to France and see some action. I knew nothing about 686, but I don't think I could have chosen a b-better s-squadron."

"Amen to that," responded Underhill, touched by Litmus's compliment.

"Hear, hear! Buy that man a beer; well a ginger beer at any rate," said 'Foggy'. "I gather you don't like bitter beer."

'Litmus' blushed again. "I-I don't dislike beer, I just can't handle it. More than one pint and I tend to keel over."

"Well don't let that worry you!" rejoined 'Foggy', "it's only a question of numbers - sooner or later we all keel over."

"What's this one?" asked Justine, wafting a silhouette past George. "Hold on!" he protested, "Hold it steady so I can get a look at it."

"Will the Germans hold steady? I think not," she retorted, whisking it past him again.

"I suppose you have a point. Junkers 88," he replied.

"Clever dick!" she laughed. "What's this then?" She wafted another. "Easy, Potez 637."

"And this?"

"Heinkel 111."

"And this?"

"Junkers 88 again."

"Hah, wrong. It's a Bristol Blenheim. You've just shot down one of your own side."

"Hmm. Not funny if I had, I need to do some more swotting." Tongue in cheek, he added, "are you this hard on your *enfants?*"

"I give them a proper education if that's what you mean," she said unapologetically, rising from the settee. "Would you like a drink?"

Alone, he glanced around the salon, at Mamam's prized possessions; fine china, ornaments, and paintings; mementos of the more affluent lifestyle that had been taken from her with her husband; and a reminder to them of how precious was this handful of days when they could pretend to be an ordinary couple, free from the shadow of war. Their idyll had been unexpectedly extended; a letter from Mamam announced that she would remain in Normandy until early March. The letter had also carried an invitation from *Tante* Lys to spend some or all of their honeymoon in Normandy. The postman had not been inactive that week – he re-read the letter in his pocket:

Our dearest George and Justine,

We are absolutely delighted to hear that you plan to marry. Please accept our wholehearted blessing. Justine sounds like a wonderful girl and we are very happy for you both. Our only regret is that travel restrictions mean we will not be with you on your wedding day. However, unless you have other plans, we would like to arrange a suite for you at the Hotel Georges V in Paris.

The rest of the family is delighted with your news too. Unlike twenty-one years ago, Grandmother Knight didn't say it's too soon and it will all end in tears!

It only remains to extend to both of you our love and best wishes for a long, fruitful and happy marriage...

As he folded it away, George felt contented. He just needed that week's leave...

Inevitably, something had had to intrude on their happiness – an invitation to visit the Battle Squadrons. Improving weather meant that 'A' Flight, including a reluctant George, went on the last day of February. An uneventful flight up and a successful rendezvous led to half an hour of formation flying and mock attacks. They did nothing to alter George's misgivings about Fairey Battles. He tried to put these and his enforced separation from Justine to the back of his mind, resolving to enjoy the evening as he climbed from his Hurricane. 686 had performed a beat-up so a reception committee was assembled when they landed. As the Squadron Leaders traded salutes and handshakes George surveyed the assembled ranks. With pleasure he recognised Peter Templeton. As 686 began mingling George found himself buttonholed by an enthusiastic Battle pilot. "Before Christmas – that's before I was posted here actually – we did an exercise with a squadron of Hurris and some Me110s tried to intervene. The Hurris saw the blighters off, though. Dashed good show!"

"I know," said George patiently, "I was there, and they were 109s."

"You were? Gosh, wizard! Have you fought many Jerries yet?"

George was beginning to feel uncomfortable. Line-shooting was the cardinal sin and that was where the conversation was leading. "Not really. I say, please don't think me rude but there's someone I simply have to speak to." He pushed his way through the throng and finally reached his objective. "Peter!"

"Good Lord! George, you old so-and-so, where have they been hiding you?" He sounded like the Peter Templeton of old, one of the 'Three Stooges' from their training days, but behind the artificially cheery greeting George could sense weariness and an air of resignation which were at odds with the man he had known. His features were strained; he looked older than his twenty years.

"Down the road, St Jean-sur-Moselle, near Epinal."

"Of course, you're one of our guardian angels."

"Don't you start; I've just been getting the Picture Post treatment over there."

"Well don't be surprised. That show in December was a big boost for morale; an oasis in the desert. Fancy a wander outside? It's easier to talk there and I've developed a preference for open spaces. Here, have another before we go." He plucked two glasses of sherry from a passing tray and handed one to George but not before his arm jerked involuntarily, causing him to spill some of it. He looked embarrassed, "Sorry, bit of a twitch. It only happens occasionally, but usually at an inconvenient moment."

"So what's been happening?" asked George, trying to hide his concern.

"As you may know, we got here right at the beginning. The French army did some sabre rattling and we were flying in support of them and pretty soon met up with the Jerries – 109s."

"Were you unescorted?"

"Yes, so they played merry hell with us. We flew in formation to concentrate our defensive fire but they picked us off at their leisure. Whatever the newsreels say the Battle is completely hopeless – no speed, little manoeuvrability and inadequate armament. We were like ducks in a shooting gallery. We all got shot to hell. It was a miracle that only three out of nine were shot down."

"Christ!" said George, "but you got away with it?"

"In a manner of speaking. I was one of the three. The rest of my crew were killed. I force landed with a dead engine and my plane shot to ribbons, just on the French side of the lines, completely bloody unscathed, would you believe? Not even a scratch." He pulled a cigarette packet from his pocket, lit up, drew deeply a couple of times and continued, "A few days later they sent us out again. We were promised a fighter escort. We never saw hide nor hair of them so the Jerries got on with the business of hacking us down again. Another four went west, including yours truly again. This time I crashed near the airfield and spent twenty odd minutes trapped in the wreckage, listening to petrol dripping from the fuel tank and expecting to be incinerated at any moment. Hence my aversion to enclosed spaces. All I got were a few cuts and bruises. My crew bought it again though. Perhaps I'm a jinx. And now to cap it all the Brass have got us training for night-flying – to drop mines or bloody leaflets. Do they really think the Jerries will chuck it all up on the strength of a few pamphlets?"

"Night flying must give you respite from the 109s though?"

"Yes, but the Battle's even more useless by night – it's a bloody death trap. We've lost several good men to accidents already."

"Why don't you ask for a posting as an instructor or suchlike; have a rest?"

He shook his head emphatically. "Bad form, old man. It would be running away. I've been shaken up pretty badly but I haven't lost my nerve. I and the other old stagers have to set an example to the new bods so its stiff upper lip and all that. I will carry on until my luck runs out. I'm reconciled now to the fact that sooner or later I will get the chop. It's strange, but now I've reached that realisation the worst of the fear has gone. Having come to terms with my own mortality it's the replacements I feel sorry for; they're just so much bloody cannon-fodder. These kids turn up, freshly scrubbed, all gung-ho and eager to face the Hun, and gradually they begin to realise how hopeless the Battle really is." He drew on his cigarette again, "Listen to me, eh, a veteran of twenty talking about keen kids."

"Is there nothing that can be done?"

"We've been promised Blenheims but I'll believe it when they arrive. Anyway, enough of this doom and gloom. Have you heard from our third Stooge?"

"Roger Carew? No, have you?"

"Yes, got a letter from him last month. He's in a Hurricane squadron, like you, but still in Blighty, completely browned off. Convoy patrols and practice intercepts," he gave an ironic laugh, "and no sign of a Jerry yet. So that just leaves you; what have you been up to?"

George felt reluctant to recount his doings since the previous summer but, like a true friend, Peter revelled in his good fortune. For the first time that day a sparkle came into his eyes and briefly he was his old self. George asked the question that had been on his mind since seeing Peter.

"Have you any leave due, because if so, come to the wedding? If nothing else I'd like you to be my best man."

"Thanks for asking. I don't know what the situation will be in March but I'll certainly come if I'm able; and thanks for listening. Don't think me ungrateful when I say it hasn't changed my view of my prospects but it has been good to blow off steam. I can talk to you in a way I can't talk to the chaps in the squadron. It's been a chance to unburden myself a bit." He lapsed into a thoughtful silence.

George knew the conversation had run its course. "I think we'd better go back inside or people will start talking." The attempt at levity went unnoticed. Peter gave him a companionable clap on the shoulder.

"You go on ahead. As I said before, I've developed a preference for open spaces."

There had been something about 686's reception which he had been unable to put his finger on until his conversation with Peter; the undercurrent of enforced gaiety – 'Eat, drink and be merry for tomorrow we die'. He felt himself moved to anger – not at them but at the politicians and the appeasers; smug, comfortable and safe, who had imposed their self-delusion onto others, procrastinating and neglecting the country's defences to the point where good men such as these would have to be sacrificed, flying obsolete aircraft, to buy time until the neglect could be remedied. He wondered whether he could match the quiet, cold courage of men like Peter. He had experienced combat and knew he could handle the heat of battle but could he climb into his aeroplane and head off to face the enemy knowing there was not much chance of returning? He hoped that he would never have to find out.

His thoughts were interrupted by 'Litmus', calling him to assist in handing furniture up to 'Roy', preferred this time to Giles, as he attempted to balance on top of it. Sullivan had talked the Battle Squadron into the game he had renamed *Blackpool Tower*. This time 686 were the veterans and duly triumphed as, amid hoots of derision, their opponents' tower collapsed at less than half the height that 'Roy' had achieved. As the beer flowed the Battle boys gained their revenge, throwing themselves into a game of indoor rugby like men possessed. It was a bruised and battered 686 that eventually staggered to their accommodation. The shouts of someone having a nightmare disturbed their sleep. In the next bed to George, Evans muttered sleepily, "Sounds like some-one's 'ad his fill." George could think of no reason to contradict him.

7: March, 1940

The sky is blue and the clouds are broken. Winter is coming to an end but patches of snow and ice have yet to melt away, their stubborn rearguard bolstered by a biting wind from the east. 'B' Flight are visiting the second Battle Squadron, leaving 'A' Flight holding the fort. The day is apparently slipping by uneventfully when the dispersal 'phone rings, cutting into a post-lunch reverie. 'Roy' answers, listening intently. He replaces the receiver, trying to suppress the look of excitement on his face, gathers his parachute and moves casually towards the door as he announces "Dornier coming this way, six thousand feet, heading home. Someone's already damaged him and AHQ want us to finish the job."

"Sounds like a job for Red Section," responds Underhill, already following 'Roy's' lead and edging towards the door, "come on George, before Yellow Section wake up and try hogging the glory." George grabs his parachute and follows them through the door as realisation comes upon the three pilots of Yellow Section who utter words of protest amid gathering their own equipment. By the time the first of them reaches the door 'A' Flight are already running headlong towards their Hurricanes, shouting and gesticulating wildly towards the ground crews who, recognising an urgency in the situation, are in the process of starting the engines. Realising that there is no prospect of overtaking them, Yellow Section stop at the door of the dispersal hut.

"Bastards!" shouts Giles. About to go back inside, in the distance he sees the Dornier approaching. He judges it is flying at about five thousand feet, on a north-easterly heading which will bring it more or less directly overhead. A thin plume of white smoke trails from its starboard engine. By now, three Merlins have burst into life and shouting will serve no purpose. He runs after them. When he reaches the Hurricanes the pilots are strapped in, ready to taxi. He catches Underhill's attention and points towards the aircraft, which is now almost overhead. A thumbs-up indicates that Underhill has seen it. He speaks into his R/T and Giles sees the others twist round and look upwards before they begin taxiing in an open-vic formation. Gathering speed they begin to judder their way across the frozen field. Off to the right 'Roy's' aircraft hits a large bump and is airborne before gaining sufficient speed. A second later it comes back to earth with a bone-shaking thump. The tail wheel, unable to stand the impact on the unyielding surface, snaps off causing the tail section to hit the ground, bouncing and slewing wildly on the rough surface. He slams the throttle closed and pulls back hard on the stick, trying to prevent the aircraft nosing over. For nerve- rending seconds he fights the bucking and twisting of the Hurricane before it begins to lose way. Eventually, it stops, just short of the boundary hedge. He flicks the R/T, "Sorry Red Leader, you two will have to manage without me."

The hiss of static doesn't hide Underhill's concern. "Are you OK, Red Two?"

"I'm OK but the bloody kite's goosed. Good hunting, Red Section." He switches off the engine and sits back to wait for the ground crew to retrieve the aircraft. "Bugger!" In frustration he thumps the side of the cockpit before taking his cigarette case from his tunic pocket. Lighting up, he finds his hands are shaking.

Meanwhile, George and Underhill are climbing hard after the Dornier. They know that the pilot will have seen them taking off in pursuit and be attempting to coax every last bit of speed from his damaged machine; nonetheless they are gaining. It takes a good five minutes before they are in range. Suddenly, George sees four specks in the sky ahead. "Red Leader, bogies, twelve o'clock."

"Roger. Can't identify them yet but they're bound to be Jerries." Underhill's mind races. With a combined closing speed of some six hundred miles an hour it won't be long before the enemy aircraft reach them. "Red Three, we've time for a quick squirt at the Dornier then beat it for home. Forget line astern. We'll attack together; you take his port side and I'll take starboard. Break away before you cross his centre line and head due west. Buster, Tallyho!" In response to Underhill's command, George pushes his throttle through the gate. Extra boost puts the needle on his rpm indicator into the red zone as the Hurricane surges ahead. They dive on the Dornier. The simultaneous attack from two directions confuses the rear gunner making his fire haphazard and ineffective. George gets the cabin area in his sights. Eight lines of tracer hammer into the target. The return fire stops. He shifts his aim onto the port engine and fires another burst. Smoke and flame erupt. Underhill has wrought similar havoc. With both engines smashed the Dornier goes into a vertical dive. No parachutes, George registers subconsciously, looking beyond the stricken machine at the approaching Germans; no longer specks but four identifiable Bfl09s. Having learned the lesson previously, he does not dwell on the Dornier's final moments but rolls his aircraft into a turn, pulling the stick hard back to make it as tight as possible. The g-forces bear down on him. He leans forward to mitigate the effects but his vision blurs as the blood is nonetheless forced from his head. Suddenly the aircraft is juddering. He realises he has tightened the turn too much – he is on the verge of a high-speed stall, which will be fatal – his pursuers will be on him before he can regain speed again. Instinctively he pushes the stick forward a fraction. The juddering stops. Gingerly, he eases the stick back again, finding the first hint of a judder then holding just short. It has taken only a couple of seconds but in that time he knows his pursuers will have gained a sixth of a mile. Rolling out of the turn he looks behind him and is startled to see that the 109s, in *Schwarm* formation, are now close behind. In under half a minute they have grown from specks into four predators, intent on clawing him from the sky. Underhill is a mile ahead. There are no clouds to duck into. Effectively, he is alone. Containing his fear he pushes the nose down to gain more speed. The airspeed indicator passes three hundred and forty mph and the rev counter goes further into the red zone. He knows he cannot run the engine for long like this without overworking it. Minutes seem like hours as the chase continues. Every time he looks back the 109s are that bit nearer. Winking lights appear on the front of the leading 109-the pilot is trying his luck at extreme range – as yet unsuccessfully. He checks his watch and the gauges. Four minutes since he applied boost. Engine temperature is rising dangerously. He flicks the R/T switch. His mouth is dry but he speaks calmly, essaying a coolness he does not feel. "Red

110

Leader, they're gaining – almost in range." Underhill's Hurricane begins rolling to the left as he makes his response. "Break left, Red Three and keep turning as tightly as you can. I'm joining you. We're back over France so they should buzz off soon."

George jumps in fright as pinging sounds come from the back of his aircraft. He feels a series of thumps behind him. His aircraft is taking hits. The controls are heavy at this speed but fear lends him the strength. As he rolls into the turn the thumping stops.

Underhill's urgent shout fills his earphones again, "French fighters, three o'clock high, coming down like the clappers. Let them know you're friendly or they might have a crack at you." George has to work hard to move the stiff ailerons but he manages to rock his wings. Ten French Curtiss Hawks swoop over him. He looks back again and is relieved to see that the four Messerschmitts are no longer following.

They too have seen the French fighters, and turned away. Pursuers become pursued for the second time in ten minutes as they are chased back into Germany. He throttles back and rpm and airspeed drop to more normal levels. He gently tests the controls and can find no evidence of damage. Despite the cold he is bathed in sweat and his heart pounds in his chest. The release of tension leaves him feeling drained. Underhill is alongside. "Well done Red Three; as the Duke of Wellington once said, that was a close run thing."

"Too bloody close, Red Leader, the bastards got me."

"Any damage?"

"I don't think they hit anything vital. Controls all seem OK."

"Take it steady on the way back. We'll still be in time for tea – and no victory rolls."

"I can't remember feeling less like doing a victory roll."

Within a quarter of an hour the two Hurricanes are taxiing back to dispersal. On one side George can see 'Roy' and Yellow Section ambling across from the dispersal hut to meet them and on the other he can see 'Roy's' Hurricane standing on supports while a couple of ground crew attend to it.

"Any joy?" calls Giles, as the roar of the engines dies away.

Underhill answers as he jumps to the ground. "Last we saw of the blighter he was going vertically down with both engines on fire. Couldn't hang around to watch though. Got chased away by four 109s."

"C-close one?" asks Litmus.

"Too close by half," says George, joining them, "they put a few holes in my kite."

"Not just your kite, unless the moths round 'ere are the size of crows," interjects Evans, "I suggest you inspect your para-chute, boyo."

George unbuckles his parachute pack and turns it round, revealing a line of four frayed bullet holes. "Bloody hell!" he exclaims.

"Sir, can you come and look at this?" The voice is that of George's rigger. George, followed by the others, returns to his Hurricane. The rigger's face is pale. "In here, sir." George and Evans climb onto the wing and look where the man is pointing in the cockpit. In the seatback are four bullet holes in a line, matching those in his parachute. "A few inches lower and you could have can-celled your wed-ding," says Evans, "mind you, if the Jerr-ies had been any nearer you could have can-celled everything."

"Christ!" George exclaims, stepping off the wing to let the others see.

"Has been somewhat merciful towards you," adds Underhill, "those bullets were just about spent when they went through the seat which is why your parachute stopped them. That'll teach you not to dawdle. What kept you?"

"Trying to avoid a high-speed stall. The whole business was pretty hairy. I think I need a beer!"

"Still an hour of readiness left. You'll have to make do with tea for now."

Mugs in hand, they waited as 'Einstein' rummaged in his desk. "Thanks for dropping back when the Jerries caught up," said George.

"What did you expect? Especially when I'd led you into it. We couldn't outrun them so I decided to out-fly them – chance to prove that the Hurri can out turn the 109 –"

"Gentlemen," interrupted 'Einstein', "time's winged chariot and all that."

He began reviewing their combat reports. "I see you crossed into Germany." Underhill answered. "We were so close to the Dornier it didn't seem right to let it escape. We were only a few minutes flying time in when we attacked. We knew the 109s were approaching but I reckoned we had time to see it off before they reached us, which proved to be the case."

"Only just," said 'Einstein'.

"My fault," said George, "I dallied a bit or else we would have got away scot free."

"It would have been a sad irony if they had got you today – a message came while you were having your seat ventilated – the back-armour arrives tomorrow. Anyway, your accounts corroborate each other so I can credit you with half a Dornier each even though you didn't see it hit the ground."

"The angel Gabriel couldn't have saved that one," observed George.

"I'll leave the Padre to speculate on what divine intervention can achieve," said 'Einstein', "and concentrate on intelligence. Did the Bfl09s adopt the usual pairs' formation?"

"Yes."

"Did either of you see any markings, so we can identify the unit?" Underhill shook his head.

"Sorry, too busy running away, although I did notice yellow spinners," said George, "just for interest why do you refer to the 110 as Me110 and the 109 as Bfl09 when they 're both Messerschmitts?"

"Although they're both designed by Messerschmitt, they're built in different places. Bf is an abbreviation for the name of the factory in Munich where they're built under licence," said 'Einstein'.

"Cripes!" said 'Roy', breaking his silence, "Is there anything this chap doesn't know?"

"I bet he doesn't know what the Jerries had for breakfast," suggested Underhill. "That's easy," George interjected, "Sauerkraut and sausage."

"Not necessarily," said 'Einstein'. "I went to Hamburg in '36 and for breakfast they had something akin to soused herrings."

"Ye Gods!" responded 'Roy', screwing up his face, "no wonder they goosestep everywhere, they daren't unclench their backsides!"

His fitter approached as he was leaving 'Einstein's' office, and saluted. "These are yours by right, sir. Dug them out of your parachute." He held out four misshapen bullets.

George indicated two. "Thank you. You can keep the others but there's something I'd like you to do with these."

Cooking smells met him as he closed the door. "Justine?" he called. *"Non!* It is I!"

"Mamam! Good to see you!" he hugged her, "You're looking well. How was Normandy?"

"It was wonderful zank you. I could 'ave stayed forever. Lys wanted me to. She wants me to go and live with 'er when you're married."

"There will always be a home with us, Mamam."

"I know and I zank you. But when the war is over, 'oo knows where the RAF will send you. Justine will follow you, *naturellement,* but I cannot. I 'ave no intention to go to Normandy soon, but one day… Before anything else, I am going to help my daughter to prepare for her wedding. But tell me, are you going to stay with Lys for your 'oneymoon?"

"Yes! Provided the Germans don't spoil it I have a week's leave confirmed. We'll spend half in Paris and half in Normandy."

"Formidable! You have been flying today?"

"Yes-just routine." He wasn't proud of the lie.

"Bon! I know as a fighter pilot risks are part of your job but it is only two weeks to your wedding. In zat time you must be especially careful!"

George is feeling restless. He has read and re-read the latest English newspapers. Since he was chased out of Germany, March has brought a thaw, but little activity. Tonight his seven-day leave starts and tomorrow at eleven o'clock he will be getting married. The combination of pent-up excitement and a feeling that he ought to be doing something useful in the meantime won't let him settle. Donning his greatcoat he decides to forsake the cosy warmth of the *Mairie* for the more elusive comforts of the dispersal hut.

"Aha! Cometh the hour," says Stewart as George enters, "Pearson has been laid low by toothache and AHQ want us to put up both sections. Fancy an afternoon in 'B' Flight, with some real pilots?"

He replies without hesitation; without thinking. "Be glad to, sir. What's the score?"

"We're covering a Blenheim recce around Saarburg. Bit off our stamping ground but I suppose it reflects our burgeoning reputation. Take-off's in fifteen minutes."

"German border coming up – eyes peeled for Jerries. Anyone seen that bloody Blenheim yet?" Stewart's usually measured delivery is suffused with frustration. There had been no sign of the Blenheim over the planned rendezvous at Thionville. They had circled for ten minutes before setting course for Saarburg; in case it had missed them and gone on alone.

From ten thousand feet there is little to indicate the existence of the border; no river, no hills. Their view of the ground is partly obscured by a layer of five-tenths cumulus, stretching for miles around. A closer inspection would no doubt reveal troops dug in, muses George, but that isn't their concern today. Within a few minutes they reach Saarburg. Still the Blenheim is nowhere to be seen. Stewart speaks again. "Begin circling. We'll give it five minutes and then head back. Good lookout everyone. The Jerries aren't going to put up with us parading in their back yard for very long." His voice is suddenly urgent. "Flak! Scatter and climb above it!" The six aircraft, formated in two groups of three, break into climbing turns in every direction as the black and white puffs of exploding shells appear in the sky around them. For George, it is too late. With a loud bang a chunk of shrapnel scythes through the cowling into his engine. White smoke streams past the cockpit as the contents of his glycol tank begin spewing out.

"Blue Leader, Green Three; engine hit and losing coolant!"

"Roger Green Three. Make for home. Green Section will cover you. Blue Section, form on me and maintain Angels fifteen."

His Hurricane is limping along in a south-westerly direction, still losing glycol, the temperature gauge already well into the red zone. As a precaution, he has the hood open. Despite the cold air the heat from the engine is becoming intense. It could burst into flames at any moment. Should he switch off and hope to glide to the border? Or try to squeeze a few more miles? The decision is taken from him. A tongue of flame appears at his feet. At any second it could become a blazing torch which will roast him alive. "Green Leader, Green Three. Engine's brewing. Baling out before I get roasted!"

"Good luck!" 'Shorty' tries to sound nonchalant.

In a flash, R/T lead and oxygen are disconnected and his straps undone. Crouching on the seat now, George rolls the aircraft and falls into space, tumbling over and over. He counts ten and pulls the handle. With a snap, his parachute opens. A sudden jolt leaves him upright, oscillating gently beneath the white canopy. Removed from the roar of engine and slipstream, the only sounds are the drone of Green Section circling protectively around him and, further away, the crack of flak bursting as the German gunners blaze away hopefully at Blue Section, who are now safely out of range. He begins studying the terrain beneath him, looking to see where he might land. From the sun he gauges that the wind is pushing him westwards. Out of the corner of his eye, he sees his blazing aircraft plough into a field. Ahead is a wood; beyond are two lakes, separated by a river in the manner of a percentage sign, and then another larger wood. His mind races – he recalls seeing them on the map earlier but can't place them – it occurs to him that he might land in Germany. Passing over the river it becomes obvious that he won't clear the second wood. Germany or no, he doesn't want to land in trees. He tugs at the control lines, quickening his descent. The ground rushes up to meet him. He lands with a thump that knocks the wind from him. Like a fish out of water he lies gasping as a car and lorry pull up on the road running between him and the trees. An officer and two soldiers dismount and begin walking unhurriedly towards him. He is still too winded to run. They are almost upon him when he rises unsteadily to his feet and raises his arms. Their uniforms are unfamiliar but don't look German. *"Vous-etes Francaises?"* he asks hopefully.

"Alas no *m'sieu*," the officer answers in almost accentless English, "you have landed in the Grand Duchy of Luxembourg." He salutes, "Capitaine Dumas of the Army of Luxembourg at your service."

George returns the salute. "P/O Knight, Royal Air Force. Luxembourg's neutral isn't it?"

"It is, and in these uncertain times we have to be seen to exercise our neutrality scrupulously; even if history suggests it will prove futile. This is distasteful to me but I must inform you that unless you are willing to give me your parole you will become a prisoner."

George knows an officer's duty is to escape captivity. "I'm sorry, I cannot do that."

"Spoken like an officer and gentleman as I would expect, *m'sieu*. Unfortunately, I was passing this way in pursuit of another, more pressing, matter when you dropped in, so rather than escort you myself as I would prefer, I must leave my men to take you to the reception centre whence I regret to say you will be sent to a place of confinement. A disappointing end to your war, I imagine…" His words are cut short by a couple of flak bursts, well wide of the two circling Hurricanes. He glances round then addresses George again. "That was our flak, merely a reminder to your colleagues that they are encroaching into a neutral zone. I assure you that we can shoot much better than that if we…" This time his words are curtailed as the two Hurricanes roar low overhead, wings waggling in farewell. A feeling of emptiness consumes George as he watches them recede. From seemingly miles away, Dumas is still speaking. "…at least they can report back that you are safe – your mother, or your girlfriend perhaps, will be spared weeks of uncertainty."

"I was due to be married tomorrow." George replies dully, beginning to appreciate the enormity of the situation.

Dumas looks moved. "My condolences, *m'sieu*! The fortunes of war, I suppose. I do hope she waits for you." They exchange salutes and he spins on his heel. About to leave he turns back, looking thoughtful. "I don't know if philosophy interests you but perhaps your enforced leisure will give you time to reflect on how the simplest of things can shape men's lives. For instance, you have landed in the south-east corner of Luxembourg; to the east, beyond the river that you floated over lies Germany. To the west, beyond the trees, lies France. If there had been no wind, you would now be a prisoner of the Germans; if the wind had blown a little stronger, and carried you over those trees and a couple of kilometres beyond, you would now be back among your allies." He looks meaningfully at George. "It is an uncertain life and we must make the most of the opportunities that come our way. *Bonne chance, m'sieu!*"

He exchanges a few words with the soldiers before striding to his car, giving a brief wave in George's direction as he pulls away. The soldiers appear reluctant to disturb George, who pretends not to notice them. He affects dejection but underneath there is a spark of optimism. Dumas has shown him the route to freedom; he has to fashion the opportunity to use it. He has been appraising his guards; tall and strong, probably farm-hands before their army service. He can't see himself overpowering them; outrunning them looks problematical too without a head start. He recalls his aerial view of the road; following the line of the wood before joining a larger road which leads northwards – to captivity. He must escape before the main road. But how?

"Zis way, pliz!" The guard is polite, almost deferential, as he indicates the lorry. Clearly, an officer, even from another country, commands his respect. The glimmer of an idea forms in George's mind. As he walks towards the lorry he staggers slightly and clutches his stomach. The guard's face registers concern. "You, o-k?" George nods hesitantly. When he gets to the lorry he reaches to climb aboard then groans and doubles up, holding his stomach, his face contorted.

"Il faut... Je dois aller a la toilette!" he begins to hobble towards the trees, some thirty yards away. The guard makes to accompany him. George looks at him imploringly, *"M'sieu, si-vous-plait!"*

Embarrassed the guard hovers, not sure what to do. *"Deux minutes, c'est tout!"*

"D'accord merci," George embellishes his response with another grimace.

Maintaining his stilted gait, he shuffles towards the wood. As he reaches the trees he glances back. The guard has been joined by the driver; both now watch him intently. The guard's rifle is propped against the lorry, within easy reach. Stepping forward, George fiddles with his trousers, as though to undo them and then steps back hastily.

The watchers tense. He calls out nonchalantly, *"Ronces!"* They burst out laughing, visibly relaxing, amused by the thought of his squatting in a clump of brambles. Using the moment to shuffle another few yards into the wood, he steps behind a couple of trees, heavily interwoven with shrubs, realising that they will screen him. Crouching down he begins loping away, trying to move quietly. Looking behind for signs of pursuit he fails to spot a raised tree-root and, with a grunt, sprawls full length over it. *"Que est que c'est?"* George can hear the alarm in the guard's voice.

"Une minute, s'il-vous plait!" He knows it is only a matter of seconds now before his escape attempt is rumbled. He keeps moving forward, steeling himself for the supreme effort.

Suddenly, a shout, *"Il est parti!"*

George explodes forward, throwing every fibre into his dash for freedom, striding out, arms pumping, charging through the undergrowth. It flashes through his mind that he hasn't run as hard as this since he intercepted a pass and covered a lightening sixty yards, chased by half a rugby team, to score the try that won the inter-schools cup three winters ago. He has run a lot further than sixty yards when unexpectedly he bursts out of the wood. He hesitates. In front of him stretch open fields, punctuated here and there by fences or small hedges and trees. Two kilometres Dumas had said. Five minutes hard running at least and not enough cover; he will be too easy to spot - and perhaps shoot. He breathes hard as he glances around. To his left the wood tails off backwards; the wrong way. To his right, it sweeps south-westwards, forward and round, like a bull's horn, ending half-a-mile away, and nearer to his objective.

Galvanised by the sound of his pursuers crashing through the trees, he darts to his right, and back into the wood, making twenty yards before dropping down behind a large tree. Like him, they burst out of the wood and stop. He can hear them debating what to do. The driver thinks he must be beyond the first hedge line a hundred metres away. The guard is not so sure – what if he hasn't gone that way, what if he has doubled back? He swings round, peering into the wood. George ducks, instinctively trying to make himself smaller. The driver is annoyed – what if – what if you hadn't let him bloody well escape in the first place? The conversation becomes heated; insults are traded and blows are ready to be struck when the driver points out that the prisoner is getting away while they argue. He prevails. Still bickering, they set off towards the first hedge. George waits until they are out of earshot before slipping away.

He has taken a watchful half-hour to reach the end of the wood. Beyond it is a road which appears to go in the direction he wants; but too much chance of being spotted now, he will wait for dark. While traversing the wood, its crescent shape has allowed him to observe his pursuers doggedly searching the fields. At last, they appear to admit defeat and begin trudging despondently back towards their lorry. He melts into the trees, watching them until they disappear into the wood. Remaining in cover he continues a listening watch in case they are trying to trick him. The distant cough of an engine starting is followed by a series of small crescendos as it is taken through the gears. The rumble of the lorry gradually fades to silence. The sun is well down the sky but it will be another hour before dusk. He sits at the base of a tree to wait. So far, so good.

Twenty minutes have passed. Despite himself, he finds the tranquillity of the wood and reaction to his ordeal are combining to make him drowsy. Suddenly, he is wide awake, roused by rustling and the cracking of twigs – they must have worked out his location and circled round behind him. He is not going to surrender again. If he can lay one of them out immediately he stands a chance. Picking up a club-like branch he found in the wood and gauging their line of approach, he moves into a position to ambush them. He listens; they are almost upon him. He braces himself to attack.

Sullivan's expression is not for those of a nervous disposition. Stewart, 'Shorty', Richard and 'Einstein' are standing at attention. "What the bloody hell happened?" 'Einstein' speaks first. "Sir, about an hour and a half after 'B' Flight left we got a 'phone call from the Blenheim boys to say their chap had suffered an electrical failure and turned back. His radio was u/s so he couldn't let anyone know 'til he returned." Stewart takes up the story. "By which time the damage was done, sir. We were stooging about over Saarburg looking for a non-existent Blenheim and George was dangling from a parachute."

"He had no choice but to jump, sir, his engine was on fire," adds 'Shorty'. "You're sure he landed safely?" queries Sullivan.

"Definitely, sir. He was standing with three soldiers when I last saw him." He walks to a large map on the wall and points, "Just here, sir – Luxembourg – at least he didn't land in Germany."

"It makes little practical difference, internee instead of p-o-w. Christ Almighty, what a shambles! We've lost a bloody good pilot for nothing." In silence he turns the matter over in his mind. "I hate to say it but there's sweet Fanny Adams we can do for him. F/L Stewart, P/O Lewis – no blame attaches to you. You may go." He turns to 'Einstein', "Prepare a report for AHQ detailing what went wrong and emphasising the need for better communications in future. By the way, its congratulations, Flight Lieutenant Howlett – your promotion in connection with the Stanhope-Smith affair has come through." His brief smile fades, "Knight's too, it would have been just in time for his wedding; instead, someone's got to tell his girl that he won't be there,"

Richard speaks quietly. "I'll do that, sir, as a friend of the family."

"Now!" yelling like a demon, brandishing the club, ready to smash the first skull that comes within range, George erupts from behind the tree – to find himself threatening a wild boar; but only for a second. Frightened by George's manic materialisation, the beast plunges squealing through the trees. Tension dissolves like a pricked balloon; he sinks to his knees, shaking with laughter.

The thought of other boars makes him decide not to remain in the wood. He emerges watchfully onto the road. Keeping to the edge he starts walking.

The sun has dropped from sight; he reckons he has covered more than a mile. He rounds a bend. Fifty yards away he sees a striped barrier and a sentry box – a border post. Before he can be spotted he plunges through a hedge into the adjoining field. Crouching, he scurries across it at right angles to the road then scrambles through another hedge. In the next field, he turns towards the borderline again and begins a cautious advance, wondering what to expect. At the end of the field, is a row of trees. This must be it but there is no fence, no barbed wire. He takes a deep breath and moves forward, alert. The light is fading fast now. No sign of life. The trees give way to cleared ground. He is almost across it when he hears a commotion nearby; a challenge, running feet, shouts, shots being fired. He dives for cover at the base of a slender tree. The hubbub dies down. Silence again. He lies still, listening. Suddenly, footsteps behind him – a command – loud in his ear. *"Haut les mains!"* He stands up, arms raised; heart in mouth. The last glimmer of daylight reveals that the slender tree is a pole; cut telephone wires dangle from it. Soldiers appear from the shadows. One shines a torch in his face, dazzling him. George speaks. *"Je suis pilote Anglais."*

In response a rifle is poked in his ribs. *"Allez!"* As he sets off, one of the soldiers picks up a metal implement from the grass near the spot where he had lain. George marches ahead of them, hands raised; a captive again, but this time he doesn't mind. A brief explanation and he will be home before bedtime.

"Did I tell you? Tante Lys is re-opening the master bedroom for your honeymoon. She hasn't used it since Uncle Remy died. She feels lost on her own in a double bed."

"I hope she airs it well."

Mamam roars with laughter. "Shame on you…that was the door. I wonder who it is."

"Probably George without his key. My nails are still drying. Can you get it?"

It takes longer than it ought for Mamam to reappear. When she does, the laughter has gone from her face. As Richard follows her through the door the blood turns to ice in Justine's veins. Richard sees her expression. He speaks quickly to reassure her. "George is unhurt, Justine, but he's been shot down. He baled out and landed in Luxembourg. It's a neutral country so he will be interned."

"What does that mean?" she asks tremulously, her mother moving to her side.

"It means that he will be there until the war ends or his release can be negotiated. It may be months, or even years; but he won't be here tomorrow – I'm so sorry."

She answers mechanically, "At least he will be safe." Then, losing the battle with her emotions, she sinks tearfully into a chair. Mamam tries to console her. Richard watches in awkward silence.

"Liar!" The back of the captain's hand hits George's face with stunning force. He can taste blood in his mouth and his cheek throbs. Outnumbered, he checks the urge to retaliate. "You are a Nazi saboteur!"

"I'm a British officer, I tell you – RAF. Look at my uniform – and these!" He pulls his ID tags from inside his shirt.

"They prove nothing. You could 'ave taken them from a prisoner. And what would a British officer be doing 'iding in a French military zone with a pair of wire-cutters?"

"They're not mine. I've never seen them before. Look, ring your HQ; they will have an RAF liaison officer who can confirm that I have been shot down…" His sentence is cut short by another back-bander.

The Frenchman fulminates. "Don't be clever with me! You well know the telephone wires 'ave been cut. I grow tired of this. This interview is at an end. Tomorrow you will be shot as a saboteur." He moves his head dismissively, *"Take him away!"* Two soldiers seize George's arms. His shouts of protest are ignored and despite his struggles, he is dragged outside and bundled into a stone shed. The door slams shut behind him and a heavy bolt slides into place. A damp, earthy smell assails him as he waits for his eyes to accustom to the dark. There is little improvement after a minute and he realises the shed is windowless. A brief spark of light through the ill-fitting timbers as a guard lights a cigarette shows him where the door is. He finds a wall and begins feeling his way along. His foot meets something solid – a pile of logs. He sits down to take stock. In his pocket he feels the bullets taken from his parachute, now drilled and ready for threading onto a string or chain. He grips them tightly.

"Luxembourg is neutral, you say. Does that mean that civilians can go there?" Justine asks. Her face is still blotchy from crying but she has regained her composure. Richard ponders for a moment. "I hadn't really thought about it but I imagine so."

"Then all is not lost. As soon as we know where he is I will visit him. Maybe they will let us get married in Luxembourg."

He has dozed fitfully but mostly George has been awake. He senses dawn is not far off. During the night, he has experienced a range of emotions; fear, self-pity, regret – a deep gut-wrenching regret that he will never see Justine again, never hear her voice, talk with her, hold her, lie with her; he knew how much he loved her before this but the prospect of losing her forever has added another, desperate, level of intensity. Now, with the coming of day, anger displaces them all; anger at the stupid bloody captain who won't listen to him; anger at the sorrow he will leave behind – Justine, bereaved on her wedding day, and his family; and anger at himself – they say never volunteer so why the hell did he? Why didn't he sit tight instead of trying to play Biggles and ruining everything, letting everyone down – and for what? Anger sparks fresh determination, replacing that which has been sapped by the night. In a short time he is going to die – but it won't be blindfolded and tied to a stake. If they're going to shoot him, it will be fighting his way out. He spends the last minutes of darkness exercising to drive the cold and stiffness from his muscles. Soon he hears the sound of marching feet. Picking up a log he stands alongside the door. The bolt rattles and the door swings inwards, allowing the pale dawn light into the interior. *"Reveillez!"* He remains motionless, pressed against the wall. Cautiously the guard starts to enter the shed. With all his strength, George brings the log down on the man's helmet. There is a dull clang and he slumps to the ground. George jumps over him and runs through the doorway. The second guard is more wily. He has remained out of sight by the door and as George emerges, he sticks out his foot and trips him up. As George measures his length on the ground he hears the click of a rifle bolt being drawn. He turns his head to see the muzzle inches from him and tenses, waiting for the bullet.

"Qu'est ce qui se passe ici? The voice is clipped and authoritative. The guard comes to attention but doesn't withdraw the rifle. George looks round to see, among others, the captain, and a colonel, the man who had spoken. There is something about his face that is familiar."

"Stand up you Nazi scum!" The captain kicks George in the side, *What more proof of guilt do you need, Colonel, he was trying to escape?"*

"Thank you, Capitaine. I will deal with this." He looks George up and down as he struggles to his feet. "Do you not salute a senior officer, whatever the nationality?"

"Not when he is about to shoot me out of hand," replies George sourly.

"That remains to be decided, although the evidence against you appears damning. Perhaps we should start at the beginning. I am Colonel Laval. Who do you claim to be?"

George knows now why the face is familiar. He comes smartly to attention. "Pilot Officer Knight, sir! Do you know of Henri Laval, *Commandant* of *GAO 549* of *L'Armee de l'air,* based at Epinal?"

120

Laval tries to contain his surprise. "Supposing you are correct – what then?"

"Call this the condemned man's last request if you like but please telephone Henri. He can confirm who I am."

The Captain interjects. "The lines are still down – as he well knows!"

"How long until they are repaired?"

Laval's ADC, a lieutenant, answers, "Probably two hours, sir."

"Then we shall wait."

"Good morning, Madame, P/O Templeton, I'm looking for P/O George Knight, I believe he is billeted here. I'm to be his best man."

"You 'ad better come in."

The Colonel breaks off from his telephone conversation as George is ushered in. "My nephew suggests that, as he cannot actually see you, I should ask a question to which he says only the real you would know the answer. If you cannot answer this I will deem you an imposter and have you shot, so consider your response carefully. When you were invited to spend the night at his HQ, you requested a favour. What was it?"

George laughs, relieved at the simplicity of his salvation. "Inform my landlady, sir."

"C'est lui. Merci beaucoup, Henri." Laval replaces the receiver and looks at George, taking in his bruised face and mud-stained uniform. "I owe you an apology. An excess of zeal on our part nearly caused a double tragedy – happily, the man you clubbed will not die either. Now, to pleasanter things; my nephew says you are to be married today – in St Jean-sur-Moselle."

"That's correct, sir – eleven o'clock – but it's nearly nine now." Laval turns to his ADC.

"How far is St Jean from here?"

"About one-hundred and sixty kilometres, sir."

"Contact this man's squadron and inform them he is safe. Ask them to relay a message to his bride-to-be – he will be back in St Jean for eleven o'clock." He turns back to George. "After what has happened here the least I can do is place my car and driver at your disposal. Before the war, he competed at Le Mans. If anyone can, he will get you there in time. Whilst the car is being readied, we shall drink a toast to your bride." He produces a brandy bottle and two glasses.

Justine and Mamam were in a tearful, joyous jig; Templeton grinned broadly. "That was a near thing. I'd be gone by now if they hadn't insisted I have something to eat."

"I just hope they haven't got him too drunk," said Richard quietly, "I was a guest of the French infantry once in the last lot – their hospitality is not for those of a delicate constitution!" He raised his voice to include the others. "I've one other bit of news about George. It didn't seem the right time to mention it last night but he's been deservedly promoted to Flying Officer." Mamam and Justine hugged again. He produced a pair of cuff-rings, the single stripe broader than that on those which they were to replace. "These need to go on his number one uniform."

They could have been at Le Mans. Since setting off the Citroen had hardly been below third gear, tearing along the straights, screeching round bends, sometimes on two wheels, scattering cyclists and pedestrians alike. George was glad there was little other traffic. He looked at his watch – almost ten. They were skirting Thionville; a third of the way there. It had been looking distinctly promising until, a few miles to the north, they had encountered a military convoy crossing their path and been forced to fret for fifteen minutes as a seemingly endless line of lorries and trailers ground past. There was time to be made up now but that was down to the colonel's driver; an intense, taciturn man, obviously focused on the job in hand. George had abandoned conversation; each attempt being met with a shrug. The only utterance the man-made was *"pas du temps!"* Seemingly, his stock excuse for every traffic violation he committed. George settled in his seat. He had slept little the night before and three large brandies downed in ten minutes were having an effect. He was becoming used to the man's driving style and felt less inclined to be alarmed by his actions. He let his eyes close and drifted off.

The sound of a whistle rouses him. It isn't the friendly toot of the tank engines he watched as a boy, as they climbed the embankment near his home, but long strident blasts. Drowsily he opens an eye. Then he is bolt upright. A hundred yards ahead – three seconds – is a level-crossing. From the right, a goods train is converging on it. Showers of sparks fly as the driving wheels skid and slip on the rails, flung into reverse by the white-faced driver who is leaning from his cab, frantically gesticulating for them to stop; and still the whistle sounds. It is clear the train won't stop before the crossing; but it is equally clear to George that his driver has no intention of doing so either. Desperately, George stamps on an imaginary brake pedal and closes his eyes but morbid fascination makes him open them again. As the car clatters across the tracks the locomotive looms over them like a mythical monster, belching steam and smoke, every bolt and rivet starkly visible, scarcely an arm's length away. Then they are clear. He looks back to see the train-driver shaking his fist at them. For the first time that day, his driver smiles. *"Pas de problem!"* George does not respond. Fear and brandy on an empty stomach have combined to create a wave of nausea. He sits back, trying to fight it, his face deathly pale. The driver mutters under his breath. *"Aviateurs – Phu!"*

At ten minutes to eleven, the Light Fifteen screeches to a halt outside the *Mairie*. George struggles out, face bruised on one side and pallid on the other, uniform dishevelled and mud-stained, to be greeted by Peter Templeton. "Morning George. Must have been some stag night!"

"Come on, let's get him inside!" urges Richard. "You've ten minutes, George. We've got hot black coffee and your best uniform ready. Because of the circumstances the C/O has agreed that your leave doesn't start now until eleven o'clock this morning, plus he's given you two extra days. And I think you need to be looking at Justine when photographs are taken."

As he entered the *Maire's* office, all his discomforts evaporated. He felt again the emotions of the day in October when they first met. He knew that to be with Justine, the vision in cream standing before him, he would endure the last twenty-four hours a thousand times. Approaching her, he could see through the short veil covering them that her eyes, though moist, were sparkling. He could sense that she, just like him, was barely containing the urge to dive headlong into an embrace. He reached out and took her hand. Their fingers intertwined eagerly. Mamam, Richard, Peter and all others present got to their feet The *Maire* smiled, adjusted his *pince-nez* and cleared his throat. *"Mesdames et Messieurs……"*

The atmosphere in the Mess was lively as they circulated. "Thank you both for the fly past over the *Mairie*. It was a wonderful surprise," Justine said to Underhill. "Sheer coincidence," he replied, conscious of Sullivan nearby, "Obviously we wouldn't knowingly do anything like that. We… erm… we just happened to be patrolling in the area and saw three strange aircraft approaching," he winked at Henri, "So we felt it our duty to investigate."

Henri returned the wink, "and we were on a navigation exercise which brought us, quite by chance, over the middle of St. Jean."

"Please pass my thanks to your uncle for the services of his driver," offered George.

"I had no idea *he* was bringing you. It's a miracle you got here. He's a madman – with a special grudge against pilots. He was turned down by *L'Armee de l'Air* you know."

"Why was that?" said George, taking a sip from his glass.

"He's as short-sighted as a badger!" He broke into laughter as George choked on his wine.

Peter had carried out his duties to the letter, seeing them and their luggage onto the train. He shook George's hand. "Goodbye old man. Today has been an absolute delight. Look after yourself and this lovely lady." He kissed Justine's hand. *"Adieu, Madame."*

She kissed his cheek. "Thank you for all you have done today, Peter; and it is '*au revoir*' not '*adieu*' for I know that we shall meet again one day."

"There you are, Peter, woman's intuition. It means that you're not going to get the chop anytime soon," said George brightly.

His laugh came easily. "I'll hold on to that – and try to avoid you until the war ends!"

They reached the King George V in time for dinner, and then danced until late, a couple in love, oblivious of everything but each other; before retiring to the luxury of their suite where, tenderly and unhurriedly, they consummated their marriage.

The following morning, Good Friday, found them enjoying the pale spring sunshine at a cafe on the *Champs-Elysees,* watching the bustle of another Parisian day. "Apart from the uniforms, you wouldn't know there was a war on," observed George, "When I was last in London it was all barrage balloons and sandbags."

"Parisians won't let a war interfere with their enjoyment of life. This is a city like no other – so much *joie de vivre,* so much to see! Let's start with the Eiffel Tower."

"Good idea! According to the guidebook, in 1914, from the top they could see the German Army advancing on the Marne, and reinforcements heading out of the city in taxis and buses to oppose them. I hope they won't get that close this time."

Her smile lost some of its radiance. "Until we go back, I don't want to think any more about the war or the Germans; just you and me, making memories."

He took her hand. "You're right. While we're here, we're Parisians, so we'll do as they do – no more thought of the war."

When they returned to the hotel, there was an envelope in their pigeon-hole, bearing only the typed legend 'M & Mme Knight'. Inside was a single folded sheet of paper on which was typed 'Maxim's 7.45'.

"Do you know who delivered this?" George asked the desk clerk.

"Non m'sieu, it arrived before I came on duty."

He turned to Justine. "What do you think?"

"I like mysteries – let's go."

"M & Mme Knight – I believe we are expected?"

"Zat is correct, *m'sieu.* Follow me please." They were led not to a table but upstairs to a private dining room. They looked at each other uncertainly for a moment as the waiter held the door open and then Justine entered followed by George.

"Surprise!"

"Mother, Father!"

After embracing George, his mother took hold of Justine's hands and kissed her on both cheeks. "Oh my dear! I've been simply dying to meet you! George has told me so much about you in his letters. This is absolutely wonderful!"

"Mrs Knight, it is…"

"Verity, please!"

"And I'm Francis." He also kissed her on both cheeks. "Sorry to butt in but this will probably be my only chance to get a word in for the next hour or so! It's wonderful to meet you."

"Well really!" Verity feigned indignation and put her arm through Justine's. "Now my dear, I'm just dying to hear about yesterday…"

"How did you get here, Father?"

"To cut a long story short, I'm doing a spot of work for the government," he lowered his voice, "Ministry of Economic Warfare. It's made your grandfather happy. He wasn't enjoying retirement so he came back like a shot when I asked. He's running the firm again now. I came over this morning to meet a French counterpart and will be going back tomorrow. The opportunity to see you both was heaven-sent so I wangled your mother a place as my secretary," his face broke into a smile, "although she's spent most of the day shopping with the Frenchman's wife! Justine's a fine girl, I must say. We Knights certainly know how to pick 'em!" He raised his voice for the one sentence and his wife's expression told him he had achieved his desired effect. "Hope you like the King George V. We're staying somewhere else though," he chuckled. "I imagine you'd never live it down if word got out that your parents were with you on your honeymoon, hence this cloak and dagger stuff." He was studying George's uniform. "I see more congratulations are due, Flying Officer!"

"I'm not supposed to tell a soul but I think I can safely make an exception for you – the promotion came out of the Stanhope-Smith affair."

His father raised a quizzical eyebrow.

"Of course, you won't know what's been going on since I saw you in October. I'm afraid you misjudged him – he was trouble."

"Sounds rather exciting. I want to hear all about it, but let's order first."

Two days later, they were on a train again, chugging towards Normandy. "It was a lovely surprise meeting your parents. Had you any idea they would be in Paris?"

"None whatsoever, otherwise I would have suggested that Mamam joined us."

"There will be other opportunities. Your father is very handsome – perhaps even more than you," she teased, "and the scar under his ear makes him look very distinguished."

"A memento of the last war, I believe, although he has never talked of it."

She sighed. "It's difficult to avoid war in some shape or form at the moment."

"At least we can lose ourselves on your aunt's farm for the rest of the week. I'm looking forward to that – and meeting your aunt."

"I think you will like her. She speaks English. Like me she was a teacher. She gave it up to be a farmer's wife when she married Uncle Remy."

An ancient taxi – so ancient that it occurred to George that it might have been one of those that had ferried reinforcements to the Marne – took them from the station out into the country. In due course, it turned down a rutted lane and after a kilometre, they found themselves in the farmyard, surrounded by stone buildings. "The oldest parts of the farmhouse date from the fifteenth century. It was begun at the end of the Hundred Years war – just after the English had been sent packing!" said Justine, with a twinkle.

"Charming!" said George, "and there you go mentioning wars again."

She giggled. "In those days half the building was occupied by the animals. Later generations built the barns and sheds to house the livestock and took the whole farmhouse for themselves."

George pointed to one corner of the farmyard. "Is that a cider-press?"

"Yes, it's still in use..." she broke off as a woman emerged from the farmhouse. She ran to embrace her. "Tante Lys!"

George could see the family resemblance. Befitting an elder sibling and widow she had a more serious, even forbidding, countenance but, as with her sister, it easily gave way to a welcoming smile.

"So you're George! I've heard a lot of good things about you so you've plenty to live up to! First, we'd better get you out of that splendid uniform and into something more suitable for a farm. I assume you'll both be willing to lend a hand?"

"We've been here four days now – what do you think of him?" They were watching George slipping and sliding in the piggeries with an enormous grin on his face.

"For once your mother did not exaggerate! I think you are a very lucky girl although he's no more than you deserve after the way you abandoned your studies to look after her. Make sure you hold onto him."

"If only it were that simple. On Saturday he goes back to his squadron..." she left the rest unsaid.

Lys squeezed her hand. *"Courage ma petite.* Put your faith in God and think positively. Not everyone dies in a war. I'm glad George is cut out for farming – one day all this will be yours." Justine looked surprised. "Well think about it – Remy and I were not blessed with children and his brothers were killed in the last war. At the moment, the farm is mine but after me... There's no point involving your brother; nearly four years without a word – he's either made a life at sea or sunk without trace. So it will be yours – you and George – with just one condition; I've invested twenty years in this already so promise me you won't flog it off to some well-heeled Parisian to use as a weekend retreat."

"I have only one reservation – I don't want to mention any of this to George now; simply because until the war is over, we must live one day at a time; we have no long term plans and that's how it must remain. Call it superstition if you like but I feel that planning something like this would be tempting fate. Does that make sense?"

Lys squeezed her hand again. *"Oui, ma cherie.* Anyway, I'm not ready to meet my maker yet – or retire – so nothing need be said until he comes marching home. Until then it will be our little secret."

The setting sun painted the few high clouds, almost motionless against the sky, with hues that varied between orange and pink, every shade slowly darkening as dusk approached. The evening, their last evening there, was eerily still; suggestive of the calm before the storm. They stood hand in hand, watching the gently undulating landscape that stretched from the apple orchards all the way to the horizon as it gradually succumbed to shadow. George broke the silence. "I never thought I'd see anything to rival the English countryside but this has to be it. I could happily live here." She felt a pang of guilt but suppressed it. Somehow she knew that to tell him of what Tante Lys had in store for them would break the fragile spell that protected him. Involuntarily, she shivered. "Are you cold?"

"No. I'm fearful of what lies ahead of us; and you in particular."

"I was wondering when to mention these. I think the time has come." From his pocket, he drew the two bullets, each now attached to a silver chain. "Three weeks ago, before we got seatback armour in the aircraft, a Jerry took a long range potshot at me. These went through the skin of the aircraft and the seatback and finished up in my parachute. By rights I should have been wounded at least – someone was looking after me that day. I suppose it's superstitious but I'm going to wear one from now on – a lucky charm if you like," he held one out to her, "and I'd like you to have the other and share my guardian angel."

She smiled. "When we first met I didn't want to become involved, because I feared losing you. In the end I followed my heart, and I have no regrets, but that doesn't mean the fear of losing you is any less. If this offers hope of your survival I will wear it gladly." She spoke again as he placed the chain around her neck. "The last few months, and our honeymoon above all, have been the happiest of my life. Thank you." She kissed him.

He returned the kiss. "It's exactly the same for me."

She looked into his eyes. "From tomorrow our lives will be back in the hands of others; tonight they are ours alone. Let us forget the war once more, make love and fall asleep in each other's arms."

He took her proffered hand and they turned for the farmhouse. They were ready for tomorrow and the days to follow and what they had in store; but first they had tonight.

8: April, 1940

The two fighters taxied to a standstill. As ground crews swarmed over them their pilots jumped to the ground and exchanged a few words before parting company.

One swapped his flying helmet for the peaked cap proffered by a fitter. Unzipping his black leather jacket, he began strolling across the airfield, heading for a man sitting on an empty oil drum. He came to attention before him, clicked his heels and saluted. The sitting man spoke first. *"At ease, Werner. How did it go?"*

"Not bad, Herr Major. A few hours and he should be the finished article."
"But?"

Werner looked blank. *"But what?"*

"Werner, we've flown and fought together for three years – Spain, Poland. I know you better than your own mother does. Come on man, out with it!"

He hesitated for only a moment then the words flowed. *"There's something about him that's not right – he doesn't belong. Not because he's English – I've met RAF pilots before the war and they're pretty much like us, though not quite as good,"* they laughed, *"but he's a cold fish and I don't trust him. I wouldn't want him as my number two in combat."*

"I agree. The Luftwaffe is the cream of the armed forces. We are a professional elite, Werner, dedicated but not fanatics like this bugger. We don't do Nazi salutes unless Der Dicke comes to inspect us," as usual they smirked at the service nickname for the corpulent General-Feldmarschall Goering, *"but he goes around throwing out Heil Hiters like a bloody semaphore. I didn't want him here but headquarters aren't in the habit of canvassing my opinion."* He bit the end of a cigar and spat it vehemently into the grass. *"I want rid of him before the proper fighting starts. Any ideas?"*

"Sorry, Herr Major. Nothing legitimate comes to mind."

A small ferret-like man with a pointed face was scurrying past. *"Otto!"*

"Herr Major?" He blinked repeatedly behind his spectacles and looked ill-at-ease. *"Stanhope-Smith, the Englishman – I don't want him here. You're our intelligence officer, so apply some intelligence and find me a reason to send him back where he came from!"*

Things had changed in his absence, reflected George. Gone were the winter routines - now the whole squadron was on dawn to dusk readiness every day and time off would be a day per week if they were lucky. The days were lengthening so longer and longer readinesses were in prospect. He saw Justine every evening but it was a wrench on her days off when, before dawn, he had to prise himself from her sleepy embrace and their cosy bed and head for the airfield. 'Their bed' – they had returned from honeymoon to find that Mamam had unselfishly taken Justine's room and given them hers. "It was too big for me on my own anyway – better suited to a couple," she had said dismissively.

"R-red Leader, b-b-bogeys, three o'clock." Litmus' voice breaks into his thoughts. He is flying Red Three and George Red Two in place of 'Roy'.

"Roger Red Three. Let's take a look." They begin a climbing turn to starboard seeking to gain the advantages of height and sun. Soon the specks have resolved themselves into nine aircraft in three vics on a westerly heading; an indication that the Germans are stepping up their efforts. Underhill speaks again. "Me110s, I don't think they've seen us. Take the rearmost vic – a quick squirt and away. Tallyho!" One after another the three Hurricanes roll into a dive, heading for the unsuspecting enemy. Underhill's tracers arrow into the cockpit of the vic leader and the aircraft begins to fall away. Then he is through the gap he has made in the formation and it is George's turn.

Surprise is gone and his target is starting to roll away from his attack. His fire only hits the rear fuselage. To his astonishment the tail section sheers off and the rest of the aircraft plunges vertically. He continues down, following Underhill. Tracers flash past his wing. Over his shoulder he sees one of the leading Me110s has turned back and dived on him, blazing away with its nose-mounted cannon and machine guns. He turns towards the attack, passing under his assailant, and uses the speed gained in his dive to start climbing – he needs to gain height now to cope with rest of the formation.

A second is diving towards him and again he turns into its attack, firing ineffectually at it. Another passes in front of him. He fires a snap burst and sees hits on the fuselage before it dives clear. Occupied with aircraft above and in front of him, he has not seen another Messerschmitt sliding into position behind, its pilot striving to centre his gun - sight on George's cockpit. A voice sounds in George's headphones – urgent but clear and authoritative. "Break right, Red Two – NOW!" Unhesitatingly, he rolls the Hurricane to the right and twisting his head round, he sees his attacker for the first time. A stream of cannon shells and tracer pass harmlessly where he had been sitting a split second before. Doomed, his assailant streaks past, sprouting flame, with 'Litmus's' Hurricane on its tail firing burst after burst into it – George knows now who gave the warning. With an unsteady hand, he touches through his shirt the bullet hanging from his neck. All at once, the sky is clear of enemy aircraft; the survivors running for home. 'Litmus's' Hurricane climbs towards him and Underhill, probably out of ammunition, is returning from pursuit of another Messerschmitt. The fight has lasted no more than a minute. From the multitude of events and sensations that have assailed his senses two predominate – the smell of cordite and 'Litmus's' call.

'Einstein' endeavoured to make himself heard over the excited chatter. "French observers confirm two Me110s downed in France and one just over the border plus three more trailing smoke. Based on your reports, I think one confirmed and one damaged by each of you is a fair…" The rest of his sentence was drowned by cheers from inside and outside his office. He leaned closer. "What do you make of the Me110?"

"Faster than the Hurri on the level or in a dive but otherwise the old girl can fly rings round it," Underhill responded.

"I'll s-s-second that!" added Litmus.

"You're stuttering again!" said George.

"I never s-stopped. For s-some reason it doesn't h-happen in emergencies."

"Well, whatever the reason, you saved my bacon, so thanks! I'd stand you a beer but I don't suppose you'll want one."

"On the c-contrary. I'm following Foggy's advice – j-just a question of numbers!"

Operation *Weserubung* was going well. On 9th April, German forces had invaded Denmark and Norway simultaneously, forcing the former to capitulate within hours and capturing the capital, Oslo, and most of the southern part of the latter. There had been losses, mainly in naval actions against the Royal Navy, but now, five days on, German troops were advancing with little opposition up the long narrow land which is Norway. Possibly the only one on the German side not satisfied with events so far was *Oberleutnant* Stanhope-Smith. His problems had begun when his *Staffel* was among those escorting troop-carrying *Ju52s* to a landing in Oslo on day one. Not all ground opposition had been suppressed at that stage so the whole armada had had to head for Denmark, refuel and try again. Stanhope-Smith had run out of fuel a few miles short of the Danish coast and been forced to ditch. After a cold wet hour in a rubber dinghy, he was retrieved by *He59* floatplane and, in due course, found himself facing his C/O. *"That was a bloody balls-up – what have you got to say for yourself?"*

"Sorry, Herr Major. Due to lack of familiarity with the 109, I misjudged the rate of fuel consumption. It won't happen again."

"Bloody right it won't! If it were down to me, I'd ground you myself but I don't have to. You're off operations!" Shock and dismay registered on Stanhope-Smith's face. The *Major* sat back in his chair and lit a cigar. Despite his tone he seemed to be enjoying the proceedings. *"It has been pointed out to me that if you had fallen into French or British hands you would have found yourself in front of a firing squad, as a result of your previous activities. I mentioned this to HQ, who agreed that it would not be right to expose you to this risk. As France will be our next opponent you are being withdrawn from front-line service. Report to HQ tomorrow for re-deployment. Otto has the details. Dismissed!"*

Stanhope-Smith's salute was a reflex. Then he stood, dazed, disbelieving, before eventually shambling from the office. The *Major* had already turned his attention to some papers and was no longer interested in him. He stumbled into Otto's office. *"You have details of my appointment at HQ?"*

Otto rummaged around and found a slip. His beady eyes were shining behind his glasses as he leaned forward and handed it over. *"Here you are, Herr Oberleutnant."* As he took it Stanhope-Smith noticed one of the *Major's* cigars in Otto's shirt pocket.

By the following morning, shock and dismay had subsided. He had had time to think. The cigar was the giveaway. He had been manoeuvred out by the *Major*. He sat in front of two senior officers with a necessarily contained but smouldering anger.

"*I believe you know the reason you have been withdrawn from front-line flying?*"

"*Yes, Herr Oberst! Is there any scope to appeal against the decision?*"

"*I regret not. But in recognition of your efforts so far we will give you a choice in your next posting. You can fly transport aircraft, ferrying officers and party officials, or become an instructor.*"

Stanhope-Smith thought quickly. Transport flying offered the possibility of a good social life – stopovers in different parts of the Reich and so on – a girl at every aerodrome perhaps, but from a flying point of view, it was a dead end. Instructing offered the chance to keep in touch with the fighter squadrons and perhaps, one day, it would enable his return to the front line. "*I'd prefer instructing, Herr Oberst, particularly if it involves advanced training.*"

"*I applaud your choice, Oberleutnant; it shows a willingness to contribute to the war effort, despite your disappointment. I shall put in a good word for you. Before you go Major Brandt has some questions for you. By way of introduction,* he turned to face his companion."

Brandt cleared his throat. "*Oberleutnant, I am sure that you are aware that we will soon be launching an attack on France. I and others have the task of obtaining intelligence to assist in selecting targets for bombing. I know that during your time with the RAF you were based at St Jean-sur-Moselle in Lorraine. Apart from the obvious airfield, are you aware of anything else in the area meriting our attention?*"

Stanhope-Smith never forgot nor forgave and now he saw an opportunity. He might yet visit his wrath on Knight's girl and the brat, whose past interference had arguably led him to his present situation. In addition, someone, anyone, was going to pay for his latest humiliation. The lie was smoothly delivered. "*Just before my enforced departure, word reached the squadron that the village was to be cleared of its civilian inhabitants and occupied by French scientists carrying out some secret project – we didn't known what but given the proximity to Germany perhaps it was poison gas or some special weapon.*"

The two officers exchanged glances. *Major* Brandt spoke again. "*We have heard nothing of this before and reconnaissance flights have shown nothing unusual.*" Stanhope-Smith shrugged. "*If they are up to something special then I imagine they would go to great lengths to disguise it.*" The two officers nodded in agreement. He had them hooked; now he reeled them in. "*I may be misinformed or they may not have gone through with it, but if you have a few bombs to spare then I think they would be put to good use there.*"

The first ripples from Operation *Weserubung* reached St Jean one week after its commencement. Red Section had landed among a hive of activity. A bowser appeared as if from nowhere and ground-crew swarmed over their aircraft. Richard emerged from his office holding an armful of files. "We're being moved to an airfield near Epernay, to support the Battles. HQ thinks the balloon's going up any time now. You've twenty minutes to collect your effects, say goodbye and get back here. I've a car – we can go together if you like."

It took five minutes to reach the School House. Richard went in to see Mamam. Justine had seen their arrival and came out of school. "What is happening?" George took her hands. "We're being moved – Epernay – we're leaving at once."

"This is – so sudden. Have the Germans attacked?" Her dismay was almost tangible. "No, but it's expected any time."

They embraced, fiercely but silently. "Please be careful," she whispered eventually.

"I will. I'll write – every day if I can."

"I love you."

"I love you too." Their lips met, just as they had once before as he had prepared to go to war.

They were still locked together when Richard and Mamam emerged. He coughed politely. "I'm sorry, but we need to be going."

Mamam, tears in her eyes, pushed a small canvas bag into George's hands. "Thank you." He kissed her on the cheek. "Look after Justine for me." Not trusting herself to speak, she nodded silently.

As Richard gave Mamam a parting kiss, George took Justine in his arms once more. *"Au revoir, ma cherie."* They kissed and then reluctantly, he released her and climbed into the car. As it pulled away he could see the tears, no longer held back, rolling down both women's cheeks as they watched him go. Behind them, at the school's windows, the children waved their bewildered farewells.

Back at the airfield there was a briefing for all pilots. "Our new base is here – six miles east of Epemay." Sullivan was pointing to the map on the wall, the only item left in the dispersal hut other than the stove. "Take off is in ten minutes." They filed out to their Hurricanes, fuelled and armed by the hard-working ground crews, and took off in Sections, forming up for a low pass over the village before setting course for their destination; George feeling as if he were being tom in half.

A week later he, and 686, had returned. His first words to her were a distressed apology for his total lack of communication. "Sssh!" she said soothingly, putting a finger to his lips. Tenderly, he clasped her hand and kissed it. Her eyes told him they were of one mind; no words were necessary as they headed for the stairs.

She was eager to tell him her news as they lay together afterwards, savouring the touch of their spent bodies. Instead she patiently listened as the frustration of the last week spilled out of him. "A complete and utter shambles! When we arrived at the airfield the only thing there was a group of tents. We had to walk to the nearest village to eat and then back again to sleep. Until the rest of the Squadron arrived the next afternoon we had no fuel or ammo and for another four days our only means of communication with AHQ was the telephone at the village bakery. Things were just about getting organised when they decided the whole thing was a false alarm and sent us back here. We didn't see a single Jerry all week. Worst of all I couldn't contact you. The only positive is that it's been decided that when things really do kick off we will be based here and operate from forward airfields each day, returning at night." She squeezed his hand in delight. "Some more good news – I've got Sunday off."

She smiled. "If it's fine, I know just the place to go."

132

"Enough talking shop. What's been happening here?"

"I went to the doctor in the week." She sounded matter of fact. He looked anxious.

"What was wrong?"

She couldn't hold out any longer. Her face broke into a broad grin. "I'm pregnant!" His head swam and he thought his chest might burst. He hugged her.

"It's wonderful, marvellous, wizard in fact!" He thought for a moment and a look of concern took over. "Should we have... what we just did?"

His inability to put such matters into words was a continuing source of amusement and endearment to her. "Not a problem – nor will it be so for some time." She almost laughed at the relief on his face. "It's due the second week of November, which means it was conceived while Mamam was away," she smiled again, "you didn't waste any time, Mr Hotshot! There's one thing though – there are people around here who will try to make something of the fact that its happened like this; people who didn't agree with my being appointed schoolmistress in the first place; so for the next few weeks I want to restrict the news to us, Mamam and Richard – and your parents of course."

He chuckled. "It's a good job I managed to escape from Luxembourg."

Sullivan's scepticism had been spot-on. In the last week of April variable-pitch propellers began to arrive; three at first, enough to provide practice. "Bloo-dy brill-iant!" was Evans' verdict, "we can compete with those Messerschmitts now."

"And climb faster," enthused Giles, "you can feel the extra bite these things give."

"I've thought of a way to avoid using them wrongly," added 'Foggy', "it came to me when I was dressing for dinner and saw myself in the mirror."

"Well, what is it?"

"Take-Off Fully Fine – TOFF!" A couple of cushions bounced off his head amid hoots of derision.

"Ignoring the line-shoot it's a damned good idea," said Underhill, "well done Foggy, I didn't think you had it in you."

"Sorry to be pedantic but what about landings – or go-arounds to be more precise?" asked Giles.

"Go Round Uses f-Fully Fine – g-GRUFF?" suggested 'Litmus'.

"Is there a dog in here?" queried 'Foggy'.

"Brilliant!" enthused Underhill, "If all else fails we'll bombard the Jerries with acronyms."

Sunday morning found George pedalling Justine's bicycle to her directions whilst she balanced precariously on the back-step, one arm around George and the other holding a large picnic basket. "Tum left, just here," she said, "another hundred metres and then we have to walk." As presaged, the track gave way to grass, already quite long. The sun was warm on their backs as hand-in-hand they strolled to a clump of trees, beyond which was a small-pebbled area in a bend of the river.

"Your own private beach!" said George.

"Alain and I discovered it as children; I have been coming here for years." Opening the basket, he extracted a rug, spread it out and began unloading the contents. "Did we bring a corkscrew?" No answer. He looked up but she wasn't where he expected. He turned, to see her clothes in a neat pile. From the middle of the river she hailed him.

"Come on in, it's lovely."

"I haven't got a costume."

"Nor have I."

"Someone might see us."

"Stop being so English!"

He looked around to satisfy himself they were alone, stripped off and followed her in.

"I thought you said the water was lovely," said George, "it was freezing."

"So I see!" smirked Justine.

It took a second before the penny dropped. "Oh, very funny! Well it's your loss too."

"In which case, I had better do something about it. You know, you've reminded me of a film I saw in England."

"What was that?"

"Wee Willie Winkie!" she shrieked and ran off. George started after her but she was surprisingly fast. It took fifty yards to catch up and drag her, laughing, onto the grass.

They stayed on the riverbank until the sun dipped beyond the far hills. Among the sights, smells and sounds of spring they laughed, lazed and loved; a few more precious hours that they had hardly dared to hope for.

To the east a giant was waking from its winter slumber. After crushing Poland, the German war machine had been resting and recuperating. Losses had been made good and plans finalised. In its first stirrings it had brushed aside Denmark and Norway. In a few more days, it would be ready to unleash its fury on Western Europe.

9: May, 1940

"Word is that the Germans are massing for an attack," said 'Einstein'.

"It has to be soon," Richard replied.

"I know this is selfish but I hope it isn't tomorrow – I'm due a day off," said George.

"Well make the most of it – I think it will be a while before you get another."

The shadows were lengthening when George and Justine returned from their day at the 'beach'. They entered the School House in high spirits to find Richard with Mamam. "Just the people I wanted to see. How about dinner at *Hotelle Manoir* in Epinal – the four of us – my treat?" asked George.

"Sounds delightful; do you mind if I ask what prompted this?" Richard replied.

"What you said yesterday. Who knows when we will get this opportunity again?"

After the taxi had chugged away, they stood outside the School House, gazing at the stars; mixing the warm glow of laughter and friendship with the cool night air. They had been the last to leave the restaurant, lingering, as though hoping to prolong the magic indefinitely. "An evening to remember," Richard had said, "good food, good wine and above all good company. Thank you so very much, though 'thank you' hardly seems adequate." Taking Mamam's hand he had continued, "I – we'd like to make a toast – to Knights present and future."

George's reflection was broken by a rumbling from the east, sporadic at first and then more persistent. "'ome just in time," said Mamam, "a storm is brewing." She was still fiercely clutching the nosegay Richard had purchased as they had arrived in Epinal, from a street vendor who had forsaken home for the fine evening and the chance it offered to clear the day's stock.

George felt Justine's hand tense within his as Richard quietly responded. "You're right my dear, but not in the way I think you intended. That's an exchange between the artillery on the *Maginot* and *Siegfried* Lines. I think, quite literally, that someone has fired the starting gun."

It seemed they had hardly gone to sleep when there was a hammering on the front door. Bleary-eyed, George opened it to an AC2. "C/O's compliments, sir. Assemble outside the *Mairie* at oh-four-twenty hours!"

By four-forty all pilots were in the dispersal hut, the undercurrent of anticipation displacing any thoughts of tiredness. They stood holding mugs of steaming tea as Sullivan addressed them. "'A' and 'B' Flights will be five aircraft apiece – a vic of three plus two weavers – and one section will remain behind for airfield defence in case the Jerries show up whilst you're away. Green Section gets the short straw first." He found their obvious disappointment encouraging. "Don't worry; there'll be other sorties today." The telephone rang. He listened intently before replacing the receiver. "The Ops boys at AHQ have got plots coming out of their ears so we are to do area patrols and deal with whatever we find. 'A' Flight – Nancy, 'B' Flight – St Dizier – Angels fifteen – good hunting!"

Half an hour of patrolling has passed uneventfully. Eagerness is giving way to frustration. Giles' breaks the silence. "Maybe we're up too early, Jerry's still abed!"

"Good thinking, I wouldn't mind going back to bed," responds George.

"Best suggestion of the day so far…!"

Underhill cuts in. "This isn't a Lyons Corner House. Remember your R/T drill!" They patrol in chastened silence for another ten minutes. Finally, patience is rewarded. "T-twelve Dorniers three o'clock low. N-no sign of an escort. I-I think they've seen us."

"Roger," replies Underhill. Inwardly he laughs at the irony; after all the talk of out-of-date tactics, the situation is ideal for a Fighting Area Attack. "No 1 attack but keep to the edge of the formation." He pauses, studying the sky. Where are the fighters? "It seems too good to be true, so keep a sharp lookout… Tally-ho!"

Following their leader, the Hurricanes roll into the dive, moving into line astern, heading for the flank of the enemy formation; avoiding the crossfire awaiting anyone naive enough to attack from the rear. In turn they make a firing pass before swinging away. The whole process takes thirty seconds but in that time two bombers have been cut down, hitting the ground with vivid orange explosions; another two are trailing smoke and lagging behind their comrades. Parachutes appear in the sky, floating on the wind like dandelion seeds.

"Form up for another pass!" orders Underhill, searching the sky for fighters again, "they're obviously carrying bombs."

"Not anymore!" shouts 'Roy' triumphantly, "they're making a run for it." Clusters of black dots fall from the Dorniers as they jettison their loads and turn towards a large bank of cloud to the north-east breaking up their formation in the process. The two damaged aircraft endeavour to follow, only to fall further behind.

"Red Four and Five, take the stragglers. Two and Three, eyes peeled and follow me!" George and Litmus set off in pursuit. George scans the sky as he moves in for the kill; still no fighters. He has no trouble overhauling the struggling aircraft and calmly, he moves into position, confident that he can tackle a lone bomber with little trouble.

He executes a beam attack with practised ease and puts a two-second burst into the undamaged engine. It is enough. The Dornier begins its downward plunge, the crew tumbling out as it falls. Having given the matter little thought before, he is surprised to find himself gladdened by their escape; perhaps the prospect of fatherhood has changed his perspective. The parachutes have emphasised that there are men in the black-crossed machines; fellow aviators. Unless in self-defence, he only needs to destroy the aircraft; the crew will become prisoners-of-war.

Looking around, he sees more parachutes appearing as Litmus despatches the second straggler. He is impressed with 'Litmus'; shy and diffident on the ground but very different in action; with eyes like a hawk. "Nice shooting, Red Five." The sky is clear. The others have disappeared in pursuit of the remaining Dorniers. "No point stooging around – let's head back!"

The rest of 'A' Flight returned twenty minutes after George and 'Litmus'. An excited hubbub broke out as they crowded into 'Einstein's' office, "No fighters – it was a duck shoot – pure and simple!"

"Three more notches on the tally-stick!" called Underhill.

"It would have been more if they hadn't scuttled into cloud!"

'Einstein' hadn't finished with 'A' Flight when 'B' Flight returned claiming two Me110s. "He'll need an assistant if we carry on like this," said 'Roy'. They were standing around swapping yarns when Sullivan called for their attention. "Well done everyone – the Jerries dropped a clanger this morning and we made them pay for it; but don't expect it to be that easy every time. As we speak, the German Army is overrunning Luxembourg. Our Battles are going to attack their columns and we will be protecting them – as soon as we get the word Red, Blue and Green Sections plus myself; Yellow Section stay behind this time, In the meantime, get something to eat."

"I'm ready for lunch. Hungry work despatching Dorniers!" said Giles.

"Lunch? Its only eight o'clock," laughed 'Roy', "but I know what you mean – we've been up for four hours already."

They bolted their sandwiches, expecting to scramble at any moment, but minutes turned into hours, with nothing happening. They waited in the growing heat of the day; talking, reading, dozing. George thought of Dumas and his scepticism about the sanctity of neutrality, now justified by events; hoping he would not have to throw away his life – the whole Luxembourg army numbered only a few hundred and could offer token resistance at best.

Through the office window, they could hear Sullivan talking to AHQ, his exasperation evident as he slammed the receiver down. He addressed them again. "Apparently, the delay is because AHQ have been waiting for permission from the French High Command to begin bombing operations; they don't want us to bomb the Germans for fear of reprisals." He shook his head as if unable to believe what he had just said. "The Battles, however, are going into action at twelve noon with or without that permission. Another squadron are escorting them initially and we have to be over Luxembourg City for a changing of the guard at twelve-twenty. We are to spend precisely twenty minutes there before withdrawing."

They have been patrolling without seeing friend or foe. The answer to the question forming in their minds is provided by Evans. "Two o'clock low – and they've got company!" All eyes turn to the north, where seven Battles, fleeing south-west in ragged formation, are being attacked. Even as they catch sight of them, one drops away, engine on fire, prey to one of a dozen Me109s; a solitary parachute blossoms. Sullivan's orders are succinct. "Green and Blue Sections, engage the 109s. Red Section, stay with me and keep your eyes peeled."

Masked by the sun behind them, the two sections attack. A *Schwarm* manoeuvring for a beam attack on the Battles receive Green Section's attention. 'Shorty' rakes his target from cockpit to propeller. The 109 rolls onto its back and falls earthwards, streaming thick black smoke. Two more Messerschmitts dive homewards, trailing coolant, hit by Gillibrand and Hewartson; the fourth flees towards his other comrades. Blue Section pick a *rotte* of 109s ahead of the Battles. Stewart fires a snap burst into the leader; a spurt of flame is followed by an explosion. He flinches as debris rattles against his Hurricane. 'Foggy's' bullets smash into number two. The cockpit canopy flies off and a dark shape falls away from the aircraft; seconds later a parachute opens. Both Sections break off, using their speed to zoom climb. The surviving 109s are now grouped together; seemingly taking stock. Six Hurricanes are sitting above them. One German pilot has probably screwed his eyes up to check near the sun and caught a glimpse of Red Section; whatever the reason, the seven Messerschmitts suddenly dive for home as one before the Hurricanes make their next move. Sullivan watches their departure with satisfaction. "Let them go. Protect the Battles – that's what we came for. Well done Green and Blue Sections!" They are close enough now to see the flak damage suffered by the Battles. None are unscathed; most holed in several places; some carrying dead or wounded aircrew.

They are back over France when Stewart speaks, "Looks like we're losing one." The plume of smoke trailing from the engine of one Battle has become darker and thicker as it drops out of formation. Sullivan responds immediately. "Red Section, cover the straggler; the rest of you stick with the others."

The limping Battle and its escort soon find themselves left behind. It is now obvious what the outcome will be. The Hurricanes circle protectively as their charge sinks towards a large field. 'Roy's' voice is suddenly urgent over the R/T, "Christ, he's on fire!" Flames are sprouting from the engine cowling, blowing back towards the cockpit as the aircraft crosses the hedge. Fire – the pilot's worst nightmare. George watches, horrified but fascinated, shouting advice that no one else can hear. "For God's sake man, get it down – quickly!" The pilot manages a belly-landing. As the aircraft slithers to a halt he leaps from the cockpit and rolls on the ground to extinguish his overalls. He staggers to his feet again and starts back towards the burning aircraft but French infantrymen have appeared and a couple get there first to pull the inert rear gunner clear. Seconds later the fuel tanks explode; the third crewman still inside.

Underhill masks his feelings with flippancy. "Show's over – time to go home!" Turning away, the Hurricanes are low enough for George to catch a glimpse of fair hair; the pilot, supported by two *poilus,* is now bareheaded – it *has* to be Peter Templeton. George's predominant emotion is relief – Peter has cheated death again and his injuries will probably keep him from flying for a while – perhaps long enough to help him avoid the inevitable carnage among the Battles.

The mood over a late lunch was ebullient. Against a background of banter 'Einstein' reported to Sullivan. "Not a bad start to the real war, sir – seven Dorniers, two 110s and three 109s without loss, plus a bagful of Jerry prisoners!"

"Thank you. A very good start, in fact, but things have gone our way so far. There may be setbacks and we shall be measured by how we handle those too. Having said that it's been a good show by all concerned." He turned to Richard, "Any news?"

"The Battles will be going out again this afternoon, sir. We're waiting for the word." They have been on duty for twelve hours when the call comes at four-thirty. Sullivan has just led the Squadron – minus Red Section – into the air when the telephone rings again. Richard leans out of the office window. "Scramble Red Section – Twenty plus bandits, east of the Maginot Line but heading our way. No other gen. Try to recall the squadron."

"If we bring them back you'll have to tell AHQ to find another escort." Underhill calls before sprinting for his Hurricane. The engine is running and his fitter stands on the wing waiting to help him with his harness. He plugs in his R/T lead and flicks the switch. "Shuttlecock Leader this is Red One – return base, repeat, return base – raid incoming!" He listens as the three Hurricanes taxi from dispersal. No reply. R/T range is very limited from the ground. He calls again. Still nothing. By now Red Section are airborne, clawing for height. It will take about six minutes to reach ten thousand feet; they may need more if the enemy turns out to be higher. He tries again as they pass two thousand feet. A few seconds later a faint reply comes through.

"Roger Red One. ETA fifteen minutes. Shuttlecock aircraft return to base – the bastards are trying to bomb us out of house and home!"

The sky is cloudless as Red Section climb but the warm afternoon sun has produced haze, hampering their view above and to the east, leaving them unable to see the part of the sky the enemy will approach from; they could be climbing into an ambush. Tension grows as they feel their way. George sees shadowy forms. He presses the R/T to shout a warning then realises it is a trick of the light. He screws up his eyes in concentration. And then, at ten thousand feet they are above the haze; relief – no sign yet of any aircraft. Glad of the chance to gain more height they continue to climb, peering into the distance. Specks, indistinct at first, take on a solid form then become identifiable. Underhill speaks again. "Twelve Heinkels, Angels twelve; twelve 110s, Angels fifteen. Red Section, line abreast. We'll take the bombers head on and try to break them up. Keep an eye on the 110s. They'll be after us like terriers when they see what we're doing. Shuttlecock Leader, engaging enemy!"

"On our way, Red One – good hunting!"

"Roger, Shuttlecock Leader. Tallyho Red Section!"

Red Section are at the same level as the bombers and now they move out of their vee-formation and open their throttles wide. The Heinkels, six abreast, grow rapidly. The large segmented Plexiglas dome on the front of one fills George's gun-sight. Behind the dome, sit pilot and navigator and prone in front of them is the front gunner. George sees a stream of tracer leave the single machine gun and arc lazily towards him before suddenly appearing to accelerate and whip over his port wing. Before the gunner can correct his aim George fires a three second burst. The dome explodes into a myriad of fragments; the tracer stops and the now pilotless aircraft drops from the formation.

Out of the corner of his eye, he sees two Heinkels collide and begin tumbling earth- wards, locked together. Through the gap he has made in the formation, he can see the Heinkel in the second rank jettisoning its bombload and starting to turn away. His bullets are striking its fuselage when he hears Underhill in his headphones. "Here they come!" He looks up to see Me110s diving down, intent on vengeance. Pulling back hard on the stick he climbs towards his attackers. Two 110s flash past firing wildly; a third breaks off and rolls away to circle clockwise for another attack. He can see three more, still above, watching the initial skirmishes, looking for an opportunity. Flashes on the ground indicate bursting bombs but the bombers that dropped them have turned for home in the remains of their original formation. Levelling off, he turns towards the circling 110, intending to cut across its arc to attack it. Glancing below, he sees the other two 110s climbing back up, looking to catch him unawares. To climb will make him vulnerable to those above; to go right exposes him to the circling one; he rolls into a diving turn to the left. Right rudder checks the dive, bringing the nose level, but he holds the turn, keeping the stick hard back into his stomach. He blacks out briefly, rolling out in time to have a quick but inconclusive shot at the circling 110 before flying clear of the melee. The haze below does not prevent him seeing straight down; he is almost back over St Jean. His heart misses a beat as a Hurricane spirals down, then he spots the parachute floating above it. A sixth sense makes him look up. The three watching 110s have chosen their target; they are coming for him. Again, his only choice is to meet their attack head-on. They are line abreast so he pulls the stick hard back, opens the throttle and heads for the centre aircraft. He can see the muzzle flashes of the machine guns and cannon in its nose. There is no need to aim – the fifty-three foot wingspan of the 110 fills the sky in front of him – simply press the gun-button and hold it. Bedlam ensues; the roar of his engine, rattle of machine guns, thumps and bangs of bullets and cannon shells smashing into the nose of the Hurricane and pinging off the sides of the cockpit. The solid block of the engine and bullet-proof windscreen shelter him but it is obvious that his aircraft is taking punishment. They are closing rapidly. He knows that German pilots are brave, not suicidal, but the problem remains – how to break from the head-on charge? The answer lies in their respective angles of approach; he must go under, and pray the German goes over. As he pushes the stick forward, there is a tremendous bang in front; engine revs go off the clock and the whole aircraft starts to shake violently. He is momentarily stunned, hardly registering the smoke and flame issuing from the 110 as it skims over him. His brain catches up. A cannon shell has blown part of the propeller away. Time to leave. He pulls at the canopy. Stuck. He tugs at it savagely. It won't budge – the runners must be damaged. He can't bale out. He'll have to land it – but unpowered – or the unbalanced propeller will literally shake the engine from its mountings, causing the plane to fall from the sky. He switches off. The shaking fades as the propeller slows to a halt; the ugly wooden stump of the blade settles in the ten-past position. An unaccustomed silence follows as he sets about trimming the aircraft for a glide back to the airfield.

"Shuttlecock aircraft, bandits galore. Fill your boots – Tallyho!" Wrapped up in the fight, George had forgotten about the rest of the Squadron. Like avenging Furies, ten Hurricanes wade into the 110s. Two fall in flames to the first pass and the remainder turn full-throttle for home using their superior speed in the dive to get away. "Shuttlecock Leader to Red Section, report in."

"Red One returning to base; minor damage but OK."

"Red Three – propeller shot off – airfield in sight – trying for home. I saw Red Two baling out."

"Bale out yourself man! To hell with the aircraft!"

"I can't sir. The hood's jammed."

There is a telling pause. "Good luck, Red Three!" Even without that, George has no illusions about his situation. Without an engine, landing on the airfield will be tricky. If he descends too quickly, he cannot regain height and will land short – probably in the woods to the east. If he arrives too high, he will have to carry on and take his chances beyond. Both possibilities offer a fair chance of a broken neck. At least he has managed to manoeuvre himself into-wind for a direct approach, avoiding the risk of stalling and spinning-in during an unpowered landing circuit. Passing over the woods, he sees the smouldering remains of a Heinkel that has gouged its way into the trees, and wonders if it was the one he shot down. He realises his approach is erring on the high side. Without the engine, he works furiously on the hand-pump to lower flaps and undercarriage – too late though to gain enough benefit from the extra drag. As the Hurricane crosses the boundary, high and fast, he switches off the electrics and tightens his harness. To one side, he can see the fire tender shadowing him. First contact with the ground is halfway across the airfield. The wheels hit with a bone-jarring thump, the aircraft bounces and thumps to earth again. A glance at the air pressure gauge shows zero – no brakes. Unchecked, the Hurricane careers towards the boundary hedge. Unable to do anything else, George puts his arms over his face and waits for the inevitable.

'Roy' is already feeling tipsy as he empties the wine bottle. Surrounded by grinning French farm-workers he describes in pigeon-French his part in the combat. *"Avion Boche – dakka-dakka-dakka – boum!"* Loud cheers; and another bottle is thrust into his hand. Five minutes earlier, they were a hostile mob, ready to lynch him until he managed to show his RAF wings and shout *'Aviateur Anglais!'* Now he is their best friend. A thought occurs. *"Telephone?"* he asks.

A Frenchman shrugs, *"Il n'y en a pas."*

"No matter," says 'Roy' taking another swig, "I'm supposed to ring my squadron but there's no 'phone so," he slaps the uncomprehending Frenchman on the shoulder, "I'll just have to have another drink."

"Are you OK, sir?" The Fitter's voice registers concern. He has forced the hood open whilst the fire crew have been giving the lifeless engine a precautionary hosing.

"I think so, thanks." George touches the bullet under his shirt then climbs unsteadily from the cockpit. His arm throbs where it intervened between his face and the gun sight but otherwise he is unhurt. He looks back at the Hurricane, its nose embedded in a thick, springy, hedge which has acted like buffers at the end of a railway track. Like most fighting men, he carries with him the unspoken conviction that he will not die – his mental armour. It has received a dent today though – a reminder of his mortality. He brushes it aside. "I suppose F/L Howlett will want to see me – can I scrounge a lift?"

Underhill looked stern. "Normally you'd get a bollocking for a landing like that." His face broke into a grin and he clapped George on the shoulder, "but in the circumstances, I think it was pretty damn good!"

"You can't class that as good," protested 'Foggy', "you know the rules – a landing is anything you can walk away from; a good landing is when you can use the kite again!"

George had heard the pilots' saw before – sufficiently often that it didn't warrant more than a wry smile – but at that moment something in him was crying out for release and he was suddenly rocking with raucous laughter. 'Foggy' looked startled. "Steady on old man, it wasn't that funny!"

George collected himself. "You're right – it's been a long day."

"And it isn't over yet," interjected Richard, "we're all invited to *le Cafe Georges* by a grateful *Maire* and villagers as a thank you for seeing the bombers off."

"I hope the young ladies of the village are as grateful as the *Maire,*" mused 'Foggy'.

George ignored him. "I didn't know the cafe had opened again."

"A few days ago – new owner. Wouldn't expect you to know that now you're a pipe and slippers man – home to wifey and all that!"

"It would be a shame," said George, "for you to survive combat with the Germans only to be found mysteriously murdered in your bed."

"Before you do that," said 'Einstein', "I want your reports."

Justine was waiting in the square as he jumped from the 'Billet Bus'. She ran to him. Oblivious to the whistles of the others, they clung to each other, emotions pushed to a new intensity by recent events. She spoke first. "I saw the fighting. I was so frightened for you; especially when a Hurricane came down – until I saw the parachute."

"That wasn't me; that was 'Roy'. Is he back yet?"

"Someone's gone for him – I think he landed in one of the neighbouring villages. Which was your aircraft?"

"The one that everyone seemed to be diving on."

Her eyes widened. "It was you who climbed up to meet them? If I'd known I couldn't have watched. That was so brave!" She sounded slightly conspiratorial, "We cheered when your opponent crashed."

He squeezed her hand. "Do you mind telling 'Einstein' that? Miserable so-and-so only gave me a 'probable'. Can we stay here for a while?" he indicated the cafe, "there seems to be a party starting."

Part of her wanted him all to herself, but another part sensed that at this time he needed to share this triumph with his comrades too. She could wait. She gave him a wink. "Wizard!"

They had laughed their way home and into bed, making love like two giggly adolescents without the gaucherie, before falling asleep. But it wasn't a sound sleep for him. Several times she was woken as he squirmed, shouted and twitched; his subconscious mind reliving the day. Each time, she soothed him back into peaceful slumber. He had once told her that it needed a team to put a Hurricane into the air – the pilot to fly it and the ground crew to maintain it. She was now part of that team; her job was to look after the pilot.

Another early start found them testing the medicinal effects of hot sweet tea on hangovers as Sullivan addressed them. "The good news first, gentlemen. Yesterday's final tally was nineteen confirmed plus another five 'probables' against one aircraft lost and two damaged but all pilots safe. Well done, all of you!" Despite throbbing heads, they cheered raucously. "The remaining good news is for Red Section. The only replacement aircraft available are the three with VP props so they're yours. Please try not to break them!" Red Section's smug looks were met with jeers and catcalls. "The bad news is that out of the Battles sent over Luxembourg yesterday, over a third were lost, virtually all to flak. They went in low because they had no escort."

All joviality ceased. "That's not our fault," protested 'Foggy', "we went where we were told, for a rendezvous, not a close escort."

"Quite so," replied Sullivan, "Meanwhile, it seems the German advance continues, they're into Belgium now, so today we shall provide the Battles with close escort."

"ETA ten minutes." As always Sullivan sounds assured and in control. George contemplates what it will be like to be a Squadron Leader – carrying the responsibility for a dozen or so other lives as well as one's own. That he might not last long enough to find out doesn't occur to him today – sleep has seemingly smoothed the dent from his armour. They are flying north-west, heading for Villeneuve, to re-fuel and pick up their charges. A layer of fluffy white cloud obscures most of the ground but not so that they can't spot landmarks now and again. George is Red Four again, sharing 'Tail End Charlie' duty with 'Litmus'. Blue Section are back at St Jean this time. To his right, well spaced out, are 'B' Flight; on this occasion Green Section plus Giles and Evans, also employing two weavers. "Four of us ought to spot something – the notion is hardly formed before it is vindicated."

Gillibrand cuts in, "109s, two o'clock high – twenty plus!" All eyes turn towards the threat; three *Staffels* of 109s – with the advantage of height.

Sullivan sounds unperturbed. "We have a pressing engagement; ignore them unless they force their attentions on us."

The two formations fly a parallel course, watching each other. It is beginning to look as if the encounter will come to nothing when, without warning, the 109s peel off into a dive. "Here they come!" intones Sullivan, "turn into them." The Hurricanes start climbing towards the down-rushing 109s, trading fire with their attackers. Somehow, the two formations slice through each other without loss and then turn back to clash again. A melee ensues. George takes a quick burst at a passing 109; pieces fly off and then it is gone. A glance behind shows one attempting to get on his tail. He rolls into a tight turn and holds it. The gap between them begins to grow and the German sheers off in search of easier pickings. George sees a Hurricane with two 109s closing in on it. He recognises Underhill's markings. "Break left Brian, now!" At the same time he fires a burst at the second aircraft. It rolls away streaming glycol. The leader, deprived of his wingman and facing the same fate, breaks off. George sees another 109 trying to slip in behind him. Again he rolls into a turn and holds it. His opponent follows.

Round and round they go but George is increasing the gap. The German must be a novice because he should have broken away by now. As they circle, a cry comes over the R/T; the desperate voice sounds like Hewartson's. "Help someone! I've two on my tail." George is caught in his own personal battle. The physical effort of holding the turn is tiring but he is now chasing the German. As he begins to close on the 109, he sees a white face looking back at him from the cockpit. He allows deflection and fires a long burst. The 109 flies into the stream of tracer and flames erupt from the engine. The canopy flies off and the pilot leaps out, tumbling over and over. No sign of a parachute opening. George suppresses a shudder as the man disappears from view. He catches a glimpse of a Hurricane spinning down but he has no time to watch as another 109 comes diving out of nowhere. He rolls inside it and, on an impulse, dives in pursuit, firing an ineffectual burst after it. The Messerschmitt is pulling away from him as he follows it, throttle wide open. His whole aeroplane vibrates, the engine screaming in protest as the airspeed indicator moves above 400mph, continuing to rise as the altimeter unwinds apace. Sudden pressure change produces sharp pains in his ears. Ice is forming on the inside of the windscreen; the result of condensation, caused by the rapid descent, freezing on the cold glass. He scrubs furiously at it, struggling to keep the 109 in view. It begins to pull out of its dive. Suddenly, its wings fold, leaving it to spear into the earth. Instantly George throttles back, looking to ease out of his dive but the ground is still rushing towards him. Air noise is reaching a crescendo. The controls are massively heavy; he needs both hands and all his strength to pull the stick back. He daren't use elevator trim in case it over-stresses the airframe. Gradually, then more positively, the nose rises. G-force crushes him into his seat as he finally bottoms out and begins climbing again. A glance at the altimeter shows four hundred feet, probably less allowing for lag. A few seconds more and he would have joined his adversary, whose final resting place is marked by a column of smoke. As George gives a silent prayer of thanks for the Hawker Aircraft Company, the R/T comes to life. "All Shuttlecock aircraft; head independently for Villeneuve." The transmission is not strong. The squadron is obviously well spread. It takes a full minute of map reading to determine his whereabouts before setting course.

George was the eighth to land. As soon as he finished taxiing, aircraftsmen began swarming over the wings, unscrewing the panels covering the ammunition bays. "Thought you'd had it, boyo," said Evans by way of a greeting, "saw you going down like the clappers!"

"Chasing a Jerry. And guess what? When he tried to pull out of his dive the wings folded up. 109s may be faster but they're not a strong as a Hurricane."

"You won't pull the wings off a Hurri – it's built like a brick-outhouse."

"What's happened to the other two?" asked George.

He spoke quietly, "Hew-ie's bought it; he had two of the sods on his tail. I managed to remove one but the other got him. I saw him go in. I don't know about Giles."

Giles! Not him, surely? George wanted to say something but, at that moment, the words wouldn't come. "What's happening now?" he asked eventually.

"The Battles left before we got here – AHQ brought the mission forward – the Old Man's hopping blood-y mad. By the time we've been refuelled and re-armed they'll be back, so the whole show has been for no-thing."

The Hurricanes had been standing ready for an hour. The Adjutant of the Battle squadron approached Sullivan. He sounded weary. "They won't be coming now - they're past their endurance so whatever's happened they'll be on the deck somewhere. They were the last of the squadron."

"What about those?" Sullivan pointed to a handful of aircraft at the far side of the airfield.

"Full of holes – the result of a strafing attack yesterday – it'll be a while before they fly again, if at all. I suppose they'll re-muster the surviving crews," he tried to sound brisk. "In the meantime, I have a message for you from AHQ. You're to spend tonight with our near neighbours." He pointed to an airfield on the map in his hand, "there's a big show planned for tomorrow and they want you on hand."

"At least they won't be able to leave without us. God alone knows why AHQ sent your chaps off unescorted."

"Ours not to reason why…" his voice faltering, the Adjutant turned away.

"How are we supposed to deal with that lot?" Even through the impersonal medium of the R/T 'Foggy's' awe is apparent.

"I can only suggest the Micawber principle," replies Stewart. "Attack the bombers and hope something turns up. Go for the leaders. Tallyho!"

The three Hurricanes roll into a dive, heading for the leading vics of the twenty plus Heinkels, ignoring a similar number of Me110s sitting three thousand feet above them. Blue Section have the advantage of height and, for their first pass, surprise, but little else. The raid is a re-run of the previous evening except that tonight there are more German aircraft and no prospect of the rest of 686 coming to the rescue. Stewart fires at the leader of the middle vic. He sees his tracers strike home. The bomber drops out of formation and begins turning away, jettisoning its bombs, black smoke billowing. To its right a Heinkel continues doggedly on despite a trail of coolant from one engine. Momentarily, the third seems untouched – until its nose drops and it plunges earthwards. A couple of nervous pilots have also jettisoned their bombs but the formation maintains its heading. The Hurricanes flash underneath the bombers then begin climbing. Stewart knows that they have done the easy part. If they are to defend the airfield, they have to keep attacking the bombers, and now the escort will be ready for them. He doesn't hesitate despite the likely consequences. "Go for the bombers again – ignore the fighters until you have no alternative. Tallyho!" The Hurricanes' climb has taken them into a loop. Now they roll off the top and dive for the bomber formation. Above them, nine fighters are already diving. "Buster," calls Stewart, "let's hit the bombers before the 110s hit us!" He tries to put them from his mind momentarily as he concentrates on the Heinkel that is growing in his sights – the one which is suddenly dropping its bombs and veering to the right.

"Something *has* turned up – look, the French are here!" shouts Reg triumphantly. Out of the south-west a mixed force of Dewoitines and Morane-

Saulniers comes hurtling into the attack; the faster Dewoitines heading for the escort and the Moranes slashing into the bombers.

"The 110s, turn into them!" shouts Stewart urgently. The Hurricanes' noses rise to meet the threat. Tracers rush past his cockpit then two giant shapes flash past either side of him. An explosion to the left rocks his aircraft. There is a ball of fire where a Hurricane should be.

"Reg!" 'Foggy's' call is followed by silence.

Stewart looks about. The 110s which dived on them have kept on going and are now heading homewards. The Heinkels, reduced in numbers, are also in retreat with the Moranes still snapping at them. Above, the remaining 110s are in two defensive circles, trying to edge eastwards, with the Dewoitines buzzing around them like angry hornets. As he watches, a blazing Messerschmitt detaches itself from one circle and plunges headlong, on its way to join the other wrecks scattered beneath them. Reg's death hasn't really registered yet.

"We've done enough, let's go home."

When Stewart reaches him 'Foggy' is standing by his aircraft, drawing moodily at a cigarette. He is shaking with suppressed emotion but his voice is controlled, matter-of-fact, "Gone-just like that."

"I know you've been friends a while. I'm sorry." Stewart inwardly curses the inadequacy of his words.

"Since *ab initio* training. Best friend a man could ask for." He takes a couple more drags before reaching a decision. "I need a drink!" He discards his cigarette and strides away across the grass.

George feels tired and irritable. The third day in a row of being up at four and he hasn't slept well either. Service beds don't compare with the School House. He has missed Justine too. Besides her more obvious attractions, he has grown to enjoy the companionship of sharing a bed; sometimes lying with his hand on her stomach, feeling for signs of their developing infant. He knows the feeling is mutual; she hadn't been able to keep the disappointment from her voice last night when he had finally managed to get through on the telephone.

He glances down on the Battle formation as it ploughs steadfastly on. Reduced to eight aircraft, 686 are providing top-cover in two groups of four, *Schwarm-style*, weaving steadily to keep in touch, constantly sweeping the sky for signs of the enemy. Between them and the Battles, is another squadron of Hurricanes. Unlike 686, their aircraft are arranged in four tight vics of three; fresh from England and wet behind the ears. He still can't believe that Giles has gone, or that no one knows what happened to him. They are over Belgium now, probably no more than ten minutes to run – and then what?

Out to the left and first to see around the intervening bank of cloud, George gets a grandstand view of the target – a three span bridge, now only a couple of miles away. He can see vehicles crossing it, east to west – obviously a German convoy. There are no signs of fighting – the front line must already be several miles to the west. He glances up – bloody hell! – there are fifty or sixty 109s, maybe more, circling or flying back and forth in order to maintain position over the

146

bridge, in layers reaching several thousand feet above 686. "Shuttlecock leader, bandits two o'clock high!"

"Roger, Red Four. Maintain present heading, Shuttlecock aircraft. We're here to provide an escort." Below, in vics of three, the Battles are starting to draw ahead; planning to run in obliquely at two thousand feet then dive bomb the bridge. "Standby, any second now the 109s will be down like a ton of bricks."

Steadily, the Battles move closer; the Hurricanes shadowing them, waiting for the assault from above... Which doesn't come. 'Roy's' voice cuts in, baffled. "Why aren't they attacking?"

The Battles are a mile from their target when his question is answered. From all around the bridge, a storm of anti-aircraft fire erupts, black shell-bursts staining the sky, so numerous that it looks feasible to step out of the aircraft and walk on them. Within seconds, the first six are shot out of the sky; some exploding with a vivid flash, others falling to earth trailing smoke and flame; only two parachutes appear, from a possible eighteen. As the first two vics are being decimated, the third and fourth take their aircraft into a dive. Soon they are at three hundred feet, going flat out for the bridge. Isolated in their cockpits the Hurricane pilots roar their encouragement. The 109s hold position. It seems everyone is focused on the drama being played out below. For a few precious seconds, the Battles have caught the flak-gunners on the hop but then, one by one, the guns are brought to bear again. One aircraft disappears in a ball of flame, a second, engine destroyed, slides out of formation, gliding towards the fields below; a third rolls onto its side, streaming thick black smoke. A body falls clear but, too low, hits the ground with parachute only half-deployed. The aircraft crashes and explodes. A quarter of a mile – four and one-half seconds to go; three left. Another explodes in midair. The fifth, riddled, rears like a stricken horse, stalls then plunges into the ground. Hit countless times, the leader remains miraculously airborne, trailing fire like a comet. It seems as if the storm of metal has deflected it from its target when, with unmistakeable deliberateness, it banks towards the bridge, then dives straight into the centre span. A column of flame shoots skywards as high explosive and aviation fuel detonate.

"Jesus-fucking-Christ," The words are delivered quietly, undemonstratively; profane yet reverent; spoken on behalf of them all. Someone, perhaps 'Shorty', has unintentionally broadcast his thoughts. George isn't bothered who. He is holding back tears of impotent rage and fighting the impulse to dive down and try to blast each and every bloody flak gunner into oblivion; deep down he knows it would be a foolish gesture, doomed to failure, which would only devalue the sacrifice he has witnessed. As the smoke and debris begin to clear, he can see the gap in the bridge. The Germans should be delayed for some time but, when he glances at it, the interrupted convoy is starting to drive along the side of the river, presumably in search of another crossing further up. He feels vaguely sick. Has all this been for nothing?

Even Sullivan sounds subdued. "Shuttlecock aircraft, there's nothing to hang around for. Head for home before that lot change their mind and descend on us."

The other Hurricane squadron begins to swing away too but, being in starboard echelon, their turn from westerly to southerly heading is a cumbersome affair; the leading aircraft slowing and the rear aircraft speeding up, like a chain of skaters. Although the mass of 109s have shown no inclination to attack, four aircraft have detached themselves unseen from the throng to stalk the British aircraft. Now they have a target of opportunity. Like the eagles they model themselves on they swoop down on the rearmost vic, whose pilots are busy trying to keep formation in the midst of a complex manoeuvre. Already over a mile away, 686 pilots see the diving 109s. Their attempts to shout a warning are in vain because the other squadron is using a different radio frequency. Within seconds, three Hurricanes are falling to earth. The victors make good their escape, letting the speed of their dive take them away from the remainder of the formation. The perfect 'bounce'.

"Hellfire!" shouts 'Roy' in disgust, "if that doesn't put the bloody tin hat on it!"

Sullivan is talking with Richard. Next door, the pilots are giving 'Einstein' their reports. The celebratory air of the last two days is absent. "It's important to get them into the air and fighting again – a chance to even the score. In the last twenty-four hours, we've not only lost three good men but had to sit helplessly and watch a dozen Battles and three Hurricanes being shot out of the sky. I actually want the Germans to attack the airfield again this evening!"

"I meant to tell you, sir. Signal from AHQ; while we're earmarked for escort duty we're not to go chasing Germans, even over our own airfield."

Sullivan snorted. "What hare-brained bloody idiot dreamed that one up? Are we supposed to sit in slit trenches and watch the Germans bomb our aircraft to bloody scrap? If anyone asks, you haven't had the chance to bring it to my attention; for the next hour or so, I'll be with the squadron, patrolling over the airfield!"

Sullivan's wish is granted. "Bandits – eight o'clock low – heading for the field!" 'Roy's' sharp eyes are the first to spot the intruders; six Dorniers in two vics of three, no more than a thousand feet above the ground, taking a south-westerly course to avoid the lowering sun, looking to achieve surprise. It is they who will be surprised as Sullivan wastes no time. A final scan of the sky reveals no sign of an escort. "Red Section stay with me. The rest of you – Tallyho! The drinks are on me tonight if none get through!" The six Hurricanes dive steeply. Their angle of attack and the low altitude of the enemy give them time for one burst before they must pull out of their dive. The task is demanding but 686 have become good at what they do. Three Dorniers fall to their guns, ploughing into the ground and exploding almost in formation. The survivors, their force shredded, and unnerved by the virtually head-on attack, turn for home. Sullivan speaks again. "Tallyho Red Section. Mop up the rest!" The remaining four Hurricanes follow their predecessors down. Sullivan, in the lead, catches the nearest aircraft, despatching it with a raking burst that shatters both engines. Underhill and 'Roy' hit the next in quick succession, sending it plummeting earthwards. George is pursuing the third, looking to get it in his sights when it explodes. Three of the first six Hurricanes swoop across in front of him. He thumbs his R/T.

"Queue-jumping bastards – I had him cold!"

'Shorty' replies. "Get your finger out then! You've got to be quick in this game- mine's a pint please, sir!"

148

In the Mess, the earlier gloom had been replaced by lively banter, vying with a 'hot' number on the gramophone. Richard made himself heard against it. "Well done, sir! They're back on form – though it'll cost you a pretty penny."

"And well worth it. A good ending to a lousy day. Some recompense too – for the Battles and the Hurricanes. Obsolete aircraft and inadequate tactics. It's criminal that we are so unprepared. I still find it hard to believe it's been allowed to happen."

'Einstein' spoke, "We're a peaceful democracy and peaceful democracies never do anything until the enemy is at the gate; 'Let him who desires peace prepare for war'."

"I've heard that before; remind me who said it?"

"Vegetius, sir; a Roman general…"

He was interrupted by a joyous roar, taken up by more voices as the reason became apparent. In the doorway, dusty and dishevelled, but very much alive, stood Giles. "You took your time!" drawled 'Foggy', "presumably you reach us via every bar in Northern France!"

"On the contrary – though, I could certainly use a drink," replied Giles. "I think I've been witnessing the end of civilisation," he added bitterly.

They waited while he drained a tankard, an appreciative look appearing on his face.

"Well go on!" prompted George.

"When the Jerries attacked, I found myself surrounded by three of the bastards – all using me for target practice – so I spun down to escape and nearly bought it because I didn't know that they'd shot half my rudder away; by the time I regained control, I was at nought feet. The engine was shot-up too so I pancaked. I was setting the old girl on fire when a squad of Frogs turned up and took me to HQ for a brandy and some transport. It was looking like 'home for tea' but then the nightmare began. The roads were chocker with refugees – from Luxembourg and Belgium I suppose – so progress was extremely slow. Then the Luftwaffe showed up."

"The radio said that Hitler has ordered them to harass refugees," Ventured 'Roy'.

A rare flash of anger entered Giles' eyes. "This wasn't harassment, whatever that might mean, it was cold-blooded bloody murder. They just bombed and strafed the lot – old people, women, children!"

"It might have been a mistake – maybe they thought it was a military convoy?"

Giles answered George with the kind of exasperation reserved by those who know the reality for those who, though ignorant of the facts, persist in airing their opinion. "Once, perhaps – but four times in a day and a half? No bloody chance! There may be strategic logic in using refugees to obstruct military movement but it's beyond the pale." He was becoming more agitated. "Forget all the guff about knights of the air – they're Nazi scum! I just want to catch the buggers doing it!"

Sullivan had heard enough. "You're not the only one, but now is not the time. How much sleep have you had in the last two days?"

"None, sir."

"After what you've been through you need a rest. Ask the MO for a pill – you're relieved of duty for twenty-four hours as of now. And Frobisher – good show!"

149

"Message from AHQ, sir – no Battle ops scheduled for today."

Sullivan turned from studying the map. "Either there is none left or they're saving them for something worthwhile. So where does that leave us?"

"Thirty minute readiness – sounds as though we're reverting to patrols."

"Good – it's depressing watching Battle crews being thrown to the lions. Only three days and it seems like forever. Is this how it was in your day?"

"Pretty much, sir," Richard replied, "although you have packed a lot into those three days. As I think you realised last night, the biggest enemy is fatigue. The bravest and the best will wilt without some respite. I saw plenty of good men pushed beyond their limit in the last lot, to the point where they couldn't take any more and were treated as cowards or they just became tired and careless and paid the price. This time around, I pray to God that the issue is better understood."

"You're right. Any more days like the last three and I intend to start resting people. If we can do it without compromising operations it ought to be two per day. Perhaps you will draw up a roster. Have a word with the MO – see if he thinks anyone should be given priority."

"Are there any other matters?" The daily meeting at *Luftflotte* HQ was nearing its end. The results of bombing operations in the previous day had been assessed and requirements for the coming day identified. A figure at the table stood up. *"Yes, Major Brandt?"*

"Herr General, I wish to mention the matter of St Jean-sur-Moselle."

The *General* briefly scanned the memorandum in front of him. *"The place identified by our British spy as the site of a secret project. What do you wish to say?"*

"Over the last three days a variety of attacks have been attempted; on the tenth-twelve escorted bombers, on the eleventh, twice that number, again escorted and yesterday an unescorted hit and run raid by six bombers. The first two raids were turned away with losses by strong formations of British and French fighters and the third was wiped out completely." A murmur ran round the table before he continued, *"So far we have not managed to drop a single bomb on St Jean. The strength of the resistance we are encountering suggests that our information must be correct."*

"Why is there no flak if the target is so important?" another officer interjected.

The *General* answered, *"If I understand matters correctly, our aircraft have not got close enough to determine whether there are flak defences or not. So Herr Major, what is your point?"*

"I believe a large raid is required. Eighty to a hundred bombers and a similar number of escorts to overwhelm the defences and destroy the target at a stroke."

The *General* considered the matter for a few moments. *"I accept your conclusions, Herr Major. However, for the next few days, priority has to be given to operations over Belgium and the Sedan area so nothing can be done immediately; but do not fret. If this mysterious project has already reached fruition, I am sure we would know about it by now!"* As laughter rippled through the assembled officers, he turned to a man on his right. *"Willi, how soon can we spare the Major his hundred bombers?"*

"It should be possible by the seventeenth, Herr General."

"The seventeenth it is. Herr Major, I will leave it to you and the Herr Oberst to organise things. In the meantime, I suggest that no further raids take place – let them think they have discouraged us. Now meinherren, I think I smell breakfast."

George woke with a start. He tensed, ready to leap up and run for his aircraft, and then realised that those around him were unperturbed. He must have dozed off under the warm sun – he didn't need much encouragement. Another night had provided little more than four hours sleep. He felt dog-tired and quietly envied Giles his twenty-four hour pill. Lack of sleep and long hours in the cockpit were taking a toll on all of them. Despite last evening's morale-boost, he could see the difference in the others. Some were quieter than usual, others a touch irritable where they would normally have joshed; at the moment a couple of beers seemed to be a restorative – but for how much longer? He looked at his watch – nearly noon. Surely they should have been airborne by now? In answer he heard Sullivan on the telephone and realised what had awoken him. "Just ringing to check the line hasn't been cut. Or have the Germans sued for peace? If not then for Christ's sake give us something to do!"

'Obviously not talking to one of the brass,' thought George.

Whomever he had been talking to, he had made an impact – within an hour ten Hurricanes in two vics of five were heading north-west. He had decided this time not to leave a section guarding the airfield; the last few days had shown that but for timely intervention three aircraft would have been overwhelmed. Better the airfield bombed than three good men thrown to the wolves.

Their orders had been slightly vague – patrol north of a line Laon-Rethel. A Flight Sergeant at Vassincourt seemed more informative as they refuelled. "Jerry's bombing everything that moves north of here. I was in the trenches in the last lot – whenever there was a major attack there was a barrage first – so I reckon that's what they're working up to!"

They have just reached the patrol line when they spot activity to the north – specks rising and falling, punctuated by the flashes of explosions. "Looks like Jerry – let's investigate."

In a short time they have closed the gap enough to see the situation. To their right, a French convoy is under attack from dive-bombers; columns of smoke twirl skywards from burning lorries. To the left the road is clear but, instead of immediately climbing away from their attacks, each Stuka is staying low and strafing the huddle of humanity which has scattered into the ditches and fields. "Giles was right!" shouts George, "The bastards are shooting up refugees – let's get them!"

"Sort them out 'B' Flight. 'A' Flight follow me – there's a gaggle of Me110s above that need our attention." George recognises the veiled rebuke from Sullivan and feels foolish. He has allowed his concern for the refugees to take over, abandoning the basics and failing to look for the escort which common sense said there would be.

As 'A' Flight move to meet the 110s, Stewart homes in on a Ju87. He is about to fire when it drops into a dive, leaving him standing. Unperturbed, he throttles back and follows it down, knowing it will have to pull out at some point. He is again ready to fire when he realises that any bullets that miss will hit the people below. Cursing, he pulls away but he has the solution immediately. Shadowing the Stuka, he loses height until he is below it, closes in and begins firing. At first nothing, then, with a vivid flash, the aircraft disintegrates. He speaks crisply into the R/T. "Take them from below – it's a piece of cake and no risk of hitting refugees!"

The Hurricanes' reputation seems to have preceded them. Instead of protecting their charges, the 110s form a defensive circle to meet the threat from the numerically inferior 'A' Flight climbing after them. "Red Four and Five, break off and get above them while we keep them occupied," orders Sullivan, "attack when ready, Tallyho!" George and 'Litmus' apply boost and climb to one side of the 110s whilst the rest of 'A' Flight force them to continue circling. From two thousand feet above, George can see his comrades, like wolves attacking a flock; darting in, firing a quick burst and pulling away. Two 110s are streaming smoke but all are still flying. Far beneath, he sees a flash as a stricken Stuka hits the ground. "Red Four and Five attacking." Pointing the nose of his Hurricane at a 110, he opens the throttle. Beside him, 'Litmus' does the same. The two Hurricanes surge downwards. At four hundred yards, George fires a two second burst then dives through the circle. He glimpses his 110 rolling onto its back belching smoke and flame. To his left 'Litmus's' target shares a similar fate. Unnerved by this, the 110s break for home, trusting in their diving speed to outstrip the Hurricanes. Their own dives have left George and 'Litmus' best placed to pursue. "Permission to chase the stragglers, sir?" George calls over the R/T, applying boost in anticipation.

"Only as far as the border, and that's an order!" responds Sullivan.

George and 'Litmus' are only gaining slowly despite the streams of coolant trailing behind the 110s. The sun highlights a strip of water ahead. "The M-meuse," says 'Litmus', "that's the b-border."

"A few seconds m... Hell fire!" A storm of flak bursts suddenly erupts between pursuers and pursued. George and 'Litmus' wrench their machines into tight turns, holding their breath and praying, temporarily blind, while pieces of shrapnel rattle against fuselages and wings. As quickly as it started, the storm of metal ceases. Gingerly they check gauges and controls – no obvious damage. They circle for a moment, breathing heavily, taking stock. The 110s are well away. "Look! The Germans are across the river in force! Where are we?"

"N-near Sedan, I think."

"We must report this. Let's get back!"

Sullivan was there as they climbed from their aircraft. "Anything to add to three Ju87s and two 110s?"

"No sir, we were stopped by flak."

"I said not to cross the bloody border."

"We didn't – the Germans have crossed the Meuse though – at Sedan – there must have been a regiment of flak, not to mention tanks and troops!"

"Bloody hell! I'd better speak to AHQ."

He returned twenty minutes later. "Apparently the French are aware of – I quote – 'a small number of troops who have crossed the river and are now surrounded'."

"They didn't look small or surrounded to us, sir!"

"I'm sure you're right but all we can do is hope they sort it out." He led him away from the others. "In the meantime, what happened earlier? Missing those 110s is not like you."

"It was the refugees being strafed, sir; I let it rattle me."

"War's a dirty business – you'll see many things like that; and need to take them in your stride. You'll be a Section Leader soon and men's lives will depend on your decisions – you can't let emotion distract you from your responsibilities."

"Yes, sir, sorry, sir."

"No need to apologise – just learn from it. Right! Let's get those of us that remain back to St Jean and catch Jerry red-handed on his nightly foray."

"Has something happened?"

"Of course – you won't know. Evans' aircraft must have stopped a Jerry bullet. Tyre burst on landing and they've carted him off to hospital. He'll be out for a few days – broken nose and concussion."

The flight back gave George time to reflect. Two things remained uppermost in his mind when he landed; firstly, he gave recognition to a feeling that he had been trying to suppress since the attack on the bridge – 686 were winning battles but the Germans were winning the war; secondly, he had to speak to Justine and Mamam.

They patrolled for over an hour without a sign of the enemy. It was gone seven when they landed to be stood down. "Jerry's either got bigger fish to fry or he's tired of having his nose bloodied!" Sullivan said with satisfaction as he dismissed them.

George excused himself and headed for the School House. Justine and Mamam were in the kitchen when he returned. "I want you – both of you – to take a few things and go to Normandy – to Tante Lys."

"Why, what is wrong?" asked Mamam.

"You mustn't talk about it outside this house but the Germans have crossed the Meuse in force – at Sedan – I have seen it myself."

"But Sedan is two hundred kilometres away – our armies will stop them."

"They should have stopped them crossing the river. My fear is that they will attack the Maginot Line from the rear – which means that they will come this way. If they can neutralise the Maginot line all France lies open to them." Mamam fell silent. She needed no reminding of the occupation of Lorraine in the last war.

Justine took up the conversation. "I can leave neither the children nor you!"

"If the Germans come this way, the children will be leaving you – as refugees – like the poor souls streaming out of Belgium and Luxembourg; and I will be moved south so you'll be left here on your own – you must go to Normandy. I'll find you a car."

"Neither of us can drive," Justine reminded him.

"Use your bicycles then. You mustn't stop here. And if anything happens to me you must go anyway. If I am only injured, I will be looked after and if not…"

She didn't want to pursue that line of thought. "How long will it take the Germans to get here, if they come this way?"

"Several days I would imagine."

"And you will see if they are coming?"

"Yes."

"Then we will go when we know for certain that they are heading this way. In fact we won't go until you get the order to pull back." Putting her arms around him she kissed him. "You are my husband and I'm not leaving you until there is no alternative. Do you agree Mamam?"

Mamam's face was a mixture of pride and determination. *"Oui, ma fille!"*

"I suppose I'll have to settle for that then," said George.

She kissed him again. "I suppose you will."

Like the cherished moments with their mugs of tea, Sullivan's remarks had been brief, "Vassincourt again, and we're back on escorts." Obviously something big was afoot; they had been roused at three-thirty instead of four. They also knew they were dog-tired, but they had no choice in the matter. He had provided a crumb of comfort. "I know you've had a hard time of it. From tomorrow, I'm going to start resting people." They took-off in the pre-dawn twilight, heading north; weariness numbing their appreciation of the splendours of the sunrise. He addressed them at greater length at Vassincourt as a rapid refuelling took place. "The Germans have crossed the Meuse and today the Battles have the job of destroying pontoon bridges that have been springing up. In a few minutes, we will be going to cover an attack near Douzy. We rendezvous south-west of the target and shepherd them in and out. They've had a rough time so far, as you know, so give short shrift to any fighters that stick their noses in!"

'Things are looking up,' muses George, 'we've found them before the Jerries.' He scans the skies anxiously; no sign of any fighters so far. Below him the first Battle peels off into a dive. Puffs of flak begin staining the sky without troubling the diving aircraft. He watches as it releases its bombs and pulls away. A brief glow and an eddying in the mist show they have detonated. One after another the remaining five follow suit, unscathed except for one unlucky one, caught by the haphazard flak, which manages to force land in French territory. The Hurricanes stay with the Battles long enough to clear the area and be satisfied that there are no German fighters around. "Job done!" announces Sullivan, "now for breakfast!"

"I think we've found the answer," said a refreshed Giles, between mouthfuls of sandwich, "attack at first light – the Jerry pilots are still abed and the ground mist spoils the flak merchants' aim!"

"Did the Battles manage to hit anything through the mist though?" queried 'Foggy'.

"We'll know soon enough," said Underhill, "because if they didn't, we'll have it all to do again!"

It was nearly lunch-time when the telephone rang next but this time there had been no champing at the bit; they had been glad to seize the chance to catch up on sleep; whether sprawled on the grass, under the wing of an aircraft or in a couple of chairs which had been conjured from somewhere. An LAC jotted down a message and handed it to Sullivan. "Mouzon this time – the attack is timed for one o'clock." He glanced at his map. "We're going to struggle to manage this one – why the hell didn't they ring sooner? Look lively you chaps!"

They had flown all the way on full throttle. At two minutes to one, Underhill breaks the silence: "Battles – eleven o'clock low." Eyes that had been searching all over the sky focus on the four approaching Battles – except for one pair.

"B-bogeys, eight o'clock high. S-seven of them!"

All eyes concentrate on the new focus. "It's OK, they're Moranes," says George.

"Are you sure?" calls 'Shorty' "because they're heading straight for the Battles."

"They're definitely Moranes," responds Sullivan, "but what in blazes are they doing?"

"They're bloody well attacking them!" 'Shorty' shouts, "For God's sake, No!" 686 are too far away to do anything except watch in disbelief as the Moranes swoop. In a single pass, three Battles are downed and the fourth is left to make a forced landing. Sullivan is incandescent. "I'll have someone's bloody hide for this; no wonder there are no Jerries around, the bloody French are doing their job for them!" They returned to Vassincourt in sombre silence, each alone with his thoughts.

Sullivan grabbed the dispersal phone and the rest of them gathered round. "... that's right sir, Moranes... yes, definitely, sir, we all saw them... absolutely certain, sir... unlike some, we know our aircraft recognition... No sir. Understood, sir. One other thing sir, if we'd been sent off in time, we'd have been with the Battles and probably able to prevent this shambles. Yes, sir." He put the phone down. "They're looking into it. In the meantime, we're not to discuss it with anyone else. Let me say this though; any hint of a repeat performance and we'll shoot the bastards down and worry about the niceties afterwards!"

"It doesn't make sense," said George, "Battles don't remotely resemble anything the Jerries have."

"Panic!" said Underhill emphatically. "The German advances have unnerved them and they're acting like headless chickens."

"So where does that leave us?"

"As the Old Man says, any sign of trouble, shoot first and ask questions afterwards!"

"Hardly ideal!"

"Have you a better solution?"

Sullivan appeared among them. "Right, we're off again. This is the big one – just about all the Battles we can muster, I gather. Sedan this time. Expect to see some more Hurricanes and no doubt a load of Huns!"

George flinches at the hammering sound from somewhere behind him. He yanks his aircraft into a tight turn and twists his neck round to see a yellow spinner and the muzzle flash of cannon and machine guns close behind – far too close – but the noise has stopped. The German is still there, trying to get his sights back on the Hurricane but George knows that provided he keeps the turn tight, that will not be possible. It is taking time – this chap is good; not good enough though and gradually George is pulling away. Any moment now, yes – there he goes, off to try his luck elsewhere or out of ammo perhaps. He had fired off a fair amount, although the word is that 109s carry more than the Hurricane's miserly fifteen seconds worth. George scans rapidly – nothing else behind or underneath. Nothing immediately in front either; his private battle has carried him from the main event which is now some two or three miles away and, judging by the flak bursts, still ongoing. He points the Hurricane towards it and opens the throttle.

They had managed to rendezvous with the Battles and the other Hurricane squadron – but that was as good as it got. Approaching the target, they had found themselves confronted by an advance guard of well over sixty 109s. Thirty or forty had dived on the Hurricanes who had had no choice but to defend themselves leaving the Battles to the mercy of the remainder. It was a classic melee, a hundred or so aircraft whirling around in a small area; as much danger of collision as of being shot down; twisting, turning, diving; as soon as George managed to draw a bead on one aircraft another would be on his tail and he had had to break off; chasing or being chased until jumped by the 109 with the yellow spinner. He had glimpsed several Battles falling from the sky and at least one Hurricane too but there had been nothing he could do.

Now, there are burning wrecks scattered across the fields, being added to as flak continues taking its toll of those Battles that have evaded the 109s, and no evidence of successful bombing – the two pontoons across the river seem untouched. Suddenly a Hurricane crosses below him, wallowing and trailing smoke, shadowed by two 109s; intent on their prey and oblivious to George. As he dives towards them, he recognises the squadron letters on the Hurricane. "Shorty, two bandits on your tail, break, break, break!" The reply is slurred and unintelligible. The Hurricane begins to roll to the right but too slowly and too late. George and the leading German fire simultaneously; both hit their target. The 109 explodes, causing its number two to sheer off but the Hurricane is now diving steeply with flames trailing behind it. "Shorty, get out man, SHORTY, BALE OUT!" There is no response. Sick at heart, he watches the falling aircraft until it buries itself in a field. He circles for a moment, checking the sky and marshalling his thoughts. Two deaths in a matter of seconds and a lot more in the last ten minutes but for some reason, he is still alive. His remaining ammunition has been used on the German. With a last rueful glance at 'Shorty's' wreckage, he sets course for Vassincourt.

"And then there were six," intoned 'Roy' morosely into his glass.

"Eight, if you count F/L Stewart and 'Foggy'," responded Giles, "just scratches and bruises so the M/O has packed them off to bed but they'll be fit again by Thursday or Friday."

"I actually meant Hurricanes," replied 'Roy', "they seem to be going west quicker than we are."

"In that case deduct the Old Man's kite. It stopped a few bullets in important places so there will only be five tomorrow. At least Hurricanes are easier to replace. I hear we'll have some more any day now."

"Believe it when it happens. Anyway, will we be here to receive them? I heard a rumour before we flew back from Vassincourt that the whole AASF will be withdrawn to the south."

"Well keep it to yourself unless it becomes official. It's the kind of thing that causes alarm and despondency. Think of George. Moving south would mean leaving his wife behind. No point worrying him unnecessarily."

"Speaking of which, where is he?"

"Gone home to aforementioned wife."

"Lucky sod!"

"Maybe, maybe not. The odds against us seem to be increasing every day so it's hard enough flying and fighting without having to worry about nearest and dearest."

"I'll bet he isn't worrying as we speak!" said 'Roy' with a wink.

"We lost four aircraft and no sign of the Germans being forced back, but at least they don't seem to be heading this way yet," said George sitting down wearily. "'Foggy' and Alistair Stewart will be OK but 'Shorty' and Gillibrand have bought it. The trouble is that there are more and more Germans and fewer and fewer of us."

Justine shared his regret. She had met 'Shorty' a few times. Like most of George's squadron friends, she found him an engaging young man, full of fun and vitality. Gillibrand, quieter, probably just shy, she didn't really know; and it was too late now. She had started making a cup of tea. Having learned of 'the cup that cheers' – that most British of panaceas – during her time in England, she knew as soon as George walked in that it was what he needed now. "I'm sorry..." she began then stopped short. There was no point continuing with her reply or the tea – he was fast asleep.

In the silence, her fears and doubts began to crowd in. How long could he go on like this? He had been fighting non-stop for almost a week now. He was clearly exhausted and needing respite. And what of the bigger picture – what had gone wrong? It was from George that she knew the Germans had crossed the Meuse. All she could get from Mamam's radio were bland bulletins and appeals for calm. Why ask for calm unless there was reason to panic? George was right – she and Mamam, and her unborn child, should go to Normandy – her first loyalty should be to her husband and family, and yet the prospect of leaving her children filled her with dismay. She glanced at George – still sound asleep. Reassured she would not be burdening him with her fears she let the tears flow.

Wednesday, May 15th, George had seen the date, next in line for a pencil cross, on the calendar in the dispersal hut. He must have noticed the dates on other days too but apart from the tenth when the balloon had gone up, they hadn't made any impression. Today had been different because a memory from another life told him that it was his brother's birthday. Edwin was fifteen today. He recalled hoping the war would be over before Edwin was old enough to be drawn into it; and then it had been off to Vassincourt again – just five of them; Underhill, 'Roy', Giles, 'Litmus' and he. Despite his tiredness, he had set off in a buoyant mood; with F/L Stewart and 'Foggy' due to return to the fray tomorrow, he would finally get some time off. The day had become a blur, with just particular moments standing out in sharp relief; the Me109 that had exploded seconds after its pilot baled out, the Dornier that collided with another as it sought to evade George's guns, the relief that George felt as 'Litmus's' parachute had finally opened after he had fallen what must have been ten thousand feet. Some divine providence had kept the Germans off his tail as, unable to drag his eyes away and ignoring all the rules of combat survival, George had followed 'Litmus's' cart-wheeling descent before the mushroom of silk had arrested his fall. With immaculate timing, Sullivan had arrived in a new Hurricane to make up the numbers again when they landed from that second sortie of the day, bringing news that the squadron had been put on readiness to remove to the Troyes area probably in the next two days. George wondered if Richard would have told Mamam yet.

Four times this day, they have taken off to intercept the packs of German aircraft which are roaming over northern France with increasing impunity, bombing roads, bridges and railway lines and harrying refugees to prevent French reinforcements from going where they are needed. As before, 686 are winning their battles; in today's four sorties they have downed at least eight Germans for the loss of 'Litmus' but it is obvious to all that they cannot indefinitely match the sheer weight of numbers. They are airborne now for the fifth time, approaching again the area around Sedan, looking for trouble; which for the first time, George does not want to find. He isn't frightened, just dog-tired. He wants to return to St Jean, make sure Justine and Mamam are preparing to leave and then to have his day of rest so that he can rejoin the fray refreshed. The day has used up his remaining energy and despite the adrenalin surge that the prospect of combat brings he feels lethargic. He is Red Five, at the left rear of the formation. In the absence of 'Litmus', Giles, four hundred yards away at Red Four, shares the 'Tail End Charlie' job.

As he looks 'through' Giles, then above and behind, George can see him reciprocating. Suddenly Giles's hand goes to his mask and his aircraft starts to roll as his urgent call comes over the R/T. "Break, break, break! Bandits seven o'clock high!" George's brain heeds the warning and instructs his hands to react but they are that fraction slower than usual – too slow; his Hurricane begins to roll but his left arm receives a kick as if from a horse. The instrument panel explodes as a storm of metal blasts into his aircraft with a din he can hear above the engine. Acrid smoke billows into the cockpit, drawn out through the shattered canopy by the slipstream. Flames will be next; through a haze something tells him it is time to bale out. He tries to disconnect his R/T lead and oxygen tube but his left arm won't work. Survival instinct overtakes the conscious thought, his right hand disconnects both; then reaches for the canopy. He is dimly aware that if the runners are damaged, he will have no chance. He tugs and it slides back easily. The aircraft is upside down now and starting to pitch downwards. Anchoring his feet to the rudder pedals, he undoes his harness and works it off his shoulders. For the first time he is aware of blood on his uniform and more dripping from his hand as his arm flops uselessly. Unhooking his feet he drops from the open cockpit. His mind is clearing now, and at the same time detached. He reasons that the quicker he gets to the ground the less blood he will lose so he allows himself to fall through space until, judging he is only about two thousand feet up, he tugs on the parachute handle. A sudden jolt and his headlong plunge ceases. Above, a canopy of white silk confirms it has deployed correctly; below, the fields, given a yellowish hue by the evening sunlight, are still coming nearer but at a less intimidating rate. He begins to feel pain in his arm and finds he can move it a bit. He clamps his right hand over it to staunch the bleeding and braces himself for impact. Unable to work the shroud lines, he cannot influence his descent. His feet hit the earth; he tumbles over and is dragged for twenty or thirty yards before he manages to hit the release button and struggle out of the harness. Vaguely aware of running men, he tries to stand, but a roaring, swirling, blackness engulfs him, as if he is being sucked down a plughole, and he slumps soundlessly back to the ground.

Justine was pacing the room. "Why have we heard nothing?"

"Patience, *ma cherie,* did you not tell me that George's friend *Gilles* took two days to get back – the roads are still choked with refugees I hear. Let us concentrate on what we have to do – the time will soon pass until you hear from him." Richard had rung the previous evening, when Red Section had returned from Vassincourt, to tell them that George had been shot down but escaped by parachute; and that was as much as he knew. By means of a couple of pre-arranged phrases, he had also imparted to Mamam, without enlightening the inevitable eavesdropper at the telephone exchange, that 686 would be moving in the next couple of days. Now Mamam was trying, in vain, to keep Justine focused on packing the few necessities they could carry on bicycles and preparing the house to be closed up for an unknown length of time.

As consciousness returned, George became aware of a dull pain in his arm, and of his head throbbing. His throat felt sore as he tried to swallow. He groaned softly. "I think he's c-coming to." The voice was familiar. His fuddled brain groped for an answer.

"About ruddy time! Come on old man, you can't sleep forever!" Another familiar voice. He opened his eyes, blinking against the sunlight streaming through the window. "Welcome to the crocks' convention!" He forced his eyes to focus on the bandaged figure in the bed opposite and a face swam into view.

"Peter! Where am I?"

"In the lucky-to-be-alive ward of Rethel Hospital. Not a ward actually; the place is chokka so they've put us non-too-serious types in an outbuilding. You know 'Litmus' – he got a knock on the head baling out and came to closer to the ground than he would have preferred – and this is LAC Osborn; my rear gunner until the Jerries shot our kite from under us, resulting in minor burns – enough to keep us out of action for a short time and a blessing in disguise from what I hear. I gather you were lucky as well – two bullets through the arm without hitting anything vital. Our guardian angels have been working overtime!"

George surreptitiously touched his mascot. "How long have I been here?"

"Twelve hours or more – it was after lights out last night when they brought you in."

"I don't recall. I must've been out for the count. Has anyone got word to Justine?"

It was early afternoon when Mamam had answered Richard's telephone call. Her relief was obvious as she replaced the receiver. "'E 'as been wounded, but not seriously – 'e is in 'ospital at Rethel."

"I must go to him!" Justine cried, and dashed upstairs to change. After nearly twenty-four hours without news, she was beside herself. In her agitation, she did not feel the silver chain around her neck snap as she tugged her dress off, or notice the bullet as it rolled under the bed. She returned in pullover and trousers, "I have to see George before we leave for Normandy."

"It is over two hundred kilometres to Rethel and the same back. Wouldn't it be better to wait until dawn tomorrow? I will come with you then and we can carry on to Normandy afterwards."

"I can travel faster on my own and without luggage. I will return by this time tomorrow and then we can leave as planned."

Mamam looked resigned. "Very well, I will wait here for you. But if you must dash off now, take this with you," she produced the Mauser pistol and some clips of ammunition, "you don't know what you might meet."

Despite the bantering of his fellow patients, fatigue and shock from being wounded had meant that George had slept for most of the day. That changed about seven o'clock when a Flight Sergeant crashed to attention at the end of Peter's bed. "Evening, F/Sgt Grey – what can I do for you?"

"Squadron Leader's compliments, sir! The order has come for withdrawal and he's sent me to remove you and LAC Osborn to Arras before the Germans get here."

"Is that where the squadron is going?"

"No, sir. What remains of the squadron is moving south but there's a base hospital at Arras. The C/O reckons there's no point you re-joining the squadron until you're properly recovered."

"I suppose that makes sense. But we can't leave these chaps behind," he gestured towards 'Litmus' and George.

"There's room for them in the car, sir."

"Good, that's settled then. Come on, George, stir your stumps – you look as though you need a breath of fresh air!"

A nurse came in as they were struggling into their clothes. She nodded sadly as Peter endeavoured to explain their sudden departure in his halting French. *"Il doit partir. Les Allemands viennent."*

George, 'Litmus' and Osborn had been settled in the back of the waiting car. Peter turned to Grey. "I assume you know the way?"

In response Grey pulled out a map. "Yes sir, we make for the Reims-Laon road and then continue north-west past Laon and St Quentin to Arras. It may take a while on account of the refugees."

"Let's get cracking then!" Peter replied, lowering himself gingerly into the passenger seat; unaware of a strangely-clad form peering round the corner of a building across the road.

"Where are the Germans?" asked Peter as they left the outskirts of Rethel behind. "Reports are sketchy, sir, but they seem to have consolidated around Sedan and are starting to push westwards. This route will keep us clear of them, though."

"I d-don't think we're l-leaving any too soon," interjected 'Litmus' from the back seat, "those look like J-jerry bombers to the north." They watched as bombs began falling from the aircraft and the muffled crump of explosions came to them above the sound of the car engine; one, considerably louder than the others and accompanied by a column of flame, seemed to come from the area they had just left. "I h-hope they missed the h-hospital." They continued down the road in silence. George had said nothing since they had left Rethel. His arm and head still ached and his mind was occupied with Justine. From the sound of it, the Germans weren't moving eastwards immediately but he was hoping that she and Mamam were now on their way to Normandy. He didn't want to be heading for Arras and away from her but he knew he had no choice; he could do nothing to help her either as a prisoner of war or as an invalid. He would try to get to Normandy as soon as he was able.

To the east, Justine was regretting her impetuosity. She hadn't covered half the distance she had expected; the farther north and west she had gone the more difficult progress had become as she encountered more and more refugees. At least there had been no air raids. It would be dark in an hour or so. She couldn't risk cycling on blacked out roads so she had only one option – to keep going until nightfall then find a place to sleep. This time of the year the nights were short; she would start again at first light and finish the journey to Rethel tomorrow.

Progress had been slow towards Laon but they had expected things to improve with darkness when most of the refugees would move off the road to rest, leaving the way clear. They had reckoned without the French army. On the Laon road, they were brought to a halt by a column crossing their route. Truck after truck thundered past, interspersed with transporters carrying huge Char B battle tanks. "That's the stuff," enthused Peter, "they'll send the Jerries packing!"

A voice called out. *"Eteindrez vos phares!"*

A French sentry appeared. "What's he saying, sir?"

"Put out the headlights. He's obviously jittery about Jerry aircraft; but they're masked." He leaned out of the window. *"Ils sont masquees!"*

By way of a reply, the sentry drove the butt of his rifle in quick succession into both headlamps. "Bloody hell – that's torn it! We're stuck here 'til dawn now."

Stiffly, Justine had mounted her bicycle and continued on her way. She had passed an uncomfortable few hours in the corner of a field, huddled under her coat with one hand on her pistol and her other arm around the frame of the bicycle to ensure no one tried to take it while she slept. At least, unlike many of the poor souls around her, she had not gone hungry. Mamam, ever reliable, had also given her a small knapsack containing bread, sausage and a bottle of water.

Morning twilight had enabled them to get under way again but their progress soon slowed to a crawl as the road became clogged once more with refugees. "Hell's teeth!" exclaimed Peter, "it's like wading against a stream in spate." He forgot his analogy as full daylight gave him his first sight of George's ashen face. "I say, you look awful!"

"I feel lousy," George shivered as he spoke, "must be reaction to being wounded."

"Well just take it easy. We should make it to Arras today – I certainly don't fancy another night in this thing!"

As the convoy rumbled away, Richard ran a hand through his hair. The last of the lorries had gone, carrying ground-crew and the squadron's spares and equipment to their new base near Troyes. Earlier, he had watched the remaining aircraft leave, to go initially to their daytime airfield at Vassincourt, probably for the last time until the war situation improves. He looked at his watch. He could give the convoy an hour's start and still overhaul them easily. Some papers to collect from his office and then time to go and say *au revoir* to Juliette and make sure that she and Justine were ready to leave for Normandy. Preparations for strategic withdrawal, or, what the words really meant – retreat, had prevented any more than hurried phone calls, to pass on the news about George, in the last forty-eight hours. He knew he might not be seeing her again for some time so he was determined to make the most of this opportunity. He was emerging from his office when he heard it – a scarcely noticeable buzz at first, growing steadily into an unmistakeable drone. Numbers and direction made identification easy. "German aircraft, take cover!" His driver climbed from the camouflaged Hillman, placing his steel helmet on his head, gas-mask case already over his shoulder. Richard reached into the car for his own 'battle bowler' and gasmask then they walked unhurriedly – he judged they had a few minutes before the enemy arrived over the airfield – to the shelter trench; sufficient against anything but a direct hit.

At the School House, Mamam, having heard the same drone and stepped outside to investigate, saw the large black swarm approaching; obviously heading for the airfield. She thought of Richard and made the unfamiliar gesture of crossing herself, then went indoors where she drew the curtains and turned the radio up.

Once more the listeners were being urged to remain calm – *tout sera bien* – all would be well.

Peter looked at his watch; his voice echoed their frustration. "Nearly ten already – how much farther to Laon?"

"Can't be far, sir. The last sign said eight kilometres and that was...!" He broke off as the sound of aircraft reached him. For a few seconds, the crowds around them were rooted, straining for identification. Then, amid shouts and screams, began a mad stampede to get off the road.

"Jerries! Everyone out!" With the throng rapidly dispersing it took only seconds to pull the car beneath the overhang of some trees and for the five of them to scramble into a ditch. For several minutes they crouched helplessly, the taste of fear in their mouths, as a group of Dorniers swept up and down the road machine-gunning indiscriminately. Eventually, the din stopped and they emerged to a scene of utter devastation. The road was strewn with personal belongings of all shapes and sizes; some dropped in the headlong flight to clear the road, others blasted from wagons, prams or handcarts by the attack. Here and there lay the bodies of those who had been too slow; mostly the elderly, but not all. A small child prodded uncomprehendingly at the still form of its mother, a dark stain sullying her flowered dress. Voices began to be raised; some in anger, others in desperation. From further down the road came a gunshot as a wounded horse was despatched.

"Bastards!" spat 'Litmus', without the hint of a stammer, "Lousy fucking bastards!"

"Christ, I wish I was in a Hurricane!" added George, between shivers, although he had never felt less capable of flying one than he had since he had awoken in hospital.

"It's a bloody bad show," added Peter, "but there's not much we can do here. We need to get moving and get old George looked at, if nothing else." It was then he saw that both offside tyres were flat. "Hell fire! That's all we need!"

"The spare is OK, sir," said Grey from the back of the car, "might I suggest we put that on and leave the car jacked up while we get the others repaired."

"Fine. You chaps hold the fort here – Osborn and I will take them into Laon."

Richard climbed from the shelter trench bewildered and fearful. Bewildered because, apart from a handful of aircraft which had punched a series of inconsequential holes across the now redundant airfield, almost the whole enemy force had concentrated their wrath on the village; fearful because Mamam and Justine were still at the School House. He summoned his driver and they set off for the village. As soon as they reached the outskirts, he had to leave the car behind and scramble across the debris, as the road in was made impassable to a car by rubble. The scene was one of complete destruction. He couldn't see a building that was untouched and most had been reduced to ruins; just a chimneystack or part of a wall and staircase was all that remained of most. It took him all of ten minutes to reach and cross the ruined square and now he was scrambling along *rue de L'Ecole,* his heart in his mouth, when he realised that he had not yet seen another human being. All too soon the scene he dreaded seeing was before him. The

School House had been reduced to rubble. He scrambled onto the ruins and began throwing aside whatever pieces he could lift, calling their names in desperation as he dug. Suddenly, as he pushed aside part of a beam he saw a clenched hand. He grasped it and moved his fingers to the wrist. It was still warm but there was no pulse, although he tried several times to find one. In the end, he gently prised open the fingers to reveal the crumpled remains of the nosegay he had bought just a week ago on that balmy evening in Epinal. He sat back sadly on his haunches. There had been so much he had wanted to say before he left, that he should have said sooner, and now… but what of Justine? He tried to shift some more debris but the area he was working had become impenetrable. He moved a few feet and tried again. Once more he was able to dig down. He froze. He had uncovered a small bullet with a hole drilled through the middle – he knew about George's bullets. Beside it, material he recognised as part of one of Justine's dresses protruded from under a large chunk of masonry that he couldn't begin to budge. There was no point digging any further now anyway. After putting the bullet into his pocket he sat with his head in his hands.

Once she reached the outskirts of Rethel, she was able to move freely but as she made her way into the city, she noticed with growing disquiet the bomb damage and the columns of smoke still climbing into the sky. Eventually she found the hospital and, amid chaotic scenes of damage and injury, a dishevelled and harassed looking nursing sister. *"Bonjour Madame, I am looking for my husband, a British airman."*

The woman had looked ready to burst into tears. *"Oh Madame, I am so sorry. All the British airmen were in the overspill; and it was bombed last night."*

They had tried two garages already. Each time, they had been met with closed doors and no sign of life. At the third Peter saw movement inside. He rapped on the window and a shadowy figure motioned him away. He rapped harder. The man approached and mouthed the word *'ferme'* and motioned him away again. Osborn had had enough. He drew his pistol and pointed it at the man, shook his head and mouthed the word *'ouvert'*. The man's face registered shock, then anger, but he had no choice; with ill-disguised animosity, he opened the door and they took the tyres inside.

It can't be true, it mustn't be true! With an increasing sense of dread, she pushes her bicycle along the street. As she rounds the corner a voice calls out. *"Hey, stop! You can't go down there. It's not safe."*

"I'm looking for my husband, a British airman – he's in the hospital outbuildings."

The Gendarme speaks again, gently this time. *"I'm sorry, madame, there's no one alive there – they're all dead – doctors, nurses, patients."*

"What happened?"

"The hospital was overwhelmed with injured so they were using the warehouse to house some of the less serious cases; but it's where they store oxygen, nitrous

164

oxide, surgical spirits, paint and so on. A bomb hit the building and it went up like a volcano; no one could have survived that inferno!"

"*Les bleus sont partis, les bleus sont partis, les bleus...*" Wearing what looks like an oversize night-shirt a figure capers past, chanting in a monotonous sing-song voice.

"*You must excuse me madame. As if things weren't bad enough, the local asylum was hit two days ago and half the inmates escaped – we're still trying to round them up. Hey you! Come back here!*" He dashes after the apparition but Justine doesn't register the surreal scene. The thing she most dreads has happened; but not in a way she would have ever imagined. At this moment nothing is real; she feels no emotion, just numbness. Automatically, she mounts her bicycle and starts to pedal away.

Richard blew the dust from his watch face. It was time he was moving. He had orders to follow and he could do no more here. With a last regretful glance at the ruins of the School House, he set off for the car. Beyond the square, and the remains of the *Mairie,* he saw life; a small white dog pawing at some rubble. He drew his pistol and took aim – the dog would surely starve so he might as well put it out of its misery – then lowered the gun and re-holstered it – there had been enough killing here for one day. He felt in one of the large pockets on the front of his tunic and found the remains of a packet of biscuits. "Here boy!" The dog ate the biscuits eagerly then licked his hand. As it did so, he stroked it, disturbing layers of dust and revealing its true colouring. "I remember you! Caspar I think you were called. C'mon Caspar!" He whistled and the dog began trotting after him.

Justine pedalled steadfastly on. She wouldn't be home before well into tomorrow but then she and Mamam would fulfil George's last wish and start the journey to Tante Lys' farm. She understood now that George was dead but she couldn't feel anything yet; not sorrow, anger, or pain – she only knew that it was important that Mamam, she and the child she carried, her remaining link with him, went to Normandy.

With a reassuring roar, the engine came to life and they nosed their way back into the tide of human misery that was still rolling along the road. In Peter and Osborn's absence, Grey and 'Litmus' had helped to bury those killed in the raid. George, one-handed, had tried to assist but was unequal to the task. Feverish and lightheaded now, as they passed the makeshift graves, he nonetheless thought of Justine and prayed to himself that she was faring better. The orphaned child had gone; he hoped it been taken in hand by someone. Peter broke into his thoughts. "The delay means we won't even reach St Quentin tonight. Can you hold on?"

George nodded, trying to show a confidence he didn't feel. 'Litmus' spoke 'Can't we go to the g-garage where you had the tyres repaired and get the h-headlights fixed?" Peter shook his head. "Even though we paid him in the end, he won't open his doors to us again. I know we have to get George to Arras as soon as possible but I'm afraid we've got another bloody night in this car."

It was already mid-morning. They were taking an eternity to get through St Quentin – it seemed that refugees were converging from all directions.

"I've been thinking," said Peter, "there are two main routes from St Quentin to Arras; one via Cambrai and the other via Peronne. They're both going to be packed with refugees, but looking at the map there's a series of minor roads that will get us there just as directly and probably be less busy. What does everyone think?" He had folded it into an oblong displaying the area in question and showed it around to murmurs of assent from all but George, who was by now drifting in and out of consciousness. "Right, Sgt Grey, that seems to be settled. You carry on driving and I'll navigate."

Justine could sense something was wrong at the road-fork before the woods. There was an unearthly stillness and a pall of dust hung in the air. As she cycled on, she could see gaps where trees had been uprooted, then damaged houses came into view. She dismounted as she reached the first of them, picked her way past the remains of the second and third and then she was facing a pile of rubble that forty-eight hours ago had been her home. Fearing the worst, she scrambled across it trying to find a way to dig down. She gave a gasp of shock as she disturbed a stone that Richard had placed, revealing, still holding the nosegay, her mother's hand. It felt cold as she clasped it. Instead of flinching, she maintained her grip and knelt down.

As soon as they had turned onto the first minor road, his idea seemed to be vindicated. Suddenly, by comparison, the Hillman was hurtling along. The place-names were passing by – Pontruet, Villeret, Epehy. They were making progress at last. He turned to 'Litmus' "How's George?"

"W-worse-he's alternately hot and cold and his b-breathing and pulse are sky high."

"He looks like death warmed up to me but if we can keep going like this we will be in Arras within two hours and we can get him some attention." A look of amazement crossed 'Litmus's' face. "What did I say?"

"N-nothing. I think I just saw a G-German motorcycle combination!"

"Where?"

"The l-last turning. C-coming down the road."

"You can't have! They're nowhere near here... Hell, you're right! It's just pulling out onto the road... They've seen us!" Peter turned to F/Sgt Grey, "Can you make this thing go any faster?" Grey pushed his foot to the floor. The speedometer needle crept painfully upwards. "He's shooting at us." There was a rattle as bullets struck the rear of the car. Osborn grunted then slumped in his seat. They rounded a bend and their pursuers disappeared temporarily from view. "We'll never outrun them."

"I've an idea, sir. Have you got your revolver with you?"

"Yes, but I can't get my finger round the trigger because of these bandages."

"I-I can fire a p-pistol but I lost mine baling out." Peter passed his to 'Litmus'.

Grey spoke again. "We're sheltered by the bend for a few seconds more which should just be time to reach this next turning. When the car stops, get out, get

166

behind it and follow my lead." He swung the Hillman into the side road. The Germans rounded the bend just in time to see the car disappearing; sensing a kill, they accelerated after it. In the side road, Grey had driven ten yards before spinning the steering wheel and pulling the handbrake on hard. The car slewed to a halt, sideways across the road. "Out, quickly."

He and 'Litmus' jumped from the car. Peter, having realised he had no hope of extracting George and Osborn, joined the other two crouching behind it. Grey spoke to 'Litmus'. "When they appear, let them approach; shoot the machine gunner first, then the driver. Three shots each at both of them. Safety-catches off. Get ready!" The roar of the approaching motorcycle faded as it slowed for the bend, then picked up and quickly died as the driver, seeing the car and sensing danger, throttled back again. "Now!" The Germans only froze for a heartbeat as Grey and 'Litmus' stood up at either end of the car but it was sufficient. Pistols held in both hands at arm's length, they fired six shots at the machine-gunner. Enough found their target to leave him sprawled in his seat. The driver was trying to bring the machine pistol slung across his chest to bear when the second volley put paid to him.

Peter gaped, "Bloody amazing! Where did you learn to do that?"

"I got the basic idea from gangster films, sir – Cagney and that ilk – and then just improvised. Can I suggest you collect the driver's gun and ammo and then we get moving – there may be more of them close behind?"

"You're right! How's Osborn?"

"H-he's dead. George w-wasn't hit but he's s-sinking fast! He can't stand any more delays."

"Hey, what are you doing there?" The shout startled Justine from her vigil. She looked round to see the local gendarme advancing across the rubble, reaching for his holster. He stopped, taking in the scene. *"I'm sorry madame! I didn't recognise you. For a moment, I thought you were a looter."* He inclined his head. *"I take it there's nothing to be done?"* She gave a brief shake of her head. *"I'm sorry. What a lousy business. I don't get it – they've flattened the village and hardly touched the airfield."*

She hadn't thought about the airfield. *"Was anyone hurt there?"*

He scoffed. *"Not very likely, our brave allies have scarpered south?"*

She spoke quietly. *"Except those like my husband who died fighting the Germans."*

He replied after an awkward silence. *"Forgive me. It was a stupid thing to say. I'm looking for someone to blame for all... this,"* he gestured angrily around the ruins, *"because the real culprits are out of my reach. It was part of my patch so it was my village too, and now it's destroyed."* He was silent for a moment. *"A few people survived by sheltering in the woods – they have headed south. What will you do?"*

"George asked me to go to Normandy with our baby. I owe it to him to do so. There's nothing left for me here except to bury my mother."

"It could be some time before anyone can excavate all these ruins and arrange proper burials – if at all."

"I realise that." Wearily, she began gathering stones.

167

"Can I help?"

"I'd rather do this alone if you don't mind."

"I understand. But you're worn out. Why don't you come back to the Gendarmerie? My wife will cook you something and there's an empty cell so you can get a good night's rest then finish this in the morning."

The RAMC Colonel looked weary but there was a hint of satisfaction in his manner that said he had helped to prevent the premature end of another young life. "It was close but the fever has broken; I was concerned that he might be falling victim to septicaemia. Whatever it was he seems to have overcome it so he should make a full recovery – though not here. The hospital is to be evacuated to Wimereux, near Boulogne – the Germans are advancing this way quite rapidly. I gather there's a counter-attack being organised but if that doesn't hold them…" He shrugged his shoulders before addressing Peter and 'Litmus'. "I'll have a nurse check your dressings. Your friend should be fit to leave the day after tomorrow. Then, as you've your own transport, I suggest you push off pronto. You'll easily make it in the day."

"Permission to speak, sir," interjected Grey, "my orders were to deliver these gentlemen to Arras and then return to my squadron."

"Who gave you those orders, F/Sgt?"

"My Squadron Leader, sir."

"As a Colonel, I outrank him and my orders are for you to deliver these gentlemen to Wimereux. Then you may return to your Squadron – Germans permitting."

Grey looked pleased as he saluted. "Sir!"

"I take it George will be well enough to travel by then, sir?" asked Peter.

"It's the lesser of two evils. He'll be over the worst but he won't be good for much other than sleeping. He's been almost at death's door so with that and the bullet wounds he'll need plenty of rest; and as little excitement as possible."

"I think that goes for us all, sir."

A small cairn now surmounted the remains of the School House, topped by two sticks bound together to form a cross. She was contemplating it in silence when the Gendarme appeared. *"Good! I've caught you before you left. My wife insisted I give you this for your journey."*

Opening the proffered bundle she found bread, cheese and sausage. Such kindness would normally have prompted heartfelt gratitude but she was still numb inside. Ingrained politeness produced a smile which she did not feel as she stowed the bundle. *"Thank her for me. I am ready to leave but now I must revisit Rethel. Doing this,"* she indicated the cairn, *"has made me realise that in some way, I have to honour my husband. Au revoir and thank you, m'sieu."*

He watched in silence as she wheeled her bicycle away. Beyond the debris, she mounted it and began to pedal, slowly but steadily. He spoke under his breath as he saluted the receding figure. *"Bonne chance, madame!"*

"How's George doing? The doc gave him more paracetamol before we left. He said he'd come to in due course."

"S-still out for the count. H-his temperature's coming down though. I could have f- fried an egg on his f-forehead when we reached Arras."

"Fingers crossed, then. We should be at Wimereux in an hour or two. We must be ahead of the German advance – there've been no refugees since we left Arras. The crossroads we're just coming to mean we're about halfway."

"There's someone in the road, sir."

"You're right. Looks like a redcap. What's he doing in the middle of nowhere?"

Refugees and hiding from strafing aircraft had cost her another day but Justine had made it back to Rethel. No one was on guard now; instead the ruins, still emitting odd wisps of smoke, were surrounded by a crude cordon, which presented no obstacle.

She had already decided on her tribute – a simple spray made from poppies gathered in the meadow where she had passed the previous night. She had knelt on the rubble to say a short prayer before leaving, but she was tired and the sun was warm. Permitting herself to sit for a few moments, she was asleep before she knew it.

Peter lowered the window. The MP saluted. "Can I arsk where you're gowin', sah?"

"Yes Sergeant. We're heading for Wimereux, near Boulogne – to the hospital."

"'Fraid that's not possible, sah. The Germans 'ave cat the roads to the norf; you'll 'have to turn sarf – t'wards Abbey-vill."

"Good lord! What's become of the counter-attack?"

The MP's eyes narrowed. "Carnter-attack, sah?"

"Yes Sergeant, there was one planned at Arras. The Germans must have overrun or outflanked…" he broke off at the sound of a pistol being cocked. F/Sgt Grey leant across and pointed it at the MP.

"What on earth are you doing F/Sgt?" Peter asked as the MP raised his hands.

"Bear with me please, sir." He addressed the MP. "A couple of questions if you don't mind, Sergeant. You sound like a Londoner. What part?"

The man glared at him. "Norf Landon – wot of it?"

"Who do you support, then?"

Curiosity replaced defiance. His answer was guarded. "The Ar-sen-al."

F/Sgt Grey relaxed visibly and uncocked his weapon. "Another Gunner! Sorry about that Sergeant; can't be too careful at the moment. I'll be glad when this bloody war's over. Then I can get back to Highfield Road to watch them again."

The response was assured now. "Me too!" The report of the pistol in the confined space of the car was deafening. The MP fell backwards, a spray of blood and brains staining the ground behind him.

Ears ringing, Peter was aghast. "Good God, have you gone mad F/Sgt?"

"No sir, he was a Jerry. You probably haven't heard with being in hospital but we've been warned to look out for enemy agents being dropped behind our lines to spread disinformation and sabotage. Some are even said to be disguised as nuns."

"How can you be sure he's German?"

"An Arsenal supporter who doesn't know they play at Highbury and a London accent I reckon he learned from Hollywood movies. I smelt a rat before he asked about the counter-attack."

"Good grief – I nearly put my foot in it there!" He thought for a moment. "He said the Germans are to the north, so if they are anywhere they must be to the south – he was obviously trying to send us into a trap."

"But if they're near Abbeville, sir, that means they've all but cut France in two and are probably intending to turn north to encircle the armies in Belgium, including our boys. We need to get moving straight away."

Jolted by the bang, George stirred. "What's happening?" he asked drowsily.

"We should reach Wimereux hospital in the next hour. F/Sgt Grey has just shot someone for not knowing where the Arsenal play," Peter added blithely, "and the Germans are overrunning France; otherwise not much." He turned for a reaction but George's eyes were already closed and, breathing steadily, he was asleep again.

When she awoke, she was disconcerted to find that only an hour or so of daylight remained. She had no map but knew that heading west would get her to Normandy. Determined to put as much distance as she could between herself and Rethel before dark, she headed towards the setting sun.

The stream of refugees coming towards her, although less numerous than previously, made her realise her mistake; in the second half of May sunset occurs, not due west, but to the north of west. She had no desire to return to Rethel to find another route, nor to take to minor roads in the gloaming; she would follow the one she was on until it either turned west or met with another that led west. In the event, it did both. It was almost dark when she wheeled her bicycle off the road to prepare for another night under the stars, having just passed a sign which told her that Laon was 43km beyond; she had gone out of her way but, with any luck, she would still reach Normandy within the next few days.

Dawn had found her hungry and thirsty and she was soon cycling along the first track she saw leading to a farmhouse; there had been no sign of life as she approached; not even a dog running to challenge her.

As she dismounts and props her bicycle against the farmhouse wall, she becomes aware of the urgent lowing of distressed cattle. A feeling of uneasiness overtakes her – no good farmer would just abandon his herd. Finding the kitchen door open, she steps cautiously inside. There are signs of a struggle – overturned chairs and broken crockery. An inner voice urges her to leave now but instead she opens the sitting-room door to find the bodies of the farmer and his wife amid a scene of horror. She staggers into the yard and retches, crying out in her anguish.

"See, I knew she had a daughter – the lying old bat kept denying it even as she died!"

She looks up to see a man in the uniform of a French soldier who has emerged from the barn, drawn by her noise, followed by another. The first is dishevelled, unarmed, carrying instead a half-consumed bottle of wine; and obviously drunk. He staggers towards her. *"C'mon girlie, don't make a fuss and we might let you live! Hey, Louis, come and hold her down for me!"* The man named Louis pauses to lean his rifle against a trough then advances, leering, in her direction. The first man stops as Justine draws the Mauser from her waistband and levels it at him.

"Any closer and I'll shoot – for your information, I'm not the farmer's daughter so the woman you butchered told the truth, not that that would mean much to vermin like you. Now raise your hands – both of you!" He is close enough for her to see his bloodshot eyes and stubble; the odour of stale sweat and rancid breath reaches her. He smiles initially as if sharing a joke with her and then, seeing the determination in her eyes, his face twists into a vicious snarl. He throws the bottle aside and, with a bellow of rage, hurls himself towards her. She fires then fires again, aiming for the torso in the way George had taught her. The two shots are enough to kill him but don't check his momentum. His lifeless body crashes into her, dragging her to the floor and sending the pistol skittering away. Pinned by his dead weight across her legs she desperately tries to squirm free to reach her weapon. Louis has seized the chance to recover his rifle and now approaches, working the bolt. As he takes aim, she turns from a last futile effort to free herself and faces her executioner, tensed for the bullet that will end her life.

"G-gin!" said 'Litmus', laying down his cards.

"I'm glad it's only for matches," said Peter, "but it's good to be playing at all. A few days here and I think I'll be as good as new." Sergeant Grey appeared. "Where've you been Sergeant? Haven't seen you since we arrived."

"I've been drafted into assisting the medical orderlies, sir. I couldn't help overhearing what you were just saying and I'm afraid you don't have a few days. I've come to tell you we're being evacuated to Blighty as soon as there are ships available. You can expect to be moved to Boulogne harbour sometime tomorrow."

She starts at the sound of the shot. But no bullet comes. Instead, Louis crumples to the ground, his rifle dropping with a clatter from nerveless hands. A soldier wearing similar uniform runs into view, rifle pointed at the body. Others are entering the farmyard, alert for opposition. One hefts the dead man off her legs, then he and another effortlessly lift her to her feet. Her situation has prompted them into swapping bawdy remarks; but this time she doesn't feel threatened; these are disciplined soldiers, not a drunken rabble. She is dusting herself down when they snap to attention. She looks up to see an officer emerging from the farmhouse. *"I am grateful to you, Capitaine; I thought my end had come."*

The look of contempt with which he was surveying the bodies disappears as he addresses her. *"Capitaine Lebrun at your service. It seems I arrived just in time – for you anyway."*

Once she would have found his dark features and easy smile attractive, but she has no place for such thoughts at present. *"Justine Knight."* She anticipates his question, *"My husband is – was – an English pilot. He was killed a few days ago."*

171

"I'm sorry. Might I enquire why you are here?"

"I came to buy food."

"Not with this I hope." With a grin he returns her pistol to her. *"German is it not?"*

"My father 'acquired' it in 1916, in a German trench."

"Then I salute a brave man as well as his brave daughter. I take it you don't live around here?"

"I'm from Lorraine, on my way to Normandy. The school I taught in and my home were destroyed by bombing; my mother was killed also."

"Mon dieu! Haven't you suffered enough without attracting the attention of these scum! I came here to investigate a report of deserters. At least I won't have to waste any further time on them when there are more pressing matters."

"How are things going?"

He lowered his voice. *"Reports are sketchy, but not well I fear. Especially when you consider that the Boche appear to be advancing westwards across France when they should be banging their heads against the Maginot Line. I suggest you aim south of west; that should keep you clear of them. Two of my men are relieving those poor cows of their milk so help yourself – and take some food from the farmhouse too – the farmer and his wife have no use for it now."*

Rain was falling steadily by the time they reached the harbour. "What a bloody shambles!" exclaimed Peter as they got their first sight. Besides abandoned military equipment, the dockside was strewn with the trampled contents of looted or discarded luggage. Cars stood here and there, some dumped; others, with mattresses tied to the roof to protect against strafing or shrapnel, still contained people, hoping for a ship and sheltering from the rain or the less savoury elements of the crowd of deserters and refugees milling around them ; some drunk, others driven by desperation to the edge of insanity.

"Thank goodness! Walking wounded for a change; well almost," the RAMC Captain said, glancing at George's recumbent form being lifted from the car. He swept his hand towards the dockside warehouse he had emerged from. "We've plenty of stretcher cases already and there's bound to be another influx now the fighting's started." He wiped his brow against his sleeve, further staining his already soiled Red-Cross armband. To emphasise his words, the rattle of small arms reached them from the south, punctuated by the deeper crump of shells. "It started a few hours ago," he added by way of explanation, "it means Jerry isn't far away. If they break through, then there's nothing to stop them turning up here and putting us all in the bag."

"We expected to find ships waiting."

"Two destroyers came this morning and landed the Guards who are holding the perimeter. They took the worst wounded and said more ships would follow but they didn't say when. In the meantime, I would appreciate a bit of help while you're waiting – nothing difficult, just handing out water and words of encouragement."

As consciousness returned, George became aware of a hand insistently shaking his shoulder and Peter's voice came to him from afar. "Wake up old man, there's a ship on its way to pick us up!"

"Where am I?" said George, trying to focus on the unfamiliar surroundings.

"In a warehouse on Boulogne dockside. You – we, were evacuated from the hospital at Wimereux yesterday to await ships to take us back to England."

The thought stood out sharply in his sleep-fuddled mind, "I can't go back to England. I've got to go to Normandy to find Justine."

"The only way you can do that now is via England. The Germans have reached the coast at Abbeville – France is cut in two. We need to get moving, can you stand?" George sat upright. He felt a whirling in his head and slumped down again. "I-I can't do it."

"Take it slowly, you've been lying down for the best part of three days." He grasped George's upper arm, "Litmus, come and lend a hand!"

"A-at least the r-rain's eased off," said Litmus as they emerged from the warehouse.

"But the fighting's much nearer than yesterday," Peter raised his voice against the sound of shell bursts, "it's to the east now as well as the south. I don't think it'll be long before Jerry gets here. Thank God for the Navy!" In the distance, two destroyers were making their way into the harbour between the twin jetties marking the entrance. Further out, they could see more destroyers firing their guns inland, presumably in support of the port's defenders. Little had changed from their first sight of the docks except for the presence of a party of Guardsmen, sweat-stained and grimy after more than a day fighting but with their military bearing undiminished and their weapons spotless, under the command of a Lieutenant.

He saluted the RAMC captain who had also come out of the warehouse. "Lieutenant Bowen, sir – Welsh Guards. I've been sent back to secure the railway quay for evacuation – we can't hold the perimeter much longer, there are just too many of them. We'd heard reports that there was a mob running amok down here."

"It hasn't quite reached that stage yet, Lieutenant, but I imagine things will liven up with the destroyers arriving. I realise you've an important job to do but is there any chance of some of your men helping me? I've seventy-two stretchers in there and the sooner we can embark them the better for everyone."

"Not immediately I'm afraid, sir, but I'll be happy to assist when the quay is secure." At that moment, the first of the destroyers was coming alongside. As two sailors leapt ashore to secure mooring lines, part of the crowd that had begun to assemble at the sight of the ships surged forward and tried jumping onto the deck. Driven back onto the quayside by sailors armed with a mixture of boathooks and rifles, they continued pressing towards the ship. A volley of shots over their heads brought a momentary silence and then they shrank back as a dozen Guardsmen arrived at the double. "No one boards these ships without permission," as Bowen spoke, the second destroyer began tying up on the other side of the quay.

A large, craggy man of about thirty, in Pioneer Corps uniform, emerged from the throng and began advancing on him. "Piss off, sonny, we're getting on that boat and you and your spit-and-polish soldiers aren't going to stop us!"

Bowen fired his pistol once. The man sank to his knees with a surprised expression then pitched forward. Bowen moved the pistol along the sea of faces. "Anyone else?" A sullen, angry silence descended. "Now get back!" He strode forward and the crowd edged away. He continued advancing, his men following, rifles with fixed bayonets at the ready. When he had gained twenty yards, he took a piece of chalk from his pocket and drew a line on the ground. He raised his voice for all to hear. "If anyone crosses this line, Sergeant, man or woman, you have my permission to shoot them."

The Sub-Lieutenant saluted. "Captain's compliments, sir and will we be much longer? The weather is lifting and that means we can expect the Luftwaffe soon."

The RAMC Captain returned the salute. "Nearly there, Sub-Lieutenant, another ten minutes should do it. And please convey my thanks to both captains." The combined efforts of medical orderlies, Guardsmen and sailors had resulted in the stretcher cases being embarked quicker than he had anticipated. He was feeling optimistic even though lack of space inside the ships meant that they had had to be placed on deck.

Peter has volunteered to continue tending them rather than face the confined spaces below with the other walking wounded so George, despite his recent trials, and 'Litmus' have felt obliged to remain topside too. On the foredeck, George, water bottle in hand, is making his way among the wounded near the front turret. Without warning, a burst of machine-gun fire rips across the deck behind him, killing several of his charges and scything down some of the seething mass on the quay beyond. As he instinctively dives for cover behind the turret, the mob, prevented from running towards the ships by the implacable line of guardsmen, scatters across the quay amid screams and shouts. He is attempting to drag the nearest patient into cover when a second burst of fire claims more lives. A loud hailer transcends the pandemonium. "Where the hell is that coming from?"

George has seen the muzzle flash from the corner of his eye. He cups his hands and shouts towards the bridge, "Brown building, your nine o'clock!"

"Gun crew to 'A' turret!" Several sailors erupt from cover and sprint along the deck, reaching the sanctuary of the 4.2-inch gun just ahead of another burst of fire. "Target – brown building, two-seven-zero degrees. Fire when ready." With practiced ease, the gun is loaded and traversed; final adjustments are made, then it barks, cutting short another stream of bullets as the building collapses in a cloud of dust, the floors concertinaing into a pile of rubble. The loud hailer cuts short a ragged cheer. "Make ready to cast off fore and aft. Lieutenant, bring your men aboard."

The other destroyer is already moving, sliding backwards round the end of the quay, the water churning beneath its stern. The crowd edges cautiously forward as the Guardsmen shoulder arms and march aboard with customary parade-ground precision. A whistling sound heralds an explosion on the quay which sends shrapnel and shards of stone flying in all directions, cutting a bloody swathe through the refugees. Still kneeling by 'A' Turret George, helpless and exposed, looks around desperately for the source of the new threat. His answer comes from the loudhailer. "Enemy tank, zero – two-zero, engage!" He spots the tank which had fired, in the eastern part of the town, about four hundred yards away, as another emerges to join it. The 4.2-inch gun has been brought to bear by now and returns fire. With a roar clearly audible on deck, the leading tank is blown apart, its heavily armoured turret and gun fluttering through the air like a child's lollypop as the hull dissolves in flame and smoke. The second tank fires. George flattens himself against the deck, trying to make himself small, the bitter taste of fear in his mouth. The tank shell screeches overhead and lands with a splash in the dock. The 4.2-inch fires again and the second tank explodes. A third has appeared but reverses rapidly back into cover. "Silence on deck!" The loudhailer cuts short the spontaneous outburst of cheering. The other ship has cleared the quay and is starting towards the harbour entrance. As his casts off and begins backing round the quay, George climbs unsteadily to his feet, fighting to overcome the effects of exertion and fear on his already battered body.

Peter appears beside him. "Thank God we're moving. It was getting pretty hairy."

"We're not out of the wood yet. The sky's cleared and if the Jerries arrive before we get out of the harbour we're a sitting duck."

They are still in the channel when his fears are borne out. A swarm of black dots in the sky transforms into eighteen Stukas. He has seen them from the air – now he will find out what the refugees have been facing. A dozen head off towards the warships outside the harbour. The two destroyers, racing seawards, have little room for manoeuvre in the narrow waterway and only two multiple pom-pom anti-aircraft guns apiece; already firing as the remaining Stukas close in. "We're for it now…" The words dry in his throat as the first attacker rolls into its dive, siren emitting a mind-numbing banshee scream, clearly audible above the rhythmic thumps of the pom-poms. It isn't aiming for the ship, it's aiming for him. He is rooted to the spot; his insides have turned to ice. There is nowhere to run to anyway. He knows he is going to die and there is nothing he can do except watch his nemesis swooping towards him.

The sign tells her she is well into Normandy. Having endured another two days of cycling, foraging and sleeping in hedges, she will reach her destination within the hour. She should be feeling glad about that but, exhausted and numbed by her experiences, she has only one thought – Tante Lys' farm. Mechanically, she hooks the pedal into place with her toes then presses the ball of her foot against it. The bicycle starts forward on the final leg of her journey.

As a black shape falls away from the Stuka, the spell suddenly breaks. "Get down!" George throws an arm around the still-transfixed Peter and drags him to the deck. The bomb detonates in the water; a curtain of spray deluges the deck and the racing destroyer heels: stretchers and their occupants begin sliding towards the deck edge; for a few ghastly seconds, it appears the vessel will capsize; then, seemingly with a shrug, it rights itself and continues hammering seawards.

"Swing with the aircraft – fire!" A Guards RSM bellows above the din of battle as his men, lined up along the side of the ship, take the fight back to the enemy, though to no avail as the Stuka climbs away unharmed. The second is on its way by now. This time the bomb hits part of the channel wall. George and Peter cringe as a storm of concrete and shrapnel pepper the sides of the ship and scythe across the deck, hitting wounded and fighting alike. There are gaps in the line of guardsmen now. The RSM, bloodied but unbowed, clutches a stanchion and barks out another command. His remaining men fire a volley at the departing aircraft. George looks ahead in time to see a bomb detonate almost under the leading destroyer, lifting its stern enough to momentarily reveal its keel before it flops back and the flailing propellers bite into the water once more. An explosion beyond the harbour entrance marks the end of one of the bombardment flotilla; caught by the dozen Stukas there, swarming and diving like angry hornets. The third attack on George's destroyer is misjudged. The bomb falls harmlessly astern and the aircraft's recovery carries it straight over the ship where the pom-poms and the Guardsmen are presented with a perfect target. Smoke, then flame, sprouts from under the stricken aircraft which staggers before crashing onto one of the stone jetties at the harbour entrance. Another round of cheering is cut short by an angry retort from the bridge, in turn replaced by the cry of "Medic!" The Guard's RSM is still clutching the stanchion, but now on his knees, as the leading destroyer passes the burning Stuka; out into the open sea where a flight of Hurricanes have appeared to drive off the remaining attackers.

"Hooray for the RAF – better late than never!" shouts a matelot sarcastically in George and Peter's direction.

Moments later, their destroyer reaches the open sea too. "Ye Gods! I thought we'd had it several times!" exclaims Peter, climbing to his feet, "Promise me one thing, George – when you get up in a Hurricane again, show those bloody Stukas no mercy!"

The shadows were starting to lengthen when Lys Deschamps glanced out of the window and saw a forlorn figure slowly wheeling a bicycle up the track towards the farmhouse. It took her a few moments to recognise the arrival. She ran downstairs, fear rising in her throat, and out of the front door. They met at the edge of the farmyard. *"Justine, what are you doing here... what has happened?"*

"Oh, Tante Lys..." In the space of a few days, her world had been shattered. She had lost her mother and her husband, her home and her school; she had witnessed refugees being strafed, invasion, the collapse of the French army; she had fought off deserters intent on rape and murder and throughout it all, she had maintained her fortitude and held her grief in check, focusing on the overriding priority of getting herself and her unborn child safely to Normandy. Now, she was eight years old again; the little girl who had fallen from one of her aunt's apple trees and sprained her ankle; who had had no need to hold anything back. As she surrendered anew to her aunt's embrace, the floodgates opened.

In the naval custom, the two destroyers had hove to in mid-channel to bury their dead at sea; sailors and others alike. An army chaplain among the evacuees had conducted the service while the survivors, with the exception of those on look out, stood or lay around. They were under way again now, making for home at half speed; George's destroyer holding back to escort her companion, slowed by damage from the near miss which had lifted her from the water. From the stern, he watched the French coast fade to a faint smudge, then nothing. Somewhere beyond, perhaps still in Lorraine, but hopefully by now in Normandy, was Justine. As soon as it was possible, he would make his way there, to the farm, and find her. As he watched, Vera Lynn's voice ran through his head, the bittersweet lyrics echoing his thoughts: *"We'll meet again... don't know where... don't know when... but I know we'll meet again... some sun-ny day..."*

Part II
The Battle of Britain

"What General Weygand called the Battle of France is over.
I expect that the Battle of Britain is about to begin…"

Extract from address by Prime Minister Winston S Churchill to the House of Commons on 18th June, 1940

10: June, 1940

Evans drew on his beer, savoured it for a moment, then gestured with his glass towards the scenery. "God's own coun-try – what we're fighting for."

"I-I'll second that!" said 'Litmus'.

Recently returned from their respective recoveries, they were sitting outside a pub a couple of miles from the aerodrome where 686 was, for the time-being, based. The sun was dropping towards a forested hill, separated from them by one of the many tributaries of the Cleddau, the river which cleaves Pembrokeshire like the trunk and roots of a massive tree. George, drawn, if only for the moment, gently but firmly back into their midst from the melancholy in which he had existed since re-joining the squadron, considered Evans' remark for a moment. The surroundings were beautiful; but so too were his native Sussex, which would always be a part of him; and Normandy, which now held nothing for him; and then there was the question of what he was fighting for. Until recently, it had unhesitatingly been king and country, but that was before the news which had spawned another less noble but equally heartfelt motivation – vengeance.

One more familiar face was expected any day – Giles, who they had heard had managed to get himself shot down a second time during the fighting retreat across France. Together, they were all that remained of the old 686; the rest having fought on for three weeks after George's departure until they had literally run out of aircraft and been evacuated to England where, exhausted by their efforts, they had been posted away for a rest; leaving the squadron to be reformed virtually from scratch. George reflected, with mixed emotions, that there were actually two more old faces still with the squadron; 'Einstein' and Richard. He had been considered well enough to be sent home to finish his recuperation and thus free-up a hospital bed for the wounded arriving from a place called Dunkirk. His father was going to London most days and his mother had answered the call for nurses so that when Richard had rung and asked to visit him, it had seemed a welcome interlude in his convalescence. Instead, his world had imploded as Richard, Adjutant and friend, had quietly recounted the raid on St Jean and what he had found at the School House. For two days and nights, he had simply sat, lost in silent thought. His mother, tearful, and his father, also silent, had watched helplessly; unable to give him comfort for the first time in his life. On the third day, he had risen from his chair, clear in his mind at least as to what he had to do. A phone call, a visit to the MO and within a week, he was on his way to rejoin 686. "We're on our own now, though," Evans cut into his thoughts – the French had concluded an armistice a few days before.

"That's no bad thing," George replied vehemently, "we can face the German assault without wondering whether our allies are going to let us down."

"W-w-when it comes," said 'Litmus', "my sister's in the WAAF, at B-biggin, and she tells me it's pretty q-quiet there at the moment."

"They'll be licking their wounds and re-organising – despite being so heavily outnumbered, we gave them a hot reception in France. But they'll be here soon enough – and I for one will be waiting for the bastards."

"D-do you think they will t-try to invade?"

A conversation came to mind that he had overheard between his father and their housekeeper in the days after Richard's visit. 'Three hundred and forty thousand British and French troops rescued from Dunkirk. Much more than we had dared hope for, Mr Knight.'

'Yes Mrs Busey, but as Mr Churchill has said, wars are not won by evacuations. It's a magnificent effort by all concerned but it still leaves us very much with our backs to the wall. Unless the French suddenly find a second wind they are going to be defeated and then we face the very real possibility of an invasion attempt.'

'Could it succeed?' her voice manifested her concern.

'If they manage to get ten divisions across. We've little or nothing to resist with at the moment; the BEF left all their equipment behind. But getting them across is easier said than done. It's not like throwing pontoon bridges across rivers as they did so successfully in France; at the narrowest point there are twenty-one miles of open sea to cross. To achieve that they need air and naval supremacy, which means defeating the RAF and then sinking the fleet. Providing we keep our nerve and everyone does their bit, I think we have every chance of surviving. Thank God, we've got Winston. At least he won't come to some half-baked compromise with them.'

Still trying to come to terms with Richard's news, George had switched his thoughts to this new issue. As a boy he had read 'War of the Worlds' and squirmed in horrified fascination as the Martians ravaged London and the Home Counties. Now the forces of Nazism, a creed as inhuman as any Martian, were poised across the channel ready to do the same; but, as his father had said, to cross twenty-one miles of water they would have to subdue the RAF and then the Royal Navy. He had by that point decided that he had to make the Germans, and the Luftwaffe in particular, pay for what they had done at St Jean, and now he added the certainty that duty demanded he subordinate his personal tragedy and play his part in making sure that invasion did not happen; it was time to rejoin the fight.

"That's down to us," he said matter-of-factly. "Fighter Command that is."

"I-in that case they haven't a hope!" 'Litmus' said resolutely.

"Fine words," Evans responded, "but we have our own rebuil-ding to do. The fighting in France cost a lot of good men, as well as planes. Its odds-on the three of us will be made section commanders so it will be our job to bring the new boys up to scratch; pass on what we've learned."

"If we're given the chance," George replied less confidently, "I've a feeling Preston operates strictly by the book and the book still says close vics and FAAs."

On his return he had met or, more accurately, been summoned to meet, the new C/O. 'Pilot Officer Knight, I trust you are familiar with King's Regulations?' had been S/L Preston's salutation.

'Yes sir.'

'Then I shouldn't need to tell you that at all times an officer will wear a collar and tie. Scarves or roll-neck sweaters are not acceptable. Is that understood?'

Out of the corner of his eye, he had seen Richard, slightly to the rear of Preston, looking directly at him and gently nodding his head. 'Yes, sir – perfectly.' His immediate impression was that in contrast to Sullivan's natural authority Preston's stemmed only from his badges of rank. Of no more than average build, he gave the impression of a man neither at ease with himself nor the world at large; manifested most obviously in an aura of irritability and cold, darting eyes; well-groomed as would be expected, wearing a precisely trimmed moustache that was broader than Hitler's but lacking the panache of a Ronald Coleman or the flamboyance of a Handlebar. Overall, he put George in mind of a minor council official come to investigate an infestation.

'It is clear,' Preston had continued, 'that things have become somewhat lax under my predecessor but I am determined to correct that very quickly. A successful squadron is an efficient squadron and an efficient squadron is one that follows the rules.'

George must have looked as ready as he had felt to protest at the slur on Sullivan because out of the corner of his eye, he had seen Richard, eyes half shut, gently shaking his head. He had bitten his lip. 'If you say so, sir.'

'I do – so I trust we won't need to repeat this discussion. You are dismissed!' George recounted this interview to the others. "I wish now I hadn't let Richard stop me from sticking up for Sullivan!"

"He w-was right, there's no sense f-falling foul of the new C/O on day one. W-what he says w-won't change anything – Sullivan's w-w-worth ten of him!" 'Litmus', who had long since abandoned his misgivings concerning beer, was becoming animated, waving his glass around.

"Stead-y," admonished Evans, "I don't need another dent in my face!"

He glanced at his battered nose. "S-something to tell your g-grandchildren; wounded fighting off Hitler's hordes."

Evans grinned, "Aww no-o! They'll hear I got this from an English boot at the Arms Park; scoring the win-ning try for Wales!"

Tante Lys was incandescent with rage. Justine tried to calm her, fearful she might burst a blood vessel. *"This is intolerable – outrageous,"* she fumed, *"in our own country, being made to register our names and carry identity cards; food, clothing and petrol to be rationed and a curfew as well. They're treating us like criminals. How dare they!"*

"Because they have won the war and we have lost," Justine said flatly.

"Well we must do something about it. We must stand up to them!"

"They crushed our army, the largest in the world; so what can you and I do against them?" She thought of the posters which were already starting to appear outside the Mairie and in other public places. *"You've seen the notices. Acts of defiance will be punishable – in some instances by death. And I don't need to remind you what happened to your brother."* She pointed to her belly. *"Besides this, you're all I've got left. Promise me you won't go getting yourself killed."*

183

The pathos in Justine's words dissolved Lys' anger. She put her arms around her. *"No my dear, I won't; but someone's got to do something. We can't live like this for the rest of our lives."*

Giles was pretty much as George had last seen him, apart from a slight limp. "Result of an argument with some 109s, but not enough to stop me flying. Good to see you're tickity-boo…" he flushed, then continued quickly, "there aren't many of us left – 'we glorious few, we band of brothers'."

"I gather you've heard," George said quietly, "from the Adj at a guess."

"Yes… I'm sorry."

"It wasn't your fault," George said dismissively. He took in DFC ribbon and Flight Lieutenant's insignia. "Congrats on the gong and the stripe; thoroughly deserved."

Giles was silent for a moment. "No more than the rest of you I think but they had to give them to somebody. I gather we're rebuilding then back to the fray; that can't be far off what with aircraft starting to arrive and several new bods on the train with me."

"What are they like?"

"There's an Aussie called Max who's tangled with Jerry over Dunkirk; a couple of sprogs with down on their cheeks and next-to-no hours on Hurricanes; and a rather odd Polish chap named Jerzy something or other."

"What's odd about him?"

"He kept staring at marks on the carriage window. When I asked him what was wrong, he said he was doing it to improve his eyesight; reckons it will make him able to see further. Interesting notion. Can't stand here talking though – I've got to report to the C/O. What's he like?"

"Name of Preston. Not a patch on Sullivan by the look of it," said George.

"Not 'Stickler' Preston?"

"Who?"

"'Stickler' Preston; lots of spit and polish and everything by the book, a prissy, ill-tempered martinet who can recite the book line by line but without an original thought in his head. Served under him briefly in '37 before they shunted him off to command some back-water – best place for him I'd say," he grimaced, "If it's the same chap then they're really scraping the barrel!"

The flight had been uneventful. The new Hurricane – his new Hurricane – had performed perfectly and he had taken a step towards meeting the Luftwaffe again; and the chance to start evening the score. It had been good to be airborne again – the first time since being shot down – losing himself for a while in the joy of unfettered flight, the aircraft becoming an extension of him once more. In the last few days, his wounded spirit had received a lift – flying and being back in the company of his friends was almost like old times – but it could never be old times again. As he had done every night since that third day after Richard had returned it to him he took the bullet – her bullet – from his uniform pocket and held it in his hand while he silently renewed his vow to avenge her. Then he placed it under his pillow and turned out the light as he sought refuge in sleep.

184

11: July, 1940

What on earth are you doing, Blue Three, have you taken leave of your senses?" Preston, leading Blue Section, can't contain himself as the propeller of the Hurricane to his left comes within inches of chewing his tail off.

"Sorry leader, I'll get it right," the voice is wretched.

"Make sure you do, you blithering idiot. Your flying is utterly abysmal. What the hell has your Section Leader been teaching you? You're here to kill Germans, not me! Now get a grip and close up properly or I'll ground you!"

George, leading Yellow Section, can't believe what he has just witnessed – Preston has torn a strip off a subordinate on open radio; not only bad for morale but also conduct unbecoming an officer and serving only to confirm his initial misgivings about the man. He looks back in turn at the two pilots in tight-vic formation either side of him, tucked in, at Preston's insistence, to the point where their wingtips are overlapping his own, like a pre-war display team, near enough for him to see on their faces the all-consuming concentration needed to maintain position. They had made their feelings known earlier when he introduced himself as their Section Leader and briefed them for the exercise. 'Stone the bleedin' crows, Skipper!' Max had exploded, 'I've been posted back to the Dark bloody Ages. We learned not to fly up each others' arses over Dunkirk but this drongo's got us doing it over again.'

'Is right,' added Jerzy, 'I come here to kill Germans, pay back what they do to my country, not fly pretty formations that will get us bloddy killed.'

George was having his first experience of relaying unpopular commands. 'We have our orders and we will carry them out however we may feel about them.' Their faces had left him in no doubt on that score.

'This is bloody madness,' he mutters to himself, echoing their earlier thoughts, 'if a Jerry appears, we won't know anything about him until he shoots our chuffs off. Jerzy and Max are relatively experienced, so God help those like Blue Three, fresh from OTU'; the threat of impending German attack has prompted shortcuts in training and squadrons like 686 are being left to make fighter pilots out of undercooked sprogs. Compounding the frustration of trying to turn tyros into aces overnight they are being asked to teach them things which he and the other seasoned pilots know to be wrong; the formations and tactics which, as Max had pithily observed, have been shown to be obsolete over France are still holy writ with many in England – and with Preston in particular. That had been made clear a few days ago. Giles – Red, Evans – Blue, 'Litmus' – Green and he – Yellow, had been summoned by Preston to be confirmed as section commanders; but that had been the highpoint as he had gone on to set out his agenda, "Group need every squadron operational as soon as possible and I have said that 686 will be ready in no more than two weeks from now. That is the goal and I don't intend my name and reputation to be sullied by your failure to meet it so to that end you will intensively school your sections in close formation flying and Fighting Area Attack drills. Periodically, I shall fly with each section to assess progress. Are there any questions? Yes, F/O Knight?'

'Sir, we learned over France that FAAs are no use unless Jerry co-operates by flying unescorted and in straight lines. Close-Vic leaves us vulnerable to being bounced. Why aren't we using the tactics that were evolved in action?'

Preston had looked increasingly furious as the question unfolded and the murmurs and nods of agreement from the others as it concluded proved too much for him. His face was crimson as he spat out his response. 'When I want a cabal of junior officers to tell me how to run my squadron, I will let you know. In the meantime, you will follow my orders and you will practise the tactics I have given you. Tactics, I might add, which were devised by persons somewhat more senior in rank than you.'

'B-but that was y-years....' 'Litmus' had begun.

'Silence! This isn't a debating society. The matter is closed!'

George hadn't been the only one left feeling unhappy, but their mood had been lifted by a more than usually practical Giles as they talked in subdued tones over a beer. 'I think we all agree that we have a problem here. We obviously can't disobey a direct order but we don't need to. The disciplines involved won't be wasted, especially on the sprogs; they need all the flying hours and ability they can get. If we train them well now, formations and tactics can be varied when the need arises as we learned in France. So let's ensure we teach them what we have been told to and then, when we judge they are capable of absorbing it, add on what they really need to know to survive.'

"For God's sake, sort yourselves out. Blue Section, you're nothing but a rabble!" Preston's continuing tirade turns George's initial dismay to anger. He wants to teach this man a lesson, to humiliate him in front of others as he has done to Blue Three. "In case, along with the rudiments of flying, you have forgotten the purpose of this exercise, Yellow Section are somewhere around, tasked to stalk and engage us in mock combat, so see if you can make less of a shambles of keeping a lookout."

From the corner of his eye, George sees Jerzy's wings waggle; observing pre-arranged radio silence. He looks to where Jerzy is pointing and sees Blue Section no more than a mile ahead, hidden until now by a bank of cloud. From their erratic motion, Blue Two and Three are obviously still struggling just to keep formation, and after what George has heard, it is clear to him that Preston's pre-occupation will be keeping an eye on them. He knows then what has to be done and motions to Jerzy and Max to go into line astern, imagining their relief as they pull away from him. Dispensing with the usual call of 'Tally-ho', he rolls into a dive, the others following. They close rapidly on Blue Section, not even bothering to use the sun for cover, and then, in a few brief seconds it is done. "Dakka-dakka-dakka, you're dead Blue Leader."

"Dakka-dakka, yor a gonner Blue Two!"

"Daka-daka-daka – you too have had chips, Blue Three." Their Hurricanes are past and diving away before anyone reacts. George can't resist a parting shot.

"Good show, Yellow Section. Piece of cake. Enemy destroyed, so let's head for home."

A terse response crackles through his headphones, "Report to me when I have landed, Flying Officer Knight."

"I don't mean to be harsh but you can't go on sitting around moping for evermore. You need something to occupy you. Almost the only time you've left the farm since you got here was when we had to go to the Mairie to register." Lys' face darkened, *"The humiliation, lining up like felons to be photographed – in our own country!"*

"We've been over all that Aunt, there's nothing we can do," Justine replied. *"I did make enquiries at the village school but they have all the people they need. I can always help on the farm."*

Lys' tone suggested there was no scope for debate. *"You'll not lift a finger on this farm until you are safely delivered of your baby. However, I think I have the solution; M Beaumont at the garage. His bookkeeper went off to war last October and he's showing no signs of returning; it's only a few hours a week – light work and it will get you out of the house."*

"But I don't know how to keep books!"

"You used to teach arithmetic. M Beaumont will show you the rest. At least try it for a month. If you don't like it after that, then make your excuses and leave."

"What, was the meaning of that?" Preston had overcome his earlier loss of composure but George could sense the simmering anger.

"You ordered us to carry out a mock attack, sir, and we carried out your order," he replied blandly. "I assume because you didn't see us coming, you weren't aware we used FAA no. 1, as you would expect of us."

"Don't be facetious, Flying Officer. You made a mockery of the exercise."

"With respect, sir, today was a taste of reality; just as we did, the Luftwaffe attack without warning at any and every opportunity and there's nothing they like better than sitting ducks; that's why we devised – had to devise, or go west – formations that allow the best possible…"

"Damn your impudence. I don't appreciate sarcasm or lectures from junior officers and if you think you can influence my decisions with displays of this nature you are sadly mistaken and will be ill-advised to try again. Blue Section are incapable of flying in formation or keeping a lookout because they are woefully sub-standard for which I blame F/O Evans as their training is his responsibility. It isn't a week since I appointed my section leaders and I am already finding reason to question my decision. My reputation rises or falls with this squadron so I will not tolerate incompetence, slackness, or, in your case, dumb insolence so make no mistake Flying Officer, if you persist in your current attitude I shall not hesitate to replace you. You may go."

"Sir, I…"

"I'm not inviting a discussion. You are dismissed, get out!"

Parsons had been listening uncomfortably to the exchange from the adjoining office. He knocked on Preston's door after George had left. "Sir, may I speak with you?" Preston's made no attempt to conceal his irritation. "Are you looking to tell me how to do things too? I have never come across such an ill-disciplined squadron."

"Sir, I must protest. My duty is to assist you in the running of the squadron and with that in mind, I wish to make some frank observations, in the light of the events of the last few days, which I offer as a positive contribution."

"Go on, F/Lt."

"I think you are being unfair to Evans if you expect Blue Section to fly FAAs and close formation like experienced pilots overnight, they simply don't have enough hours on Hurricanes – and to what purpose? Your section leaders' misgivings about tactics stem from experience not insubordination. We learned in France, and more recently over Dunkirk, that the 'book' is out-of-date. More young lives will be wasted if we have to learn those lessons yet again in the coming days. I mean no disrespect when I suggest that, until you have gained some combat experience yourself, you should at least listen to these men. They are only junior officers as you say, but they are currently among the most experienced in the service, or indeed the world, in the practice and tactics of modern air fighting."

Preston's reply was icy. "You can now do the courtesy of listening to me as I have listened to you. I'm glad I did as I have now identified another of those who are seeking to undermine my authority. Thank you, F/Lt., for pointing out my lack of combat experience. However, when I do go into battle, I shall do so armed with a well- considered and ordered method of fighting, not something cobbled together on the spur of the moment as a result of a few set-backs, which were probably brought about by the indiscipline which seems to characterise this squadron. I am not in the habit of seeking advice from junior officers, nor of allowing my command to be run by a committee. I alone am in charge of this squadron and as long as I remain so I will not tolerate dissent; if necessary I will have every last one of you court-martialled or posted away, and, as for tactics, they will be changed when I am told to do so by my superiors and not before."

"… and those were his very words," said Richard wearily as they walked along the perimeter track, Caspar roaming in front, trying to sniff out rabbits.

"Oh, for goodness sake…" cried George, "we're not trying to stage a rebellion, just open his eyes."

"I know that but he seems to have a paranoia; and after today he'll be keeping an eye on you in particular so watch your step or he'll replace you as Yellow leader."

"I wouldn't care if he did. It would leave me free to hunt Germans, without having the responsibility of a section."

Richard was silent for a few moments, collecting his thoughts. "I know Justine's death has hit you pretty hard, and I can understand your desire for revenge, but you can't do it singlehandedly; modern air warfare requires teamwork or you won't last five minutes – plus you're too young to throw your life away like that. It doesn't seem like it now, but take it from me that time is a great healer – one day you'll meet someone else and your life will begin again."

George was tempted to flare but his respect for Richard told him that what he had said was well intended and he tempered his response. "That's not going to happen because there can never be anyone else. Part of me died with Justine and that which remains alive has only one reason for doing so; which is to go on killing Germans. You say I can't do it alone. What about the aces of the last war – Ball, Mannock, McCudden?"

"Things were different to begin with. Air warfare was in its infancy and there was room for individuality; but flying became more organised and individuals gave way to formations. None of the aces lasted; same on the German side – Immelmann, von Richtofen. They all got tired or complacent; either way they bought it."

"I'd settle for any of their tallies. And I'm not on my own. I hear Jerzy has a score to settle too. We can look out for each other."

"It grieves me to hear you talk this way."

"Grieving is a part of my life now. That and the feeling that I should have been there to look after her and wasn't. That hurts most of all."

Cloud is scattered as they sweep along the coast, heading into the morning sun. Away from Preston's gaze, George has opened the formation out. He is beginning to tire of mock battles and, like the rest of Yellow Section, yearning for real action.

"This is more like it. I can fart now without bumping into you blokes."

"Save the chatter, Yellow Two, and concentrate on keeping a good lookout – Red Section are somewhere around looking to bounce us."

"No worries, they couldn't bounce a baby!"

"I shan't tell you again."

"Yellow leader. Is Yellow Three. I see German, high at ten of clock."

George screws his eyes up but can't see anything. "Are you sure, Yellow Three?"

"Positive – is German – probably Dornier. We climb up?"

"Can you see anything Yellow Two?"

"Negative, leader!"

"Maintain course and lookout, Yellow Section."

"You say you want kill Germans. We don't kill them sitting here!"

George understands the frustration but doesn't appreciate the backchat. "I shan't tell either of you again about R/T discipline. We're on an exercise and Preston will have our hides if we go swanning off because someone thinks they've seen something. Plus, while we're chattering like schoolgirls, Red Section are probably lining us up so keep your eyes peeled and don't speak unless you've something useful to say."

After two minutes of heavy silence Jerzy speaks again. "Yellow leader, German is now eight of clock. Sparkle very prettily in sunshine!"

George is about to issue another rebuke when he catches a tell-tale glint. "Hell, you're right! He's at least Angels twenty and turning for home. Buster Yellow Section! Steer two-twenty for an intercept. Red Leader, we're after a Jerry, south of Swansea."

Giles' voice comes faintly. "We were delayed; still west of Pembrey so you can count us out. Good hunting!"

189

Using emergency boost, the three Hurricanes swing onto a south-westerly track as they begin their climb. A magneto problem in his Hurricane has meant George is in one of the older reserve aircraft, fitted with a fixed-pitch propeller – adequate for training sorties but no match in rate of climb for its variable-pitch companions – so he is soon lagging behind. "Don't wait for me, Yellow Section! It'll be close but you can catch it before it reaches those clouds." The Dornier has obviously spotted them and is already in a dive, trading altitude for speed as it strives for the sanctuary of a large bank of cumulus to the south.

The turn to intercept has placed Max ahead of Jerzy so he is first in shooting range after several minutes hard climbing. The Dornier has almost reached safety as he fires a long burst into its underside. Black smoke trails as its outline begins to blur in the outer fringes of the cloudbank. "Bugger, he's getting away!"

"Is not gone yet!" As Max banks away from the cloud, Jerzy's Hurricane passes underneath and ploughs straight into the murk.

"Come back you crazy drongo – you'll run straight into it!"

There is no reply. After half a minute, George speaks into his R/T. "Yellow Three, this is Yellow Leader, come in please."

Silence.

"Yellow Three, this is Yellow Leader, come in please."

"Hell fire, he must have collided with it!"

"Yellow Three, this is Yellow Leader, come in please." George has now caught up with Max and joins him circling. For several minutes the R/T remains silent. "I don't know what's happened but there's no sign of him. We'd better head back."

Justine hadn't needed a month to make up her mind. With M Beaumont's tuition, she had taken easily to bookkeeping; its inherent order had provided her mind with a much-needed antithesis to the upheaval of recent weeks.

She is sitting at the old-fashioned desk in the back room of the garage; it is already warm so the large windows to her left are partly open, producing sufficient movement of air to keep her cool but not disturb the paperwork spread out in front of her. The peaceful atmosphere is threatening to become soporific. Suddenly, the door flies open and a farm labourer skids in, his face largely obscured by a bushy moustache and a baggy cap. *"You must help. There are Germans after me!"*

Instead of giving way to the shock of the intrusion, she finds herself instantly springing up and opening a cupboard, taller than the man, set into the wall behind her seat. *"Quickly, in here, and don't make a sound!"* As the door closes, she draws a table across the front of it from under the window before transferring one, two, three files of papers from her desk. She pushes the windows wider then tips another file onto the floor and gives a scream. Seconds later, two more men dash in to find her standing among her scattered papers, hand on chest and breathing hard. As a result of her exertions, it is not difficult to appear distressed. *"Oh messieurs! A man – burst in – a robber or a vagabond – and then went out of the window – I was so frightened – for a moment I thought he might..."* Her voice tails off as they clamber through the window without a word. She retrieves her papers and puts them on her desk, allowing her breathing to return to normal and collecting herself for what she knows is still to come. Silence is broken by a grating sound as the table begins inching across the floor. Fingertips curl around the edge of the cupboard door. A flick of her hip slams the table against it prompting a muffled cry from within as the fingers vanish. *"Don't dare move until I tell you to!"*

All the way back to the airfield, George has been calling, without response. Max's shout forestalls his next attempt. "Look leader. On finals!" Picking its way over the ridge guarding the approach from the south is a solitary Hurricane.

"It must be him. Let's see what he's been up to."

Sitting at her desk, the pile of muddled papers in front of her, she tries to sort them but her mind is racing so much she can scarcely begin to concentrate. As she had expected, the two men soon return. One is a gendarme; tall and apparently unaffected by his exertions, obviously used to pursuit. The other; shorter, wearing a leather overcoat despite the fine weather, is sweating profusely, his flabby face bright pink; only his pig-like eyes lack warmth. The gendarme speaks. *"There's no sign of him. Are you sure he went that way?"*

"Of course, monsieur. He charged in, had a quick look round then pushed me aside and went out through the window – then you arrived." With the file – strewn table in front of it the potential of the cupboard is not immediately obvious. She wants to look at it, to satisfy herself it is closed, but she knows she must not lest she gives the game away. The flabby man begins to look around the room as he peels off a glove. She has to deflect him. *"Is he a robber?"* She pauses then widens her eyes for effect, *"or something worse?"*

He turns his gaze onto her and moves closer; she catches a hint of rosewater; his tone is as cold and unfriendly as his eyes. *"He is wanted in connection with subversive activities."*

She gives him an uncomprehending look. *"Quoi?"*

"He has been posting slogans prejudicial to the occupying forces and will be severely dealt with when we catch him." His voice takes on a more menacing tone. *"As will you or anyone else we find has been helping him."*

Despite the warmth of the day, his words chill her to the marrow. She channels her genuine fear into a show of panic. *"I know nothing – I have never seen him before and, anyway, the war is over; as the posters say – further resistance is futile!"*

"Good – so you won't hesitate to tell me if you see him again." He moves to the door; then pauses. *"You can contact me through the Gendarmerie. My name is Herr Glauber of the Gestapo."*

After they have left, she resumes her work. It isn't long before scratching comes from the cupboard. Moving to the table as if to check a document, she hisses again at her unseen charge. *"Stay there and be quiet. I'll tell you when you can come out."*

Clearly excited, Jerzy is holding court to a handful of aircraftsmen as George and Max reach him. "What happened?"

"I follow black smoke through cloud until seeing shape of plane. Let him have it - hundred and fifty yards, maybe. I fire all bullets. There are flames as I pull away. I try to call but radio dead – now I know why." He indicates the aerial mast of his aircraft, neatly severed by return fire.

"Well bloody good show," George claps him on the back, "and I owe you an apology; you really must have the most phenomenal eyesight."

"Maybe you don't think me mad now…"

Giles pushes through the crowd and addresses George. "Sorry to break up the party but the C/O wants to see you, right away. He's in the most awful bate because you abandoned the exercise. I told him you'd spotted a bogey but he's not listening. He wants your guts for garters!"

"We downed a Jerry for God's sake… Surely even he can't find fault with that!"

"Once again you have chosen to flout my authority."

"It was nothing of the sort, sir. We spotted a Jerry, or at least Jerzy did. His eyesight is phenomenal."

"You were tasked to carry out a combat exercise!"

"My apologies, sir, but I imagined that engaging the enemy for real would take precedence over swanning around pretending to."

"I warned you about your impudent attitude! I'll have you court-martialled for this. You flagrantly disobeyed an order."

George realises he has overstepped the mark. He modifies his tone "With respect, sir, Red Section were nowhere near and we destroyed an e/a."

"What e/a? All we have is the word of some madman who claims to be able to see through cloud. I've a good mind to court-martial him too for…" A knock on the door stops him. "I said no interruptions!" he barks.

Parsons face is impassive. "Sorry to barge in sir, but I thought you should know that we've just had a signal that Yellow Section's Dornier was seen going into the drink by a destroyer in the Bristol Channel. It must be theirs – Group have confirmed that no other squadron was in the area at the time. Oh, and they send their congratulations on 686's smart response to the intruder given that Sector Control hadn't been notified that we were airborne and therefore couldn't task us with its interception."

Preston for a moment looks as if he will choke on his own tongue. George knows his head is off the block. He tries to sound matter-of-fact. "It seems the claim is corroborated. Will that be all, sir?"

"Get out of my sight, damn you! But don't think you've heard the last of this."

Nearly two hours have passed before she puts her pen down and goes out to the forecourt. *"I have done all I can for today, unless there is anything else."*

M. Beaumont is working on a lorry, his head under the bonnet. *"Merci, ma petite. Enjoy your lunch, and take care going home – you never know who is on the road these days."* She catches his meaning. She can see that the road in front of her is empty. As they talk, she leans nonchalantly against the lorry, so that, via its wing mirror, she can see the road behind – and there, parked almost behind a tree five or six hundred metres away, is a black Citroen. She narrows her eyes and can make out two figures within. Without looking towards the car, she turns and casually re-crosses the forecourt. Inside, casualness becomes urgency as she dashes into her office and pulls the table aside.

The cupboard door opens and the man emerges, blinking against the light. *"Merci mad..."*

"Not now. They are waiting out at the front. Leave by the window and keep away from the road." He hesitates. *"Go quickly!"* Fear lends strength as she propels him to the window. Before he can speak, she gives him a violent push. *"Just go, NOW!"* He hits the ground with a thump and a yelp of pain. Without checking on him, she pulls the shutters together and locks the window then replaces the table in front of the cupboard. Grabbing her hat and basket she dashes from the office, reverting to casual as she emerges onto the forecourt. She strolls nonchalantly to her bicycle, threads the basket onto one handlebar, spends a moment adjusting her hat and then steps on a pedal, hoisting herself onto the saddle as the bicycle gains momentum. With a cheery wave in M. Beaumont's direction, she describes a half-circle and sets off up the road, steering with one hand and holding her hat to her head with the other. The man is gone so she has nothing more to fear – as she passes the Citroen, she gives a demure smile. She catches a flash of teeth as the Gendarme smiles in return. Glauber, looking sour, takes a notebook from his coat.

"Thanks for getting me out of that scrape Adj."

"Have you completely taken leave of your senses? You can't bandy words with superior officers like that!"

"I know but the man's a bloody fool. It's hard to maintain any respect for him, superior officer or not."

"Remember that you salute the uniform not the man and that without discipline the service would fall apart. You show respect, obey orders and get on with it, like it or not; or face the consequences."

George took a few moments to reply. "Of course you're right, Adj. It was stupid of me but..."

"On the whole, the system works and sooner or later Preston will be found out for what he is so knuckle down or you'll miss your chance to face the Luftwaffe again; which is coming sooner than you think."

"What do you mean?"

"The signal's just come through. As a result of Yellow Section's exploits, we're being moved into the frontline the day after tomorrow. Your old stamping ground – sunny Sussex by the sea."

"Shuttlecock Red Leader, this is Bluejay Control. We have trade for you. Twenty-plus bandits at Angels twelve. Vector two-three-zero and make Angels fifteen."

"Roger, Bluejay Control," Giles' sounds his usual imperturbable self as he leads Red and Yellow Sections onto their new course.

Twenty minutes ago they had been sitting in deckchairs or on the grass at their new airfield, hiding their nervous tension with a lively debate of the pros and cons of *The Barley Mow,* their latest watering hole, when the telephone in the dispersal hut had jangled. A bellowed 'Scramble 'A' Flight!' and six pilots are pelting the short distance to their mounts, which are already bursting into life in the hands of the ground crews. By the time George grabs his parachute, placed ready for him on the tail-plane, the accumulator trolley which had fired up the engine has been unplugged and rolled clear by his fitter while his rigger has scrambled from the cockpit onto the wing ready to strap him in as he pulls on his helmet and makes a quick check of oxygen, radio jack and 't's' and 'p's'. Thumbs up, chocks away and his rigger drops from the wing, dodging the advancing tailplane, and in no time he, Max and Jerzy are rolling across the bumpy grass in pursuit of Red Section. Climbing away, it occurs to him that this is his first 'real' scramble. It has been a long year since the squadron practised the controlled interceptions which they never got the opportunity to repeat in France.

By seven thousand feet, they have cleared the six-tenths strato-cumulus which had been frustrating their sunbathing and above them the sky is endless blue. To their right, the Isle of Wight lies in the sparkling sea, protecting the approaches to Portsmouth as it has since long before the first English Navy had sailed from there. Nearer, a coastal convoy is heading for the Dover Straights – more than likely what the approaching Germans are after he thinks. Before leaving, a pilot in the squadron 686 had come to replace told him that the Germans had been attacking convoys for the last couple of weeks and that they could expect to find themselves undertaking escort duties; an armchair strategy session at dispersal had come to the conclusion the Germans are doing it to test the defences. For no particular reason Justine comes into his mind. Angrily, he dismisses the thought. She is dead and he can't bring her back but at least he is about to begin avenging her. "Shuttlecock Red Leader this is Bluejay Control. Trade is now thirty miles south of you at Angels twelve. Change course to two-two-fiver and continue climbing Angels fifteen."

"Roger Bluejay control, changing course to two-two-fiver." They will intercept within four minutes, by which time they should have height advantage. Unsurprisingly, Jerzy is the first to make a sighting. "Is Yellow Three, bandits at eleven of clock!"

Almost a minute passes before Giles acknowledges during which time two groups of dots have resolved into a dozen bombers at twelve thousand feet and a similar number of what must be twin-engined fighters three thousand feet above them. "Roger, Yellow Three. Bluejay Control, bandits sighted. Regret to inform you some are rather higher than angels twelve." Then a laconic question. "Yellow Three, can you use your remarkable eyesight to check for top cover?"

After a few moments Jerzy replies, "I see nothing, Red Leader."

"Splendid! Yellow Section, deal with the Heinkels as you see fit while we go for the escort. Good hunting! Tally-ho Red Section!" Giles and George have worked out tactics together for situations such as this. Their experiences in France have shown them that the Hurricane handled well is more than a match for the Me110 so with no sign of 109s, they can look to cause maximum havoc.

"Yellow leader to Yellow Section – line abreast for head on attack – pick your targets and give them hell – tallyho!" Max and Jerzy move from the widely-spaced vic that George prefers to operate out of Preston's sight into line with their leader. As one, they accelerate towards the enemy. George knows they can't hope to shoot them all down but he is using a head-on attack to unnerve them – a well-organised formation of twelve aircraft can produce formidable defensive fire but if panicked into scattering then they will become vulnerable to the fighters.

At the first sight of Red Section approaching, the 110s have abandoned their task and formed a defensive circle so before Yellow Section is within shooting range, the bombers, recognising that they are no longer escorted, begin turning away and jettisoning their loads. The aircraft George has his sights on disappears behind another as the enemy sections wheel about. He fires a couple of inconclusive bursts and swings away but before he has the chance to try again, several aircraft have recovered some semblance of formation and his second attempt is met with defensive crossfire, forcing him to break off again. As he does he sees Jerzy attacking a Heinkel on their flank, so close to his target he wants to shout a warning. Jerzy opens fire. From such short range the effect is devastating. Pieces fly off in all directions. He continues firing. *'Niek Zeeyer Polska!'* The unfamiliar phrase issues from the R/T as, with a vivid orange flash, the bomber ceases to exist. For a moment it appears to have taken Jerzy with it before his Hurricane emerges from the cloud of debris. Momentarily, George is stunned, then remembers why he is there. Whilst most of the fleeing enemy are back together a pair are trailing, striving to re-join their fellows. They are echeloned ideally for him to attack each in turn and, from almost side on, he swoops; calmly and purposefully, controlling the desire for vengeance within him. He fires into engine, fuselage, engine, repeating the process with the second, his finger on the firing button until his ammunition is spent, a wild exultation now coursing through him as he deals death and destruction to those he holds responsible for his pain. He wheels his aircraft around in time to see the first aircraft falling towards the sea. By some miracle, the second is still staggering through the air, the smoke from engines and fuselage combining into one thick black plume, when Max's Hurricane appears and applies the finishing touch. "Hope you didn't mind me gate-crashing the party, skip, but that drongo was trying to leave without saying goodbye."

"So that makes three confirmed for Yellow Section to add to a couple of probables for Red; and no losses from the Squadron. Not a bad morning's work gentlemen," said 'Einstein'. He turned to George. "Was Jerzy really so close...?" Before he could say more Preston stepped through the open doorway.

"Sorry to interrupt F/L but I couldn't help overhearing the conversation. Did anyone, see F/O Knight's 'kill' hit the water?" He looked at them in turn. Jerzy shook his head reluctantly.

"Sir, I didn't actually see it hit the water but I saw it falling before I shot its cobber down and there was no way it was going to recover," said Max.

"You didn't actually see it hit the water?" repeated Preston

"No sir."

He turned to 'Einstein'. "In that case, F/L Howlett, I suggest you alter F/O Knight's claim to a 'probable' and I would advise you to be a little more thoroughgoing in your debriefings in future. I don't want my squadron to get a reputation for exaggerated claims. There was enough of that in France I believe. F/O Knight, I'd like to see you in my office in fifteen minutes. Good day gentlemen."

They remained at attention until he had left the room. At least twenty seconds were allowed to pass before anyone spoke.

"What a bastard!" said Max.

"Is large hole-in-arse!" added Jerzy.

"I'm sorry about that rather uncompromising interpretation of the rules," said 'Einstein', "with that one 'confirmed' you'd have been in line for a DFC."

"Scores and gongs don't matter," said George heading for the door, "I know I got the bastard – that's enough for me."

When George entered Preston's office, he was surprised to find Giles there, standing stiffly to attention and looking straight ahead. He came to attention beside him and saluted. Preston finished writing something before he looked up from his desk. "I'll start with a question. Are there any regulations or orders that you and the rest of Yellow Section consider worth obeying?" George couldn't miss the dangerously heavy sarcasm. Out of the corner of his eye, he tried to read Giles' expression but Giles, in plain view of Preston, remained impassive.

"All of them of course, sir."

"Really? Have you heard of what is colloquially known as the 'Dowding Spread'?"

"Yes sir, our guns are harmonised so as to concentrate the fire from all at a point four hundred yards ahead of the aircraft."

"Indeed; so why was P/O Paderewski firing at his target from less than one hundred yards? On the way back here, I took a look at his aircraft and it is covered in dents and scrapes of varying sizes, not to mention various patches of scorched or burnt fabric. It is little more than a miracle that he didn't go the way of his victim. We cannot afford to lose aircraft or pilots, even the hare-brained ones, at a ratio of 1 to 1, so this nonsense has to stop. He is going to be the first of those I post away. There is now a purely Polish squadron under training so they can have the benefit of his antics."

"Sir, please let me speak to him. I share your concern but as I was summoned here I've not had the chance yet."

"You agree with me!? Wonders never cease! Next you'll tell me you approve of the Dowding Spread." Whether he saw a trap or not, George went in with both feet.

"In France, I was one of those tasked with testing guns harmonised to two hundred and fifty yards, sir. The results were disproportionately better."

"So you know more than the commander-in-chief also!"

"I didn't say that, sir, but I do know that the latest all-metal German bombers are capable of absorbing punishment so, within reason, it makes sense to get closer and hit them harder."

Giles made to speak but Preston cut him short. "Thank you F/Lt. I will be calling on you in a moment. I'll come to the main point, F/O Knight; it seems from what I heard of F/Lt Howlett's rather lax debriefing that your attack on the enemy bombers failed to use any of the prescribed formations the squadron has been practising."

"That's correct, sir."

"Would you care to explain yourself?"

"Yes sir. In the circumstances, a head-on attack seemed appropriate."

"I see. F/L Frobisher, I asked you to be here so you could bear witness to the fact that F/O Knight has admitted failure to carry out prescribed tactics thus compromising fighting efficiency and imperilling the lives of men under his command."

"I disagree, sir," said Giles firmly. He looked exasperated; an unusual emotion for him thought George.

"I beg your pardon?"

"Sir, as Flight Commander, I gave him orders to attack as he deemed fit and I am happy to accept responsibility for that because having fought alongside him for several months, I have complete faith in his abilities, as a fighter pilot and latterly as a Section Leader. In the circumstances, I consider he performed commendably – a force of bombers larger than his were made to jettison their loads and driven off in disarray, sustaining losses without harm to Yellow Section or their intended target. I fail to see how he could have done better."

Preston was silent for what seemed an eternity but George was now familiar with his efforts to keep control of himself. At length he spoke, "Obviously this whole squadron is determined to defy and undermine me. So be it! Until I have managed to have the main offenders replaced, I see no alternative henceforth but to lead formations myself whenever possible and ensure first-hand that my orders are obeyed. Flight or Section Leaders will fly as supernumeraries on these occasions. You are both dismissed."

George had never seen Giles so irate, even after the episode of the refugees in France. "What the bloody hell is wrong with the man? Is he on our side or theirs? I doubt Stanhope-Smith could have been more antipathetic."

"He's definitely got it in for me."

Giles gave a hollow laugh. "It's gone way beyond that. He's the Emperor bloody Nero, simply not fit to be in command, and the sooner we're rid of him the better. The Germans know they won't win the war by bombing a few coastal convoys. As we've already discussed, they're just probing our defences. The real attack is coming soon though – and God help 686 if Preston's still in charge!"

The pale glow in the eastern sky silhouetted their aircraft and the erks standing ready to fire them into life. George had loved the cool freshness of a summer dawn ever since, some ten years ago, that first time his father had dragged him reluctantly from his bed to go and catch trout for breakfast – another age, another world. Today it wasn't trout he was after but reconnaissance aircraft. At least the early start meant Yellow Section wouldn't be on the convoy patrol, which Preston was going to lead following yesterday's decision. That dubious honour was going to Blue Section; today at least. "So what time did you roll in last night – and how the hell did you get past the guard?" he directed his question at a rumpled looking Jerzy.

"I prefer not say in case of self-incrimination."

"Hope she was worth it; bearing in mind what the skip said last night," added Max.

Momentarily, Jerzy's face lit up. "She was."

"Well don't let it happen again," snapped George irritably, then added more calmly, "You're a grown man and I don't want to treat you like a child but if you're going to fly effectively you'll need all the sleep you can get; particularly when things hot up."

"Don't worry," Jerzy grinned, "today I fly like angel and fight like devil."

"Make sure you do." After his meeting with Preston, Max and Jerzy had insisted he accompany them to the *Barley Mow*. Over a beer, he had gently reprimanded Jerzy about being too close to the Dornier.

'Don't you British want to win this war?' had been his response.

'Of course we do and that means getting nearer than four hundred yards but I think you overdid it yesterday. Did you see the state of your aircraft?'

Jerzy had nodded ruefully. 'OK, maybe I was little too near. Lesson learned.'

'Good, because it seems you're on your last chance with Preston – one more blot and you're off to join your countrymen; perhaps you'd prefer that?'

His face had fallen. 'No. Have cousin in 302 Squadron. Every day they ride tricycles and have English lessons – but don't fight. I come here to kill Germans not ride bike around; and I speak already bloody good English'

'Well you'd better watch your step then. And one more thing – battle cries are all well and good in Hollywood films but they block the R/T when we need to communicate. Shout your head off in the cockpit but keep off the air. OK?' Jerzy nodded. 'So what did it mean?'

'Long live Poland.'

'I'll drink to that – Long live Poland!'

Max had stood up. "Hold on you blokes, I've an idea." He headed for the bar.

Jerzy stared moodily into the distance. George had waited a while before speaking,

'Are you OK?'

'Talk of Poland brings bad memories. No matter.'

'I'm sorry if I've opened an old wound.'

'No matter – these things are with us always, as you know also I think.'

Before George could reply, Max had returned with three whiskies. 'One of the books I read on the boat over here was the Three Musketeers. I reckon that's us, defending our King against foes near and far.'

'I know this book,' from Jerzy.

'Preston has to be Richelieu,' George had added.

'That settles it,' Max had concluded, 'all for one and one for all,' raising his glass for them to join the toast.

After draining his glass, Jerzy had glanced at his watch and stood up. 'Forgive please, have,' he frowned in concentration, 'as-sig-nation.'

'I think I know who Aramis is. He's cutting a swathe through the WAAFs as well as the Germans,' Max had said lightly, watching him go, 'a bit of Polish gallantry and they're falling over like skittles. Still, after what he's been through he needs some enjoyment.'

'I've not yet had a chance to talk to him beyond operational matters.'

'He's usually pretty reticent – it all came out one night when he'd had a few more than usual. He spent the first week or so of the war having aircraft shot from under him – their biplanes were no match for 109s. When there was nothing left to fly, he made his way home to find his mother and sisters raped and murdered. I think that would have driven me round the bend but instead he spent weeks making his way across Poland to Rumania, dodging Germans all the time, then to France where he volunteered for their air force but they seemed to regard him as a bit of an embarrassment and kept him on the sidelines. When France collapsed he managed to get to England and here he is; eager to fight and nursing a great deal of hatred for the Germans – but then I don't think I need to tell you anything about that?'

'No, you don't.' He was silent briefly, his face working as he battled with his emotions. 'Just be thankful you don't have a wife to protect.'

'Actually I do,' he gave George just enough time to register what he had said before continuing, 'Connie, my lovely English Rose. Met her a few days after I got off the boat and we married within a month. I left her in Norfolk near my last airfield. She keeps badgering to come down here. I'm not sure – it's pretty close to the Jerries.'

'Now they hold the French, Belgian and Dutch coasts they can bomb East Anglia just as easily as Sussex. At least here you'd have her nearby. I wasn't there when Justine needed me.'

'If you'll permit me to say it skip, I think you're being too hard on yourself. I heard tell you were wounded and the bastards flattened the whole village – what could you have done?'

'I don't know – I'm sure I could have done something – but I'll never know now.'

'I think you're right about one thing though – I'll see if I can get through to her tonight.'

'You're due a 24. Wangle some extra petrol and shoot up there and fetch her. In that MG of yours you'll be there and back in no time; I doubt you'll regret it.'

They were climbing hard. Although their quarry was still a good mile above them, its progress was made clear by the vapour trail it was leaving in the cold air. The three Hurricanes would be creating their own trails soon but George expected they would be much closer to the intruder before that happened; until then they were hidden against the dark channel waters beneath them where dawn was still minutes away. It was another early morning flight come to gather weather information for the coming day. How much it had already managed to radio back to its base, he did not know but he was determined that radio messages were all that would be returning. A few months ago, he would have felt a certain respect for the crew, flying an aircraft, albeit armed, which stood little chance if intercepted by Hurricanes or Spitfires; now his main feeling was the desire to put them vertically into the channel. RDF had picked up the Dornier before it left Normandy and the warning thus provided would enable Yellow Section to intercept before it reached its intended landfall in the Portsmouth area. "Line astern, Yellow Section, and make every shot count – we may not get a second chance." The Dornier was flying above 20,000 feet where the air temperature exceeded minus thirty and he knew that, once the canvas patches had been blown off the gun ports by the first firing pass, the oil in the guns could well have frozen by the time they had turned for a second attempt, rendering them useless. He had heard talk of diverting exhaust heat to the gun mechanisms to prevent this but 686's Hurricanes as yet lacked this modification. They were closing fast now and the Dornier crew had yet to spot them. In many ways the approach reminded him of his first shared kill over France, but with two big differences; he was section leader now instead of number three and there had been no Justine to see him off this morning. Grimly he checked t's and p's, adjusted the reflector sight, moved the safety ring to the firing position and pressed the R/T. "Tally-ho!" At that moment, the ventral gunner spotted him and loosed a wild burst well wide of the mark. The Dornier started to bank away from him but he followed the turn allowing the gunsight to cover the gunner's position and fired a long burst, manoeuvring his aircraft to rake forwards along the cabin. There was no return fire as he banked away to allow Yellow Two and Three to follow up. Within a minute, it was all over as Max and Jerzy completed the execution and the Dornier's turn had degenerated into a spiral dive. They circled to watch until it disappeared into the waters below. There were no parachutes. "Bluejay Control, Shuttlecock leader. Bandit destroyed. Home for tea and a bacon sandwich."

"Roger, Shuttlecock Leader. Good show and *bon appetit.*" He realised that he felt no great elation this time, just grim satisfaction that another German aircraft and its crew had got their just desserts. He permitted himself a wry grin as the thought struck that even Preston would struggle to find fault with this morning's work.

Lys caught the brief flash – and knew it for what it was; sunlight reflecting off binoculars. She had seen it more than once when her husband was alive and they had hunted game together; but she had no knowledge of a hunt today so someone was watching the farm; and she was determined to find out who. She decided not to rouse Justine; she hadn't actually been sick so far, but she hadn't been at her best in the mornings either so Lys saw little gain in disturbing her. Pausing only to pick up her shotgun, she whistled her two retrievers and slipped out of the back door of the farmhouse. It would take five minutes to reach the watcher's location unobserved.

The Hurricane slid to a halt three-quarters of the way across the landing field; the blades of its propeller bent backwards over the engine cowling like the leaves of a wilted plant. Crash tender and ambulance skidded to a halt alongside and men ran to lift the pilot from the cockpit. A second Hurricane, wisps of smoke issuing from its engine and holes the size of a man's fist in its rear fuselage, landed heavily to one side, bouncing three times before settling onto the grass. George rose from his chair and approached it as the growl of the Merlin died away. The pilot jumped down from the wing and threaded his way through the aircraftsmen converging on it.

"What happened; where are Blue Two and Three?" George asked.

"Not a roar-ing success," replied Evans quietly, removing his helmet. A flash of malevolence briefly lit his face, "but it could have been – we nearly lost the C/O! Instead Bartholomew and Godley have bought it. They didn't stand a chance – silly bastard led them into it. He ought to get an Iron Cross for this day's work. As usual he had us flying closer than fleas on a blood-y dog, but being 'supernumerary' at the rear I managed to drop back enough to keep a decent look-out. I spotted this horde of one-oh-nines coming down on us like a ton of bricks and called 'break', but instead of turning into the attack like I've been drum-ming into them they both followed Preston and flew straight on. He was telling them to hold formation and await his command – God knows what man-oeuvre he 'ad in mind!" he shook his head in a mixture of sadness and frustration.

"Probably none," said George bitterly, "the book doesn't cover being bounced by 109s." He sensed Evan's mood. "For God's sake don't blame yourself; after the brow-beatings he's given them they didn't dare do otherwise."

"Easy to say-but why did he have to survive? De-vil looks after his own, I reck-on." Richard and then Giles joined them. Richard spoke first. "Preston's stopped a couple of bullets; only minor wounds but he'll be out for a while..."

"That's a shame," interjected George, ironically.

Richard gave him an admonitory look, "... which means that Giles is acting C/O."

"Not a mo-ment too soon," said Evans.

Giles' was immediately business-like, seemingly untouched by events. "So pass the word around, I want all pilots at dispersal in 15 minutes, along with you, Richard, and I need a word with 'Einstein' right away."

Lys motioned to the dogs to stop. Each pressed its chest to the ground and watched expectantly for her next signal. She carefully crept the last few yards, took a deep breath and thrust the shotgun through the bush in front of her. *"OK, put your hands..."* She didn't continue because there was no one there; but there had been. Her husband had taught her how to track deer so one fairly clumsy human was no problem. Flattened grass showed where he had been lying and she was able to follow a trail the few metres to the edge of the road where tyre marks completed the picture. She made a mental note to have a couple of man-traps set. If the watcher returned he wouldn't find things so easy next time.

The expectation was almost tangible as Giles began speaking. "I don't intend to waste words. For the next few weeks, I will be acting C/O," he ignored the rumble of approval from his audience, "and for that time we shall do things my way. After today's fiasco close vic and sections of three are out," more approbation, "and I intend to give the Jerries a taste of their own medicine – quite literally – by copying their tactics. That doesn't mean they're better than us – they've just had more time to sort out the best way to do things. Our four sections of three will become six sections of two. Generally these pairs will be combined, so effectively we shall be three sections of four – somewhat more widely spaced than hitherto." Ironic laughter. "This will make both formation flying and lookout-keeping easier. You will engage the enemy as one or more pairs, each leader covered by his wingman. The Adj will post a roster shortly. Also I want you all to study the diagrams that I have asked 'Einstein' to draw. They show cross-over turns – which allow two, four, six or eight aircraft to change course without breaking formation. Put simply everyone but the leader turns inside the man in front and the new formation is a mirror-image of the previous one. Any questions?

– No? – Good. Sooner or later we are going to face an onslaught from an enemy who is powerful and ruthless; but not superhuman – so with God's help and our own guts and determination we will prevail. Good luck to you all, gentlemen."

12: August, 1940

"This last week has been a Godsend," said Giles, "scarcely a Hun to be seen. It's allowed us to practice the new formations without any rude interruptions."

"And the new boys have fired shots in anger on morning patrols – one damaged and one probable," reflected Richard, "If you ask me, 'Litmus' and Evans have done a good job with them."

"Hopefully they've learned enough to stand a chance of surviving. The first few hours are the most dangerous."

"Nothing new there then," rejoined Richard

"My father never tires of saying 'there's nothing new under the sun'; and he's probably right. I'm not going to repeat Chamberlain's mistake and say they've missed the bus but they are taking their time. If they intend to invade this year they've less than two months realistically; they can't expect to get troops across the channel after that."

"I think William the Conqueror invaded in October, but things were probably simpler then. So we just have to play a straight bat until the end of September."

"Nearly eight weeks. Easier said than done I'll wager. Put Blue and Green Sections on the dawn show again tomorrow."

"Some of the other chaps are starting to get restless."

"They can have whatever convoy patrols come our way. It's important just now to give the sprogs as much time in the air as possible. Pretty soon everyone's going to see all the action they could wish for."

Through the open window came the sound of approaching aircraft, and nearer, the sound of Max's voice. "It's the morning glory boys!" Giles and Richard moved to the window to watch.

"No glory today though," George was sitting in a wicker chair, shading his eyes with one hand as they came in to land, "their gun patches are intact."

"It m-must have s-spotted us climbing," said 'Litmus' at dispersal a few minutes later, "because it s-scarpered for home b-before we got anywhere near."

"Well at least they couldn't have achieved much of a reconnaissance."

"P-probably saw all they n-needed. There's a big convoy steaming w-w-westwards so I b-bet that will be th-the target today."

"Good morning, Mme. Is M Beaumont available?" The man proffered his business card which announced him as Pierre Lagarde, traveller in vehicle and machine parts.

"I'm afraid not, he's gone out to mend a tractor; and," Justine added tartly, *"even if he were, he doesn't see commercial travellers without an appointment."* She found herself riled by the way this stranger, with his flashy suit and hat pulled down over his eyes, had swept into her office unannounced, expecting to see M Beaumont as if by right. Rationing imposed by the 'occupying power', as the Germans liked to style themselves, had already sparked the beginnings of a *'marche noir'* and she found herself wondering if this man dealt in more than spare parts.

"That's fine, but an appointment won't be necessary; it's you I really came to see."

"I've no idea why. I don't know you."

"Actually, you do," she couldn't restrain a gasp of recognition as he removed his hat.

"I don't remember your name... Capitaine something."

"Don't try. Its Victor now and so it will remain until we have rid France of the Boche; and that's all you need to know. I'm here for two things; one of which is to thank you for helping me."

"I don't understand, you saved me."

"I'm obviously better at disguise than I hoped. As a soldier, I saved you, but do you recall a farm labourer pursued by the Gestapo?"

This time she stifled any trace of surprise. *"I do. You are something of a chameleon. I suppose that makes us even."* She narrowed her eyes. *"So what is the second thing?"*

"To ask you to help me again."

"To do what – chalk slogans on walls and end up getting shot? I don't think so!"

"I'm trying to build an organisation to resist the occupation."

"In case you've forgotten, the Germans defeated our army so how can you and I and a few others hope to beat them?"

"We can't. But we can help those who can. The British are still fighting. We've lost the first round but we're going to – we have to – win in the end and you're the sort of person I – and France – are going to need. I've seen you in action, how you took in your stride a situation that would have overwhelmed many people – you can think on your feet and you're brave and resourceful. Plus you live on a farm – out in the country away from the Gendarmes and the Germans."

"How do you know where I live?" Surprise gave way to anger, *"You knew who I was – it wasn't a co-incidence when you barged in here and risked my life."*

"No, I swear I had no idea then that you worked here. I recognised you immediately but there wasn't time to say anything before you put me in that cupboard Then, you pushed me out of the window – and sprained my wrist," he gave her a winning smile, *"for which I forgive you,"* and received a wan response. *"I had to lie low for a couple of weeks then I made enquiries about you."*

"Well I'm sorry that you've wasted your time but I've no intention of joining you. Among other reasons, I'm pregnant – hardly an ideal condition for ducking and diving from the Germans."

"That's no problem. At this stage having the farm as a place to..."

She cut in, her face suffused with anger. *"Don't you think I've lost enough? Husband, mother, home, school, pupils and a whole village and now you want me to risk my aunt and my child by helping you to annoy the Germans. Forget it! And don't come here again peddling your hare-brained schemes much less to the farm because you won't be welcome. I thank you again for saving my life but as you've pointed out I saved you so I don't feel any further obligation to you. I would love to see France free again but the reality is we're occupied and we're going to have to make the best of it."* For the second time in as many months she found herself propelling him from the office; this time via the door. *"For what it's worth, I wish you luck, but you'll have to manage without me."*

'Litmus's' prediction is confirmed. For the second time in the day, he climbs away from the airfield, this time as one of eight instead of leading three others.

"Shuttlecock Leader, Bluejay Control. Vector two-one-fiver and make Angels ten. Convoy under attack off Isle-of-Wight. Be aware of friendly aircraft."

"Roger Bluejay Control." Giles wants to arrive above the enemy fighters. "All Shuttlecock aircraft make Angels twelve."

Crossing the coast near Thorney Island, they see ahead of them tiny shapes swarming over a spread of ships, fountains of water erupting like small stalagmites, and columns of smoke. "Steer two-four-zero. I want to be up-sun." Soon the picture becomes more distinct. Four ships are burning and another lying on its side while the remainder are spread over a wide area, making them more difficult to defend. Above the convoy, Stukas in twos and threes are diving and releasing their bombs. RAF fighters are managing to harass some but are mostly being engaged by the more numerous Me109 escort. Giles permits himself a second's satisfaction; by now they have the sun at their backs and are above the melee. "Go for the Stukas and keep at them until the 109s come after you. Break into Sections and pick your targets. Tallyho!" In pairs, he and Max, now his no. 2, George and Jerzy and Litmus, Evans and their respective wingmen roll into a dive. Unseen until they are through the screen of 109s, they are unopposed. The Stukas are in vics of three, four abreast. Giles points his Hurricane at the leader of the leftmost vic and, closing rapidly, opens fire, oblivious to a burst of return fire from the rear gunner which is cut short as the Stuka explodes in a ball of flame. The blast knocks its companions sideways but George doesn't have time to watch the outcome as he is now firing at the leader of the next vic, his bullets tracking along the fuselage and into the engine. Gushing smoke it falls away and then he and Jerzy are beyond the formation and arcing into a climbing turn for another attack.

"Yellow leader, 109 on tail. Break right." George rolls away to the right in response to Jerzy's call and tracers pass harmlessly by.

"Thanks, Yellow Two. Reform and we'll try again." George's evasive action has taken him away from the whirling mass of planes so he turns in again towards them. From the corner of his eye, he sees Jerzy easing into position on his starboard quarter.

"Four 109s, 12 of clock high," intones Jerzy.

"Roger Yellow Two. I see them. Buster, break towards them." George pushes the throttle through the gate and hauls back on the stick, pointing his aircraft at the down-rushing enemy. He opens fire at extreme range and the tracers to his right tell him that Jerzy is following suit. The 109s return fire without effect before breaking away in search of easier pickings. "Stukas two o'clock high." They turn and begin climbing towards them. More 109s come from the side. "Yellow Two, Bandits nine o'clock. Break left!" Again they turn into the threat, firing a quick burst at the fleeting targets with no obvious results. "Let's give it another go." George hauls his aircraft round to the right and tries again to climb up to the remaining Stukas. Another gaggle of 109s falls upon them and once more, they turn into the attack. As before, the return fire is wayward but this time the 109s leave it later before breaking off.

"I hit one!" calls Jerzy as they flash past.

George rolls the Hurricane onto its back in time to see them, already well below him, heading for France; one trailing a thin white stream of glycol. He rolls level again, wanting to pursue more Stukas but, by the now-familiar magic, the sky around is suddenly clear of aircraft, except for Jerzy, steadfastly protecting his tail. Now he becomes aware that he is tired and wet with sweat from the effort of hauling his Hurricane around the sky, frustrated that the 109s have prevented him taking a toll of the Stukas but with a measure of satisfaction. "That was hard going but we got a couple of the bastards at least. Home time. Good show Yellow Two. How's it go – 'Neck Zia Polska'?"

"It's 'Ni-ek Zee-yer Polska', but best I hear yet from an Englishman!"

Their return added to a lively debriefing room. "A damaged 109 for Jerzy, and a probable Ju87 for me," George called over the hubbub, by way of salutation, "I saw it fall away but I didn't –"

"M-make that confirmed," interjected 'Litmus', "it hit the water j-just before mine."

"That puts you in line for a gong," said Einstein, "good show!"

"It isn't me you should be congratulating," said George, "It's Giles. His formation worked like a charm; offensively and defensively. If we'd been flying Preston's vics we'd have been massacred today."

"Hardly my formation. As you know I pinched it from the Jerries."

Evans grinned. "Hoist with their own pet-ard then – and all the swee-ter for that."

"There were so many 109s we couldn't get near the Stukas after the first pass."

"That's something we'll have to live with," said Giles, "we know they out-number us and I've a feeling that the brass don't want us getting into big battles at this stage, so they won't be committing us wholesale. I can't speak for other squadrons today but despite being few in numbers we despatched at least four without loss. Carry on like that and *we* will wear *them* down."

"Why are they s-still attacking convoys?"

"I really don't know but it can't last. They'll have to try something different soon because they're not going to win the war by sinking a few coasters; and the Stukas are sitting ducks if we can get past the escort. Today's not over yet though. Richard, I want the sections which haven't flown yet on standby. There's a pint at the Barley Mow tonight for everyone who flies today."

Late afternoon sees White and Black Sections airborne, accompanied by Red and Yellow, heading to repel another attack on the same, somewhat depleted, convoy, now passing Weymouth Bay. They track beyond Portland before leaving the coast with the sun at their backs. As in the morning, the advantages of height and sun enable them to avoid the defending 109s and set about the Stukas. Giles sends the leader spinning down: Rear gunner and pilot jerk like crazy marionettes in a storm of bullets before George's target falls satisfyingly earthwards; Jerzy takes the opportunity of a deflection shot as he spears through the formation behind George and exults at the resulting explosion. P/O Bardsley, leading White Section, is frustrated to see only wisps of white smoke from his while Sgt Bannerman, his counterpart in Black Section, opens his account by shooting the propeller off another. As they swing round looking to attack again, the escort respond and now it is Max's job to remove a 109 from Giles' tail. A burst into the wing-root prompts the pilot to jettison his canopy and take to his parachute as flames begin to lick back along the fuselage. His comrade endeavours to manoeuvre onto Max's tail but the sound of Bardsley's bullets bouncing off his armoured seat-back persuade him otherwise. There is consolation for the Germans as Black 2 turns on its back, glycol and smoke mingling in a grey plume. P/O Judd, in his first combat, drops from the open canopy and tumbles through the air for heart-stopping seconds until a blossoming parachute jerks him upright, to drift on an onshore wind and live to fight another day; and then, once more, the sky is clear and they are riding the ebbing tide of adrenalin back to the promise of pints all round.

The *Barley Mow* was already pretty full as George and Jerzy stooped beneath the low doorway. To a background of excited chatter they worked their way through the throng of pilots, WAAFs, always magically there to add feminine company to a celebration, and locals; some hoping to benefit from free-flowing drinks, others more than willing to put their hands in their pockets to show their appreciation of the 'boys in blue'. Giles was perched on a stool at one end of the bar, holding court to a small group. "George, glad you could make it. Pint?"

"Yes please, and one for…" He turned but Jerzy was no longer following. He was several yards away, already deep in conversation with an attractive brunette.

"Good job there are no WAAFs at Angels fifteen or you'd be minus a wingman. He spots more than Jerries with those eagle eyes."

Before he could reply, he felt a hand on his shoulder. "George, I want you to meet the wife. Connie, this is George."

"Pleased to meet you, Max has told me a lot about you," she spoke softly, almost shyly.

"As you can see, Skipper, I took your advice and brought her down here. We've a room down the road at *The Stag.* Can I get you anything?"

"Thanks, but I've one on its way from Giles."

Max grinned. "I've had mine but I'm still thirsty. Can I get you another, Con?"

"Gin-and-it. Please." As he set off through the crowd towards the bar, she turned her large blue eyes back to him.

"I believe I've you to thank for my being here; you helped him make up his mind."

He found the words with difficulty. "I hope it works out for the best; it's what I'd…"

She put her hand on his arm. "I'm sure it will – don't say any more – I understand; I don't know what I'd do if anything were to happen to Max."

George knew he couldn't maintain the conversation and his composure. Salvation came in the form of Max and a slightly inebriated Evans, the latter proffering one of the two beers he carried. "Cheers boyo! Comp-liments of the C/O (act-ing)." He lowered his voice, "'Ave you seen what's 'app-ening over there?" George looked to see 'Litmus' holding the rapt attention of a buxom civilian who could have won the part of Nell Gwyn in any repertory company in the land. "If 'e doesn't lose 'is cherr-y tonight, 'e never will. Mind you, by the look of 'er, she'll prob-ably kill 'im."

"He's made of sterner stuff than you may imagine, but better her than the Luftwaffe?" suggested George, quietly grateful to Evans who had now dissolved into laughter.

George finally fathomed what had been gnawing at him since their introduction. He had felt drawn to Connie and thereby disloyal to Justine. Blonde but shorter and more slender than Justine, Connie too was beautiful, but now he knew that wasn't what had moved him; it was her air of vulnerability that had struck deep into a soul still racked with guilt and grief; he didn't want her for himself – he wanted to protect her. His mind now cleared of pre-occupation, he began feeling for the bullet under his pillow but sleep put paid to his search.

"I'm not surprised they stayed at home yesterday," said Bardsley, "even the birds were walking, but the day before was fine and they didn't show."

"Ours not to reason why," said Max, "just be grateful for the respite. There's obviously something brewing today though or they wouldn't have put the whole squadron at Readiness." Scarcely had he spoken when the scramble call came and he was formatting on Giles' starboard quarter as they climbed skywards once more.

Twenty-five thousand feet later they are again approaching Weymouth Bay but this time there is no convoy in sight. Fifty-plus bandits they had been told; below, they can see probably eighty bombers approaching the coast. Higher, but still below them, twenty or thirty Me110s have already formed a circle offshore. To right and left at their altitude are two more circles, of Bf109s, about thirty in each. "Shuttlecock aircraft; take a pot at the 110s – deflection shots – carry on over the circle then drop onto the bombers and away. Remember that 109 and 110s are faster than us in the dive so watch your tails. Tallyho!" Giles goes into a shallow dive. He fires at a point in front of a 110 and is rewarded with the sight of it flying into his tracer stream, staggering and then falling away, but he can't watch it go down. Max, echeloned starboard and two hundred yards apart, fires his guns and leaves the next in line trailing smoke. George, in the manner he has learned from Jerzy, draws closer to his target before firing, so reducing the margin for error. He too has allowed the right amount of deflection and the 110 immediately bursts into flame. Jerzy sets another ablaze. "Yellow Section, maintain altitude and form up on me. All other Shuttlecock aircraft proceed as ordered." Giles has continued beyond the circle and is now curving in the direction of the bombers but has maintained his altitude. George and Jerzy close up on Red Section while Blue, Green, White and

Black Sections in turn make their firing passes over the circling 110s then point their noses at the bombers below. George is impressed; Giles' plan of attack means that without leaving the circle the 110s can't bring their formidable forward armament of cannon and machine guns to bear on the Hurricanes and greatly reduces the likelihood of being hit by their single free-swinging rear machine guns. The Me110 is named *Zerstorer* – Destroyer – by the Germans. Today they are destroying the Destroyers.

Several 109s are dropping from their two circles in pursuit of the diving Hurricanes. "Yellow Section, take the Huns on the right. We'll deal with the others; and watch your own tails, there'll be more following. Shuttlecock aircraft – be aware of bandits in your six o'clock. Have your squirt at the bombers, head for the deck and then home like the clappers!" So saying Giles leads Max into a dive and George, realising he has witnessed an object lesson in fighter tactics, begins his pursuit with Jerzy following; their task to reach the 109s before they get in range of the Hurricanes which are now bursting through the bombers. Three are falling and a couple more dropping out of formation but 686 alone can't inflict enough damage to turn back the tide which is now crossing the coast and starting its bombing run. Like an unrolling carpet of mushrooms he can see advancing explosions interspersed with gouts of flame. Larger than usual flashes and billowing black smoke indicate oil tanks being hit. In a straight dive he would be unable to match the 109s but their relative courses mean he has been aiming for an interception and he is fast reaching that point as the 109s in turn are closing on the other Hurricanes. A speculative burst at extreme range is wide of the mark but sufficient to cause the 109s to abandon the chase and turn inside him. The Hurricanes are far enough ahead now to be safe, although he can see one is leaving a thin white glycol trail, probably, he reflects, caused by return fire from one or more of the bombers.

"Yellow Leader, bandits closing!"

"Break Yellow Two, break!" responds George and, turning his head, he can see Jerzy's Hurricane swinging out to the right with two 109s further back but still chasing. Two to one – not good odds he thinks – for the Germans! A quick scan shows two behind him also; flashes at the propeller boss and on the wings telling him they are firing. His ears are hurting due to the sudden pressurisation of the dive and a quick glance at the rapidly unwinding altimeter shows he is passing through 5,000 feet. A few black puffs appear around him and he hears the rattle of shrapnel from somewhere behind him – flak from Portland AA guns. He isn't feeling particularly grateful for their intervention until another look back shows that one of his pursuers has given up the chase. The other is still there though, obviously determined to make a kill, and to emphasise the point a line of tracer zips over his port wing. At three thousand feet he starts easing out of the dive and begins jinking to avoid becoming a sitting target. He is nearing two thousand feet and still his pursuer is there, gaining slowly and firing short but, so far, ineffectual bursts. Sooner or later the German will have to turn for home but that might prove too late for George so he decides to force the issue. He throttles back abruptly, bringing a gout of smoke from the exhausts, then begins a gentle climb. The 109 is now closing rapidly but holding fire, the pilot confident and looking to make sure of his kill. George watches, gauging the distance. A sighting burst punches some holes in his tail plane. He kicks in full rudder and hauls back hard on the stick. The flick roll tumbles the Hurricane through the sky like a blown leaf. The German is taken by surprise and overshoots. George centres the rudder and pushes the stick forward, bringing the Hurricane under control again. Opening the throttle, he has become the pursuer, just as he did against F/L Underhill a long year ago. He fires a burst and pieces fly off the wing. The German is weaving now but George is determined to down him. Another burst starts a thin stream of glycol. He presses the gun button again but this time nothing – out of ammo. He is cursing in frustration when it occurs to him that the longer he can detain the German the less his chances of making it back across the channel. He continues twisting and turning after the jinking aircraft, as if trying to get it in his sights. The glycol trail has thickened considerably by the time the German pilot decides he must risk all by breaking southwards. George knows his bluff has been called so he makes no effort to follow; convinced that the 109 is destined to end up in the drink. He scans the sky above and behind him before pressing the R/T. "Yellow Two, do you read me?"

"Roger, Yellow Leader." Jerzy's reply is faint but firm.

"Report position."

"South of Isle of Wight – returning base."

"Proceed independently but keep your eyes peeled. Any joy?"

"One Boche in drink, the other might get home!"

"Good show; the beers are on me tonight." Several Germans won't be drinking beer again so for him and Jerzy in particular it has been a good day – over already because the met forecast for the afternoon is rain and poor visibility which will preclude any raids of the magnitude they have just witnessed; a few hours relief from the knotted stomachs that afflict veterans and sprogs alike as they sit at dispersal awaiting the call to action. Dark cloud is already building up in the west. It has also been a different day – the bombers have struck in numbers at Portland Harbour instead of convoys. Is this the beginning of the major assault? It is nearly mid-August – it must be.

The cup wobbled slightly as she picked it up and the liquid within threatened to slop over the sides onto her paperwork. Liquid was the best word for it since it bore little resemblance to coffee as she had known it in the past – just one more consequence of occupation. The wobble was the result of a sleepless night. All her life when something had been troubling her it inevitably turned up in her dreams and now was no exception. She had seen herself, accompanied by Lys, pushing a pram through the village when the escaped lunatic from Rethel walked past on the other side of the road, pointing down the road and mouthing something she couldn't hear – he had appeared in several of her dreams since Rethel, always incoherent, and she still hadn't divined his significance. A black Citroen had screeched to a halt beside her and Glauber, the Gendarme and two German soldiers leaped out, seized the pram and began searching it. The first soldier unwrapped the bundle of blankets within. All it contained was a china doll which was cast aside, breaking into fragments. The second delved deeper and triumphantly extracted some cans of paint and brushes. There was a shot and Lys fell to the ground beside her. She turned to see Glauber snarling the word 'bitch' and levelling his pistol at her. As he pulled the trigger she had awakened. The import of her dream seemed clear; helping Victor would be courting catastrophe for her and her remaining family.

George was feeling frustrated as the morning sun beat down on him. He and Jerzy had again been denied the chance to take further toll of the Luftwaffe by Giles' continuing insistence on letting 'Litmus' or Evans take the less experienced pilots on the early morning patrols in search of reconnaissance aircraft. That he knew Giles' decision was tactically the right one didn't make it any more palatable so he continued to fret as the sun climbed higher. The dispersal phone had already rung several times and each time he had tensed, ready to spring from his deckchair into a headlong dash for his aircraft, but still he found himself waiting. He glanced across at Jerzy, sitting cross-legged, moodily tearing up tufts of grass as he stared into the distance. Was he mirroring George's frustration; exercising his eyes again, or perhaps reliving the horrors he had witnessed since the war had begun? Whatever the answer, he couldn't think at that moment of anyone he would rather have to protect his tail. He had come to value this man and their friendship; measured as yet in weeks. Then the waiting was over – the jangling phone, 'Squadron scramble', pelting headlong to his aircraft, bouncing across the grass airfield until the sudden release as it became airborne, followed by the long haul skywards, clawing for the height needed to be above the enemy when they met; twelve aircraft in groups of four, a relatively new formation but already comfortingly familiar.

Lys stepped out of the farmhouse to meet the battered truck that she had seen chugging its way up the lane. It sputtered to a halt in front of her and the driver alighted. He lifted his hat and at the same time, with a small bow, handed her his business card. *"Bonjour madam, je suis..."*

She glanced at the card, which confirmed what she expected, and returned it dismissively. *"Save your breath m'sieu. You are Victor; my niece's description of you was as good as a photograph. So what brings you here in her absence? To conduct marche-noir business or invite me to commit suicide with you?"*

"I'm no black-marketeer, madame, nor do I wish you to commit suicide. I am a patriot who comes to ask you to join with me for the sake of France."

"You have already had my niece's answer. What reason do you have to suppose mine will be different?"

"None madame, but if I am to serve France then I don't give up at the first setback."

"Fine words, m'sieu, but it will take more than those to free France from her chains; it will require the gathering of people and resources under the very noses of the Germans; and it will require a clear idea of how they are to be used. It will also require an organisation that is resilient because at some point, it will come under attack; people will be caught and made to reveal what they know, probably tortured, or there may be those who choose to betray it, who side with those who have scuttled to Vichy; so the organisation must be compartmentalised to limit damage; like the watertight doors in a ship."

"You sound as if you have done this kind of thing before."

"I haven't – but I have given the matter thought because like you I want to see France free again and some form of organised resistance has to be a first step."

"So you will join me?"

"I haven't said that – on the other hand I haven't said I won't. I can help you with a couple of things. But if I were to, it will be on a number of conditions."

"Go on."

"I'll come to the conditions. The first thing I will do is give you some pamphlets. Ten years ago a dear friend of mine fell head over heels in love with a communist, worshipped the ground he walked on; but he was a hothead and ended up getting killed in a street-brawl. She went to pieces, asked me to dispose of his effects. His papers were mainly standard communist drivel but there were some pamphlets on creating networks and cells; codes and ciphers; infiltrating organisations; subversion; sabotage etc. They made fascinating reading so I kept them but now you should have them because they are a blueprint for what you need to do and they will be worth your while to study. The second thing I can help you with is field-craft."

"They taught us that in the army."

"Perhaps that is why we lost the war then because yours is non-existent – it was you surveying the farm with binoculars from over there a week or so ago?" She pointed to where she had seen the telltale flash. He nodded sheepishly. "If this were a German outpost you would be dead by now; or rotting in jail. You're obviously a townsman. You need to learn to blend in and exploit the natural cover provided by the countryside."

"I would like that. So what are your conditions?"

"Regarding the farm. You want to make use of it, I gather, for your operations. That won't happen for some time. I'm not going to put the safety of all this in the hands of a beginner – a puppy-dog, full of energy and enthusiasm but no idea what to do with it. So build your organisation, learn what I will teach you and prove that you can do it all well enough to stay alive for the next six months. Even then the farm will depend on my niece. By then she will be safely delivered of her baby, and can make a choice whether to become involved. If she won't then the farm won't be available."

"Do you think she will?"

"Quite honestly I don't know. She has suffered grievously in the last few months, perhaps enough to crush her spirit permanently."

"If what I witnessed is anything to go by, then I think it is no more than bruised. What other conditions do you have?"

"I believe I have a nose for people and now I have met you I begin to feel you are a man who could achieve what we are talking about, otherwise we wouldn't be having this conversation. So the first thing you do is stop running around chalking slogans on walls – there's no sense getting your head shot off doing something you can leave to street urchins."

"I've actually realised that myself. Next?"

"You must openly approach the farm only in your disguise as a salesman – and then at appropriate intervals, consistent with your occupation – otherwise only in the most exceptional circumstances. While I am teaching you we will meet in the woods – and for that you must come on foot – so don't park your truck anywhere near here. You mustn't compromise our safety."

212

"OK – anything else?"

"I would like to know a couple of things. How will you support yourself while you're doing all this; and have you made contact with the British?"

"I really am a parts salesman. I have an uncle with a factory in Rennes who is prepared to employ me and not ask questions. It means I have a vehicle, and a permit to travel about. I have made a tenuous contact with the British – via a trusted friend with a fishing boat who has managed to slip across the channel a couple of times under the guise of fishing trips. How long that can last I don't know because as the Germans tighten their grip on the country they're bound to restrict the movement of fishing vessels. So I have asked the British to supply me with a radio."

"And have they?"

"Not yet, but I'm sure they will soon – they must recognise the help we can provide."

"Tres bien. Then on the terms we have discussed I will assist you. I think you should be going now – you've had ample time to conduct your business should anyone be observing us. I suggest we meet at noon in two days' time – from where you spied on me. Be careful as there are some surprises there now – your first lesson can be to find them. I will bring you the pamphlets then. Now, would you like a bag of rotten apples – they are very good for blocking exhaust pipes; especially German ones?"

"Yes, I will, please. I know an urchin who will enjoy such mischief."

"Bravo, it seems you are learning!"

'Damnation' thought George, 'we're not high enough'. They had been vectored to meet a large raid heading towards Brighton, but, while they were still climbing to meet it, it had swung westwards and was now heading for the Solent – Portsmouth harbour – so they had been redirected and found themselves too late and too low. Too late because something like a hundred Junkers 88s were roaming freely over Portsmouth, bombing at will, but there was nothing 686 or the other RAF aircraft already there or still arriving could do except wait to catch them as they left; to enter the 'box' over Portsmouth invited being shot down by the Portsmouth AA guns, who tended, not unreasonably given what they had to defend, to fire and ask questions later, currently blazing away as if there were no tomorrow. He saw a Ju88 blown apart in the distance but it was obvious from the explosions and fires below that far more damage was being wrought than suffered by the attackers. Too low because above them he could see a circle of Me110s and higher still two more circles of 109s; seemingly waiting to defend the Ju88s as they withdrew. A few 109s, like medieval knights seeking individual combat, had detached themselves and come to lay down challenges. None got within range of 686 as they had been despatched by other RAF aircraft who, although massively outnumbered overall, enjoyed local superiority. And then the bombers were withdrawing, heading out through the gap in the balloon barrage by which they had entered. Like sharks, the defenders moved in for the kill but only a handful of 88s had been despatched, and none by 686, when their comrades swooped down and mayhem ensued. For ten or fifteen minutes George twisted and turned, alternatively fearful and angry, firing short bursts but never able to take proper aim before he had to avoid the attentions of one and then another, ducking and diving as tracers shot past him from different directions and trying to avoid collision in the crowded sky. Jerzy was scarcely able to help him as he, too, found himself constantly shaking off assailants. Suddenly, like a flock of migrating birds, the Germans had gone and the sky was clear and the British pilots were easing aching muscles and bringing pounding hearts under control; and wondering what more they could do against such odds.

"That was bloo-dy hairy," said Evans at de-briefing, "there were so many there was no hope of fighting them – I was just trying to stay alive."

"It was the same for all of us," replied Giles, "The trouble was we were at a total disadvantage. When we're outnumbered like that we need height so we can dart in, knock a few down and dart out again; we can't afford to turn up several thousand feet lower than their fighters. This isn't the first time we've been too low but it's the first time it's really mattered – things are hotting up now so we can expect to face large formations regularly. Since landing I've had a word with Group; they're going to try to get us off the ground a bit earlier – but it isn't easy because if the Jerries change course like they did today, we can be on a wild goose-chase. As for height, the system's still pretty new and there remains a margin for error so I propose quite simply to add three to five thousand to whatever Angels we're given. Well done everyone – we didn't bag any of theirs today but we didn't lose any either. Tomorrow's the thirteenth – so let's make it unlucky for them!"

"Bandits one o'clock low. Far too many to mix it with so no heroics, just a quick squirt and away. Tally-ho!" George makes a rough count of sixty 109s in twos and fours, sweeping westwards along the coast as he and Jerzy follow Red Section down. They have height again today; their two Sections having been scrambled early enough to give them that advantage; but not only that. They have had time to position themselves off the coast so that they are attacking with the morning sun behind them. Now they have to put it to good use. Giles' target is one of a *schwarm* at the rear of the formation and George watches his tracers striking home. The 109 begins to fall away with white smoke pluming behind it. Now it is his turn, but the other three are reacting; two rolling underneath and the fourth turning towards him, trying to bring its guns to bear. George fires a snap burst and sees strikes forward of the cockpit but then he is past and the rest of the formation are already a mile or more away with the gap growing by the second. "Bluejay Control, Shuttlecock Leader, customers have departed, any more trade?"

"Negative Shuttlecock Leader, pancake at your discretion." Reluctantly, George and Jerzy follow Red Section for home.

Three hours later and still before noon, Yellow Section are airborne again, this time as one of four sections vectored to Portland to intercept twenty-plus incoming bandits. "Red Leader, one-one-ohs ten of clock!" As usual, Jerzy is first to spot the enemy. Giles is his usual crisp self. "Roger, Yellow Two, turn port all Shuttlecock aircraft; Go!"

214

"Red Leader, Hurricanes two o'clock." P/O Bardsley has spotted a squadron to the west but closer to the German formation, which on seeing them swings away to retreat back to France but not quickly enough to prevent one of its number being despatched by the leading section. Still out of range there is nothing for 686 but to turn for home.

"That was a bloody waste of time," said George vehemently.

"Not altogether," said Max, "they were sent packing. I don't get what they were doing though. They weren't carrying bombs or escorting anything."

"I'd suggest they've missed a rendezvous," answered 'Einstein' quietly, "which just goes to show that the 'master-race' aren't so perfect after all."

"Would have been fair dinkum if the bombers had shown up instead of the 110s," responded Max with a grin.

"Well they bloody well didn't!" snapped George, "Fact is all we have to show for today is Giles' 109. We need more than a handful of aircraft up at once. It will take forever to win the war at this bloody rate."

"Can we have a word in my office, George – in five minutes." It was a command couched as a request; Giles had gone unnoticed at the back of the room.

Victor grinned as the jaws of the second man-trap snapped together, again narrowly failing to trim the stick he had used to spring them. He felt a small glow of satisfaction. He had arrived ahead of the appointed time and already dealt with two 'surprises'. Were there any more, he mused, as he stepped back, perhaps… a cold metal cylinder pressed into his neck, *"Hande hoch, schweinhund!"*

"Seven weeks," said Giles, motioning George to occupy the seat across from him, "if we're still around in numbers in seven weeks then it will be too late for Hitler to invade and we will have won. For that reason we can't afford to be drawn into large fighter actions, because even if we manage to shoot down two or three of theirs for one of ours they can afford those losses as they will have aircraft left when we have none. I know it's frustrating but that's how we must play it."

"So we just let them fly up and down with impunity?" An edge of bitterness came into George's voice.

"Hardly. We showed them today that the English coast is a dangerous place to be. They came trailing their coats and one and," he inclined his head towards George, "possibly two, paid the price. The 109s can fly backwards and forwards for all eternity and if we don't take the bait they will achieve nothing. So if they want to draw us into any sort of a fight they will have to send their bombers and when they do we will knock them down."

"In penny numbers."

"Not necessarily, but certainly without risking large-scale losses from our side for the next few weeks. It looks like they've finished with attacking convoys so it will be attacks on the mainland now. It's been decided on high that Hurris will primarily go after the bombers and Spits will deal with the 109s. I haven't just called you in to discuss strategy though. I know that you want to shoot down as many Germans as possible – come to that, we all do – and the last couple of days have been frustrating for you but today it led you into quarrelling with a fellow officer. Don't think I'm unsympathetic to your loss but for the good of the squadron, I can't permit your personal crusade to conflict with your duties as an RAF officer so you need to get things into perspective. We've all got to pull together and we're here for the long haul so you will have plenty of opportunity to achieve what you seek but not if you become a loose cannon. I'm speaking to you now as a friend and colleague but as Squadron Commander I shall not hesitate to act if you ignore this warning. How much leave have you had recently?"

"None since I returned but…"

"But nothing. Too much work makes George a dull boy. Remain on duty today but tomorrow you will have a 24. I want you to spend it thinking about what I have said and hopefully come back in a different frame of mind. Oh, and 'Litmus' is due a break too so you can lead the dawn show on the 15th. That should give you a chance for a pop at something with a Swastika on it."

Victor's mind raced even as his body froze in the posture of a surrendering scarecrow.

The command was in German but delivered by a voice that, although essaying a low register, was obviously female. He began to lower his arms. *"Hande hoch, oder ich schiesse."*

His arms jerked upwards. *"Who are you?"* he ventured. The response was not immediate. He waited, uncertain.

"Luckily for you, neither the Gestapo nor the Wehrmacht. But very disappointed, why the hell did you spring the mantraps?" The voice – now obviously Lys' – registered frustration.

"You told me to."

"No I didn't, I told you to find them; I said nothing about interfering with them. There will be times when you're going to have to act with subtlety; come and go silently and unremarked, leaving things untouched – like a cat perhaps, not a wounded elephant."

Already piqued by the ambush and the dressing-down he was receiving, it was too much for his pride when he turned to face her and saw that she had been pressing a brandy-flask into his neck. *"It doesn't matter two centimes – it was only an exercise."*

Her face became a mask of rage, her eyes blazing. *"It damn well does matter – everything we do, training or for real, is to be treated as a matter of life and death, because sooner or later that's what it will be; so if you can't handle that then it finishes now before any damage is done. I'm beginning to think I made a mistake getting involved with this."*

Her eyes continued to bore into him but he met them with a steady gaze. Eventually, without breaking contact, he spoke. *"You're right; I'm sorry."*

"Yellow Two, do you confirm no fighter cover?"

"Red Leader, I see nothing."

"Splendid! All Shuttlecock aircraft – Christmas has come early – pick your birds and make sure you pluck them. Tally-ho!"

Eight Hurricanes had been scrambled from 686 along with elements of other squadrons in response to RDF plots but at this particular moment the only aircraft in the vicinity were twenty-plus Stukas in loose vics of three, wallowing with their half-ton bomb loads towards the Dorset coast. Those further back were already jettisoning theirs and diving away as the leading sections tried to close up for mutual support; to no avail as 686, in groups of four, slashed into them from their undefended flank. One had exploded and three were tumbling seawards as the Hurricanes wheeled around and despatched another two, left by the first pass as sitting ducks, whilst three of their seemingly more fortunate comrades, trailing smoke, dived away to attempt to nurse damaged aircraft some one hundred and twenty nerve-shredding kilometres back to their Normandy bases.

Giles jumped from the wing of his aircraft as George and Jerzy were passing. "Just the one for me; any joy?"

"One sure and one probable," said Jerzy, enthusiastically.

"Same here," added George.

"Everything comes… now make good use of your 24."

As the four Hurricanes climbed steadily higher, George, satisfied that they were keeping formation, allowed part of his mind to revisit the previous day. It had started late for him; he hadn't woken until nearly eight o'clock, a good four hours later than Blakely, his batman of some two months, was presently in the habit of rousing him with a mug of scalding tea. He had remonstrated with Blakely who had observed in the blunt manner he had become accustomed to that 'it were no use 'avin' a 24 if tha's getting up afore t'bloody crow'; and having considered it in that light he had felt glad of the precious sleep gained. Blakely, it was said, had been in the RAF since its birth in 1918, and although he had never risen above the rank of AC2 that he had started with it seemed generally accepted that he could offer his forthright opinion on any matter to whomsoever, regardless of rank.

Still smarting from his interview with Giles and unable to face the prospect of sitting at dispersal and watching his colleagues taking to the skies without him, he had persuaded Max to lend him his MG for the day. After driving around for a while, he had found himself on the coast, a few miles west of Brighton. Barred from the beach by a combination of coiled barbed wire and notices proclaiming 'Danger – Minefield' he had sat on a grassy embankment, barely ten feet above sea level. To his right, through a light haze he could see, beyond Littlehampton, the outline of the Isle of Wight on the horizon while to his left the coast curved round past Brighton to the chalk promontory of Beachy Head; without turning to look he knew that behind him fields, some yellowish, some green and various shades in between, rose steadily to become the Downs. This was his country, and his father's, and his father's before him and so on back for tens of generations and hundreds of years; and at once he had felt two emotions; sadness that he hadn't been able to show this land to his wife and a burning anger that those who had killed her were trying to take it from him and every other free-born Englishman, coming over in their war machines to visit death and destruction on all who opposed them.

A group of tiny ants was scurrying seawards across the sky and he realised they were fighters – perhaps 686 among them; he had no way of telling – heading towards a swarm of larger ants coming in from the south. The two groups met and milled around until the larger ones began to turn and retreat, but not before a couple of them fell away to splash into the sea. A wild exultation had gripped George and he had leapt to his feet waving and yelling, 'take that you lousy fucking bastards!'

'Are you alright, sir?' He had turned to find a constable studying him; after nearly a year of war the gas-mask case slung over his shoulder still looking incongruous against his police uniform. 'Only I couldn't help hearing you shouting and all.'

George had blushed. 'I'm sorry for the language. I just got carried away seeing a couple of Huns getting the chop.'

'I shouldn't worry about that, sir – there weren't any ladies present and we're both men of the world. I'm more concerned about that,' he indicated the MG parked a hundred yards away, 'have you immobilised it?'

His heart had sunk. Briefly, he had been tempted to bluff but thought better of it. Instead he had stammered, 'I'm sorry... didn't think there would be anyone around...'

'There could be a Nazi spy lurking anywhere, so they say, and there's a fine or imprisonment for failing to immobilise a vehicle.' His face was deadpan as he pulled the MG's distributor cap from his pocket. 'So it's a good job I did it for you before my sergeant happened along. Let that be a lesson to you and make sure it doesn't happen again.'

'Thanks... very much...' George had stammered.

'Makes no sense locking you up when you could be shooting down Germans, does it? I know we haven't so many pilots that we can afford to play ducks and drakes with them.'

'Do you know someone then?'

'In a manner of speaking. My nephew was, but he bought it, I think he would have said, over Dunkirk.' He had fallen to silent reflection for a few moments before continuing. 'Strange really, if you speak to soldiers who've come back from there, they all say, "where were the bloody RAF?" I can't speak for all of them but I know where one was.' He had articulated his grief with a quiet, uncomplaining dignity. 'Anyway, I can't stand here talking all day – there's a war on and we've all got our parts to play. Take care now, sir, and good luck.' Had Giles stage-managed the encounter, he could not have brought the point home to George any better; in the weeks since he rejoined 686, he had been losing the balance between self and duty.

"Yellow Leader, Bandit, two of clock high. Dornier."

"Well spotted Blue One." Jerzy had decided he wasn't going to be left on the ground while George was hunting Germans and, with little difficulty, had persuaded Evans to have a lie-in. "All Shuttlecock aircraft continue climbing, he hasn't seen us yet and by the time he does we will be between him and home." Minutes later they were in position, above and astern, off the starboard quarter.

"Yellow Two, follow me in and do as I do. Chance to make the buggers pay for shooting you down."

"Wilco... leader," P/O Judd's reply sounded vague.

"Blue Section, finish him off if we don't." A quick glance over his shoulder showed Judd's Hurricane was there but further back than it should have been. "Close up now Yellow Two. Tallyho!" He pushed the stick forward and headed for the Dornier, his practised eyes and hands preparing his aircraft for battle without any conscious thought as he closed with the target. Before the ventral gunner had a chance to fire he had been annihilated by a well-aimed burst. "Give him a squirt, Yellow Two!" As he swung away from the Dornier which had gone into a descending turn to port, looking to lose its assailants with speed, he saw Judd's Hurricane turning the other way. "Where are you going, Yellow Two?"

"Low oil pressure, sir – need to pancake."

Meanwhile, Jerzy had anticipated the Dornier's response and led Sgt Greening, the newest of the sprogs, into a dive across the arc it was describing. At two hundred yards and closing he poured fire along the wing and into its port engine before diving underneath it to avoid collision. "OK, Blue Two, like me, in from side then under." Without further invitation the Hurricane reprised Jerzy's attack, but laying off his aim so that the Dornier flew into his stream of bullets. Its dive began steepening as Greening's shots tore into it, removing his intended escape route.

George realised what was going to happen, but too late. "Break right, Blue Two, break right!" Instead, the inexperienced Greening had pulled back on the stick to pass over the stricken bomber and, as he did so, a line of tracer sprang from its dorsal machine gun into the vulnerable underside of his aircraft. It jerked up into a steep climb before, with awful slowness, standing on a wing then falling into a spin. "Bale out, Blue Two, jump man!" There was only silence as the stricken Hurricane began spinning faster. George knew that, even if he were unhurt, unless he stopped the spin Greening would be pinned in his seat by the force of the rotation. Nothing changed. With a sick feeling he and Jerzy watched the Hurricane drill itself into the sea only a few hundred yards from where the Dornier had met its end without any parachutes; the gunner who had done for Greening either trapped or too badly wounded to escape.

Giles voice was sympathetic. "Don't blame yourself, either of you. Inexperience killed him – pure and simple. We must learn from this though – all new bods must have it drummed in from the word go not to expose their undersides to return fire."

"I gather the poor blighter only arrived yesterday afternoon; half his stuff isn't unpacked yet." Said George sadly.

"Is pity, he was good shot," said Jerzy.

"I put him on this morning's show because he was keen to get cracking and it seemed like a safe bet." Giles turned to Richard. "Does he have any next-of-kin?"

"Just his widowed mother in Derbyshire."

"Poor devil."

"I'll make a list of his worldly goods – anything she doesn't want can be auctioned in the Mess. Scant consolation, I know."

"I've been over S-Sugar's engine and I can't find anything wrong with it, sir," said F/Sgt Robertson, "but it needs a complete strip-down to be absolutely conclusive."

"So not impossible but pretty unlikely?" countered George.

"That's about it, sir. But you recall that situation in France with your guns."

"What are you saying, Flight?"

"With respect sir, I was in France in the last lot and saw a few young gentlemen who couldn't cope and what became of them. I want to be absolutely sure before I help to condemn someone.

"Me too. Thanks Flight."

He found Judd near dispersal, sitting apart from the others. He looked pale and nervous. It was only three o'clock but it had been a fraught day for them all, since the early morning patrol the squadron had been at readiness but nothing had materialised despite the dispersal phone jangling into life on several occasions, grating everyone's nerves and prompting a couple of pilots to bring back their lunch behind the hut.

"Are you alright?"

"Yes, thank you, sir. Just not enjoying the waiting."

"None of us do. So, what happened earlier?"

"I don't know, sir. I was checking t's & p's to follow you into the attack and the oil pressure had suddenly dropped. I had no choice but to pancake. Strange thing was, it came back just before I landed."

"Really?" said George, "I was just talking with F/S Robertson and he said he couldn't find anything wrong with it." He was silent for a moment, looking for a reaction but none came. "Tell you what – as you missed out this morning you can be my no. 2 if anything blows up in the rest of the day. I'll have a word with the C/O and fix it."

"Gosh!" said Judd, "Really?"

"Is that a problem?"

"No, sir, its… it's… spiffing!"

"Have I wrought this change? Forsaking Jerzy for Judd, a complete novice."

"I'm not sure about him, sir, whether he funked it when he turned back or whether it was for real. He looks frightened to death sitting at dispersal but on the other hand he sounded keen when I said he could be my no. 2."

Giles thought for a moment. "He's had a rough start being shot down so soon after he arrived so I'm not surprised if he's feeling a bit flaky. We all feel frightened a lot more than we care to admit but we cope with it. LMF, if that's what it is, is a serious business so we'd better get to the bottom of it sooner rather than later. Take him up by all means, but be careful you don't find yourself out on a limb; and report back."

It was late afternoon before 686 were in action again, tasked to intercept a plot apparently heading for Portsmouth. George, with Judd as his no. 2 and leading a formation of eight Hurricanes, had time to route north of the Isle of Wight to a position where they could attack with the sun at their backs. Jerzy, not passing up an opportunity to shoot at Germans, was as usual the first to spot the enemy. "Thirty plus bombers and same number fighters." George was spared the dilemma of how to divide his small force between attack and defence because just as he was focusing on the fighters above him they were suddenly assailed by four vics of Spitfires and the two formations began to diffuse into a whirling mass.

He seized the chance, "Shuttlecock aircraft – go for the bombers, firing pass and then beat it for home. Tallyho! Yellow two, sit on my tail and see how it's done, but keep an eye on the Jerries above."

"Sorry, Yellow Leader, oil pressure gone again, got to head for home." George looked back in time to see Judd's Hurricane falling away eastwards. A blind rage overtook him momentarily but he suppressed the urge to vent his feelings over the R/T.

Instead Jerzy spoke, "OK Yellow Leader, Blue Section is covering you." Seeing their escort involved with the Spitfires the mixed formation of Dorniers and Ju88s was already jettisoning bombs and turning away as the remaining seven Hurricanes tore through them. George saw his tracers hitting two aircraft in turn but no obvious result. By now the bombers were heading for France and, although initially scattered were starting to coalesce into defensive groups. Looking behind him he could see the other six Hurricanes, all seemingly unscathed whilst two columns of black smoke, already thinning on the wind, showed that two of the enemy weren't going home. "Permission to chase stragglers?"

His impulse was to say 'yes' but then Giles' words came back to him; they had downed two, driven off the rest and gained another day – no sense spoiling that by losing Jerzy – 109s were disengaging from their combat with the Spitfires and forming protective umbrellas over the retreating bombers. "Negative Blue Leader, maintain formation and head for home. Well done everyone." Besides, he had another matter to deal with.

Judd was standing to attention in front of Giles' desk. On either side of Giles were George, who was giving Judd a hostile stare, and F/Sgt Robertson who was giving particular attention to a spot on the floor just in front of his feet.

"So, P/O Judd, what have you to say for yourself?"

"Nothing sir," said Judd, "there's nothing more I can say beyond what I've already told you."

"The suggestion is that you turned and ran from the enemy. If that is true it is a serious matter."

Judd's face flushed and he looked near to tears. "That's not true, sir. On both occasions I found myself with no oil pressure."

"But it came back each time before you landed?"

"Yes, sir."

"F/Sgt Robertson, is this possible, and if so, how?"

Robertson broke off from his study. "Yes it is possible, sir, particularly if some foreign object has got into the engine."

"But you haven't found anything?"

"Not on a limited inspection, sir. We would have to strip it right down and that needs time which we haven't got at the moment."

"I'm sorry, F/Sgt, but due to the serious nature of this situation I will have to ask you to make the necessary time. How long do you need?"

"If I put two men on it right away we should be able to give you an answer by this time tomorrow; but that will hold up routine work."

"I understand F/Sgt; and thank you. In the meantime P/O Judd you are grounded until F/Sgt Robertson reports to me."

"Sir, if I could have another aircraft…"

"No, I think it's better this way. Make use of the time to rest. Dismissed."

With a hunted look, Judd saluted, turned and marched way. George's expression had softened. "I'm not so sure he is LMF now, sir. I mean he asked for another kite…"

"I agree, and that's why I refused because I don't want him doing anything foolhardy to prove he's not. If the F/Sgt can show there is a fault with the engine it will be a better outcome. So make sure your chaps are absolutely thorough please F/Sgt – as always I'm sure," he added with a smile.

"S-stukas, loads of the b-bastards, 10 o'clock." All heads turned in the direction 'Litmus' had indicated. 686 had been vectored to intercept an incoming raid heading for the Isle of Wight but the raiders had seemingly arrived early. At least thirty Ju87s were sliding past on a reciprocal course. Giles realised the import immediately. "They're after the airfield – turn port now, buster!" Twelve Hurricanes swung as one in pursuit but Giles knew that even with emergency boost the nearness of their base meant that they couldn't overhaul the Stukas before they set about their deadly mission. As they tore after their quarry he looked anxiously over both shoulders. He could see a melee higher up. "Looks like the Spits have the escort in hand so we can concentrate on this lot. Tallyho!" As they finally caught up, bomb-bursts were sprouting like mushrooms across the aerodrome accompanied by gouts of flame and black smoke as hangars, buildings and aircraft were blasted into oblivion, helped on their way by exploding fuel bowsers, and ammunition. The rear of the Stuka formation was still waiting its turn to add to the mayhem below as 686 sliced into them. By the time the whole squadron had passed through, seven Ju87s were among the airfield wreckage and several more were limping away, unlikely to make it home. "Good show, Shuttlecock aircraft, now pancake Satellite B."

"Hope it doesn't rain to-night," said Evans looking at the row of tents.

"Or the rest of the week," added Bardsley, "I don't see us back home soon, and after the pasting it took I bet we'll be under canvas there too."

"Me, George and the C/O started the war un-der canvas. Didn't do us an-y 'arm."

"You're starting to sound like my father. You weren't on the Somme as well?"

"Cheeky bugg-er!" He made to cuff Bardsley, who in avoiding the blow backed into the newly arrived Giles and burst into profuse apology.

"May I ask why you are attempting to strike a junior officer?" Giles enquired lightly.

"Sprea-ding gloom and despond-ency, sir. Told me we could be 'ere for a week."

"He could well be right – the airfield should be useable again tomorrow, it doesn't take long to fill in craters once the Sappers have sorted out the unexploded bombs, but I gather the buildings took a pasting – they won't be fixed overnight. Still, we have all the essentials here; admin, hangars, fuel and ammo – and plenty of tents." Giles laughed as Evans' face fell. "I think we will be billeting you in local hostelries as soon as Richard can arrange things. Talking of which, has he showed up yet?"

As if on cue, Max's MG came across the field, carrying Richard, whose face and uniform, begrimed with a mixture of soil and dust, were in stark contrast to that of Max, just returned from a 24, and the car. Caspar's head poked out of the neck of Richard's tunic, taking a keen interest in the goings-on.

"He looks OK, at any rate," ventured Bardsley.

"Must be gett-ing used to being…" Evans stopped, realising his gaffe.

"Luckily for you George is currently out of earshot," said Giles with a hint of exasperation. "Richard, thank God you're alive. How are things?"

"Thank you, sir. Not good but it should be flyable again by tomorrow. We have restored most of the telephone lines already. Hangars etc. won't be so easy. Seven other ranks and two civilian workers killed and twenty-three wounded; plus P/O Judd who is now in the Cottage Hospital having a couple of bullets removed from his leg."

"Caught by a strafing Hun?"

"Shot down, actually. In the middle of the raid, with the help of a couple of erks he managed to get a Hurricane airborne. Saw off one Stuka at the bottom of its dive and he was after a second when another got him from behind. He managed to pancake on a local golf course."

Giles' smile was born of relief. "Good show! It's an ill-wind etc. F/Sgt Robertson will still have to finish dismantling his kite though, to find out what's wrong with it."

Richard's smile was rueful. "I believe the Germans took care of that, along with the hangar it was in. Happily, Robertson and his men were in a shelter trench at the time. Oh, and the Golf Club secretary rang to ask how soon we can remove Judd's new kite. Apparently, it's blocking the seventh fairway and playing havoc with the four-ball."

For a moment it seemed Giles was going to explode but instead he began to shake with laughter. "Tell me it's April the 1ˢᵗ please, Richard."

Richard remained deadpan. "No sir, it's England; what we're fighting for."

"Good show," said Giles, "there'll be a gong in this I shouldn't wonder." Although there were only five of them, it was crowded in the small hospital room where they had shuffled in, two either side of the bed and one at its foot. They were there because the sky was clear; not only of cloud but Germans too. They had waited until late-afternoon before Group had decided they could be released from Readiness. "In the meantime, something you might enjoy more; where can we hide these?" As he spoke they produced the bottles of beer each had secreted in their uniforms. "I take it you do drink beer?" he added as an afterthought. Judd had to settle for nodding as Giles continued seamlessly. "I know, in your flying boots – you won't be needing those for a while I imagine." He stuffed four bottles into the fur-lined boots standing in the corner, one still showing the bloodstains caused by his wounds, and pushed the fifth under his pillow. "One for after lights-out. What's the score anyway?"

"The doc reckons I'll be here for at least a couple of weeks."

"D-dashed bad show," said Litmus, "just when t-things are g-getting interesting."

"I shouldn't worry," added Bardsley, "there'll still be plenty of the bastards..."

"I'll thank you to moderate your language in here, young man." Matron had glided soundlessly into the doorway, beyond which she found her progress blocked, "and it's time you all were leaving – this young man needs his rest. Come along now."

Facing 109s was one thing, Matrons another. Without argument they shuffled from the room. George was last; he hung back slightly. "I want to apologise, for judging you too hastily; and when you're in one piece again I'd be pleased to have you as my no. 2." Unable to speak for a different reason now, Judd, eyes shining, nodded his appreciation.

"Shuttlecock Leader, make Angels fifteen and orbit base, repeat, orbit base."

"Bluejay Control this is Shuttlecock leader. Angels fifteen as directed but no, repeat no, sign of bandits." To George, Giles sounds irritated, for him an unusual frame of mind. It is only a couple of minutes but it seems like ages as they circle, although Giles makes sure they gain some more precious height.

"Shuttlecock Leader, vector two-three-zero, buster. Sixty-plus bandits approaching coastal installations. Engage at will. Be aware of friendly aircraft joining your 4 o'clock."

His irritation is understandable, reflects George. From his first day in command Giles's abiding concern has been to take 686 into combat in the most favourable situation. Now, events are forcing him to operate at a disadvantage. They will arrive after the enemy and be vulnerable. Echoing his thoughts Giles speaks again, "Eyes peeled everyone. We're late so Jerry will be waiting for us."

But fortune is with them today. As they draw near to the coast they can see Stukas milling around, waiting their turn to dive in twos and threes onto their targets below and already being attacked by another Hurricane Squadron; better still, Spitfires have also arrived and are engaging the escort. However, Giles isn't taking any chances. "Green Section, stay with me in case any 109s get past the Spits. George, take the rest of the Squadron and tackle the Stukas like we did in France."

A host of memories flash through George's mind but the one that Giles meant stands out; how F/L Stewart dropped with the diving Stukas and picked them off as they pulled out of their dives. "Pick a Stuka and follow it down then blast it. Tallyho!" He latches onto a Stuka that has just commenced its dive and curves in almost alongside it, throttling back and raising his nose to lose speed and keep pace with it. He can see the rear gunner looking across at him, talking animatedly to his pilot, unable to do anything because George is outside his arc of fire. His no. 2,

Bardsley today, is shadowing him and to his right he can see Evans following another Stuka accompanied by his wingman. George's Stuka drops its 500kg bomb and begins to pull out of its dive. 'Crossed controls'; rudder and aileron applied in opposing directions, enable him to drop faster and sideslip beneath his target, again out of the reach of the rear gunner. As the white dot in his gunsight centres under the Stuka's cockpit he presses the button and eight streams of tracer smash into the defenceless aircraft. Immediately flames and black smoke erupt and it resumes its near-vertical attitude of a few seconds before; but this time with no prospect of recovering. "Bastards," George intones under his breath. To his left another Stuka has levelled out and is looking to head back towards France. "Follow me, Yellow Two – eyes peeled." Instinct has already made him check the sky above and behind and satisfied he is in the clear, he sets off in pursuit. Within twenty seconds he is firing into the fugitive. "Break left Yellow Leader, Stuka." He yanks the stick to the left as two lines of tracer flash over his wing. His assailant is already trailing smoke as it wallows past him, Bardsley pouring fire into it, before it begins to curl down towards the waters below.

"Good show, Yellow Two. Let's see off the other one." The Stuka he had been firing at is still airborne, but trailing white smoke and obviously in trouble. It takes little time for him and Bardsley to overhaul it and apply the coup-de-grace. The sky around is laced with columns and trails of black and white smoke; testament to the toll that has been taken. George thumbs his R/T button, "Shuttlecock aircraft, fun's over, rejoin leader."

From somewhere overhead Giles adds. "Good show, chaps, time to go home."

Low grey clouds and squalls of rain were scudding across the airfield when Giles and his flight commanders assembled in Einstein's temporary office. The Squadron had been stood down as there was no expectation of significant enemy activity that day; providing a release for once from the nerve-stretching vigil from first light to early evening, over twelve hours of waiting and false alarms interspersed with the real thing, which were proving as exhausting as the actual flying and fighting. "First of all, good show yesterday. We and the other Hurris despatched twenty Stukas, to add to the dozen or so two days previously; and the Spits downed several of the escort; all for three casualties, none of which, happily, are from 686. So, a small victory. But don't get carried away; we've bloodied their nose but the bulk of the Luftwaffe is intact and we've still got six weeks to survive. The Met boys reckon we're in for poor weather for the next three or four days which means the Jerries won't be able to mount major attacks. But they're not going to leave us to lie in bed; there'll be recce flights and nuisance raids to react to. We'll do this with small formations; two or four aircraft only. No one will be at Readiness for more than three hours a day because I want everyone to have some respite. When the weather picks up we can expect the Jerries to redouble their efforts as 'Einstein' will explain."

'Einstein' stood for a moment and collected his thoughts. "The raids along the coast which you intercepted yesterday were directed at Ford, Gosport and Thorney Island. As you know, none of these are Fighter Command airfields so that's fortunate for us. Given the attack on our airfield a couple of days ago and attacks on airfields in Kent and Surrey in the last few days it seems obvious that having failed to draw us into major battles by attacking convoys and then ports and factories, they are going for our airfields; so we either have to fight or be destroyed on the ground. Yesterday looks like faulty 'gen' on their part but, if only by a process of elimination, they will find the ones that matter. By the time they can resume their attacks there will be only a week left in August. Time is running out if they're to attempt an invasion, so they're going to come at us with everything they've got."

"Thanks, 'Einstein'. So, gentlemen, quite simply we are entering the decisive phase of the battle. The next few weeks will decide our fate and the fate of our nation."

For different reasons similar weather was equally welcome in the small fishing harbour in Normandy. Gusts of wind were sending sheets of rain sweeping across the stone quays. *This will keep the buggers' heads down; nobody likes a bucket full of water down the back of their neck,*" The voice came from somewhere inside a large set of oilskins; the hat which topped them off inclined briefly in the direction of the guard-post.

"Couldn't have come at a better time – no prying eyes. Which box is it in?"

"Third one down, under a layer of fish – wrapped in oilcloth. You'll make sure the fish get to market – I can't afford for that lot to go to waste?"

"Henri will have them, and his van, in an hour or so! Just need a small detour first."

"Where are you going to put it?"

"Better I don't say. What you don't know you can't be made to tell." Victor allowed himself a quick smile. Lys would have approved of that. He had every reason for a big smile. He had got his radio – the British were taking him seriously. *"One day, France will thank you for what you have done."*

"Some of it perhaps, but not those bloody collaborators in Vichy. It feels good to be giving them a poke in the eye as well as the Boche; but that is likely to be my last trip to England. Any day now a patrol craft is due here; henceforth all fishing boats will go out together and be chaperoned by the Kriegsmarine. A day like this might provide a chance to slip away but there would be a lot of explaining to do afterwards. It would probably be smarter to stay in England and join de Gaulle's lot."

"Enemy should be ahead and below, Shuttlecock Leader."

"Repeat – no sign of Jerry." Giles is tetchy again, uncomfortable because he feels once more they are too low. He glances upwards, "Christ – bandits four o'clock high, break Shuttlecock aircraft, break, break, break!" They split into four sections of two, some, having glimpsed the diving 109s, pull upwards to face them, others turn inside their dives, but for some it is too late. As George and Bardsley, his no. 2, turn into the attack streams of cannon shells hammer into the noses of their aircraft. Black smoke interspersed with white streams of glycol billow past George's cockpit and the temperature gauge climbs. The whole aircraft is vibrating badly as the damaged propeller continues to revolve. As he rolls his stricken Hurricane onto its back he is relieved to see Bardsley's parachute blossoming below him. He jerks open the canopy and undoes his straps preparing to take to his own 'brolly'.

The slender man in Home Guard uniform continues to watch the vapour trails being etched in the sky as he speaks. "Those young lads are giving a good account of themselves. It can't be easy."

His stouter companion shrugs, "Ruddy Brylcreem boys – you should see them of an evening in the *Nags' Head,* showing off to the girls; they don't look like they're in much difficulty then."

"I don't know about that Bert, they're fighting and dying to protect dear old England – like Mr Churchill said 'never in the field of human conflict was so much owed by so many to so few'

"They should try a spell in the trenches like we did. Or a day's work and evenings and weekends on guard duty. This generation has had it too easy – they've no sense and no application. Take that dopey apprentice of mine – the other day I asked him to set the points on a lorry."

"So...?"

"So he comes back to me and says he's done it. I says 'is it right?' and he says – God help me – 'it's near enough'. What sort of an answer is that? So I says 'near enough? That's no bloody good! It needs to be right – so go back and make sure its bloody right'. Eventually he comes back and I says 'so, is it right?' and he says – 'it's right'."

"So what did you say?"

For the first time Bert gives a small grin, "... that's near enough." He is about to say more when he glances skywards. "Look Joe, up there!" he points, "it's a bloody Boche!" He closes his shotgun and raises it to his shoulder.

"Hold on, how do you know it's a Boche – could be one of our boys? We've been told to make sure before we fire at parachutists. We should wait until he's lower."

"...and give him first shot? Not bloody likely! 'Course he's a bloody Boche, and there's another of the bastards in the distance."

He fires both barrels, "take that you Nazi bastard!"

Dangling in his parachute harness, still coming to terms with his narrow escape, George can see the two khaki-clad figures below him. He is about to wave when with a start he recognises the flash of the gun firing and a second later he feels the impact. Fortunately Bert has rushed his shot, firing at extreme range so that the pellets are all but spent; but still with enough momentum to penetrate his uniform. He lands two fields away, collapsing to absorb the impact but, prompted by the stinging sensation in his buttocks and the realisation that the two Home Guardsmen are heading his way, he is immediately on his feet and has shed his harness when they come panting through the gate; Bert pointing the shotgun in his direction. *"Handes hoch!* You bloody Boche!"

Already aware of Bert's trigger-happy propensities George raises his hands and tries to contain his annoyance. "I'm an English pilot, you bloody fool."

"Don't give me any of them Nazi tricks."

He points to the wings on his tunic, "Look – RAF."

"You understand German. You could be a spy, dressed up as one of our boys."

"Listen you stupid wanker, I'm an English pilot who you've just bloody shot and I'm not very happy about it. And if you don't point that bloody gun somewhere else so help me I'll stick it up your arse and pull the bloody trigger."

"Just you try it, I'd love an excuse to shoot you, you Boche bastard."

George turns to Joe, who is looking much less certain of the situation than his colleague. "Can you tell this cretin to put the gun down?"

"He's got the stripe. I can't tell him what to do."

"He won't have a bloody stripe when I've finished with him." He turns back to Bert. "Right, enough of this bloody nonsense. I need medical attention so take me to your C/O – IMMEDIATELY!" he barks out the last word and for the first time Bert begins to look less sure of himself.

He makes one last effort to remain in control. "Right, you walk on ahead, and no tricks because I've got the gun."

As George hobbles off in the direction indicated Joe sidles up to Bert. "I don't think he is German – if he were he'd have called you a stupid vanker."

The Home Guard C/O was writing as George was ushered in so all he could identify immediately was the balding top of his head and double shoulder pips of a lieutenant, but there was something familiar.

"Prisoner, sir, claims he's English but I'd say he's a Boche spy!" announced Bert.

"I want to make a complaint about this trigger-happy moron who has shot me and to demand immediate medical attention."

The lieutenant raised his head and George found himself looking into the eyes of Dorothy's father. The spark of recognition wasn't a warm one. "I'm afraid you've got it wrong on two counts, L/Cpl – I know this man and can vouch for him. Send for Dr Morris and then I suggest you re-read standing orders about shooting at parachutists – we'll talk later."

"Sit down." He continued writing until his men had gone.

"I'd prefer to stand, thank you, in view of the job your L/Cpl has done on me."

"Had it been anyone else I'd have his stripe, but not in this instance I think; and don't you say 'sir' to a superior officer?"

His tone was harsh but George was unimpressed. "The fact you were a Brigadier in the last lot doesn't count now. Our present ranks are equivalent but as the Home Guard was formed in June your commission only dates from then whilst mine predates that. Therefore it is you who should be addressing me as 'Sir' but, unless you insist, I'm not looking for formality whilst we're alone."

"In view of the way you have treated my daughter I don't see any reason for 'chumminess'… sir." He pronounced the last word with obvious resentment. George's mind went back to the day before his return to 686 when Dorothy had appeared unexpectedly; or so it seemed. 'Oh Georgie, I'm so terribly, terribly sorry to hear what's happened. Is there anything I can do?' She had always called him Georgie but suddenly it was grating; the air of concern seemed to his raw emotions to contain a hint of smugness, triumph even. His response had been instantaneous, feral. 'Yes, you can clear off and not come bothering me again!' For a moment she had been stunned. Then tears had welled in her eyes and she had run from the house. His mother had appeared, her tone more shocked than critical. 'George, how could you?' 'Quite easily. I've already made it clear that she and I are a thing of the past and now, of all times, I don't need her trailing after me like a lovesick puppy!' For a moment she had looked at him as if she didn't recognise him, then, her own eyes filling up, left the room.

"I regret the way I spoke to Dorothy and make no excuses. I want you to know this though; I have loved Dorothy as long as I can remember, and still do, but I now know that that love is as for a sister. When I met Justine in France, I found a different kind of love; one that I will never find again. When you lost Dorothy's mother I was a child and unable to comprehend but I understand now how much you must miss her." Her father's eyes had been blazing angrily but, for a fleeting moment, they showed his pain; the anger did not return as George continued. "I believe Dorothy would readily have taken me back and for some men it would have been easy to take advantage of that, but she deserves better."

For a few moments there was silence. "Perhaps," he cleared his throat, "... perhaps I've judged you a bit hastily. Having known you all your life, I should have thought better of you, but it isn't easy to see your only daughter heart-broken, she's all..." George raised his hand as if to silence him and then extended it. The elder man rose to his feet and took it with a firm grip.

"If you see her before I, let her know please I'm sorry for the way I last spoke to her."

"I will, though I hardly see her myself these days. She's in London – doing something 'dreadfully hush-hush'." He smiled with pride. "Now, we'd better get you patched up and back to the fray; and on second thoughts, I shall have that idiot's stripe!"

It is bearable, but the added G-force pressing his tender posterior into the seat makes George feel distinctly uncomfortable as he pulls hard back on the stick to loop and half-roll off the top back towards the remaining Me110s, of which he has already downed one on his first pass. At least he can vent his feelings on the enemy, unlike poor Evans who is destined for a few days in the cottage hospital after yesterday's bounce resulted in him crash landing and breaking his nose on the gunsight for a second time. He puts a burst into the engine of a Me110 and then breaks off as the rear gunner of the next fires a stream of tracer just over his cockpit. He doesn't know why he finds Evan's mishap amusing but, having endured at dispersal several hours of music-hall jokes about his own predicament, he allows himself that he is no more insensitive than his fellows. The 110 is now spiralling down but there are too many enemy aircraft around for him to pay it further attention. He could have justifiably had a day or two off duty but his determination to exact revenge for Justine allows no such self-indulgence and two kills are compensation for his discomfort. He looks around for a third but the remaining 110s are now drawing away to the south. "Still there Yellow Two? That's how it's done. Time to pancake."

"Roger leader," P/O Enderby sounds as if he is speaking through gritted teeth. Another replacement pilot with nowhere near enough hours on Hurricanes; having come up for a training flight and been vectored onto the incoming raid, George knows Enderby will have been pushed to the limits to keep up with him never mind admire his handiwork. At least he has experienced combat and lived to learn from it.

The AC2 saluted as George hopped off the wing. "F/L Frobisher's compliments, sir and can you join him in his office as soon as possible."

"Bagged two 110s and managed to bring the sprog back in one p..." George snapped to attention as he saw the two senior officers who had been hidden by the door; beyond them Richard was also in attendance.

Giles suppressed the urge to laugh. "George, this is Air Commodore Meadows and S/Ldr Matthews from Group. Gentlemen, this is F/O Knight who, as a result of yesterday's events, is effectively my second-in-command."

Meadows spoke; his age and his medal ribbons, similar to but slightly more extensive than Richard's, marked him out as a veteran of the last war. "Glad to meet you, F/O. We are here because your squadron is one of those which, even after yesterday's misfortune, are reporting a pleasingly high ratio of kills to losses. We have come to see if we can learn anything from your experiences which can be passed on for the benefit of other squadrons. Acting S/L Frobisher and F/L Parsons have already told us a great deal about the tactics and formations you have been employing; now we would like to hear your views as one of those who has to put them into practice."

"Forget that you are with senior officers; what we are discussing is of vital importance so we want to hear what you really think – warts and all," Matthews had said this, with a flourish of his hands. For the first time, George saw the bandages, the angry redness of his forehead and neck and the absence of eyebrows. "Bounced by 109s over Dunkirk; lucky to get out lightly toasted," he answered George's unspoken question.

"Cheers," Giles swallowed a draft then held his glass up to the light, appraising the contents as he spoke, "and thanks for the complementary things you said."

"All true," said George, "as was what I said about Preston."

Giles laughed. "I think you pushed your luck there. The Air Cdre was looking a bit hot under the collar by the time you'd finished."

"If it means we don't see Preston here again it was worth the risk."

"On the subject of 'here' I think in causing us to be billeted here the Luftwaffe might have done us a small favour," he took another draft, "this beer is really rather good, fancy another?"

"We're turning into the bloody matinee squadron; I don't like waiting for anything," said Max, stubbing a cigarette out at the side of his deck chair, "especially bloody Germans. And what's keeping them – I thought they were supposed to be stepping up their efforts?" For the third day in a row, they had been on standby for the whole morning and now well into the afternoon, waiting. Waiting; he recalled describing it to Connie, reluctantly, because he didn't want to burden her, but she had been insistent. 'You want the dispersal phone to ring and the shout of 'scramble' to get you running for your aircraft because that brings a rush of adrenalin and a release from the tension. It's bad enough just sitting there as the minutes drag by; but when some drongo from Wing rings to query a spares requisition or something it brings everyone to the brink. Nothing happens and you all sink back but it ratchets up a little more each time. Some blokes curse, some laugh, some go round the back of dispersal and throw up.' She had said nothing; just held his hand a little tighter.

"They are," answered Richard from behind him, "but most of it is being directed at the south-east at the moment; we're getting the finale each day." Jerzy glanced under his eyebrows at 'Litmus'– his sister was at Biggin – but saw no outward reaction.

Oblong, wooden, and with numerous windows; raised off the ground by a brick base and separated from the rest of the world by a wire fence, to the casual observer these huts were little different from many that had over the last year appeared like spring flowers, in clumps, across the British countryside. To a more inquisitive watcher, whose scrutiny would have been a matter of concern to the guards at the gate or patrolling the perimeter, these huts would have been marked out from their fellows by the profusion of aerials and wires connected to them. Inside, a clerk checked what she had just transcribed against the original Morse. Satisfied, she removed her earphones, rose from her desk and walked past several rows of her colleagues to the officer sitting at the large table at the head of the room. She handed the message to him wordlessly and waited while he glanced through it. "Thank you," he said, initialling it. She turned to return to her station as he dropped it into one of several wire baskets arrayed in front of him. The afternoon sun illuminated what she had written. *'Goods received. Ready to commence business. Victor'.*

George would rather have been almost anywhere and doing almost anything than this. He had asked himself why he was here. He knew the answer; because he had volunteered; because he somehow felt responsible that she was here. He was standing by the reception desk of *The Stag* when she appeared, two-stepping lightly down the staircase. Her smile froze when she saw his face; comprehension was instant. She approached him warily. "It's Max, isn't it? Is he…?"

"Missing," said George flatly.

"What happened?"

"We turned back a crowd of Heinkels heading for Portsmouth. In the scrap Max caught a packet in his engine. He baled out OK but the wind was offshore and it took him out to sea. We lost sight of him during his descent because we were occupied with 109s. We searched until lack of fuel forced us back to base. A lifeboat is still out looking and he might have been found by a boat with no radio, so don't give up hope. The sea is at its warmest at this time of year." He realised he was trying to convince himself as much as her.

Her eyes met his only briefly; otherwise she focused somewhere over his shoulder.

"Thanks for telling me, and your words of encouragement – but my father used to take my sister and I sailing when we were little so I know what he's up against. It won't stop me hoping though. He was a lifeguard at home so he's a good swimmer."

"Is there anything I can do?"

"Forgive me – I'd rather be alone just now. But keep me informed please – good or bad." She gave his hand a quick squeeze and before he could say anything she had turned and was running up the stairs.

"As we're 'released' at the moment Jerzy and I would like to take a section apiece and search for Max. It's not eighteen hours since he baled out – he could still be alive."

"Go ahead," said Giles, "take Enderby and the other new boy as your no. 2s; the practice will do them good – but no sneaking off to France looking for trouble."

"No fear of that. I took on board what you said; plus we're not in the habit of throwing sprogs to the wolves."

"Good show – and good luck. I wish I was coming with you. Max was – is a good chap."

"One more sweep westwards and then we'll have to pancake." George was conscious that his, and therefore everyone's, fuel was running low. His earlier optimism had evaporated as their search had produced nothing. He knew he was going to have to pin his hopes on Max having been picked up either by a fishing boat that hadn't returned to port yet or, better a p.o.w. than the alternative, by the Germans. Another example of the criminal neglect of preparedness for war of the British authorities – there was nothing organised to retrieve downed pilots from the sea – they had to hope to land close to a boat or within swimming distance of the shore. Yet the Germans, who had only come to the channel coast ten weeks ago, had floatplanes and fast motor boats to search for theirs…

"Shuttlecock aircraft. Steer two-five-zero and make Angels fifteen to intercept bogey."

"Roger Bluejay Control. Changing course." Within five minutes Jerzy's sharp eyesight had identified a lone Heinkel 111. The low cloud base which had existed when they began their search had been thinning and lifting throughout so that the Heinkel, which had presumably been relying on the reverse, now stood out starkly in the clear sky. "Blue Leader, take out the rear gunner if you can and then keep your eyes peeled for other Jerries. Yellow Two, Blue Two, attack in turn after Blue One, go for the engines and then break away. Do not, repeat, do not, cross behind the rear gunner. We've only fuel enough for one pass so make it count. Tallyho!" The enemy pilot had seen them now and was turning away initially westwards but with practised ease Jerzy, leading the formation, was making use of the Hurricane's superior speed to position himself for a quarter attack. His tracers ripped into the fuselage near the rear gun position and the ineffectual return fire ceased. He climbed away to provide top cover as Enderby made his attack, firing at the starboard engine before banking away.

232

Sgt Westridge, newly arrived, followed suit and as he pulled clear, the first smoke was trailing from the engine. George had used the crew's preoccupation with the other Hurricanes to take position on the port quarter, closing to within two hundred yards before he put a long burst into that engine. The Heinkel flew on for several seconds streaming flame and black smoke before suddenly flipping over and spiralling seawards. There were no parachutes. 'That's for Max, you bastards,' he thought with no hint of remorse. "Good show you new chaps. Pints are on me tonight."

They met in reception again. Her eyes, despite the blotchiness around them, ablaze with hope; which George had to pour cold water on. He didn't mention the fruitless search, merely that there was no news, and he refrained from the empty platitude that no news was good news. Instead, just as he had yesterday he asked if there was anything he could do. "Yes, bring me Max!" she retorted; then, after a pause, "I'm sorry. I'm sure you're doing all that you can. Please don't think me ungracious but I need to go back to my room." Just as yesterday, she squeezed his hand before running up the stairs, leaving him to deal with his own emotions.

As usual they are climbing hard, but in an unusual direction. 'Steer 070, make Angels twenty and expect 100-plus bandits in your three o'clock' had been the message acknowledged with his usual sang-froid by Giles.

'Their course is taking us across a line from northern France to London so we must be protecting Croydon, Kenley, Biggin Hill or all of them perhaps;' George muses, 'as well as their new tactic of going for the airfields, the Germans with increasing frequency have been arriving in force and then splitting up to attack several targets.' 686 number ten aircraft today, in their customary pairs. With Evans unavailable Giles has opted not to have a sixth section comprised of two sprog pilots.

"Bluejay Control. Shuttlecock Leader. 150-plus bandits in sight and there isn't a single bomber among them." To their right and on a level are eighty or ninety 110s – too many to count – and above them, a similar number of 109s, stacked up like an overhanging cliff.

"If there are no bombers, don't engage, Shuttlecock Leader."

"No choice Bluejay Control – they've seen us and they're coming after us. Bandits 2 o'clock high. Shuttlecock aircraft – turn into them. Fight your way through and disengage as soon as you're able. Tallyho!" As one, the five pairs angle upwards to meet double their number diving down on them; the remaining 109s continuing their northward advance. The opposing groups slice through each other, guns blazing. "Take over command, Yellow Leader, I'm hit and baling out."

George has survived the charge unharmed. Beneath him, he can see two parachutes blossoming and the smoke trails of two Hurricanes falling to earth. The remainder of the squadron, also apparently unscathed, are around him. The 109s have used the speed of their dive to zoom climb after their fellows, content with the classic attack and the toll they have taken. The Hurricanes' battle climb has left them above and behind the 110s. For a moment, George's impulse is to attack and ignore orders not to engage free-chasing fighters. Discipline prevails. Reluctantly, he flicks the transmit switch. "Return to base, all Shuttlecock aircraft."

Richard rose from his desk as George entered. "Congratulations; until Giles, Evans or Preston return, you are acting O/C 686 Squadron."

"I had hoped we'd seen the back of Preston."

"Until we hear differently, he is still officially squadron leader and will resume command as soon as he is able."

"God help us if that day dawns. What news of Giles and…" He searched his mind for the name of Red Two, another recent arrival.

"Sgt Porter is unharmed and will be back with us later today – someone's gone to pick him up. Giles got a bang on the head baling out so he's in Redhill hospital for 24-48hrs observation, which means effectively that he will be back the day after tomorrow. So, what are your orders?"

"I don't presume to alter what Giles has put in place. If the opportunity arises, have 'Litmus' and Bardsley take a couple of the new boys up and give them some combat practice. I'll look to do the same but whilst we're at readiness we can't have more than one section airborne at a time. Otherwise, carry on as normal."

George clapped P/O Rodway on the shoulder as he stepped away from his Hurricane. Leaving 'Litmus' to deal with any early morning recce flights, he had seized the chance to give one of the new pilots the benefit of his experience. Rodway had proved a receptive pupil and George was content that he had made a significant contribution to his chances of survival. After spending yesterday waiting for a call which never came he was glad to be airborne again. Max's words about waiting, uttered before his last scramble, had come back to him while he was sitting at dispersal. Unlike what he had heard of squadrons based around London who were now scrambling three or even four times a day 686 had seen no activity at all yesterday, not even a call to aid their colleagues, but had nonetheless spent the entire dawn to dusk period at readiness. Without even the questionable release of action, the effect was as draining as heavy fighting. He knew he and, with the exception of recent arrivals, the other pilots were tired but, by Giles' timetable, they still had to hold out another month or so even though the pressure was increasing. Above all, if he were to stop now he would be failing Justine and he wouldn't be able to live with himself in those circumstances… "Good show. Just digest what you've learned today; particularly keeping a lookout and not flying straight and level when there are Jerries about and you'll be OK."

"Thanks, sir. That was wizard flying, especially the flick-roll – I enjoyed that."

"It has its uses, as does keeping your turns as tight as possible or using your rudder trim to skid your turns – it confuses deflection shooting."

The conversation was halted by the arrival of an A/C 2 who came to attention in front of George. "You're wanted in the C/O's office immediately, sir!"

"Thank you. So F/L Frobisher's back already?" Giles was due to return from hospital but word had been received requiring him to attend Group HQ en route.

The airman's face was impassive. "No sir, S/L Preston."

'Christ' thought George, managing not to utter the word.

234

"He did say 'immediately', sir, and he didn't seem to be in a very good mood."

'No change there then,' he thought, heading for the single hut which in their temporary home was serving as office for both Squadron Leader and Adjutant. Not a problem for reasonable people like Giles and Richard but Preston??? He caught a glimpse of the latter in the dispersal hut. As he entered, he could see that Preston was busy re- arranging the duty roster from Giles' six sections back into four 'threes'. "You wanted to see me, sir?"

"In my office, as I recall. Wait for me there."

"I gather that you were O/C immediately prior to my return?"

"Yes sir, due to the temporary indispositions of F/L Frobisher and F/O Evans."

"So where were you when I arrived this morning?"

"While things were quiet, I was teaching one of the new boys some of the basic skills he will need to stay alive – sir."

"And what would have occurred if there had been a scramble while you were absent?"

"Not an issue, sir. The squadron was on thirty-minute readiness when we went aloft, and I had left word to recall us if there was any advance in state. I was never more than five minutes away and I had a spare Hurricane fuelled and armed if needed."

"You seem to have thought of everything F/O," he replied acidly. Well we are now on immediate readiness and I shall be leading the next scramble – in four sections of three – the proper way, not the groups of two I observed on the Ops Board."

Already smarting from the initial rebuff, George wasn't in the best frame of mind to engage with Preston.

"Until Giles, Evans or Judd return we only have eleven pilots, counting you, fit to be scrambled. Two or three of the new boys need more training before they are sent into battle – to scramble them now would be tantamount to murder."

"I shall be the judge of who is fit to fly and when, thank you. I see these back-of- envelope tactics espoused by F/L Frobisher and yourself have resulted in losses."

"A few of the casualties have been from return fire whilst attacking bombers but the majority have arisen because we have been scrambled too low and then bounced. Things have changed while you have been away. The Jerries are sending over huge escorts of 109s and 110s now."

"As I expected you blame everyone but yourself when your ill-discipline leads to the inevitable consequences. It's a good thing I've returned to restore some order." George could feel his anger rising. Had Richard been present, he might have defused the situation, but he was elsewhere. The strains of a telephone reached his ears, the surge of adrenalin it triggered further suppressing any inhibitions.

"Might I point out that in the month you've been away, whilst we have lost kites, we have only suffered one fatality and one missing. You managed to kill two sprog pilots and get yourself and Evans shot up in one sortie with your outdated ideas!"

"Damn your impudence! I'll have you court-martialled for this!"

235

George was beyond any restraint now. "That's all you know isn't it – how to wave a rule book, not how to command. You're a petty-minded hide-bound fool who isn't a shadow of our last C/O or Giles and you're not fit to run a whelk stall on Brighton bloody beach let alone this sq –"

"SCRAMBLE!" The shout from the dispersal hut and the ringing of the bell brought George's diatribe to a halt. He turned to head to his aircraft.

"You are going nowhere F/O Knight. As of now you are grounded and under open arrest for insubordination. I will deal with you when I return." So saying Preston grabbed his flying helmet from a desk drawer and ran from the hut, leaving a stunned George in his wake.

George's head is throbbing and his mind is in turmoil but through the confusion a cogent stream of thought appears. He has just effectively ended his flying career; even in wartime, if the charge of insubordination is proved he will probably end his days handing out flying kit in a store somewhere. He has let himself, his country, his family and his friends down but most of all he has failed Justine. Her death will now go un-avenged. A feeling of utter desolation overcomes him and he sinks to his knees in despair. As he does so the parachute pack he hadn't had time to discard catches on the edge of the desk and a wild idea comes into his mind. He will fly one last time and destroy as many Germans as he can – kill or be killed – it no longer matters. He looks out of the door. The last of the engines have started and the Hurricanes are arranging themselves into now unfamiliar threes. He has to let them take off so Preston won't see him and try to stop him; and to hope nothing has been said. With throttles wide, twelve aircraft surge across the field; Preston has included the new boys to make up his precious vies. Before their wheels have left the ground, George is running for the Hurricane he had earlier put on standby. A fitter sees him coming and waves for a starter trolley as he jumps into the cockpit. By the time George arrives, the engine is running and the man is back on the wing ready to assist with his harness. George shouts "no time!" above the roar of the engine and waves him away. A thumbs up and a second fitter pulls the chocks away as the first leaps from the wing and rolls clear; before he has got to his feet George is accelerating across the grass. A couple of bounces, and he is airborne and climbing away in the direction taken by the rest of the squadron – eastwards again today.

He is following the squadron at a distance – without his helmet he has no radio to guide him – knowing the limitations imposed by Preston's formation will allow him to tail them unseen. At 15,000 feet they level off; he adds another two thousand before doing so. To his right he catches a glint and then a large formation of bombers becomes visible. The squadron have obviously not seen them; but that isn't his concern. He rolls into a dive towards the bombers; with his throttle through the gate he closes rapidly and, with a savage exultation, sweeps across the top of the formation holding the firing button for a count of eight seconds – half his ammunition. He sees strikes on one, two, three, four machines but has no chance to assess the results; then he has pulled back on the stick and is zoom climbing towards a stall turn to enable another pass. As he climbs, he sees 109s high above peeling off into a dive; but they are not coming for him – with a stab of regret, he realises they must be heading for the squadron and there is nothing he can do to warn them. With mounting ferocity he dives again, the roar of the slipstream past his open hood adding to his battle madness; there are now a couple of gaps in the formation and smoke trailing back from two machines; and then he is sweeping, diagonally this time, across the massed ranks, hosing bullets, screaming a battle cry as generations before had done, aware of return fire but seemingly untouchable until the clatter of his guns gives way to thuds and his ammunition is exhausted. He zoom-climbs again, this time out in front; he can see more gaps created by his second pass but the survivors continue rolling onwards like a production line. He has no more ammunition; there is only one thing left. He pushes the stick forward and aims at the leading aircraft. He feels strangely at peace as the distance between them diminishes. Some small part of his brain registers the large plexiglass cupola at the front of his target and for the first time, he is conscious that he has been attacking Heinkel 111s. As the horrified faces of the pilot, flight engineer and front gunner come into focus another part of his brain determines that now is not the time to die and makes his hand pull back on the stick, lifting the nose of his Hurricane just enough that instead of slamming headlong into the Heinkel, it skids along the back until part of its port wing is severed by the tail fin. The unbalanced airframe flicks violently and the craziness that has led George to this point saves him; unimpeded by harness or radio cord, he is thrown from the cockpit like a stone from a slingshot. As he tumbles through the air, the damaged Heinkel veers away and collides with its neighbour. A second later their combined bomb loads detonate, the blast claiming two more aircraft. George, seeing the flash, curls into a ball as pieces of red hot metal fly out in all directions. He feels a thump and a burning sensation and swats at his trouser leg as it starts to smoulder. Within seconds all that is left of five aircraft is a cloud of black smoke. Shaken by the ferocity of the attack and the violence of the explosion, the rest of the formation are jettisoning their bombs and turning away. Now several thousand feet below, George holds his breath and pulls the ripcord. With a jolt the canopy opens and he is relieved to find that it is undamaged. His relief is short-lived. Against the background of retreating Heinkels, a 109 has detached from its fellows and is diving towards George, seeking revenge. For the second time in minutes, he is facing death, but this time his subconscious can't save him. He has done all he can; but remains defiant to the last. "Bastard!" he yells, balling his fists.

Justine looked up from her desk as she sensed his presence. Standing in the doorway doffing his hat and smiling was Victor. *"Bonjour madam, ca va?"*

"Ca va," she responded without enthusiasm, *"and the answer is still 'no'."*

Victor essayed incomprehension. *"I haven't asked anything."*

"Well I've saved you the trouble; and you know perfectly well what I mean."

"In which case I will indulge in small talk. I see you are not sitting as close to your desk as the last time I was here."

Despite herself, she found she was suppressing a smile. *"You're right. He, for I'm sure it is 'he', is starting to make his presence felt."*

"Another fine son for France – she will need all of her sons if she is to be free again."

"I'd rather not think of another generation of Frenchmen cut down in their prime; especially if one of them is to be my son." She turned her head away.

"I'm sorry madame, it was clumsy of me. I will leave now before I cause you further distress. I will be back in a few weeks though, if you can suffer to receive me then."

She continued to look away as she spoke. *"Sell your wares to M Beaumont by all means; don't try to sell your schemes to me and I will be content to receive you."*

"I shall look forward to it. Au revoir, madame." When she turned back, he was gone.

He hears machine gun fire and senses bullets passing close by but he is unscathed. Comprehension is immediate. He is a small target, about two feet across compared to the thirty-odd of a Hurricane or Spitfire, and, like his own aircraft, the 109's guns will be harmonised to a certain point. So he has a few more seconds to live until it finds the correct distance. Another burst of gunfire – but followed this time by an explosion. He flinches then opens his eyes to see the burning remains of the 109 falling away as a Hurricane sweeps across. Through narrowed eyes he makes out the squadron letters on its side – Jerzy! His former wingman has appeared like an avenging angel. He waves as the Hurricane banks and settles into a protective orbit around him, only breaking off as he enters a stray clump of cumulus cloud.

When he emerges beneath it, brushing off water, Jerzy has gone, but there are no other aircraft about and he is only a matter of seconds from the ground; euphoria at having survived flickers briefly then begins to fade in the face of what is to come.

The juddering of the carriages over the points brought him awake and he tried to gather his thoughts. Compared to his last parachute descent, his reception this time had been exemplary. The only thing the PC who was on hand when he landed fired at him was a couple of questions to satisfy himself of George's bona fides. After that he was taken to the local police station and plied with tea laced with something stronger while his whereabouts were phoned through to the squadron. Before he knew it, he was on a train back to his airfield with good wishes ringing in his ears; a world away from the reception awaiting him.

His original mood of belligerence, which had started to rekindle as he emerged from the station, was slightly confounded when he found Richard leaning nonchalantly against a three-tonner. "Best I can offer; the C/O's car hasn't been replaced yet," he said apologetically.

George had nothing left to lose, so even Richard's calming presence wasn't going to completely pacify him. "It'll do. No armed guards then?" Richard looked quizzical. "I take it you're here to re-arrest me?" Richard's expression became more quizzical. "Preston left me grounded under open-arrest but as soon as he took off I followed, so if I wasn't going to get a court-martial before I am now."

"Preston is dead – shot down."

"Bloody marvellous! Three cheers for the Luftwaffe!"

"I'll pretend I didn't hear that, or your last few sentences. They were bounced - Bardsley and 'Litmus' force-landed, most of the others managed to fight their way out with a few bullet holes but the two new boys bought it too."

"Poor buggers! I told him they weren't ready. I hope he burns in hell." Parsons frowned disapprovingly. "So what happens now? I was under open-arrest."

"What passed between S/L Preston and you is known only to you so unless you are determined to talk yourself into a court-martial, I suggest you pipe down, get in the cab and let me drive you back to the airfield where I strongly advise you visit the MO and get a sleeping pill. You are clearly tired and overwrought, making no sense and of no use to the squadron or yourself in your present state. Do I make myself clear?"

As the full import of Richard's words seeped into his inflamed consciousness George smiled briefly. "Yes Adj, as crystal."

Richard put the truck into gear and began turning it around. "By all accounts, you single-handedly broke up a massed bomber formation. You're a hero and you'll probably get a DSO," pursing his lips, he looked at George and nodded slowly in confirmation. They burst into laughter. George was still laughing as they set off down the road.

Evening shadows were lengthening across the airfield, accompanied by the scents of a summer evening and an incongruous mixture of birdsong and the metallic clinks and clangs of aircraft being serviced, as George approached the squadron 'hut'. Giles was signing paperwork proffered by Richard. "What ho, Rip van Winkle," he said, looking up from his desk, "you timed that well; bumph all sorted so we're off to the *Barley Mow.*"

"I can do with a beer, I'm parched; I must have slept all afternoon – what's so funny?" he asked as they dissolved into laughter.

"You haven't just slept the afternoon," explained Richard, "you've slept for thirty-odd hours – it's the 31st of August."

"Hell fire," said George, "why didn't someone wake me?"

"Because you obviously needed it," said Giles, "that was your second rest day since June; you can't keep on like that; and," he added mischievously, "it gives the rest of us chance to shoot down some Germans."

"Har, bloody har," said George sourly, "so how went the day?"

"Hard," said Giles, "not many 'kills', but no casualties from 686. We scrambled twice, both times over Kent and Surrey. It's obvious Jerry is after the airfields – Biggin, Kenley and Croydon are all taking a pasting and there are so many damned escort fighters it's bloody difficult to get near the bombers. Along with the other squadrons we managed to turn a lot of them back but some are bound to get through by sheer weight of numbers. Things are coming to a head and I think over the fields of Kent and Surrey is where they will be decided."

George passed a foaming tankard to Jerzy who took a deep draught. "I needed that, has been tough day – for some of us anyway." He added with a grin.

"Don't you start. I wanted to say thanks for saving me. That Jerry would have done me for sure."

"Is pleasure. Is twice pleasure – save you, kill German." He emptied the tankard with another swig just as the pub door opened and a WAAF with dark, curly hair entered. Her face lit up as she spotted Jerzy. "Excuse, please," he said.

"I know," George smiled. "you have an assignation." He sipped at his beer, leaned back against the bar and looked around. In one corner, Judd and Evans, now restored, Bardsley, Enderby, Porter and Rodway and the latest new boys were having a noisy game of darts. In another, darker corner 'Litmus' was sitting with one arm around 'Nell Gwyn' and with his other hand in the air appeared to be sketching out a quarter attack. Jerzy and his WAAF were standing close near the fireplace. At the other end of the bar, Giles, 'Einstein' and Richard were in deep conversation. 'Take away the military trappings,' he mused, 'and it could have been another night at the local; but of course it wasn't.' It was the most bizarre of situations; probably never before in history had it been possible to spend the day fighting the enemy and then retire for an evening at the pub, and then back to the fight the next day followed again by another evening in the pub, and so on for as long as one survives. Tomorrow will usher in September. One month to go by Giles' calculations but with the intensity of the Luftwaffe's attacks stepping up day by day. How many of them will be here at the end of September, or indeed will be back tomorrow night, or the night after, or else replaced by more fresh eager faces; the only indication of their having existed being their hastily scribbled signatures on a wall next to the bar? A roar from the darts corner told him that someone's aim had been true. On young men such as these rested the fate of a nation.

13: September, 1940

It had been another 'hard' day as Giles put it. Two more scrambles to protect the airfields in front of London against formations of bombers escorted by larger numbers of 109s and 110s. They had managed to penetrate the fighter screens and George had downed a Dornier, damaged a couple more and duelled inconclusively with a couple of 109s but most of his time had been spent whirling around dodging attacks and firing snap bursts at fleeting targets until, with fuel running low or ammunition exhausted, both sides had disengaged.

Once 686 had been stood down, he made his way to *The Stag*. "I'm sorry I haven't been to see you…"

It had been three days since he had seen her and she had regained much of her composure. "It's OK," Connie said. "Your adjutant rang to say that you couldn't make it and that there was no more news about Max."

"It's still possible he's been captured," said George, "in which case it will be some time before we hear anything."

"I hope you're right." She was silent for a few moments. "I gather you've been quite the hero."

"Oh, for heaven's sake, I managed to knock down a couple of bombers, that's all."

"That's not quite how I heard it."

"I hope they mentioned Jerzy, too. But for him I'd have been turned into a colander." As soon as he had spoken he wished he could have retracted.

"Could that have happened to Max? Shot in his parachute?" Her smile had faded now.

He looked her in the eye. "Honestly, I doubt it. The sky was pretty well clear on Friday whereas we lost sight of Max because of the amount of cloud there was then. If we couldn't see him nor could the Jerries."

"I'm sorry, I shouldn't have asked that. It was unfair. Forgive me, I'm not myself. Will you come again tomorrow please?" He nodded assent. "Thank you." She squeezed his hand and before he could react, she was heading up the stairs once more.

Late afternoon finds them over Kent in response to their second scramble of the day. The first had been in vain as they had arrived too late to engage the retreating Germans.

This time they aren't late. To their right and above, they can see massed formations of aircraft. However, as these draw closer, it becomes apparent that there are only a small number of bombers relative to fighters. Nonetheless, they have to be attacked. "Eyes peeled all Shuttlecock aircraft," Giles' commands are as crisp as ever, "try for a squirt at the bombers then break off; don't look to mix it with the fighters."

Before they can begin their attack, a shout from Jerzy disrupts their plans. "Bandits, five of clock high!" Instinctively, George looks back over his right shoulder and straight into the glare of the afternoon sun. That tells him enough. Even as Giles gives the order, George is swinging his Hurricane into a tight turn inside the line he estimates his unseen attackers are taking. Judd, his no. 2 today, has turned inside him and is in position as his wingman. Squinting into the sun, George can see black shapes bearing down. Tracer flashes past his cockpit, a shadow rushes over the top of his aircraft and the threat has passed as quickly as it came.

"Pancake, all Shuttlecock aircraft!" Dodging the attack has meant that they have lost touch with the main force and won't have enough fuel to pursue or wait for it returning so all they can do is head for base. Looking about him, George spots a single Hurricane, below and behind, trailing a thin stream of smoke. He drops back, Judd following suit, so they can escort it. Closing in, he recognises Sgt Northwood, another of the 'new types' giving a cheery wave. As they near home, he and Judd fall back and fan out so they can land in a vic. Northwood guides his aircraft onto the ground but the hydraulics have apparently been damaged; one brake locks and it goes into a ground loop. Without warning, flames appear and the aircraft is quickly ablaze.

"No!" shouts George, opening the throttle and taxiing towards it. He jumps from his aircraft and runs across the grass but is forced to pull up by the intense heat.

The crash tender arrives and men disgorge and start to deal with the fire. One of them calls to him. "Keep back please, sir – there's nothing you can do." Sickened and powerless to help, he turns away.

"As if that wasn't bad enough," said Richard, "I've just heard that Max has been found – dead of course – he was washed ashore near St Catherine's Point."

"Drowned I suppose?" asked George.

"Actually, no," replied Richard quietly, "he'd been machine-gunned."

"Bastards!" spat George vehemently.

"I agree... but it happens." He was silent for a few moments. "Someone's got to break the news to his widow. I can go tomor –"

"I'll go," said George in a tone that invited no argument.

Half an hour later he was at *The Stag* once more. As soon as she saw him, she knew.

"Where?" she asked.

"Isle-of-Wight."

"Drowned?"

"Probably exposure. He had a Mae West on." He hated the lie but couldn't see how she would benefit from the truth.

She tried to sound matter-of-fact. "A friend of my father died that way – they say it's painless." He waited for her to speak again. "Over the last week, I have imagined this moment and worked out how I would deal with it. But now it's here…" He stepped forward and put his arms around her and held her as she dissolved into wracking sobs. He lost track of time; it may have been five, even ten minutes before she became still. "Thank you," she said eventually.

"Is there anything I can do?"

"Yes please, if you have the time, come again tomorrow; but I need to be on my own just now." She turned and moved slowly, painfully, to the stairs.

The shortening days at least mean we don't have to get up so damned early, reflected George as he made his way to dispersal. The thought did little to lift the feeling of gloom which enveloped him, mainly the result of the previous day's events, but added to those, the war was a year old today. So much had happened in that year; he had gone from youthful optimism to fighting for survival and revenge – immediate future uncertain and further future empty. Within that year, he had loved and lost Justine; Mamam and so many friends and comrades gone – 'Edge', Reg, 'Shorty', Max and several whom he had known so fleetingly, he couldn't remember their names any longer if he had known them at all. He shook himself from his thoughts – he had things to do. Giles, as always, seemed irrepressible. "Morning, George. Following a signal from Group, when the rest of us scramble, presumably, eastwards, I need you, Jerzy and 'Litmus' with your wingmen to take-up a standing patrol on this line." He traced his finger across the map on the office wall. "While we and others were fending off 109s yesterday, a number of bombers that came in with the horde of Huns we encountered, sneaked off and tried to bomb the Hawker factory where they make nice new Hurris for us. Naturally, the Brass take a dim view of this, hence your mission."

Apart from one scramble to investigate what turned out to be a flight of Blenheims on a training exercise, 686 were not called upon that day. Released from immediate readiness by teatime, George headed for *The Stag.*

Connie had obviously spent the day crying but put on a brave face. "You're early."

"We weren't needed today; the Jerries must have been operating beyond London. I've brought Max's car – it's yours now."

"Thank you, but I can't drive. If I can find a buyer, I shall sell it. I've had some happy times in it so I'll be sorry to see it go – but memories don't pay bills."

"How're you fixed?"

"The room is paid until the 21st and Max and I have a few pounds in the bank – we were saving towards a house after the war… that won't be happening now." She paused and gathered herself. "So, in answer to your question, I can survive the next few weeks in which time I must decide what to do next."

"I may be able to help. Sometimes when a chap has bought it, his brother officers auction those of his possessions which aren't wanted by his nearest and dearest."

"It sounds like a good idea."

"How much are you hoping to get for it?"

"Max told me he bought it for £12.10s, so I suppose that's about what it's worth."

"OK. I'll take it back with me and we'll arrange an auction in the Mess." He looked at her as he spoke; she was pale and drawn. A thought occurred to him. "When was the last time you stepped outside?"

She thought for a moment. "The day Max disappeared."

"Come on," he said, "I'll take you for a last spin." She looked uncertain. "The fresh air will do you good."

They have only been patrolling for five minutes or so when they see them. Fifteen Dorniers in vics of three, moving fast at low level – and unescorted. George has a new call-sign to avoid confusion with the rest of the squadron. "Dogfish aircraft, line abreast for head-on attack. Pick your targets. Tallyho!"

They are already diving as they slide out of their pairs into formation. George picks the lead aircraft of the foremost vic – the formation commander or perhaps just keen; either way with little time left to regret it. He commences firing from three hundred yards and is immediately rewarded with an explosion – his instinct says lucky shot – probably a tracer bullet hitting a fuel tank. He pulls back hard on the stick to avoid all but a patter of fragments and climbs hard into a loop using the speed of his dive. About him the other Hurricanes are climbing too. Almost as one they half-roll off the top and dive again. Ahead and below, the Dornier formation has been shattered, but the survivors are pressing on regardless in ones and twos, forsaking the protection of rejoining formation in exchange for the chance to reach their target ahead of their pursuers. A tiny part of George feels respect for their courage but this is as nothing compared to his desire to knock them down. "Dogfish aircraft, Buster, don't let the bastards get the factory." The surge of extra power from the Merlins makes the Hurricanes leap forward. Slowly they start to gain. To his right one Dornier is gradually falling behind its fellows and Jerzy, without deviating from the chase, chops it down with a burst into one, then the other engine. George is shouting above the roar of his engine, urging his mount onwards. He is closing on another when a line of tracer floats lazily towards him then, at seemingly the last moment, rushes past. He aims a burst at its source and it stops. He fires again but as he does so, black objects fall from his target and then it is climbing and swinging away to the right. Others ahead have done the same. Explosions from the ground tell him that the black shapes are bombs. "Balloons, break!" he shouts into the R/T as he sees the reason for the Dorniers' evasive action and drags his Hurricane round. He glances at his temperature gauge – well into the red – his engine will soon seize or be irreparably damaged at this pace. He throttles back. Hopefully there will be other British fighters between here and the coast. "Break off pursuit and pancake, all Dogfish aircraft." He glances back – the balloon barrage is now riding above a carpet of smoke and flame. Sick in the stomach, he sets course.

The atmosphere could only be described as gloomy as 'Einstein' finished checking and collating their combat reports. "Seven downed – of which six already confirmed by Observer Corps reports – and two damaged – not a bad haul if I may say so."

"And one factory destroyed," said George quietly.

The ringing of the telephone caught their attention and they braced for another scramble; but no call came and they began to relax. 'Einstein' had used the time unsuccessfully searching for something to say that didn't sound platitudinous, when Giles' appearance solved his problem. "What I am about to say is not to be discussed beyond this gathering. The call was from Group, who are far from disappointed with your efforts today. It's clear from the fact that the Huns continued their attack, despite the ferocity and effectiveness of your defence, witnessed by the Observer Corps, that they were an elite unit; that, and greater numbers, made it inevitable that some of them would get through; but your continued snapping at their heels meant that when they got there, they didn't have time to float around and pick their target so they ended up in haste bombing the wrong factory." He paused to let his words sink in. "Yes, the wrong factory. No consolation to the poor devils on the receiving end but the damage done is of no consequence to Fighter Command's immediate needs. So, good show; which means you can wipe away those morose looks and form an orderly queue in the pub tonight – the beers are on me! One more thing, when the Huns send a recce flight across today or tomorrow, we're not to shoot it down. Even as we speak bods are burning oily rags and throwing rubble around our precious factory, so we want the Huns to get their pictures of destruction in the hope that they won't want to try again. Finally, you're released for today; so – until tonight."

It was a warm sunlit evening and, relieved of the despondency of apparent failure, George made short work of the mile and a half walk to the *The Stag*. To his surprise, Connie was sitting outside, catching the last of the sinking sun.

"Has the car been sold already?" she asked, sounding, he thought, a little put out. "Not yet. The Adj will hold the auction as soon as he can gather a reasonable number of us together – probably the next time we're weathered in."

"So the car – my car – is still available. Could you bring it over again please – I'd like another spin before it goes; last evening was lovely – a real tonic."

"Of course. I'd go for it now but by the time I get back it will be going dark. Fresh air seems to agree with you – how about a quick stroll while it's still light."

She pondered for a moment. "Why not?"

Three times this day he had led the 'Dogfish' sections to yesterday's patrol line but no enemy aircraft came to trouble them. Nonetheless three scrambles in a day were no sinecure and it was a weary George who drove up to *The Stag* to find Connie outside again, sitting on a bench. He called across. "Evening ma'am; your carriage awaits."

She climbed in beside him. "Thank you so much for doing this."

"My pleasure. How are you?"

"Just existing, day to day. It's nice to have a few moments away from reality." In their close proximity she could see his face was tired and drawn. "What about you?"

"Much the same. Giles reckons we have to hold out until the end of the month."

"Can you do it?"

"There's no alternative – and in a strange way that helps because there's no soft option to distract us. We have to stop the Germans – it's do or die. And we owe it to Max and all the others who've bought it already not to give in." He wondered if he'd said too much and was relieved to see her nod slowly in agreement. "Enough of this talk; let's enjoy the countryside."

To Stanhope-Smith, the Paris blackout, although punctuated by chinks of light in seemingly all the right places, was a surprise after Berlin; ablaze with light on his last leave, except for an hour when RAF bombers had had the temerity to pay a visit. They had already visited several bars when he and Reinhart, his travelling companion, found themselves under a dimly lit sign which proclaimed 'Le Chat Noir'. A face appeared at a small window in response to their knock. Seconds later, the door swung open and they were ushered up a dingy staircase. The interior was as dark as the name suggested, lit only by a number of feeble wall lights; the atmosphere fetid and claustrophobic. Here and there a cigarette glowed as its owner inhaled. Coming from the dark outside it didn't take long for their eyes to acclimatise. Apart from a bar, a dance floor and a small group playing an erotic-sounding jazz the rest of the room was given over to tables and chaise-longue type seating. The dance floor was full of couples shuffling and smooching to the music and the chaises were occupied either by women draped languorously across them, cigarette holder in hand, or more couples. With a start, he thought he saw two men exchange a kiss but some people pushed in front of him and he lost sight of them. Intermittently, he noticed a strange sweet smell that he couldn't place but which reminded him vaguely of incense. It occurred to him that despite the war it was business as usual here. The women, apart from a handful wearing suits and short hair in the Marlene Dietrich style, were uniformly brassy, while the men were a mixture of pimps, villains, military and collaborators. A year ago it would have been pimps, villains, businessmen and politicians. 'Plus ca change,' he thought sullenly. He hadn't wanted to come here. That he had was down to Reinhardt. They were on their way to Luftflotte 2 HQ near the channel coast when problems in the overworked rail network had forced a stopover in Paris. 'The best whoring in Europe' Reinhardt had announced gleefully before disappearing upstairs to confirm it, leaving him here. He wasn't averse to women himself – in fact the opposite – but he had already found that the Luftwaffe uniform had them falling on their backs like ninepins so he didn't see the need to pay for the services of a Parisian tart and probably end up with more than he had bargained for.

The evening's drinking was starting to catch up with him and he was beginning to feel the worse for wear. He wasn't sure whether he had momentarily dozed off but when he raised his head with a start there was a woman at his side. Her German was halting, she obviously hadn't had time to adapt fully to the changed situation. *"'allo, m'sieu Pilot, you want dance with me?"* He studied her for a moment. Underneath the heavily applied makeup, her features were delicate and, he thought, quite pretty. She had black curly hair, green eyes and a slender figure. Attractive, but he felt no desire for her.

"No thanks," he replied at length.

She tried again. *"Perhaps you like buy champan? I 'ave nice room to share it."*

"No thanks."

She thought for a moment and then added waspishly. *"Perhaps you prefer dance with my brother?"*

It took a moment or two for her meaning to sink in. The vision of the two kissing men flashed across his mind. He felt the colour rush to his cheeks. *"I certainly do not."*

"Well, what do you want?" she said angrily.

"I want you to bugger off!" he snapped.

"Asshole!" She tried to slap his face but he caught her arm and twisted it causing her to cry out.

The disturbance caused another Luftwaffe officer to turn around. He was holding a girl and a half-empty champagne bottle and his face and partly unbuttoned shirt were covered in lipstick smudges. He swayed as he tried to focus, as though on the deck of a ship. *"Good God! The Englishman. What brings you here?"*

Stanhope-Smith didn't try to conceal his bitterness. *"Fat lot you or your bloody Major care! If you must know I'm on my way to Luftflotte 2 as part of a fact-finding mission – to discover why we haven't swept the RAF from the skies yet."*

For a moment, Werner wanted to hit him but the champagne was far too expensive to waste and he wasn't sure that if he took his other arm from around the neck of the girl he could still stand up; so he restrained himself. *"You're right about one thing. 'My bloody Major' doesn't care – not now anyway – because he's feeding fishes at the bottom of the channel. I saw him ditch and sink like a stone. I'll live with that for the rest of my days because it was my fault. I was his wingman and his friend and I let a bloody 'Tommy' put a burst into his engine. He tried to make it back but the bloody channel was too wide. As for why we haven't swept the RAF from the skies, I'll tell you in two sentences – They're good and well led; we had a foretaste at Dunkirk, but no-one recognised it. We're good too but we're led by a puffed-up idiot."* He saw the look on Stanhope-Smith's face and gave a weary laugh. *"Go on party man, report me if you like but it's the truth. He might have been a hero in the last lot but he's a clown this time. First he tells us to go after the RAF fighters, then he tells us to stick with our bombers. Now we're being told to protect the 110s as well and they're supposed to be bloody fighters. If they can't cope on their bloody own, they should bloody well stay at home. As a result, by the time we get across the channel, we've hardly any fuel left to take on the Tommies before we have to turn around. So we're all flying back watching our gauges and wondering if we're going to have to ditch and go the way of the Major. It's grinding men down – in case it hasn't filtered through to Berlin yet the word is 'Kanalkrankheit' – 'Channel sickness' – so go back and tell that to fat fucking Hermann. You should be thanking 'my bloody Major' for keeping you out of it. I heard you went to be an instructor anyway?"*

"I did, but I kept asking to join a front-line squadron. In the end, because I'm English, they moved me to a staff job to help with the invasion planning. Being an ADC is cushy but I still want to fight."

Werner was silent for a moment. *"It does you credit,"* he lowered his voice, *"Enjoy your cushy number while you can. I have a cousin in OKW and I know for a fact that they've started planning for war in the East next summer. Keep it under your hat because it isn't official yet."*

"Russia?"

"The very same. So bide your time because they'll need every pilot they can get and you won't have to worry about landing amongst the Tommies."

Stanhope-Smith felt a surge of elation. *"I'll tell you something in exchange. Don't go criticising the Reichsmarschall in public and you might still be around next summer."*

Werner bowed his head and attempted to click his heels. *"I may well not be anyway but that sounds like good advice. Auf weidersehn!"* He unhooked his arm from around the girl's neck and she squealed as he slapped her rump. *"Come wench, I have need of you upstairs!"*

A few minutes later, a re-invigorated Stanhope-Smith pushed through the throng with a bottle and two glasses and caught sight of the green-eyed girl, sharing a cigarette with a colleague; *"We got off to a bad start – still wanting a drink?"*

They are climbing for the second time in the day – as a full squadron again; George and his fellow 'dogfish' re-absorbed; 'factory duty' having been rotated to another squadron. The day's first encounter had been a bruising one; as they sought to attack the bombers they had found themselves fending off hordes of 109s. Bardsley had been shot down, baled out and returned in time for this scramble, but Sgt Westridge's Hurricane was seen falling earthwards without any sign of a parachute – another new type gone before he had had a chance to learn his trade properly. The rest of them had survived but achieved little to deflect the bombers. Could they last until the end of September, Connie had asked the previous evening. As he had said, they had to but, in truth, he did not know, they could only try. For the last two weeks, the Germans had been using more effective tactics; sending massive fighter escorts to protect their bombers, so ensuring that more were achieving their aim of battering the airfields around London; and thus obtaining the dual benefits of engaging more of the defenders in attritional fighter-to-fighter combats and destroying the bases without which the RAF could not operate; more than once in the last fortnight he had seen one or another covered in smoke and flame – it was miraculous that squadrons were continuing to operate from them. By comparison the Sussex and Hampshire airfields had got off lightly, so far, but that could change at any time. Little by little they were being ground down; they needed some respite, but even the weather was against them, the last fortnight having been nothing but fine weather. The glint of sunlight on Perspex catches his attention just as Giles' voice crackles inside his helmet. "Bandits, two o'clock low. Aim for the bombers and try to avoid the fighters. Tallyho!" This morning they had crossed most of Kent to meet the enemy but now they are still over their own county. He banks towards the enemy formation, seeing that the bombers and fighters are about equal in number; Judd, his no. 2 again, following with the practised ease of a veteran of a week or more. Perhaps the Germans are feeling the strain too, because they have made a mistake. He can see, as he expects the other seasoned pilots can, that the 109s providing top cover are too high, even though some are now diving; and those flying on a level with the bombers are too low, to intercept 686 as they arrow into the bomber formation. He picks a Heinkel 111, and fires at its port engine, then kicks the rudder bar, swinging the Hurricane's nose and spraying his fire along the cockpit. From the corner of his eye, he sees flames issuing from another Heinkel.

"Shuttlecock aircraft, Bandits four o'clock high." A glance is enough to see that the diving 109s are not yet in range so, instead of turning into them, he steepens his own dive. Another glance tells him that although Judd is still with him, the 109s are not; obviously under orders to stay with their charges. Using the speed of their dive to climb again, they curve in towards the rear of the formation. The monoplane fighter's blind spot is astern and below, and the pilots alongside the bombers aren't looking for attacks from there; their attention being divided between matching their speed with the slower Heinkels and the threat as other British squadrons dive into the fray. George picks a *rotte* at the rear, closing rapidly and firing up into the wingman's underside. A spurt of flame and before it begins its final dive he has transferred his sights onto the leader. A long burst, the canopy flies off and a body tumbles clear. The empty aircraft flies level for two seconds, streaming smoke; then a wing drops.

"Yellow Leader, Four bandits, seven o'clock high."

"Roger, Yellow Two. Buster and turn into them." Throttle through the gate, George pulls into an inside loop then rolls upright, Judd beside him as their aircraft, hanging on their propellers, claw their way upwards. As if on cue, both sides open fire. The recoil of eight Brownings is too much for the labouring Hurricanes and each topples into a spin, but not before George's bulletproof windscreen suffers a couple of spider's web indentations. "Hold the spin, Yellow Two." He watches the hands whirl round as his altimeter unwinds – fifteen, fourteen, thirteen; they are passing through twelve thousand feet when he gives the order to pull out. Full opposite rudder, stick centred and forward then wait. They are below five thousand when the rotation stops and they ease into level flight, taking a good look around.

"I think I got one – Hun with a red spinner." Judd sounds excited as his aircraft draws into formation. "I say, sir, it looks like you're losing coolant."

Judd's observation is confirmed by the engine temperature, which hasn't dropped as it should have with the reduced revs. "That blasted Hun must have hit the glycol tank as well as the windscreen. I'm going to try to get her back – we've not far to go." He opens the hood in case he has to jump in a hurry and reduces the revs further but the temperature obstinately continues to edge up. For several minutes, he creeps across the landscape, tensed for the first lick of flame. Finally, in the distance he can see the airfield. Until now, he has had sufficient altitude to bale out but if the engine catches fire on the descent, he will have the choice of being burnt alive or jumping to his death. He turns off the magnetos and closes the fuel cock. The roar of the engine subsides to leave only the rush of wind past his open cockpit. The propeller is still windmilling in the slipstream so he leaves it in coarse pitch to lessen resistance – he won't be looking for a go-around. Gradually the field grows in his windscreen. He begins working the auxiliary pump to lower the undercarriage. The heat which had been building up in the cockpit is reducing, but still sufficient to have him sweating with effort. He gives a grunt of satisfaction as the wheels lock in place and two green lights confirm. Now all he has to do is land the thing. Certain now that he will make the field he porpoises – nose up to shed speed then back down to avoid the catastrophe of a stall. His approach is still fast but without the engine it has to be flapless. Judd has preceded him and flown low over the airfield waggling his wings.

Thus alerted, someone has spotted George's silent approach and the crash tender and ambulance are racing for position. George flares as he crosses the boundary hedge and the Hurricane sinks quickly in the warm afternoon air. First contact is hard and the aircraft bounces but George works the stick forward and back to control pitch. The second bounce is less and the aircraft settles at the third contact, still travelling fast but the wind direction has allowed landing into the longest dimension, and the dry uneven grass strips the speed off, bringing it to a halt before the far boundary. George is climbing unsteadily from the cockpit as the crash tender arrives, closely followed, on a pushbike, by 'Litmus'. "G-good show. A-are you OK?"

"Yes thanks – but I think it's time I took up smoking."

Not for the first time in the day, George glanced across at Jerzy, who was sitting in a deckchair reading, seemingly oblivious to all about him; apparently at peace in the midst of a war. Not for the first time too, he thought back to the previous evening's conversation. He had been about to get into the MG to visit Connie when Jerzy had approached and given him a small silver crucifix. 'You have been good friend and I hope I have been same. So I want you to have this in remembrance.'

'Have you been posted?'

'No, but soon I am gone.'

'I don't understand.'

'Last night, my mother came to me. She said that soon I will be with her and not to have fear.'

'You've been dreaming, that's all. We live with death and destruction every day so it's bound to be on your mind.'

'I think not. It did not feel like dream – but if it is, you can keep cross.'

'Try to put it from your mind – Richard told me that in the last lot people thought they were going to die and it became a self-fulfilling prophecy, because they gave up.'

'I have not given up. I will fight Nazis to my last breath; but if it is to be…'

George checked his watch – two o'clock. He couldn't shake off a sense of foreboding. It wasn't because of what Jerzy had said. The fine weather of the last fortnight had stretched into another day; the ideal English summer just when it was least wanted, perfect conditions for continuing the onslaught; yet there had been no sign of the enemy at all. Two weeks of mounting pressure had mysteriously given way to the relative luxury of thirty-minute readiness. Was this the prelude to invasion? If it was going to happen everyone knew it had to be soon. He looked around. Apart from Jerzy's, the faces reflected the same unease, bewilderment even, which he felt.

250

Just after four o'clock they were advanced to immediate readiness; half-an-hour later, airborne. It became clear from their heading that they weren't aiming for any part of the coastline or the airfields and factories they had previously been defending – they were vectored to London itself.

Emerging from a belt of haze to the west of the capital, they meet with a sight that George knows he will never forget. Like some biblical plague a massive formation of aircraft, several miles across and thousands of feet high is advancing from the south- east. There must be eight or nine hundred, even a thousand of them. A momentary feeling of despair, replaced with visceral anger and an even deeper hatred for the Hun than he already held. To him it is obvious – Rotterdam. Just as they did in Holland, they are looking to force surrender by devastating the capital city; the massive attack feared a year ago has arrived. His next emotion is admiration; for Giles. Faced with the same horde, he sounds as unflappable as ever. "Shuttlecock aircraft, no shortage of sport today – ignore the fighters as far as you can and get after the bombers – Tallyho!" As they close with the enemy, George sees other British squadrons hurling themselves into the fray. Escorting 109s begin peeling from the formation to bar the way and more are diving down from above. "Yellow and Green Sections, form on me line abreast, take the 109s, the rest of you keep going for the bombers." Giles and Bardsley, George and Judd, and 'Litmus' and Enderby point their aircraft towards the advancing Germans giving them no choice but to reciprocate. The two groups close rapidly, then burst through each other's lines, their firing having no obvious effect. "Now for the divers." They pull into a loop, half-roll and push their throttles to full boost, charging through the diving 109s. Again, no hits are scored but they have gained height and turn towards the first group, now arcing round below them to renew the joust. "George, throttle back for a few seconds and stay with me, 'Litmus' take their flank." Red and Yellow Sections cancel boost as they begin their third headlong charge, to give 'Litmus' and Enderby time to swing wider at full power before turning in at an angle to the converging aircraft and opening fire. Streaming glycol, a 109 falls away and, faced with this additional threat, his comrades dive away under the advancing Hurricanes. "Good show, let's have a squirt at the bombers before any more of the buggers spot us." George can see that the 109s which dived on them are now engaged with other British fighters so there is a brief window to the bombers. Giles leads, he and Bardsley shooting a Dornier down. George heads towards another. He fires into the Dornier's engine but his ammunition runs out. His frustration is allayed when Judd follows up with a killing burst – how he misjudged him only weeks before. They are diving away as 'Litmus' and Enderby despatch a third. If George's ammunition is spent, then the rest of them must be in a similar situation. Confirming his thoughts, 'Disengage, all Shuttlecock aircraft and pancake' comes through his headphones. For all the damage 686 and their fellows have done, sheer weight of numbers has carried the attack through. The East End and docklands have disappeared from view under a pall formed of dust thrown skywards by countless explosions and black smoke boiling up from the resulting fires. Even as he is trying to come to terms with this vision of hell, the next radio message makes his blood run cold.

Justine opened the door as Lys reached it. *"Where have you been? I was starting to worry."*

"No need, my dear, just checking fences; making sure they are adequate and secure. Autumn is coming and there is also the possibility of poachers now food is rationed."

"Can't one of the farmhands to do that? You were out for ages last Saturday too. I was beginning to wonder if you have an admirer."

"As you will learn when the farm is yours, there are some things you will always want to do for yourself. Unfortunately I don't have an admirer; but what a nice idea; maybe I should put a note in the window of the Tabac – 'refined lady seeks tall, dark, handsome man for country walks. Vichyites need not apply', how does that sound?"

"Now you're making fun of me."

"Just a little, my dear – you were beginning to sound like our occupying power."

Jerzy's voice was strained, his words faltering, "Goodbye... my... friends – is over. *Niek... Zeeyer... Po...*" The message cut off abruptly. Before George could gather himself to do so, Giles called. "Blue Leader, Shuttlecock Leader, come in please."

Sgt Rodway answered, his voice unsteady, "Shuttlecock Leader, Blue Two – Blue Leader... has... has... bought it."

"Roger, Blue Two, disengage when you are able and head for home."

George didn't register the *sang-froid* in Giles' response. He was numb. He wasn't aware of the flight back to the airfield; only that he was in the little group which gathered as Sgt Rodway, close to tears, climbed from his aircraft. "He just kept going so close, as if he had nothing to fear – he shot down three at point-blank range." He looked at Giles, "when you called us to disengage, he went for his fourth but he was caught in a cross-fire from several of them – I fired at a couple but it was too late – I saw their tracers hitting his cockpit and I knew he'd had it. His kite staggered for a moment, he spoke on the R/T and then he flew straight into one of them. There was nothing more I could..." He turned away from them to gather himself. Evans laid a consoling hand on his shoulder and led him away as George recalled what Jerzy had said the night before, '...I will fight Nazis to my last breath'.

George hadn't noticed Giles detaching himself from the group to speak to Richard and 'Einstein' who had arrived in some haste. After a brief conversation, he turned to address them, looking grim, "Gentlemen, the codeword 'Cromwell' has been issued – invasion imminent. All ranks are to be armed and we are to be on the alert for attack on the airfield, whether by land or from the air." Underlining his words they heard for the first time the pealing of bells from the village church.

Sunset had been several hours ago but sufficient light for 'Litmus' to read the time, nearly midnight, was provided by the red glow on the northern horizon – London in flames; the nightmare had come to pass. He and George were in the middle of their turn in command of the watch. All quiet so far; no sounds to concern them beyond the rustle of nearby trees in the night airs; although he had heard it said that the only warning of glider troops was the swish as their transports swooped in to land. George had said little during the hour they had been together but 'Litmus' had understood his reluctance even though he quietly craved reassuring conversation in this moment of peril. What would the next hours bring? Would they soon be dead like Jerzy, or in a living hell in the grip of the barbarous regime that had ravaged his homeland? He thought of his own sister, who had already endured the attacks on Biggin Hill, and shuddered. As if reading his thoughts, George spoke, "I'm sorry, I'm poor company. Everything's pretty bloody at the moment."

"I-I know. D-do you think they're c-coming?"

"I don't know. If not, why this alert? But if they are I think they're pushing their luck, trying to cross the channel without seeing off us or the Navy – and whilst bombing London is pretty rotten, I really can't see it making us throw in the towel. Can you?"

'Litmus' thought for a few moments. When he answered he looked perceptibly brighter. "No," he said emphatically.

Today was probably going to be the day he would die, thought George, not greatly disturbed to find he could contemplate it with such detachment. He was dog-tired, browned-off and in no fit state to go to war; but today of all days, with the invasion underway, he could hardly report unfit for duty. Although his watch had finished at 2 am, he had hardly slept. Every time he had closed his eyes, although he hadn't actually witnessed it, he could see Jerzy's final act of defiance and, when he managed to get beyond that, with his nerves drawn taut by the expectation of attack, he was woken or kept awake by every unusual sound the night had to offer. It was coming light when a mug of hot tea appeared beside him. "By 'eck, tha looks rough. Ah s'pose tha's bin on't wild goose-chase wi't rest of 'em."

"What?" George found conversing with AC2 Blakely a challenge even on a good day.

"Don't tha know? There's no invasion; t'ol thing's bollocks."

"God in Heaven!" exclaimed George wearily, "are you sure?"

"Aye, av'eard it from t'Einstein feller. Call t'stand down come ten minutes since. An't squadron's released too fo't time bein' so tha's no call t'go anywhere in a 'urry. Some daft wazzock's goin' t' get 'is arse reet royally kicked for this. Ah reckon it all comes of these posh folks sending their idiot sons in tot'army. If we're goin' t'win this war we're goin' t'ave t'ave a bloody good sort out. Mark my words…" He turned to emphasise his point but George was sound asleep. "Bloody 'ell, mek 'im a 'ot cuppa an' he falls asleep ower it." He gently pulled a blanket over George's recumbent form and crept out of the tent.

Six hours of uninterrupted sleep had done much to revivify George. He wasn't going to put aside the loss of Jerzy that easily but he had largely shaken off the cloak of despondency which had enveloped him that dawn. The squadron had returned to 'released' from the thirty-minute readiness to which he had awoken, even though it was only early afternoon. Richard had seized on the unexpected lull to organise an impromptu auction of the MG so, with a feeling of mild anticipation, George joined his fellows, grouped around the item in question.

"Gentlemen, I believe you are all sufficiently familiar with this fine example of the genre for me not to have to give any further description. So who's going to start the bidding at ten pounds?" Silence. "Nine then?" More silence. "Eight?"

"S-seven pounds t-ten," called a familiar voice.

"Eight," instantly followed.

"N-nine."

Ten pounds came quickly but then things began to drag. Eventually the bid crept up to twelve pounds ten shillings.

"I have twelve pounds ten," said Richard, "any advance on twelve pounds ten?" He looked around, "No? Then going for the first time… going for the second time…" George didn't really know what made him do it other than he wanted to believe that someone would have done the same for Justine had she been in Connie's shoes. "Fifty guineas!" There was a stunned silence, broken eventually by Richard.

"Can I just confirm that you said 'fifty' rather than 'fifteen'?"

"Five-oh, fifty," said George.

"Very well; any advance on fifty guineas?… Going for the first time… going for the second at fifty guineas… gone – to a Knight in shining armour." A ripple of laughter ran through the gathering before they began to drift away leaving just Richard and George. "That was a very decent thing you just did; and I daresay I know why."

"Poor girl's all on her own."

"Oh, I wouldn't say that – not with you for a friend."

As the readiness state had remained at 'released' all afternoon, with less than an hour to sunset, George felt able to head for *The Stag*. It was a dull evening so he found Connie inside.

"I didn't know whether you'd be coming, what with the invasion scare."

"I'm sorry I wasn't able to 'phone you yesterday; it wasn't permitted."

"I understood when I heard the church bells. I must say I was quite frightened; I didn't sleep until the all-clear came this morning. What about you?"

"Frightened and browned-off at the same time. They bombed the daylights out of London and Jerzy was killed yesterday."

"Oh no! Max spoke so highly of him."

"We were the three musketeers. I daresay they're waiting for me to rejoin them."

"You mustn't talk like that."

"You're right. Its bad form to dwell on things. Time for some good news. The car's been sold."

"I'm wishing now I hadn't asked; I shall miss the drives."

"No you won't, I bought it!"

She looked at him suspiciously. "How much did you pay for it?"

"Only fifty guineas. It was a hard-fought auction."

"Only? That's forty pounds more than Max paid for it!" Her eyes brimmed with tears. "Oh George, you shouldn't," she stretched up and kissed his cheek, "but thank you so very much."

He pulled a cheque from his uniform. "Put it away before you make the ink run."

With something between a laugh and a sob she folded it and put it in a small pocket in her skirt. He could see her eyes brimming again so he spoke first. "Bit late tonight but, Jerry permitting, do you fancy a spin tomorrow?"

They stood around him sipping early morning mugs of tea as Giles spoke. "I've had a signal from Group to say that, in response to the large formations the Huns are now using against London, Squadrons are to work in pairs – it should give us more of a chance to break through the fighter screen and get among the bombers." Amid nods of agreement, he continued. "Obviously we will normally be paired with one of our near neighbours and hopefully be vectored to meet up before interception. We won't have direct radio contact with them so we will independently follow the controller's instructions and hope to arrive together; however, we should be able to achieve a concerted effort. Now all we need is a bunch of Huns to try it out on."

For most of the day they have again been 'released', sparing them hours of knife-edge tension. Late afternoon brought, in quick succession, thirty-minute then immediate readiness before they are once again going to war. To George's surprise they are heading along the coast, rather than for London, and to his satisfaction they meet with their companion squadron without a hitch. Scarcely, have they done so than they see the enemy, few more than one hundred aircraft instead of the hordes of recent times, but on their way back from the capital, with other British fighters snapping at them. "Shuttlecock Aircraft, Bluejay Control, engage escort."

Earlier attacks have separated the fighters from the bombers and both 109s and 110s have adopted defensive circles as they wait for their returning charges. Giles gives his instructions. "Yellow and Blue Sections, have a crack at the 110s. The rest of you follow me. Tallyho!"

George heads for the 110s, using height gained on the approach to dive down on them. He makes a deflection shot but doesn't have time to see the results as the following 110 breaks formation to attack him. As George pulls up over the circle, Judd fires a burst at it, forcing it to dive away. "Thanks, Yellow Two." As he turns to make another pass he can see that the remaining 110s have broken their circle, seemingly no longer mindful of their escort duties, and used their superior speed in the dive to draw away, minus one of their number spiralling down as a result of Blue Section's attentions. The bombers, now with only the 109s to defend them, although still under attack are also far enough ahead to dissuade him, after turning hopefully in their direction, from pursuit. He has not long led Judd and Blue Section into a turn for home when he hears Giles recalling the rest of the squadron.

"Did anyone see what happened to my 110?" George asked as they made their way to see 'Einstein'.

"Engine smoking, but still flying; much the same as mine," Judd replied.

"Two damaged then," he said wistfully. "I was especially hoping to get one today." Evans' rich Welsh baritone emphasised his delight. "Ours went down in this lovely spiral, see; like wa-ter down a plug-'ole."

"That was for Jerzy," added Rodway.

"Good show. Music to my ears. I'll stand a round for that," said George.

"You seem a lot brighter." Connie shouted above the wind as the MG bowled along. "Things are looking brighter;" he replied, "in the last three days the weather has given us some respite; we've only had one scramble – bit of a scrap over the Isle of Wight – so we've had the chance to get some rest; and we're a bit further through September; I'm beginning to believe we can last the course."

"It's Friday the 13th tomorrow, so be careful."

"I'm not worried by 13 – triskaidekaphobic do they call it?"

"Well, be careful anyway... I'd miss these outings." He laughed as she gave him an impish grin.

Surviving Friday the 13th hadn't proved difficult; he had passed the day reading and falling in and out of welcome slumber, as 686 relished the unexpected bonus of being at 'released' throughout. At some point, he had found himself pondering why, after three weeks of relentless assault, the past few days had produced comparatively little activity. On a couple of days a break in the weather had been a factor but otherwise, had the Germans become disheartened at the continuing and, with the use of paired squadrons, increasing numbers of defending fighters, or were they gathering for a final massive effort to overwhelm the defences and pave the way for invasion? The soft embrace of sleep had reclaimed him before he had found an answer.

The question has arisen again. Saturday afternoon, a week on from the first massive raid on London, the loss of Jerzy and the invasion false alarm. Despite being bombed every night since, London, he has heard, is still largely intact, Jerzy is only a memory and the invasion remains an unfulfilled threat; and once more nothing is happening.

The third phone call in the space of ten minutes sees them running for their aircraft – and a sense of deja-vu; 'Shuttlecock aircraft, Vector one-six-fiver, Angels ten, 10+ bandits'. Just like July, George reflects as they claw their way skywards. Within five minutes, they can see about twenty aircraft in two groups, already dropping bombs on the coastal towns beneath them.

"No sign of escorts, give the bastards hell, Tallyho!" calls Giles. Instinct has caused George to make his own scan and with a sharp pang he recalls how they had been helped by Jerzy's eagle eyes over the past few weeks. Regret quickly turns into cold fury as they close with the enemy planes which, having seen 686's approach, have jettisoned their remaining bombs on the town below and turned for home. George and Judd catch up with a group of four Dorniers. Co-ordinated bursts from the rear gunners tells George that these are experienced campaigners so he veers to starboard and pulls out wide before arcing in once more. Applying full deflection he fires a burst at the nearest aircraft and with a savage joy sees it flying into his tracer stream. Flames erupt from the starboard engine and it begins to drop from the formation. Its companions have no realistic choice but to carry on without it. Deprived of protection, within seconds it is being raked by Judd. Its descent becomes a steep spiral but they lose sight of it as they turn in pursuit of the other three. The density of their exhaust fumes shows that they are all at maximum power as they endeavour to escape. George and Judd are gaining gradually when the recall comes. For a moment he is tempted to apply the Nelson touch but they are already well out to sea and could soon find themselves facing fresh fighters sent to cover the retreat. Discipline and experience prevail and he reluctantly leads Judd into a turn for home.

"Thank you," said George, accepting the proffered pint of beer. Despite the ongoing threat of invasion, *The Barley Mow* was busy and the atmosphere far from subdued. "So what do we make of it?" Giles threw the question to the 'older' heads – George, Richard, 'Litmus', Evans and 'Einstein' – grouped around him.

Richard spoke first, "To begin with I have to say that the last week has been most welcome but it doesn't make sense; to me at any rate. To use a boxing analogy they had us on the ropes and then stepped back and allowed us a breather."

"I t-thought last Saturday's blitz on L-London was meant to be the kn-knockout punch, like Rotterdam."

"Or else the prelude to invasion – but they haven't followed it up."

"Not yet anyway. I spoke on the 'phone to Peter Templeton yesterday. He's flying Blenheims now and spending his time bombing barge concentrations in the channel ports – he says the numbers are still increasing despite all."

"Rotterdam was different because the Dutch were on their last legs anyway," said 'Einstein', "the shock was the straw that broke that camel's back. Perhaps if they had tried to invade last Saturday it would have proved equally decisive – I think we all felt pretty browned-off and jumpy last weekend – but they didn't. Instead they've carried on bombing London every night since; not pleasant for Londoners and frustrating that we can do so little to prevent it at present, but it has already lost its shock-effect. It has become another matter of endurance and you," he swept his hand around them, "are proving that the fight goes on unabated despite it. I know the weather has interfered with their plans to a degree but I think they have made a big mistake in easing off the pressure. Looking at you all, I can see that this week has made a big difference – you are clearly refreshed and ready to see this through. As for invasion, well that's still an obvious possibility but," he glanced at Giles, "as has been said previously, they have to make their move soon or not at all. So unless they've lost their focus my feeling is that they're winding themselves up for one big effort; and if that fails they'll have to forget invasion until at least next spring." He drained his glass then looked around, inviting comment.

"Bravo!" said Giles. "I think that warrants a refill. If you hadn't previously, you've justified your status as Intelligence officer tonight," he added to laughter.

Blakely had brought a mug of hot tea before first light so George was wide awake when Giles spoke to him. "Group want a standing patrol over the coast for the first couple of hours of daylight." He traced the patrol area on the map in front of them. "The rest of us will be at Readiness. Take our newest recruit, Sgt Bryce; give him the chance of a pot at a recce kite."
"How many hours on type?"
"Just about into double figures."
George closed his eyes and shook his head. When he spoke it was on a different subject. "When this mist bums off it will be gin clear. Group are obviously expecting something; I've a feeling this is the day we talked of."
"Me too," said Giles.

Bryce was waiting for him at dispersal exuding the mix of eagerness and trepidation he had seen in other new boys. "Morning Sergeant. How many hours on type?"
"Ten and a half, sir," he replied proudly.
"Have you fired your guns?"
"No sir," he said reluctantly, before adding, "we were going to last week but the weather intervened and then I was posted here."
George held back a number of retorts that instantly came to mind. "So, do you know how to use a reflector sight?"
"No, sir." He could see Bryce's self-assurance deflating with each question.
"OK. We've a few minutes to spare. Hop in your kite and I'll give you a run-down."

"Shuttlecock leader, you have trade. Vector two-one-zero and make angels two-five." George was encouraged to see that Bryce had more or less held position as they banked round onto their new heading. Slightly to the south-west a flash of sunlight off Perspex told him what he needed to know.
"Roger Bluejay Control, bandit in sight. Engaging." Instead of going for a direct intercept George aims more to the south, anticipating being spotted. His expectation is correct and the e/a begins a 180 degree turn away from him. The Hurricanes' margin of speed over that of what is now obviously a Dornier means that within a couple of minutes they have caught up to it. "Okay Yellow two, stick to me like glue; and watch out for the gunners. Tallyho!" He pulls wide to port and then curves in. The Dornier tries to turn away but George uses boost to maintain his relative position for the few seconds he needs. Pressing the firing button he sees his tracers striking across wing and engine and into the fuselage beyond, before breaking away to port again. Over his shoulder he sees Bryce's approach. His first attempt at firing is wild and high. The German pilot recognises his inexperience and swings away again to allow his dorsal and ventral gunners to get a bead. Preoccupied with trying to bring his sights to bear, Bryce hasn't recognised his

danger, but George has. "Break left, Yellow two. Break left now!" Bryce responds to the instruction but too late to dodge the stream of bullets from the dorsal gunner.

"I'm hit, Yellow Leader, in the leg!" he cries into the radio.

"Can you make it back?"

Silence for a moment. "I-I don't know. Bleeding quite badly."

"Take your helmet off and tie the R/T lead as tightly as you can around your leg. You don't need R/T – just waggle your wings when you 're ready and follow me."

The Dornier is heading southwards in a shallow dive, trailing a long plume of smoke from its damaged engine. He knows that unhindered it will probably make it home but he has a pilot to save. Bryce's wings waggle and George moves from alongside into the lead, heading northwards.

"Probably a blessing in disguise," said George at dispersal, between bites of a sandwich, "if today turns out as we expect, he probably would have got the chop – it's pointless sending these poor sods to us half-trained."

"Well, he'll live to fight another day and by the time he's fit again there should be time to complete his education," said Giles, examining his sandwich. "Any idea what's in this?"

"I believe it's called Spam; I heard one of the erks say 'something posing as meat' –"

"Well don't say any more," interrupted Giles, "it actually tastes quite good."

An hour later, ten Hurricanes from 686 are heading for London as they have so many times in recent weeks; but today is different. Not one, but three other squadrons have joined them by the time they sight three hundred bombers and fighters approaching from the south-east. As usual the core of bombers is surrounded by an outer layer of fighters but these are already being engaged by numerous other British fighters. The four squadrons continue headlong towards the oncoming mass. "Good Lord, look to your left!" exclaims Giles over the R/T. George catches his breath in a mixture of surprise and excitement. Five squadrons of Spitfires and Hurricanes have appeared from the north heading for the German flank. They drive into it at the same moment as George and his companions open fire from the front. Like a bomb-burst in a beehive the bombers scatter in all directions, their formation shattered. As he flashes past, George fires at a Dornier, rakes another and then fires a burst as a 109 crosses in front of him. Curving round he spots another 109, looking to slide in behind him but Judd fires, leaving it to fall away, and then ahead of him are three more Dorniers trying to close together for mutual protection. He fires into the fuselage of the nearest. It immediately drops back from its fellows and bodies begin tumbling out. As George turns away Judd rakes the second, setting it ablaze, before swinging to follow him.

All around are bombers in small groups, jettisoning bombs haphazardly in their quest to escape, and 109s attempting the impossible task of shielding them from the scores of RAF fighters going after them like angry hornets.

George sees a 109 lining up an unsuspecting Hurricane and fires at it. Its canopy flies off and the pilot rolls the aircraft before tumbling out; the white silk of his deploying parachute stark against the blue sky and trails of black smoke from falling aircraft. Another Dornier swims into view. He sets it squarely in his sights and fires. A few rounds tear into an engine and then the clunk of empty breechblocks means that for him, the party is over. "Out of ammo, Yellow Two. See if you can finish it then we're going home." Aware of his vulnerability now, he searches the sky for 109s as Judd sweeps past and in seconds finishes what George had started, before rejoining him on their homeward course.

"Anyone know what happened to Bardsley?" asked Giles.
"A 109 got him, but I saw him take to his brolly." Rodway replied.
"Splendid!" said Giles, "Everyone accounted for."
"It was bloody marvellous. I've never seen so many of our chaps," said George. "More to the point, nor have the Huns," said Giles," it must have been a bit of a shock to say the least. Now you can see why we have only been sending up penny numbers. We've been waiting for a day like this; and I don't think it's over yet." All around him was a hive of activity as ground crews were striving to re-fuel, re-arm and repair minor damage as the squadron remained on immediate readiness. "I must say all this excitement is making me hungry. Are there any more of those Spam sandwiches?"

At 2.45 pm, they are heading for London again and by the time they reach the outskirts they are one of not four, but eight, squadrons heading directly for the mass of bombers and fighters they can now see advancing from the south; more numerous than they had been in the morning but again beset by scores of British fighters, snapping at and harassing the escorting Messerschmitts. For the second time in the day the five squadrons of the Duxford Wing appear again from the north and tear into the German flank. The whole scenario strikes George as a repeat of the morning on a larger scale, but with one difference; the formation of which he is a part is the last to arrive this time and now he is in the vanguard of the charge that irretrievably smashes the German attack. Heinkels and Dorniers scatter in all directions in response to the deluge of fighters, dumping their bomb-loads before turning south, attempting to flee back whence they have come. He has read of when British musketry broke Bonaparte's columns at Waterloo and now he is part of the aerial army smashing another tyrant's forces. He fires at one Heinkel, then another. A third bursts into flames and flips into a spin. Despite his elation he hasn't lost his senses. He spots a 109 trying to bounce him and turns inside its dive. The buffet of an explosion tells him Judd had seen it too. Overhauling two more Heinkels, dense exhaust trails indicating their desperation to escape, he sideslips to the right as their dorsal gunners fire at him, then silences the nearer gunner with a short burst, followed by a longer one into the fuselage. The aircraft drops away. He throttles back allowing Judd to overtake him, "Your turn, Yellow Two," and slides into the wing-man's position; scanning the sky automatically as Judd dispatches the second Heinkel.

All around scores of individual combats play out as fighters challenge fighters whilst others are attacking fleeing bombers. Here, a Spitfire spins down trailing smoke and flame; there a 109 disintegrates and beyond it a Dornier explodes, obviously too slow in shedding its bomb-load. Judd is stalking a lone Heinkel when a 109 slides in behind him. George fires a burst. Pieces fly off the wing and the pilot immediately noses into a dive, aware that to follow him George will have to half-roll into a dive and lose a few vital seconds. "Forget him," said George, "we must be low on ammo so let's use what remains on the bombers." To their right and a little below a lone Spitfire is attacking a vic of three Heinkels, dodging and weaving to avoid return fire and aiming short bursts at them. "Looks like that chap at 3 o'clock could use some assistance,

Tallyho!" With Judd still no. 1 they dive into a beam attack once more. George can see the nearest Heinkel's Perspex nose shattering before it rolls into a downward spiral. "Out of ammo, Yellow Leader."

"Roger, Yellow Two; head for home, I'll be right behind you." Yellow Section's attack has given the Spitfire the chance to concentrate on the Heinkel furthest from them so with a savage exultation. George exhausts his remaining ammunition in a prolonged burst into the vic leader. He leaves it ablaze, a fiery comet plunging earthwards, as he sets off after Judd.

He doesn't relax his vigil on the homeward flight, continuing to look for any hint of marauding 109s, but his battle-fury ebbs away and is replaced by a feeling of optimism he hasn't felt for a while. The Germans have been not just mauled, but routed twice this day; defeated by a greater number of British fighters than he has ever seen in the air together, and yet still less than half of Fighter Command's strength. Under these circumstances the invasion cannot hope to succeed.

As he taxied towards dispersal, he could see two figures dancing around slapping each other on the back like barn-dancers in a cowboy film. They resolved into 'Litmus' and Evans as he drew nearer. Climbing from his Hurricane he found an atmosphere reminiscent of a church fete – smiling faces, laughter, the babble of voices – with groundcrew gathered around their pilots as they recounted the victory they had won, and could not help contrasting in his mind the mood of just one week ago. "Make sure you're there tonight, George," a beaming Giles interrupted his thoughts, "the *Barley Mow* will witness the biggest bash it's ever seen – we're all going to get screechers."

He opened the door of the *Barley Mow* to a wave of exuberance. The place was packed pilots, WAAFs and locals all pressed together in a merry throng. He glanced at the clock behind the bar – ten to nine; later than he intended because he had been with Connie at *The Stag.*

He had gone to tell her of the day's events and ask her along to the *Barley Mow* to join the celebration. 'Thank you, but no. It wouldn't be the same without Max.'

'I'm sorry. It was insensitive of me.'

'No – it wasn't. It was very kind; but it's too soon and there are too many memories.' Before arriving, he had been expecting them to be on their way to the *Barley Mow* within minutes but he realised that he couldn't just leave her. So he had sat for an hour sipping a gin and tonic as they, or mainly she, had talked about Max. Suddenly, as if waking and finding herself somewhere unexpected, she had said to him. 'I shouldn't be keeping you here like this – you should be celebrating with your friends. Please join them while there is still time; and thank you so much for listening to me.'

No sooner had he closed the door than Giles was there with a pint in each hand. "Come on, young George, you've a bit of catching up to do."

"Thanks." He took the beers and downed one in two draughts. "I needed that."

"Problems?"

"Not really. I went to ask Connie to join us but she felt she couldn't face all this so soon after Max."

"Pity – this is Max's party too, and Jerzy and all the others who helped to make it happen." He turned back towards the bar so George followed him, easing his way through the throng. Giles plucked his beer from the bar and turned to George. "Cheers!"

"Cheers! So you think we've done it?"

"Undoubtedly. We'll probably see some more skirmishing but I'm convinced the battle has been won, thank God! Hold on a second, it's nearly nine." He leaned over the bar and signalled to the Landlord. "Quiet everyone," he shouted, "for the nine o'clock news." It was at that point that George realised how far the party had progressed without him. Whilst most immediately went quiet, some of the more inebriated continued talking and laughing causing other inebriates to begin 'shushing' them and being 'shushed' in turn by their more sober fellows. Against this hubbub the wireless was warming up and speech gradually becoming discernible. '… news read by Alvar Liddell. By eight o'clock this evening one hundred and sixty-five German…' The rest was drowned out by a roar of triumph that shook the ancient wooden beams that supported the thatched roof; beams that if able to talk could have recounted news of the victories of Marlborough, Rodney, Nelson, Wellington – and the end of the over-optimistically named 'war to end all wars'.

"Hell fire," said George amid backslaps from colleagues and handshakes from civilians, "a hundred and sixty-five! That definitely warrants more beer."

"By 'eck, tha looks rough." Despite his pounding head, George recognised he had heard that line before. "So tha'll be glad t'ear't squadron's released. Looks like 'Uns 'ave 'ad their fill – for a while at any rate. Just as well from't state o'thee." George winced as the mug of tea crashed down beside him before Blakely's face broke into the first smile he had ever seen from him. "Well done lad, you an' t'others – tha's bloodied 'itler's nose good an' proper."

"I c-could get used to this," offered 'Litmus', "two scrambles in f-five days is a lot b-better than five in two."

"Not only that," added George, "but Peter Templeton told me today that he's sure there's been a small reduction in the number of barges. It looks like the invasion threat is receding."

"And still only the 20th of September," said Giles, "never have I been happier to be proved wrong. The hiding we gave them last Sunday must have made up their minds."

"Well, they haven't been back since in anything like the numbers…" George broke off as two Spitfires, one with the long snout of a Hispano cannon extending proudly from each wing, swooped overhead and banked into a curved landing approach. "What's their game – no squadron letters?"

"That's because we will be painting them on," said Giles. "Group has decided our faithful old Hurris are becoming *passe* so they're giving us some Spits to play with instead. There will be more arriving over the next few days; Mark 2a, Merlin XII engines with 110 extra horsepower. Faster rate of climb and higher ceiling."

"You sound like a salesman," quipped George.

Giles smiled. "I don't think I'd have any trouble selling these. The cannon job is a Mark 2b for us to try out. I know you're on a 24 tomorrow but can I ask you to delay until noon so you can give it a flip before you buzz off. That way you'll get a lie-in on Sunday and with a bit of luck, you might run into a Hun to test the cannon on; the technical bods have been making some improvements."

"Wizard!" he said, outwardly enthusiastic, although inwardly with mixed feelings. He was happy to fly a Spitfire but he knew that attempts to fit cannon to Hurricanes and Spitfires had so far met with limited success. "I wasn't going anywhere before noon anyway."

"Splendid. 'Einstein' has some Pilot's Notes waiting for you to give the once-over. Try not to dent her and let me know what you think."

"Morning Flight. Everything tickity-boo?"

"Yes sir, everything's spot on. She's a real beauty, and no mistake!"

He had spent the previous evening boning up. The extra power of the Merlin XII and lower all-up-weight compared to the Hurricane pointed to the improved performance heralded by Giles, although he was disappointed to see that his favourite flick roll was not permitted; the filly was perhaps not as robust as the destrier he had been used to. Also, he was amused to read, spinning could only be carried out with the C/O's written permission, which might make things difficult in the middle of a dog-fight. As the fitter adjusted his straps he scanned the cockpit; smaller than the Hurri's but sufficient to accommodate him. Barring a few extra knobs and taps it was pretty much what he was used to. The icing on the cake was the bubble canopy – no framework to obstruct his view – and, on top of the windscreen, a rear-view mirror. How he could have used that in recent weeks!

Start-up and taxiing were much the same as the Hurricane; the nose was a little higher so the same weaving technique applied. It was when he opened the throttle that the differences became apparent. The Spitfire raced across the grass and would have been airborne sooner had he allowed it. When he did, after raising the undercarriage with the same hand-switching ritual he had used in Hurricanes, it soared into the fastest climb he had yet known, carrying him swiftly to fifteen thousand feet where he proceeded to explore its aerobatic capabilities. His exhilaration had shown no sign of abating after ten minutes when the R/T came to life. "Shuttlecock aircraft, Bluejay Control, we have trade for you. Vector two-three-zero and make angels two-fiver."

The sight of a condensation trail ahead prompts the thought that the bandit is perhaps a bit higher than angels twenty-five. George swings a little southwards with a view to climbing to thirty thousand feet so he can attack with the sun at his back.

The Spitfire has made light work of the extra altitude when he banks westwards and there below him is a Dornier, on a northerly heading, seemingly oblivious to his presence; despite the reduction in daytime bomber activity the Germans are still undertaking reconnaissance on a regular basis. Checking temperatures, pressures and the sky is second nature to him but today he has the additional task of operating a valve to cock the cannon. The Spitfire leaps forward as he lowers its nose. The gap between them closes rapidly and he is still unseen when he gets within firing range.

There is an extra firing button on the joystick. Instead of the familiar staccato rattle of eight Brownings, pressing it produces the steady thump of cannon-fire. He is unprepared for the result of a one and one-half second burst. The starboard engine explodes and half the wing falls off, toppling the Dornier. After a quick check he follows its descent through ten thousand feet in which time two crewmen manage to take to their parachutes. Satisfied it is accelerating to its doom and he has no need to follow it further, he pulls into a loop and a victory roll before heading for home.

"Can I keep it?"

"I don't see why not. I gather it met with your approval," said Giles.

"If we'd had a few hundred more of them I don't think it would have taken until mid-September to see the Huns off. The cannons are absolutely wizard. I feel disloyal to the dear old Hurri saying it but this Spit is the bee's knees."

"The Hurricane has served us well but every dog has its day. Anyway, things are quiet so I suggest you buzz off on your 24. We'll look after the Spit while you're gone."

As he pulled up outside *The Stag,* she came out to join him, radiant in her summer frock. "I'm so glad you could make it!"

"My pleasure. What do you fancy doing?"

"It's a lovely day, let's have a stroll for a change."

They had been walking for nearly an hour when George noticed the change in the sky. "Uh oh! – looks like rain on the way. I think we should head back."

They were little more than halfway when the black clouds he had seen caught up with them and the heavens opened, subjecting them to a deluge. In no time they were soaked to the skin; Connie's frock became almost translucent and George's uniform a few shades darker. They had run all the way back to *The Stag* and now they stood outside, drenched but laughing.

"You'd better come in and get dry," she suggested," I've a fire in my room. She saw George's surprise. "It faces north; it never really gets the sun so there's always a fire." There was no sign of life as he followed her in, up the stairs and along to the door at the far end of the corridor. When they entered, the fire had burnt down and there was already more than a hint of chill. She walked over to it and with practised ease swirled the embers with a poker and added some more coal. Within a few minutes, flames were dancing up the chimney and warmth was returning. She threw him a large towel.

"Here," she said, "get out of your wet clothes – I'll change in the bathroom."

She returned a few minutes later, clad in a large dressing gown; a towel turban-like around her head. He couldn't help noticing that barefoot, her gait was catlike; smooth and seductive. His uniform was already beginning to steam as he arranged her clothes next to it on the fireguard. "Shouldn't take too long," he indicated.

"Don't be in too much of a hurry to rush off – I've got crumpets."

"Hot buttered crumpets! I haven't had any for ages. It's really quite cosy here."

"Today, with the two of us, perhaps, but actually it's been quite bloody. I sat here on my own for weeks, waiting for Max to return each day, not knowing if he was alive until I heard the car pull up outside. And since the news came that he was dead there's been nothing left here but memories and might-have-beens."

"I'm sorry."

"Of all people you've least cause to apologise. Since he died you've been wonderful. I don't know what I would have done without you. I owe you a great deal."

He looked into the fire, lost for words. There was a faint rustle. "George." Her voice had become husky.

He knew what to expect before he looked. The towel and dressing gown were lying on the floor and she was standing with her arms outstretched towards him. He rose, divesting himself of his towel, and moved to her. They clasped each other fiercely and fell onto the bed. Their lovemaking was frantic, almost frenzied; each searching desperately for the thing that, deep down, they knew the other could not provide. Eventually they fell asleep, spent but unfulfilled.

When he awoke, he felt a massive guilt; Justine was dead but every fibre of his being told him he had betrayed her. Connie was sitting on the edge of the bed, staring out of the window. She turned to look at him and his face confirmed what she already knew. "There won't be anyone else for either of us, will there?" she said.

"I don't think so." She resumed looking out of the window as he dressed.

When he was ready to go, he took her hand in both of his, holding it tenderly. She turned to face him one last time, her eyes brimming. He squeezed her hand. "I'm sorry." He paused at the door, wanting to say something to ease her pain, but knew it was beyond him. As the door closed, she put her face in a pillow and began to sob.

"Cheers all!" said Giles, raising his glass and then drinking deeply from it. "Here we are at the end of September, as near as dammit, and it's quite obvious that the Hun has had to abandon his evil design…"

George nodded inwardly as he drank. Another chat with Peter Templeton had told him that more and more invasion barges were disappearing from the channel ports, and on the two occasions in the last week when the bombers came in any number it was in tens rather than the hundreds of earlier times. Yesterday the Master Race had shown itself fallible when fifty or sixty Ju88s and a similar number of Me110s had arrived ahead of the 109s that were supposed to be guarding them. By the time their escort caught up eight squadrons of Hurricanes and Spitfires had downed twenty per cent of their numbers. He had been delighted to see a Ju88 explode as a result of several seconds of cannon fire and then used the rest of his ammunition to leave a 109 to limp back to France with no certainty of getting there.

Giles brought him back to the present,"… but that's not why I asked the three of you here tonight. Group have decided that they want me to use whatever talents they think I have with them for the next few months; so I'll be leaving in a couple of days. If I'm honest I can't say I'm sorry to be getting a breather," he looked around 'Litmus', Evans and George, "we've been on the go pretty solidly since May. As a result Group have told me that any reasonable transfer request you chaps come up with – training sprogs, fighter control etc. won't be refused, because you've all jolly well earned it. Just think about it and let me know before I leave."

"Provided a good sort replaces you I would prefer to stick around," said George.

A brief flicker of disappointment showed on Giles' face; he, and the other two, knew it was no use trying to argue the point. "I think you'll approve – his name is S/Ldr Underhill."

"You mean…?"

"The very same!"

"Then let's drink to that."

14: October, 1940

George was feeling browned off – in fact somewhat beyond that. The lift to his spirits provided by the events of September had been eroded by a combination of things.

He was angry with himself for his betrayal of Justine and for the hurt he had left Connie with; not to mention the effective end of their friendship. His best and closest comrades were gone, or about to; Giles to Group, Evans to Sector Control and 'Litmus' about to leave for a spell instructing. They had fought together through the madness of France and the onslaught of August and September to their eventual triumph; and now the others were going for a well-earned rest. But he couldn't allow himself to rest – he still had his mission to avenge Justine; and even this troubled him. A part of him was awakening to the truth that others had warned him of; he had killed a score or more of Germans since June but it hadn't brought her back. But another part impelled him to carry on; because to admit that truth would be to recognise that she was gone forever. And suddenly killing Germans had become more problematic. Since the hidings meted out to them in September, they had stopped sending large numbers of bombers. For the most part it was now 109s carrying small bomb loads at heights above twenty-five thousand feet covered by masses of unencumbered 109s still higher and in a position to bounce RAF fighters climbing to intercept the bomb carriers. Three times in the first half of October, 686 had been bounced on the climb, losing yet another sprog, and George had brought his Spitfire back each time with fresh holes in it and nothing to show in the way of kills. Strategically, these nuisance raids would never achieve anything but tactically they were frustrating, particularly to George. Added to this, bombers were still roaming freely at night and little was being achieved in the way of interceptions.

"Telephone call for you, sir." 686 were back at their home airfield, which had been restored sufficiently to enable their return. He acknowledged the Mess Steward and made his way to the phone. When he picked up the receiver, the voice at the other end was quiet, hesitant.

"This is Veronica, Connie's sister; she told me how to get in touch with you…I'm afraid she's dead." His stomach lurched. There was a moment's silence. He could sense her fighting to maintain her composure. "She left a letter for you but I wasn't sure where you are."

He felt a need to get away from the Station, to be out in the open for a while. "I'm off duty tomorrow, I could come and collect it. What's your address?"

He found the house without much difficulty – a semi among many. He walked through the gate. What had once doubtless been a neat little suburban garden had been given over to 'Dig for Victory'. He could see several rows of what he took to be winter vegetables poking through the soil in search of a reluctant sun. The front door opened before he had the chance to knock. In terms of appearance, Connie's sister had little in common with her; pale, tall and slender, almost painfully thin, her dark hair hung lankly. She looked tired. 'Not surprising,' he thought to himself. Not many bombs had been dropped this far out but no doubt the nightly alerts were taking their toll – trying to sleep in an Anderson Shelter was by no means easy – she was probably missing her children too, evacuated but still cause for concern; and now this.

She gave him a limp handshake. "I'm Veronica, you're obviously George. Come in please." He followed her into a small parlour; neat, unostentatious. "Please sit down – would you like a cup of tea?"

"I won't, if you don't mind, but thank you." There was an awkward silence. She seemed to be struggling to find where to begin. "What happened?"

She gathered herself. "When, is easier – a week ago. We'd reported her missing but it was two days before they informed us. All they found was her handbag with her ration card, near Rotherhithe, after a big raid."

"Could her handbag have been stolen and discarded there?"

"I don't think so. Apparently she walked the streets there every night until dawn. The ARP wardens thought she was a prostitute to begin with and ordered her into the shelters but at the first opportunity she would give them the slip." She took a deep breath. "I think, quite simply, she was trying to get herself killed."

"Did she say anything?"

"With the benefit of hindsight, yes. She said how kind you had been to her and how she thought it was a new beginning, but then something had made her realise that she could never replace Max." She stopped for a moment, composing her thoughts before continuing. "We had seen very little of each other in the last few years – a silly quarrel – I didn't even know she was married until she contacted me after Max had been killed; but when she came to us three weeks ago, she wasn't Connie. She was withdrawn, almost in another world. She spent her days in her room and then as soon as evening came, she went out and didn't come home until the following morning; but she wouldn't talk about it. I know why now..." She tailed off into silence.

"You mentioned a letter."

"I began sorting her room yesterday and found this." She crossed to the mantelpiece, extracted a white envelope from under the Bakelite radio set and handed it to him. He glanced at the legend. *'To George Knight, in the event of my death.'* He wanted to rip it open and read the contents there and then but he suppressed the urge. She had begun talking again, this time only partly to him. "... just a silly quarrel... if only we had made up sooner... there is never as much time as you think..." she had her head in her hands and he could see tears running through her fingers.

He crossed the room and put his hand on her shoulder. "I'm sorry."

She looked up and attempted a smile. "Don't be – it's not your fault – and thank you for coming."

"No trouble at all. Thank you too – for this." He indicated the letter. "Don't get up- I'll see myself out…"

He drove to the end of the road, turned the corner and parked. With unsteady hands he opened the envelope and began to read:

'Dearest George, if you are reading this, I am re-united with Max, so don't grieve for me. Don't blame yourself either. Our time together showed me, just as it did you regarding Justine, that Max is irreplaceable. Without him, I don't want to go on with this life and that is why I have done what I have done. Also, don't reproach yourself about what happened between us. You were still of this world and Justine was not. I don't think she will blame you for trying to find love again any more than I think Max will blame me. I would like you to know that your kindness and your company brought me as near to happiness again as was possible. For that my everlasting thanks.
Until we meet again, Connie.
PS – When we do, let's make-up a foursome!

He struggled to read the last few lines through misty eyes then re-folded the letter into its envelope and placed it in his pocket. He sat in thought for a few minutes before starting the car. As he set off for the airfield, he knew that he had yet another reason to kill Germans; and he knew now how he was going to go about it.

Underhill was signing bumph as George entered his office. He glanced up briefly, "Morning George!" he offered before continuing.

George came to attention and saluted, "Morning sir, I'd like to request a transfer to a night-fighter squadron."

Underhill's attention was with George now. "Why?"

"Things have gone pretty quiet by day. Just the odd skirmish with 109s and that's it."

"After the five months you've had, you need a rest. The word is that in January we'll start offensive sweeps – taking the war to them."

"By night they are pounding our cities to rubble, killing women and children – I want to get after them now."

"You're a first-rate Flight Commander, George. Two or three months more and you'll be ready to lead a squadron; but not if you kill yourself first. I know what's eating you. Ever since you lost Justine, you've been on your mission to kill as many Germans as possible – and no thought other than to carry on until one day your luck runs out."

"And when it does, I'll get that rest. Until then I carry on; I've really nothing else. Can I have the transfer, sir?"

Underhill looked at him with a wistful expression. "There's nothing I can say to make you change your mind?"

"Sorry, sir, but no."

"OK, I'll speak to Wing."

"Thank you, sir."

After George had left, Underhill continued to sit at his desk, the paperwork forgotten. Eventually he rose to step outside. Spying the waste-paper bin he gave it a vicious kick. "Damn this lousy bloody war!"

Peter Templeton watches the Blenheim plough into a French field with mixed emotions; glad he had got out but sad to see the old girl go like this. He and *P-Popsie* have somewhat miraculously survived nearly three months together, bombing invasion barges in the fraught days of August and September and then, when the dissolving barge concentrations had signalled that an invasion would not be a possibility for the next six months at least, the emphasis had changed to 'hitting back'. Raids had begun on installations in occupied France; along the coast initially, then gradually further inland. Hanging from his parachute he relives *Popsie's* last mission; to attack an aero-engine factory near Le Mans. Despite easterly winds, there was cloud cover across northern France and the formation of six Blenheims reached their target unobserved. Their sudden emergence from the clouds meant there was no time to scramble fighters but the ubiquitous flak-guns took their toll. Climbing away from the target, *Popsie* took a shell burst in her port wing and engine. Fire had broken out immediately prompting Templeton to order his navigator and gunner to bale out while he held the aircraft level – the proximity of the escape hatch to the starboard propeller made baling out of a diving Blenheim tantamount to suicide. He was considering his own chances of escape when he realised that the fire had burnt out, leaving the engine running on reduced revs. Regretting his prompt dismissal of the crew, he decided to stay and nurse *Popsie* homewards. Fifteen minutes later, he knew the end was near. The gauges showed nearly empty – obviously *Popsie* was losing fuel. Leaving her trimmed for level flight he tumbled from the hatch. As he did so, he heard the first splutterings of fuel-starved engines. Perversely, the damaged engine kept running the longer and the aircraft swung away from him as he drifted on the wind. Perhaps it had been *Popsie's* last brave gesture – unless his descent was spotted the Germans would go to the crash site and begin their search for survivors from there – she had given him a few miles headstart.

His mind returns to the present. He is approaching the ground quickly now – farming country by the look of it – rolling fields punctuated by hedges and trees. As he lands, he allows his legs to give way and he rolls to absorb the impact; the hour he spent chatting in a railway waiting room with a member of the newly-formed Parachute Regiment has paid dividends. Scrambling to his feet, he begins gathering his parachute, wishing he had paid more attention to the lecture on what to do if shot down. He is wondering how best to dispose of it when he hears a voice. He freezes, then realises it is calling to him in a mixture of French and English. *"M'sieu,* over 'ere!" He looks round and sees a figure beckoning to him from among some trees. He hesitates briefly then starts running, trying not to fall over the bundle of silk spilling from his arms. *"Bonjour, m'sieu,* welcome to France. I am Victor."

"Bonjour, Victor. Peter Templeton, I must say its jolly lucky…"

Victor holds up a hand. "Later, *m'sieu*. I 'ave seen your descent so others, including the Germans, may have done so too. Therefore we should leave this place at once. Follow me, please!"

Peter holds the parachute out. "What about this?"

"Bring it with you. I know some ladies who can put the silk to good use." Beyond the trees is an old lorry. The parachute is quickly stuffed into a large chest on the back, half-filled with wood, next to a strange, stove-like, contraption. From under the passenger seat Victor extracts a roll neck sweater and a moth-eaten beret. "Put these on, they will withstand a casual glance. It is necessary to get you to a safe place to wait while we arrange for your return to England."

"I was going to say that it was jolly lucky finding someone who speaks English, but I have a feeling its better than that."

"*Oui*. I am one of the few people in Normandy 'oo can get you 'ome again."

He wrinkled his nose," I think something's burning."

"It is the device which converts wood into fuel to drive the lorry. We 'ave 'ad no petrol since the *Boche* took over. But pay attention, please! In a few minutes we will come to a village. Appear bored and don't look directly at anyone, especially if there 'appen to be any Germans about. As we pass the fourth 'ouse on the right, regard the windows and tell me what you see."

The immediate appearance of Victor had occupied him until now but suddenly it comes home to Peter that he is in enemy occupied France and one false move can bring disaster; on him and the man trying to help him. He takes several deep breaths, trying to still the nerves which have erupted within him then slouches in his seat and leans his head against the window, gazing sightlessly into space. The entire length of the main street is empty as they enter the village. Without moving his head, Peter focuses on the fourth house as instructed then returns to his apparent trance. Ahead, two German soldiers wheeling bicycles, rifles slung across their backs, emerge from a turning. They look at the approaching lorry. "Don't move a muscle, stay exactly as you are!" hisses Victor, staring straight ahead. Heart in mouth, Peter remains motionless, fighting the urge to look at them. Two out of focus shapes draw level; then they are past. Transferring his gaze to the wing mirror he watches their receding backs. Victor exhales loudly. "They 'aven't 'eard about you yet, or they'd 'ave stopped us."

"What would you have done if they had?"

"With you without papers?" He dips his hand into his coat pocket and briefly slides a pistol into view. "Only one thing. What did you see at the 'ouse?"

"A curtain half-drawn in an upstairs window, otherwise nothing."

"*Zut!* We cannot go there today."

"I assume that's a problem?"

"*Oui*. It will be dark before we can get to another safehouse. We cannot risk being out after curfew." Deep in thought he drives out of the village. "There is one 'ope! It means asking another favour of a lady."

After driving up a bumpy track in the gathering dusk, the lorry draws to a halt outside a farmhouse. "Wait 'ere." Victor strides to the door and knocks loudly. It opens but despite the light from within the occupant is hidden from Peter's view by Victor. He hears a woman's voice. The tone of the conversation grows more

271

urgent, Victor is gesticulating extravagantly; it is obvious things are not going well. He hears a second woman. Feeling there is nothing to lose Peter slides quietly from the cab and goes to join Victor. For the first time he can see past him.

"Good Lord! Justine Knight!"

Surprised, she peers into the gloom. "Peter-Peter Templeton!"

"What are you doing here? George thinks you're dead!"

She stands rooted to the spot as his words sink in. Her face turns ashen and she hesitates in her response, fearful he will not give the answer she so desperately wants to hear. "George is… alive?"

"Well, he was when I spoke to him two days ago!"

She looks ready to faint; he pushes past Victor and supports her. "Please, come in!" Lys takes her other arm and they help her to a chair. Victor closes the door behind them.

Tears are running down her cheeks and she is shaking. "I thought he was killed in the hospital in Rethel. It was bombed. When I got there it was just rubble."

"I know – I was there with George, 'Litmus' and another chap. My Flight Sergeant came and took us away in the nick of time."

Suddenly it all made sense – the capering lunatic – *'les bleus sont partis'* – 'the blues have gone'. If only she had understood before. "How is he?"

"He'll be a lot better for knowing you're alive," he glances shyly at her swollen belly, "and your baby. Richard found your lucky bullet in the ruins of your house and reached the obvious conclusion. He rescued a little dog while he was there and took it back to England with him. Caspar I think it's called." Tears well in Justine's eyes at memories of Gaspard and Pascal as Peter continues. "To tell the truth, I think part of George died when he heard Richard's news. He lives now only for revenge – to kill Germans; and that's not a healthy thing."

She clasps his hand in hers, looking at him earnestly. "You must let him know."

"I will, as soon as I get back, whenever that is." He turns to look questioningly at Victor, who in turn addresses her, with a hint of exasperation.

"May I take it now that he can stay with you?"

She looks at Lys, who nods imperceptibly. *"Of course. And you must stay tonight also. How long will it be…?"*

"A week at least – arrangements have to be made and the tides won't be right before then. Can you keep him that long? It could be dangerous if the Germans come."

"We'll manage." She makes to rise. *"We must…"* The cry comes from deep within her and she slumps back into the chair.

Lys is at her side in an instant. *"My dear, what is it?"*

Her teeth are clenched against the contraction *"The baby, it's starting!"*

"Mon dieu! It must have been the shock." She turns to the two men. "Help her to her room and then," pointing to the kitchen, "start boiling water – lots of it! I'm going to fetch Mme Lafarge; I'll be back within the half-hour. And stay out of sight when I bring her back."

"What if it comes before then?"

"Just pray it doesn't!"

The doctor had attended early the following morning. *"A little premature but with his mother's nurture he will grow up strong and healthy,"* his face clouded a little, *"like his father was, perhaps?"* She nodded, trying to match his gravity and resisting the temptation to correct his use of the past tense. The fewer who knew her news, and how it had come to her, the better.

After he had gone, as she watched her son sleeping, the hopelessness of it all came upon her; France lay prostrate under the jackboot and her husband, his father, was separated from them by more than just the width of the channel. It might be years before they were together again. She had lain for a few minutes, sobbing quietly, when a gap in the clouds allowed a shaft of sunlight to fall through the window onto her, somehow creating certainties that had seemed a nonsense only minutes before; France would be free and proud again; and she and George would be reunited – but before either of those things would occur, and despite earlier rebuttals of the idea, she knew now that she would take her place in the struggle.

There was a knock and Peter and Victor, accompanied by Lys, entered the room. Joy and pride were obvious as Justine spoke first to Peter, "Now you can also tell George he has a son."

"What are you naming him?"

"George Alain Richard," she smiled, "I think his father will approve."

She addressed Victor, a serious look on her face. "It was wrong of me to try to turn you away yesterday and also to refuse when you asked me to join you," she indicated baby George, sleeping beside her. "I know that now."

"I would have thought all the more reason to keep out of the fight," Victor replied.

"On the contrary; I want him to grow up in a France free from fear and oppression. That hope will not be realised by wishful thinking. Across the channel the British, his father among them, are continuing the fight and we in France must do whatever we can to help; such as returning Peter and men like him; and hindering the Germans at every opportunity. I must first attend to my son for a few weeks, but when he is strong I will join you."

"Bravo, madame," said Victor quietly, clearly moved.

"Amen to that!" added Peter.

"And now *m'sieu*," Lys took Peter by the arm, "there are things we have to do."

Two days later, a lorry is seen entering the farm track – German soldiers. By the time it reaches the farmhouse, Lys and Justine are at the front door. Lys' throat is dry but she manages to sound authoritative. *"Yes, what is it?"*

The Iron Cross at the throat of the officer in charge testifies to his courage but his resolution is tested before her imperious gaze. *"Good morning, madame! Leutnant Priller. A British flyer parachuted near here a few days ago. Have you seen him?"*

"No."

"It is necessary my men conduct a thorough search. If you will permit me..."

"I doubt it would make the slightest difference if I refused, so just get on with it." Beneath her *hauteur* icy fingers clutch at her vitals. *"One thing, Lieutenant – there is a new-born baby asleep upstairs so I would ask you to avoid his room."*

The *Leutnant* is stiffly courteous. *"I am sorry, madame, but all rooms must be searched."*

The search is carried out thoroughly but correctly. Attention is given to every cupboard, hatch and trapdoor in every room in the house; floorboards are tested. Especial, but careful, attention is given to the room where the baby lies asleep.

Similar attention is given to the barns and outbuildings; the hay is pitch forked and all chums and large containers are investigated. In the midst of the search, a man emerges from the pigsty, slightly stooped, dressed in a grubby shirt and stained corduroy trousers, a battered beret partially covering his salt-and-pepper, almost white, close-cropped hair. He is pushing a barrow load of pig manure, destined for the slurry tank.

Suddenly, the wheel hits a rut and his malodorous cargo slops onto his boots and trousers. Without removing the unlit remnant of a *Gitane* from the corner of his mouth, he explodes into a string of Gallic oaths, evoking laughter from the searching troops. Drawn by the noise, Leutnant Priller dashes from the house. He doesn't consider searching farms to be suitable employment for heroes of the Reich and his reception has done nothing to improve his mood. His subordinates feel his wrath. *"What do you think you are doing standing about? Get on with the search or I'll have you all on a charge."* The soldiers disperse to continue the search. He switches to French. *"As for you. old man,"* he is advancing on the barrow when the full stench of the ordure soaking the man's trousers hits him; he feels suddenly queasy, *"Get on with your work and stop distracting my men, or you'll have cause to regret it!"* Muttering truculently under his breath, the man wheels his barrow away. Hand-in-hand for mutual support, Lys and Justine watch the progress of the search from the farmhouse.

Eventually the troops return to their lorry. The Leutnant is politely correct once more as he addresses Lys. He feels her disdain and is keen to be away from it. *"Thank you madame, all is in order."*

Her response is terse, *"Never doubted it, Lieutenant. Good day."*

The lorry bumps away down the farm track watched by Lys and Justine. As it reaches the far end, the man from the pigsty shuffles up to join them. He watches the lorry turn onto the road before he speaks. "Can I stand up straight now?"

"You must maintain your disguise until you leave." She breaks into a smile despite the smell that accompanies him. "I will find you some more trousers though – and bravo *m'sieu!*"

The moon is completely obscured by cloud. There is no other light. Peter is walking gingerly down the cliff path, his boots wrapped in rags to muffle sound, holding on to a piece of string tied to the battle-dress of the man in front. Peter is tense, not to say scared. Although he is a pilot, he has a fear of heights, or more accurately, a fear of falling off something high. Stumbling down a cliff path in the pitch dark is not his idea of fun. Behind him another man holds the string tied to

Peter. There are five of them altogether; two more RAF men, to Peter's regret not his crew, and a couple of soldiers who have been on the run since Dunkirk. Victor leads the column. He knows the path well and can negotiate it safely in the dark. Even so, he periodically stops; to check his whereabouts, with the pencil thin beam from a small torch; to listen for any potential threat; and to allow his charges a rest. Some have been in hiding for weeks, cooped up in small rooms and cupboards, and are not as fit as they should be.

As he relaxes his aching legs, Peter's mind goes back over the last few hours. It was an hour after dusk when his guide had appeared at the farmhouse, as if from nowhere, ending his week-long wait. He had been told to expect it and had managed to soak away the smells of the pigsty in a hot bath, although it would be a while before his hair was back to its usual colour. Justine had tucked the expected envelope inside his coat. "For George." He had tested it briefly with his fingers; it felt well filled. She had read his thoughts. "I had plenty to say." He knew she had typed it out over the previous week; Victor had anticipated a letter and insisted, lest it fell into the wrong hands, it should neither be handwritten, signed, nor identify the farm or anyone involved. Amusement had flickered briefly on her face, "I would kiss you for George but I doubt you would pass it on." Then she had looked serious again and squeezed his hand meaningfully, *"Au revoir,* Peter. Until we meet again."

"Au revoir, Justine. And au revoir Madam Lys. You have added a new dimension to the French language for me, though I doubt the *Cure* would approve."

Lys laughed as he hugged her. "I think even he would forgive me on this occasion." The guide was showing signs of impatience so without further ado they had set off across the fields. Despite short rests, the pace had been ferocious and three hours later, when they finally halted, Peter was exhausted. The moon had broken through the clouds to reveal what looked like a small cottage, the rendezvous. After a few minutes' vigil the guide cupped his hands and made two hooting sounds. Seconds later he received a response. Cautiously they had approached the cottage…

A hissed command brings him back to the present. They start downwards again. There is a stumble further along the line, a muffled curse and the sound of stones clattering down the cliff-face, seemingly magnified a hundred times. They freeze, hearts thudding in their chest, and wait; fearing a guttural challenge, the flash of torches and perhaps shots. But there is no response, no patrol. Admonished to 'be careful' they set off again. After ten minutes, to Peter's intense relief, they are walking over shingle and then the going becomes soft. "Take off your bindings!" As Peter stoops, he can feel sand and the sound of gentle surf is close now. A brief thinning in the cloud cover is sufficient to show that they are in a small bay, thirty yards from the sea. "Keep it quiet!" After stuffing their rags into a sack, Peter and the others are dispersed amongst some large rocks. From his hiding place, Peter can see Victor repeatedly checking his watch. At last, he walks to the water's edge and flashes his torch out to sea. There is no response. He waits a full minute before going back among the rocks. Fifteen minutes later, he tries again –

no answer. Tension mounts among the waiting group. Before setting off, they had been briefed that they would only stay on the beach for half an hour. Peter knows that if there is no response this last time they will have to repeat the nightmare of the cliff path back to the cottage, hoping to remain undiscovered for another twenty-four hours. With bated breath, he watches Victor once more emerge from cover and make his signal. Seconds pass. Victor is about to turn away when the answering flash finally comes. A wave of relief passes through them all. Minutes later, a dinghy pulls through the surf and grounds on the beach. A figure in a reefer jacket and wellingtons jumps out, approaching Victor with outstretched hand.

"Sub/Lt Doyle RN. Sorry we're late – spot of bother on the way."

"I am Victor. As arranged, there are five packages." He beckons to his charges.

"Let's get them aboard then. I'm sure you don't want to hang about here any more than we do!"

Seated in the dinghy, Peter finds an oar thrust into his hands. "Ever rowed, chum?"

"Only on holiday."

The voice behind him brightens. "Better than nothing, chum. Just follow my calls."

"Ship oars!" The dinghy bumps alongside the waiting MTB. In a flash strong arms are helping the occupants up. "All aboard the skylark! Trips round the bay – one and a tanner!" Moonlight re-appears briefly. Peter can see bullet holes and splintering in the wooden deck; a dark stain off to one side.

Doyle sees him studying the damage. "As I said, a spot of bother. Shouldn't have happened – we were promised cloud cover. You should see the other chap, though! Can any of you handle m/gs?"

One of the RAF men speaks. "We're both air-gunners, sir!"

"Grand!" he indicates a machine gun mounted on each of the two torpedo tubes, "Choose your weapons!" He turns to Peter and the soldiers. We have wounded; I'm afraid there's only room below for two of you."

Peter still prefers to avoid confined spaces. "I'll be happy to remain on top, if that's the correct phrase."

"I'd suggest the after-deck; you won't be in the way there."

The dinghy is aboard and secured. The boat vibrates as its two engines come to life and it starts turning, almost in its own length. Peter makes his way aft, passing the bridge. The moon disappears behind cloud again, but not before he sees dents in the armour-plated side. Suddenly, the throttles are opened wide. The stern dips as the twin screws bite into the water and the boat surges forward. Caught off balance, he totters sternwards. He grabs on to a dark object and wedges himself between it and its neighbour. Secure now, he sits back to enjoy the ride. Even without the moon, the phosphorescence of the wake leaves a white trail – seemingly stretching all the way back to Normandy. Lulled by the steady pulse of the engines he succumbs to sleep.

The deceleration of the boat awakes him as it slows before entering a blacked out harbour. Cold and stiff, he eases himself painfully from his resting place. He recognises Doyle by the dim light from the chart lamp on the bridge. "Where are we?"

"Weymouth. You've slept all the way across; I take it you felt secure between the depth charges!"

The MTB had been secured alongside a jetty. At the top of the ladder, an army officer was waiting for the evaders. "Welcome back to England, and congratulations to each of you on a damn fine show! I'm Captain Fuller. You're to come with me now to a hotel where a hot bath and crisp clean linen await. In the morning, I shall begin hearing from each of you in turn your experiences and any information you may have. After that a leave pass and rail warrant are yours. In the meantime, you will remain incommunicado."

15: November, 1940

Alphabetical order meant that it was late in the evening before Peter was released. The first thing he did was to head for the nearest telephone.

"George, is that you?" He listened to the reply. "I've just got back from there – and have I got some news for you..."

Underhill's words had been brisk but not unkindly meant. "HQ have asked us to put up a patrol. As you're determined to go to night-fighters you might as well be the man to do it. It's a chance to gain some experience if nothing else. Good hunting!"

George was donning his flying gear when the Mess Corporal's head appeared round the door. "Telephone call for you, sir."

He picked up the receiver wondering who it might be. "Peter, you old dog! I was told you'd been shot down over France!"

The moon has disappeared behind a bank of cloud to the south so the only illumination is the soft glow of his blind-flying panel. It is his first night flight in over a year and his first in wartime. The steady, uninterrupted drone of the Merlin is comforting. His mind is buzzing as he prowls across the night sky in search of the elusive enemy. The exhilaration generated by Peter Templeton's call hasn't even begun to evaporate. In a matter of minutes, his life has changed completely; or at least his perspective of it. Justine alive! And he has a son! And with their resurrection, he can feel a new life within himself. His joy is tempered by the knowledge that they are in enemy territory and for the foreseeable future he has no chance of being with them.

He will have to shoot down a lot more Germans before that dream becomes reality, so has anything really changed? Yes, it has. Revenge will no longer be his *raison d'etre*. Instead of an empty victory the end of the road, however far off it may be, will bring fulfilment. The fighting will go on for a long time yet and he will be in the thick of it but he has two aims; to overcome and to survive – and by God he will!

"Foxglove One, Moonbeam Control, I have some trade for you," The controller's voice drags him from his reverie, "vector one-six-fiver and make Angels fifteen, Buster. He's six miles ahead of you."

"Wilco, Moonbeam Control." The Spitfire leaps forward as he applies boost and rolls onto the required heading.

Several minutes have passed. "Foxglove One, bandit is half-a-mile ahead of you and below – you should be able to see him."

George peers through the windscreen. His vision ahead and below is largely ruined by the glow from the exhausts. He tries turning to one side and then the other but he can see nothing. "Negative, Moonbeam Control."

"You're just about on top of him now; you must be able to see him!" The Controller is almost beseeching him; interceptions are all too rare.

"I can't see a damn thing. Hold on, I'm going to try something." George throttles back and lowers the nose. He drops a thousand feet.

"Foxglove One, he's gained on you. He's half-a-mile ahead."

"Roger, Moonbeam Control. Let me know when I've caught up again." He moves the throttle to boost once more and begins searching the sky above him. Despite the cloud to the south and west, to the southeast, it is still clear and stars are visible. George begins to feel cautiously optimistic.

"Foxglove One, you're gaining rapidly."

"Roger, Moonbeam Control." He eases the throttle back and redoubles his search. He is looking for one thing; a patch of sky without stars.

"Foxglove One, you're almost underneath him."

His eyes are beginning to water with the strain. The stars are starting to disappear… but only in one area. He looks away then looks back. The blank area is still there, keeping pace with him. He's found it! "Moonbeam Control, bandit in sight!" He opens the throttle slightly. With bated breath, he edges closer. The black patch begins to assume features. An occasional sparkle from the exhausts pinpoints the engines. He can make out a faint silhouette now – Heinkel 111. Subconsciously, he has been running the usual checks – temperatures, pressures, cannons ready to fire. He eases out gently to the left, positioning himself for a quarter-attack. The Heinkel flies on, the crew oblivious to his approach. He expects that they are alert but he knows from his first attempt the difficulty of spotting another aircraft against the blacked-out countryside without moonlight. He's in position. A final touch on the rudder pedal then a two-second burst. His Spitfire shudders under the recoil of its cannons as he watches the target. He can see his shells exploding across the wing and then flames begin to appear around the engine, rapidly fanned into a torch-like blaze. He throttles back sharply to maintain position as the Heinkel begins to lose way. The moon appears briefly through a hole in the clouds. He is preparing for another burst when one-two-three dark bundles tumble from beneath the aircraft followed shortly afterwards by a fourth. He glimpses the white flashes of parachutes deploying. The crew have baled out; no point wasting ammo. Almost the whole wing is ablaze now and gradually it begins to dip as the stricken aircraft starts its final descent. He turns away knowing he does not need to follow it down.

He controls his excitement. "Moonbeam Control. Bandit destroyed. Four crew baled out." He glances at his gauges – still adequate fuel. "Any more trade?"

"Negative Foxglove One. Vector three-four-zero for base. You have sixty miles to run. And well done!"

Back to base. Tea and a bacon sandwich waiting with any luck; and Justine's letter on its way to him. All in all it has been a good night. He has achieved his first night-kill and he isn't even officially on a night-fighter squadron. But that is as nothing compared with the news that Justine and his son are alive. Nothing will ever compare with that. It will be a long hard slog, but one day he will be with them.

The words of the song were running through his mind as he began a long gentle descent towards the airfield. By the time he was making a low-level circuit to pick out the lines of glim lamps from the first hint of ground mist, he had started humming it. As he curved in past the chance light on final approach, he had progressed to la-la-la-ing it. The Spitfire bumped a couple of times and then settled onto the runway. He opened the throttle to taxi the remaining distance to dispersal. Against the roar of the engine, he bellowed the concluding chorus, not the Vera Lynn version but the up-tempo rendition he had heard by Lew Stone and his Orchestra: *"We'll-meet-again, don't-know-where-don't-know-when – but I know we will meet again – some sun-nee day-y-y!"*

Epilogue

He was surprised that there were no guards, only the all-too-familiar pile of sandbags around the entrance, as he entered the building for the first time. It looked to him as if it had been a hotel before its present use – probably, like many in London, no longer enjoying its Victorian heyday. Inside, he found marble floor and wood panelling; both had seen better days but retained more than a hint of their former grandeur. The guards he had expected were inside; two of them, standing to one side of the door, deep in conversation. They looked at him briefly, decided his army uniform meant he posed no obvious threat, and returned to their discussion. He crossed the floor to a large desk, the only item of furniture to be seen, but not looking as if it had been there in hotel days. Behind it, typing with surprising speed, sat a large, plump woman, with iron-grey short-cropped hair and wearing an iron-grey suit. She looked up at him with a stern expression – it occurred to him that the guards were probably superfluous – and demanded, rather than enquired, "Can I help you?"

"Captain Fuller to see the Assistant Director!"

She consulted a clipboard. Recognition brought an incongruous smile. "Ah, yes! You're expected. Second floor; last room to the right and on the right. The lift's out of order so you'll have to use the stairs."

His train journey from Weymouth had been uncomfortable, the carriage packed as was the wartime norm, so he was glad of an opportunity to stretch himself. He took the stairs two at a time, followed the corridor along and found himself knocking on a door bearing the legend 'Assistant Director'. He entered a large, high-ceilinged room – the hotel had clearly once been very grandiose. A single bed and cupboards mostly filled one wall, unlikely to have been original furnishings either; the opposite wall was lined with filing cabinets and as he closed the door he saw hanging next to it a large-scale map of France. There were unopened boxes scattered around the room suggesting that a lot of unpacking was still to be done. In front of the filing cabinets, was a large desk similar to that of the iron-grey lady at which sat the Assistant Director, dark haired, dressed in a suit. Fuller had wondered whether or not he would be a military man.

"Fuller, thank you for coming." His eyes took in his cap badge. "West Sussex Yeomanry, my old regiment!"

Fuller smiled. "I take it you were with General Allenby, sir?"

That's right – heat, dust, camels and flies, and that was the good part! Still, it wasn't all bad – I met my wife out there. Oh! Excuse my manners – do have a seat."

"Thank you, sir." As he sat he slid a folder across the desk, through a gap between two telephones and some box files. "As ordered, I interviewed five evaders – there's a separate report for each. Four of them provided routine information – a few more pins in the map – it's the fifth one you might find interesting."

There was silence as the Assistant Director skimmed through a couple of reports. "These are well put together – I take it you've done this before?"

His initial experience of his work had been immediately after Dunkirk. Speaking passable German he had been asked to assist in interrogating the handful of German prisoners that had been brought back. As their fellows had deferred their plans to follow them to England, he was then given the task of debriefing returning stragglers. The whole thing had been rather ad hoc and disjointed but he must have impressed someone because he then found himself interviewing evaders, culminating in the trip to Weymouth on behalf of this – to him – unknown department. However, he hadn't joined the army to be a clerk. "Yes, sir."

"Fancy joining our growing band? We could use you."

"I've applied for commando training, sir. I'm due in Scotland in two days' time."

"Pity, but well done you! Another of Mr Churchill's good ideas; as was this setup, incidentally. If things don't work out for any reason do come and look me up."

"Thank you, sir."

"Now, tell me about this fifth report."

"Our chap landed by parachute in Normandy and had the good fortune to run straight into a Frenchman called Victor, who seems to help evaders."

"I know of him. I understand we supplied him with a radio a couple of months ago."

"For some reason his intended safe house wasn't available so he took our chap to a farm where he spent a week waiting to be picked up. While he was there, the Germans searched the place but they didn't manage to find him. It seems the widow who runs it is nobody's fool. Apart from her there's her niece, who has a baby. While our chap was there they volunteered to help Victor on a permanent basis; I imagine a setup like this could prove very useful."

"I agree. Do we have names?"

"He only knew the aunt as Lys but he knew her niece from earlier times; Justine Knight. Married to an English pilot apparently but separated by the invasion."

After Fuller had gone the Assistant Director sat and read the report that he had just heard in summary form. As he sat there, the sinking sun reflected off a window opposite and, had anyone been there to see it, highlighted in passing the neat scar that ran from his ear to the angle of his jaw. He sat thinking for a while longer, grappling with a problem, before he got up, went to a cupboard and poured himself a whisky.

He sat sipping it as he re-read the report. It was dark when he finally reached across to one of the telephones, lifted the receiver and pressed a button. He could have said nothing, allowed the report to sink into the morass of the filing system and thought no more of it, but his late-Victorian/Edwardian upbringing, having instilled a sense of duty which tolerated no interference from personal considerations, demanded the decision he had come to; although what that decision

282

might cost he preferred not to think about any longer. He could hear a telephone ringing in the Director's office, across the corridor from his. The ringing stopped. The Director's voice crackled in the receiver. "Hallo?"

"Francis Knight, sir. Can you spare me a minute? Something's come up that I think you ought to hear about."

Glossary

'AHQ' – Area Headquarters – overseeing RAF forces in France 1939-40.

'Angels' – height above the ground. E.g. – Angels fifteen meant 15,000 feet.

'Bandits' – enemy aircraft.

'Bogeys' – unidentified aircraft.

'Bounce' – a surprise attack, commonly out of the sun, involving a firing pass intended to shoot down one or more of the enemy and escape before the remainder could react.

'Brass' – senior officers, usually of staff rank.

'Bumph' – paperwork, official forms etc.

'Buster' – using maximum revs from the engine, usually only in emergency situations.

'Dogfight' – the aerial melee which resulted when large numbers of opposing fighters engaged in combat. Contrary to inter-war thinking, the higher speeds of contemporary fighters simply meant that the dogfight took place in a larger area.

FAA' – Fighting Area Attacks – prescribed tactics for dealing with individual or several bombers developed between the wars when the expectation was that the increases in fighter speeds would render the dogfights of WWI impossible, thus leaving the fighters to deal with the massed bomber forces which were envisaged.

'Flights' – RAF fighter squadrons were usually divided into two – 'A' and 'B' – Flights and these in turn were sub-divided into Sections – typically Red, Yellow in 'A' and Blue, Green in 'B' although further Sections were added dependent on numbers of aircraft and tactical dispositions.

'GHQ' – Group Headquarters.

'Gong' – Medal.

'Guinea' – in pre-decimal coinage one pound and one shilling (£ 1.05); fifty guineas amounted to fifty-two pounds and ten shillings (£ 52.50).

'ITMA' – It's That Man Again – a popular wartime radio comedy series starring Tommy Handley and others (television, in its infancy, had been suspended for the duration leaving radio as the principal medium of popular entertainment).

'LMF' – Lack of Moral Fibre. Somewhere between a euphemism for cowardice and an indication that someone had reached the end of their tether. Courage, like physical strength, is finite and some possess it in greater measure than others.

'Observer Corps' – The task of the Royal Observer Corps was to visually (or aurally) locate, plot and report on enemy aircraft movements after they had crossed the coast because, in its early years, RDF could only track aircraft approaching the coast.

'OKW' – German Army High Command.

'Ops' – Another name for Sector Control who issued 'scramble' instructions.

'ops'– Operations.

'OTU' – Operational Training Unit – the final stage of training before joining a squadron.

'Pancake' – Land.

'PTI' – Physical Training Instructor.

'RDF' – Radio Direction Finding (later known as Radar) the system of spotting and tracking incoming aircraft by means of emitting and receiving radio waves reflected from them.

'Readiness' – the state of preparedness of a Squadron to be able to 'Scramble' ranging from 'Standby' or 'Immediate' through 'thirty minutes' to 'Released' (not available).

'RFC' – Royal Flying Corps – the 'army air force' of WWI which merged with its sister Royal Naval Air Service on 1st April, 1918 to form the Royal Air Force.

'Richard Hannay' – fictional hero of 'The 39 Steps' – a popular pre-war spy novel and film.

'R/T' – Radiotelephony, the means of communication within the squadron in the air and with ground controllers.

'Scramble' – The take-off of some or all of a Squadron in response to approaching enemy aircraft.

'Sidcot suit' – One-piece insulated flying overall invented by aviation pioneer Sidney Cotton; to combat the cold experienced at altitude in open cockpit or otherwise draughty/unheated aircraft.

'Sprog' – Novice pilot.

'Through the gate' – Opening the throttle to its fullest extent – see also 'Buster'

'Vic' – Vee-shaped three or sometimes five-aircraft formation.